I0739356

Division One: Tour de Force

by Stephanie Osborn

Chromosphere Press

Huntsville, AL

Table of Contents

Chapter 1

Alpha One was just returning home from a long, hard mission in South America—a Veelsi had gone berserk and was threatening the ancient Incan citadel of Macchu Picchu; given its size, it was capable of razing the time-worn city, and it had been up to Alpha One to stop the creature's rampage. The attractive, athletic Agent with the long, platinum-blonde braid known only as Omega entered her quarters, her partner following on her heels.

"HOME! Finally! I dunno about you, but I'm starved," she told him.

"Me too," agreed the tall, rugged, veteran Agent known to friend and enemy alike as simply Echo.

"Okay. I'll fix something quick for dinner if you'll help out."

"That was never in question, baby. C'mon. Let's hit the kitchen and see what you got that looks good, fast, and filling."

"Depends if you want hot or not," Omega decided, rummaging in the kitchen cupboards as Echo opened the refrigerator door and surveyed the contents. "Hey, don't just stand there holding it open! The cold air is all on the floor now."

"Uh, sorry," Echo mumbled, closing the door. "I wasn't thinking; I'm a little tired. And I don't care if it's hot or cold, just as long as it's human-edible and has a shit-ton of calories."

"Okay, lemme grab the loaf of bread, an' we'll just make sandwiches. Oh wait, I got hoagie rolls! You get out the lunchmeat, cheese, and condiments. I oughta have some fresh lettuce in there too, but I think I'm outta tomatoes and onions."

"I see pickle chips in here, too. I got some onions and tomatoes in my kitchen, if you want me to run over and grab 'em," Echo offered, swiftly fishing out the requested sandwich ingredients and dumping them on the adjacent countertop, before closing the refrigerator door again.

"If YOU want 'em, go get 'em," Omega replied, reaching for a couple of plates. "I'm gonna go with what we already got here. If I wait any longer to eat, I'm gonna keel over."

"Low blood sugar?"

"Yeah, a little, I guess."

"You're not hypoglycemic or something, are you?"

"No way in hell," Omega grumbled, slapping together a huge sandwich with sliced ham, turkey and roast beef, with Swiss and Cheddar cheeses, a substantial portion of the head of iceberg lettuce, a handful of dill pickle chips, and all but dripping with mayo and spicy brown mustard. "We burned a bazillion calories on that mission, Echo! I don't think I need any other explanation."

"Okay, okay," he murmured, putting together his equally-large sandwich with similar ingredients. "Point taken."

"Sorry. I don't mean to snap, Ace. It's just that I'm tired, I'm grumpy, we spent months on this mission in a couple o' days, and I need some food in me," she said around a mouthful of her sub.

"Yeah, me too, I guess," Echo agreed, and took a big bite of his own submarine sandwich.

They ate in relatively companionable silence for a few minutes, then Echo rummaged in Omega's fridge and fished out a couple of longnecks.

"Here," he said, twisting off the caps before offering one to her. She took it and knocked it back, chugging several swallows.

"Mm, that's good," she sighed, then returned to her three-quarters-gone sandwich.

"Feeling a little better now?"

"Yeah, a little. Still tired."

"I hear ya. Me, too. Well, things have been pretty busy lately, I guess. I can always put in for Alpha One to take some leave time, a little vacation or something. I think we've earned it."

"Maybe. I didn't get the impression from Fox that things looked like easing up any time soon, though. At least tomorrow is our day off."

"Yeah. But given your partner is the department manager, I expect we could wangle a short vacay if you wanted it. I'm sure game." Echo smiled. "So, what do you think you'd like to do when things settle down and we take that vacation? Maybe find, um, 'somebody special' to spend some time with?" he offered the gentle hint; he had recently come to realize that he cared for his partner rather more than he had expected to do. Initially—and based on past, painful experience—he had decided to ignore the potential romance, but advice from others, most notably Agency Director Fox, had convinced him to at least see if it was worth pursuing. And, he found, he was seriously starting to hope there was something there to pursue...though he had yet to see any signs of it in his partner.

"Nope. I'm gonna nap for three weeks, then go to some deserted beach all by myself—where it's quiet," Omega declared, vehement, then started foraging in the cabinets again. "Hey, want some dessert? I think I got a package of cookies in here some place..."

"What? Oh, no thanks. Rather have your homemade ones," Echo murmured, staring down at the last few bites of his sub, his appetite suddenly gone. *Damn,* he thought, discouraged. *Shot me down in flames. I thought at least she'd be interested in spending some of her vacation time with her partner. After all, India swears she considers me her best friend.* Echo sighed silently. *Maybe that's the problem. Maybe I've been friend-zoned. Hell.* He sat the unfinished sandwich back on the paper plate Omega had provided, and picked up his bottle of beer.

"Um, listen, Echo, I hate to run you off," Omega said just then, interrupting his glum thoughts, "but I had notions of doing some observing tonight when it gets good and dark, to finish up my data set for the class to use, and after the kind of day—make that last couple of days—we've already had, I need to take a nap if I'm gonna do that..."

"So you need me to leave," Echo finished for her, in a flat tone. *Dammit, she's even kicking me out. I thought we might at least pop in a movie and watch it together to wind down for the day.* He sat the mostly-empty beer bottle down on the counter rather harder than he'd intended, and added, "Sure. Whatever. See you in the morning," and walked out.

* * *

Omega blinked and stared after him in some surprise.

Well, shit, she thought. *I thought he knew I was pressing to finish that observing run, so I could have it ready to use in the astronomy class at Division One University next semester. But evidently I offended him somehow. He sure seemed fixated on the notion of a vacation, too. I wonder if he's starting to want some extended time off and...* Omega paused, thinking. *Maybe he was thinking about taking a joint vacation or something, and wanted to spend tonight planning it?*

Not that I mind. She shook her head. *I think that would be a hell of a lotta fun. And maybe...just maybe...something more might come out of it.* Omega sighed, wistful; she had realized some months before—the previous autumn, in fact—that she had fallen hard for her partner. *Not that I'm holding my breath. But right now, I don't have the wits about me to think about it, anyway. I'm just...I'm tired, I still got a long night of observing ahead of me, and I need to catch some sleep or I'll fall asleep at the 'scope. And if I put it off much longer, my target object will be gone, lost in the daylight until next fall, which will be way the hell too late for the class.*

Omega tossed the empty longneck bottles into the recycle bin and headed for the back door.

"Echo? Everything okay?" she wondered, peeping through.

But the lights were dimmed in his den, and his bedroom door was closed, a minuscule sliver of light emanating beneath it. No answer was forthcoming; given the soundproofing in the agent quarters, it was doubtful he'd even heard.

Huh, maybe he's just tired and cranky too, she decided, withdrawing and heading for her own bedroom. *I'll do something nice for him by way of an apology. And given how he raved over certain images in my astronomical textbooks, I think I know just what to do. And I can even run it tonight, I think, especially if I start the observing a few hours earlier than I'd planned. It'll mean cutting short my sleep, but maybe I can make up for it by sleeping late in the morning.*

* * *

In his bedroom, a certain morose male Agent stripped down, throwing his black Suit and its accoutrements into the laundry chute. He stared at the neatly-made, empty bed for a long moment, pensive and somewhat yearning, before going into his bathroom, climbing into the shower, and sluicing off his tall, muscular form under the hot, soothing spray.

Using a skill honed over years of missions, Echo blanked his mind and bottled his emotions. By the time he emerged from the shower and toweled off, he had retreated mentally and decided to forego any other activities for the evening; Omega had had a point. It had been a damned long, tough mission, rounding up that Veelsi before it destroyed Macchu Picchu, and he was tired.

So he combed his hair into place, brushed his teeth and generally prepared for bed. By the time he walked back into the bedroom, his hair was dry. He yanked down the bedclothes and crawled between them, turning out the light on the nightstand, leaving only the soft orange glow of the nightlight in the corner.

Echo lay alone in the semi-darkness and stared at the ceiling for a long time, a wistful expression in the brown eyes.

* * *

An exhausted Omega slept hard for several hours, then rose and dressed in black jeans and black turtleneck sweater. She fished her overcoat from the coat closet—it was still winter in New York, and tended to get windy into the bargain—and headed for the Headquarters roof.

Once there, she slipped into the small but efficient and Agency-state-of-the-art observatory dome, unsheathed the big black telescope which Echo had given her for Christmas only weeks earlier, activated the clock drive, and booted the computer, before sitting down at the tiny table off to one side, to make an observing run.

"Let's see," she murmured to herself with a smile. "Orion sets around a quarter to four in the morning this time of year around here, and it's already past eleven o'clock local. PLUS I got south Manhattan to my west to cut in on that setting time. And it's gonna take a while to get the sort of thing I want. So I need to go ahead and look at grabbing that image while I have time to get a decent exposure...."

She bent over the laptop and began keying in commands.

* * *

When Echo got up the next morning, he was a little bit more sanguine about matters—but only a little.

After all, he had decided, *it's entirely possible, as tired as we both were, that we just misread each other. Maybe a similar talk over breakfast will give me a different reaction. I gotta figure out how to find out how she feels about the idea without actually giving a lot away just yet. 'Cause if she doesn't like the idea, but I've already given myself away, it is gonna make for some DAMN awkward interactions on missions. Maybe enough that she'd decide to put in for a transfer. Which I would NOT like. And which Fox would not like either, 'cause it would break up Alpha One. I'd love to have her as...as my lover, wife, whatever, if she wanted it too, but I'd rather just stick with what we've already got than lose her altogether.*

So he threw on his robe over his nude body, went into his kitchen, pulled a breakfast casserole from the freezer—one of several such ready-made meals that he and his partner had prepared together on their last day off, and frozen for those times when they were too tired or rushed to cook from scratch, but wanted something better than a standard microwave dinner from the grocery—turned on the oven, and slid it in to cook.

Then Echo went to the back door and looked into Omega's apartment.

There was no one there.

The bedroom door was closed, however, indicating she hadn't yet gotten up, and there was a sticky note affixed to the door. He moved to the door and removed the note.

* * *

Hey Ace.

Got the observations done—finally!—but it took longer than I thought. I only just did get it all in before the thing got too low to see in the Manhattan glare. If I'm still asleep when you get up, and I probably will be, go ahead and run errands without me. I'll run my own errands whenever I wake up, and we'll catch up later today.

—Ω

* * *

Dammit, he thought, feeling intensely frustrated. *Well, I'll back-burner it for now. It isn't like either of us is really going anywhere, any time soon, I suppose.*

Echo moved to the end table and grabbed a pen and the very same sticky-note pad Omega had probably used before she went to bed, and wrote his own note in reply.

* * *

Meg,

Got your note. There's your half of a breakfast casserole in the oven, warming. Ping me on my cell phone when you're back from running errands, if I'm not back home by then myself, and I'll meet you someplace. We can do coffee and a snack, or dinner if it's late enough. Maybe even a movie if we're not still too tired.

—E

* * *

Then he stuck it on her bedroom door—making sure to put it in a different place, so she'd recognize that it was from him and not her old note—and wandered back to his kitchen to finish preparing and eating a solitary breakfast.

* * *

As he was putting his breakfast dishes in the dishwasher, having already covered the casserole so it wouldn't dry out and returned it to the oven to keep warm for his partner, Echo's cell phone rang, back in the bedroom where he'd inadvertently left it earlier that morning, having been too preoccupied with talking to Omega to think of it. He unceremoniously dumped the dishes into the washer, then sprinted for the bedroom, grabbing the phone and activating it before the caller could hang up.

"Echo here."

"Good morning, Echo; it's Fox."

"Oh, hey, Boss. What's up?"

"Well, I know it's your day off, but a little diplomatic something has come up. No need to throw on your work clothes, but if you could pop by my office in the next hour or so, it would probably be good."

"Do you need me to wake Meg? She was up late last night—most of the night, I gathered—with her little observatory on the roof, getting data she can use for that class she's teaching at the university next semester."

"Ah. Yes, I was glad to hear about the class. It's great that someone of her calibre will be teaching it. She's still asleep, then?"

"Yeah. And since that South American mission turned out to be such a pain in the ass, I think she'll be in a better frame of mind if we let her sleep until she's ready to get up."

Echo heard a laugh on the other end of the line.

"I'll bet. Yes, that's fine. Given the nature of the diplomatic request, Omega will be filling a backup role on this anyway, I'm afraid. I hate it like hell; it's exactly the sort of thing she's been hoping for. But the Cortians are really fixated on their requirements."

"Cortians?" Echo said. "I don't think I've ever heard of them."

"They're from the core of the Sagittarius Dwarf satellite galaxy, looking to start diplomatic and trade negotiations. It's the first diplomatic overture from the Sagittarius Dwarf we've had, and the Council is interested in finding out more about 'em, so I have orders to cooperate as much as I can, and see what we can do. I'll tell you all about 'em when you get here. Or at least, what we know so far."

"Okay, gimme a half an hour to actually get dressed—"

"You're not dressed?!"

"Nah, not yet. Runnin' around in my bathrobe."

"But you two still keep the 'back door' open all the time?"

"Uh, yeah..."

There was a silence on the other end.

"And Omega is all right with that?" Fox finally queried.

"Aw, hell, Fox, as long as we've been together by now, yeah. We both do it. I mean, we don't run around in the buff or anything, but if either of us has just gotten outta the shower or whatever, throw on the bathrobe and we're covered decently."

"Well, that's interesting," came the amused reply. "I suppose that Christmas and Hanukkah gift from Zebra and myself was a good idea, after all; I have to admit, it was Zebra's idea..."

"Oh, you mean that black silk robe? Yeah, Meg loves it. It's like her new favorite or something."

"That's good to know, I guess. How...do YOU like it?"

"Um," Echo hedged, "it's pretty, I guess." *Prettier on her than on the door hook, for sure,* he amended mentally, but did not say.

"All right, Echo, I'll see you in half an hour. Fox out."

"Echo out."

* * *

When Omega finally hauled her tired body out of bed, showered, donned her own robe—though it was the black terry, not the black silk, which latter tended to go over her pajama top—and went to see what was going on with her partner, she found the note he had left on her bedroom door. So with some gratitude, she polished off the last of the breakfast casserole for her own meal, sitting at his dining table. Then she deposited the dirty dishes in Echo's dishwasher and set it going, heading back to her bedroom to dress for the day.

On her way out, however, she popped into her study and grabbed a certain quantum flash drive and stuck it in her pocket, grinning from ear to ear.

As she headed out her front door, instead of targeting the exit at the front of the building, she aimed for the photography lab.

* * *

Echo returned to his quarters later that morning from the unexpected meeting with Fox to come face-to-face with a gift. A huge, poster-sized full color print of the Orion Nebula was propped carefully in the recliner in his living area. Echo stood there studying it for a long moment. The gas filaments in the nebula were sharp and clearly defined, the colors vivid, the stars crisp and bright but not overexposed. The giant sheet of paper on which it was printed was high-quality photo stock. This was no off-the-shelf poster; this was the personal work of a professional astronomer. A skilled professional astronomer.

Thoughtfully he lifted the image and flipped it over to check the photographic paper. It was from the Agency photolab. He nodded to himself, the corners of his mouth curving slightly.

Wow. Just...wow. Somebody, he decided, *must have realized I was not happy about being thrown out last night, I think. After all, it wasn't like I tried to hide it. And I'll just bet this is an apology. A pretty cool one, too.*

He laid the photo back down with care and went to the back door. Upon seeing Omega's quarters empty, he shrugged, and headed into his own kitchen to grab some lunch.

* * *

Later that day, Omega returned to her quarters from running errands, and knocked on the frame of the connecting 'back door,' calling to her partner.

"Hi, Echo, I'm back..." Omega paused as Echo glanced up from re-reading H. G. Wells' *The Invisible Man* to look at her from his prone position on the couch.

Over the couch now hung the only adornment on Echo's walls, the Orion Nebula photo she had made and printed, which had, in the interim, been beautifully matted and framed in jet black. The overall impression created by the framing was that the nebula itself extended onto the wall, while at the same time it highlighted the beauty of the delicate colors. More, Echo's position on the couch seemed calculated to allow him to glance up at it whenever he was not actively reading.

She studied the framed picture silently for a long moment, startled but pleased, and he watched her reaction equally silently, with dusky brown eyes.

"...Did Fox call?" Omega finally finished.

"As a matter of fact, he did. It's not anything you have to worry about. But it DOES look like I'll be going off-planet for a couple days."

"Just you? What for?" She moved farther into the room, an odd, disturbed sensation running through her being.

"Yeah, it's a first contact, and they're scheduled to arrive in a couple of weeks; sorry about that. I know you're dying to do an exo mission. Especially since the Agency co-opted you just as you made astronaut. But the Cortians are new to us, the Pan-Galactic Council is eager to connect with 'em 'cause they're from the Sagittarius Dwarf Galaxy, and the situation's a little complex. Seems they follow a strict protocol in making diplomatic overtures. One of the rules they've laid down is one agent, and one only. They also had some interesting requirements regarding gender and physical ability."

"What? Physical..." Omega's eyes narrowed, and she frowned, as imagery of a particularly unpleasant nature popped into the back of her mind while Echo talked.

* * *

"What's wrong?" Echo asked, noting her expression.

"I...don't know," Omega admitted. "I've just suddenly got enough bells ringing in my head for a five-alarm fire. I don't like the sound of that, Echo."

"It sounded pretty routine to Fox and me." He shrugged. "Nothing really unusual."

"I don't think you should go."

"Why not?"

"Call it a hunch. Women's intuition. Whatever. Just don't go."

Damn, he thought, biting his lip. *I was afraid she was gonna take it hard. Especially coming so soon after the South American mission, when she's still tired. Hell, when we're both tired.* He pondered how to let her down easy.

"Meg, look. I know you'd love to go, but...you can't. I really am sorry. I'll try to arrange with Fox to get us both an offworld assignment as Alpha One as soon as I can."

* * *

She stared at him, shocked, then a little glint of anger kindled in the depths of her eyes.

"You think I'm trying..." Omega turned on her heel and stalked toward the door. Over her shoulder she said, "I thought you knew me better than that, Echo. You've sure preached about it enough in recent months. But damn, are you off this time, Ace."

* * *

Alpha One reported to Fox's office the next day for first-contact preparations. As she sat next to Echo in Fox's office and listened to the two men discuss plans, Omega tried desperately to shake yesterday's feelings of disquiet, which had become today's feelings of foreboding anxiety.

Why do I feel like a sword is hanging over our heads? she wondered. *Like...something is about to happen, and I don't know what...and it can't be stopped...*

"...No," Fox was saying to Echo, as Omega's attention returned to them, "I think it will be fine if just the three of us are there. I've got a small situation developing in China that I'd like Romeo and India to keep an eye on, and the rest of the Alpha teams are on other assignments already. We might call 'em in for the departure, but you, Omega, and myself should be

11

sufficient for the arrival protocol. Especially given the, um, picky nature of the Cortians."

* * *

"That's fine," Echo responded. "Where are we bringing 'em in?"

"Chicago Station spaceport," Fox replied. "That's the best location, given the landing window. Chicago Office ground ops is reserving Hangar 16."

"Gotcha," Echo replied. "Catch that, Meg?" He'd noticed her preoccupation.

"Chicago Station Hangar 16," she reiterated, not missing a beat. "Time of landing?"

"PGLEIA 10:00," Fox told her. "CST of...let's see—"

"Greenwich Mean'll do," Omega responded.

"All right, that's 0600 Zulu," Fox replied.

"Copy that. 0600 Ephemeris Time; midnight Chicago time," she converted without hesitation, and the two men raised impressed eyebrows.

"Right." Fox nodded.

"Ephemeris Time?" queried Echo. "I haven't heard that one."

* * *

"Yeah," Omega answered, quirking a slight grin. "Astronomer-ese for Greenwich Mean Time. Also—and most often, actually—called Universal Time or UT, though for the Agency, that term no longer makes sense, which is why I've started using the term, 'Ephemeris Time.' Anyway, it got modified a little bit to ensure consistency with the atomic clock standards and junk, so they don't officially call it Greenwich Mean anymore, but it amounted to the same difference, in the end." She saw Fox's expression and elaborated, "An ephemeris is an equation of time we use to calculate the state of a regularly varying object, like the phases of the Moon, or a variable star. Or the rotation of a planet." She shrugged.

"Ah," Fox responded with a smile. "Foreign language, eh?"

"Something like, I guess," Omega chuckled.

"That reminds me," Echo told Fox. "I'll need to put in an order for a BLT, Fox."

BLT? It's not lunchtime, Omega thought, glancing surreptitiously at

12

her wrist chronometer. *What's he doing asking Fox for that, anyway?* This time, Fox caught the expression on Omega's face, and his eyes twinkled in amusement, but HE didn't elaborate.

"I'll have it delivered right away, Echo," Fox told the Alpha Line department chief. "I've already got sufficient to have it ginned up."

"Good."

"What else will you need?"

"Just the usual, Fox. A couple Suits, my shaving kit. Something to read."

"Gonna travel light, huh?" Omega remarked.

"Yep. Ever lose your luggage on a domestic plane flight?"

"Once. Never again. Have carry-on, will travel."

"Exactly. Trust me, Meg, you don't want to have to worry about luggage on an interstellar flight."

"I believe you," she said with a grin. The grin faded as a powerful sense of dread gripped her. *If that's all you lose, Echo, you'll be lucky...*

* * *

As they sat at their desks in the Alpha Line meeting room right off the Core, and studied up on the files that the Cortians had sent in advance, Omega found herself becoming more and more perturbed.

I don't believe it, Omega decided, flipping through a summation report in the dossier on the planet. *These guys are just too good to be true. Their exports, the gross planetary products, all of that. I don't see what we've got to offer them. Oh, maybe PGLEIA all together, sure. But they have no real reason to want to connect with Earth in particular, if I just go by this shit.*

"Echo," Omega murmured, "this seems kinda over the top to me."

"Huh? What does?" Echo wondered, glancing up from his own studies.

"This stuff." Omega waved the tablet, denoting the files on it. "The whole Cortian dossier."

"Oh, that. Yeah, take it with a building-sized grain of salt, Meg," Echo said. "Pretty much every diplomatically-motivated first contact, somebody does shit like that. They wanna make sure we see it as worth our while to meet with 'em, so they pad the résumé, sorta."

"'Sorta'? This is a helluva lot of padding," Omega observed in serious disgust, waving the tablet again. "To hear this tell it, the only thing they can't do is walk on water, and the only resource they don't have is adamantine ultradiamond. Why would they need us? It's overkill."

* * *

"Well, it is," Echo agreed. "But Fox and I have seen just as bad before. Truth is, when we were discussing it the other day in his office—that was the day you slept in—we both had a really good laugh about it."

"It doesn't bother you?"

"Nah." Echo studied her. "I take it, it's bothering you?"

"Hell, yeah."

"Can you tell me why?"

"...No."

"Can't, or won't?"

"Can't," Omega sighed. "Because I don't know why. I just don't feel good about it, Ace."

"Well, I know that getting left behind doesn't feel good, baby," Echo offered in a soft voice. "And I'm sorry about that. But I'm not the one setting the terms. FOX isn't even the one doing it. It's the Cortians, and they won't budge. Fox already tried. And he's got orders from the Ennead—the Galactic Council—to do whatever it takes to make this contact happen."

"Then lemme talk to the Ennead," Omega grumbled, and Echo blinked.

"Meg...you can't be serious."

"As a heart attack."

"Do you know how that would come across? If you go over Fox's head to the Ennead and demanded to be put on this mission?" He shook his head. "Baby, you would be scuttled from EVER going out there, and might even be thrown out entirely, by way of sanctions. Which would mean, since we can't brain-bleach you, that we'd have—" Echo broke off and took a deep breath. "Look, Meg, I don't want to see you thrown in a PGLEIA prison for the rest of your life."

"You still don't get it! I don't want to go ON the mission. I want to stop it from occurring. Period."

"Well, it ain't happenin', baby. Regardless of how you're trying to spin it, this IS going forward."

"HELL!"

Omega turned and threw the tablet against the wall. It bounced off, ricocheted off her desk, and skittered across the floor, finally stopping when it nudged Echo's foot. He picked it up and checked it quickly, but it was undamaged; Agency equipment was intended to be tough, because sometimes it had to be. *This wasn't expected to be one of those times, but whatever works,* Echo decided. *Wow.*

But by that time Omega was at the door of the Alpha Line room.

"Where are you going?" he asked.

"I'm going for a walk," she declared, "before I really DO break something."

And she was gone.

* * *

Omega made her way up to the ceiling of the Core. There on the ceiling could be found the giant holographic projection map of the Milky Way Galaxy, one of her favorite places in Headquarters...even if she was hanging upside-down with respect to the rest of the Core's volume as she walked through it. The walking paths through the map were empty at the moment, much to Omega's gratitude and considerable relief; she found it a soothing place to stroll and ponder whenever matters were troubling her.

And boy, are they troubling me today, she thought, morose. *I just wish I could get Echo to stop and actually HEAR what I'm saying. I am so antsy about this I can hardly sit still. But it's anything BUT wanting to GO ON the mission with him. It's wanting the mission not to happen at ALL. I don't trust these... 'Cortians'...any farther than I can throw 'em. I just don't know why. But if Echo leaves with 'em, I'm scared to death something bad is gonna happen, and I'll never see him again. And I don't think I could stand that. After losing Mom and Dad and Grandmomma, to lose him too...I dunno if I want to even try to keep going, if he's gone too. I'm not sure if there's a point to keeping going. I just wish...I wish I thought he felt about me the way I do about him.*

Then again, she realized, as she strolled through the representation of the Perseus Arm, *I'm a no-longer-human, alien-enhanced...construct, intended to be a weapon—targeted against HIM specifically. And damn, but*

15

Slug's machinations nearly worked. She shivered. *The image of his head in my blaster's sights...I think it's permanently branded in my mind. I can't get rid of it no matter HOW hard I try. So...yeah. No way in the twelfth level, raised to the thirteenth power, of hell...is Echo ever gonna look at me like THAT.* She sighed. *I don't suppose any decent, healthy straight guy would, for that matter. I haven't been human since I was twelve. I just didn't know it.*

Meh. That's neither here nor there, I guess. Omega dismissed the consideration. *The important thing at this point is how to keep...whatever's gonna happen...from happening to Echo. Whether he wants it or not.*

But to do that, I need to know what it is that's gonna happen, and I got no clue. Except that I don't think they're gonna let him come home once they've got him. Alive or dead.

Another series of jumbled images flashed into her mind's eye for a few moments as she looked out across the galactic map—some sort of largish spacecraft, though it was too confused to allow her to identify even an overall model; yellow feathers; a canary in a bird cage...except the canary kept morphing into Echo; Echo dead, Echo dying, Echo behind bars.

Ahh! Omega thought, intensely frustrated and annoyed. *I can't make plans if I don't know what I'm planning for! And I'm just not seein' it!*

You don't need to see it, baby, a calm voice seemed to say; it sounded vaguely like Echo's, and she suddenly grasped that part of her subconscious was using his logic and her own feelings for him to project a possible solution. *All you really need to know is that Echo better not get on that spacecraft. All you really need to DO is to prevent that happening.*

But if I do that, she told the 'Echo voice,' *it's like he said—I'll end up in jail for the rest of my life. Or worse.*

Then you have a decision to make, don't you? the 'Echo voice' said. *How much is Echo's life worth to you, and how much is your own life worth?*

Are you telling me...

No, I'm asking you. Are you willing to become expendable to ensure that he stays alive, and free...and SAFE?

Omega responded without hesitation then.

YES.

Then you know now what you have to do. And everything you do, everything you say, everything you observe, from this point out, must be with this focus—do what you have to do to keep Echo OFF THAT SHIP.

Omega took a deep breath, and nodded to herself.

She walked over to the wall and down it, headed for her quarters.

* * *

Echo spotted her walking across the Core and left the Alpha Line room at speed, headed straight for her. She appeared preoccupied, because she didn't see him until he reached her.

"Meg? You okay?" He had carefully pondered how to approach her when he next saw her; her stereotypically Celtic temper was apt to flare if she was stressed, and after her display of anger in the department room, he had come to a realization that that stress level was a lot higher than he'd thought. He didn't want to make it worse; another department chief might have reprimanded her for her temper, but Omega was normally a very easy-going sort, and massive flares of anger were usually few and far between. *And usually MEAN something, when they DO happen. Oh, she's got her quirks, and she's as driven as I am, but I get that,* Echo thought, watching as she startled a bit, then glanced up at him. *I do the same thing sometimes. I can't fault her for my own faults. And they're not always faults, anyway.*

"Huh? Oh—Echo! Hi," she murmured, flushing a bit. "Um, yeah, I think I'm all right for now, anyway. I, uh, I had to work some things out in my head, I guess."

"And do you? Have it worked out, I mean."

"I think so, to a point. At least for now."

"Okay, good. Look, it's almost end of shift. Let's go to the break room and grab a cup of coffee. If you need to talk, we'll talk. Then what say we go out tonight? I think we earned it after Macchu Picchu. We can go over to that pub we both like near the Barclay Center, then maybe go to the big cineplex and catch a movie. No work talk allowed from the time we leave Headquarters to the time we get back."

"I...think I like that idea, Ace," Omega said with a smile.

Echo drew a deep, relieved breath and smiled back.

"Then let's go, baby," he said.

* * *

Omega said little of significance over coffee, though she did apologize for losing her temper, and Echo didn't push it.

Then they went to the vehicle hangar, hopped into the 'Vette, and headed for the pub.

"Kinda nice to eat good food we didn't have to fix, for a change," Echo decided as they chowed down on juicy steaks with mashed potatoes and Brussels sprouts drizzled with balsamic vinegar, accompanied by a bottle of a nice cabernet, having already polished off Caesar salads and bowls of gazpacho.

"Amen to that," Omega agreed. "Or else do without, because we were too damn busy to eat."

"That, too."

"Is there a reason there isn't a cafeteria or something—at least a food court—in Headquarters? I mean, something besides the thing down in Grand Central Station for the tourists passing through..."

"Well, we used to have one, years ago. Problem was, we needed like twelve head chefs and all kinds of foodstuffs to cover all the different countries here, let alone all the different sentient species we got in the various embassies. And then you'd get infighting over whose particular version of the homeworld's signature dish was authentic, and it just went downhill from there. In the end, I think the bean counters decided it wasn't very cost-effective."

"I guess that makes sense."

"Hey, you want dessert tonight?"

"I might could be talked into it, Ace. What are you gonna get?"

"I was trying to decide, baby! I was hoping you'd choose."

"What? Are you wanting to split it?"

"Maybe. Just order one, with two spoons. The portions are pretty big here, remember?"

"Oh yeah. Okay. In that case, how HUNGRY are you?"

"Mm. The steaks are good-sized, and we ordered extra sides. So it doesn't have to be too big, I guess."

"How about ordering the crème brulée and splitting that, then? I like crème brulée, and it's relatively light..."

"Works for me." Echo signaled the waiter and placed the order, then worked on polishing off the last of his steak. "I assume you're wanting to go see that latest movie in the fantasy franchise you like?"

"You bet! Wait—do you NOT wanna see it?"

"No, I'm game. I'm not quite as into it as you are, but I like it."

"You're sure?"

"Yeah, I'm sure. We'll go, we'll have fun, I'll crack jokes about the quest all the way home. While you laugh yourself silly."

Omega laughed, and Echo grinned.

* * *

As the days progressed, Omega grew increasingly uncomfortable while a heavy sense of foreboding steadily built within her. It was a struggle to keep it from being noticed, especially by Echo, who appeared to be particularly adept at reading her in the last few days—at least, to a point. *But he still doesn't understand about the Cortian mission,* she thought in frustration.

Today, though—the third Division day after notice of the first contact—whatever was going on in Omega's subconscious seemed to have reached a peak, and it had taken everything Omega had to even keep focused on her work. Fox had chided her for inattention, and Echo had had to cover for her several times.

* * *

"What's wrong, Meg?" he'd asked, as they did an abbreviated patrol after the meeting with Fox.

"Having a day." She shrugged.

"What kind of day?"

"You know—one of those days. Murphy's Law and all of the corrolaries." She winced.

"Headache?" Echo asked sympathetically.

"Yeah," Omega replied. "Any dolocet in the medikit?"

"Yeah, there should be." He watched as she crawled part way into the warp seat of the Corvette to access the trunk as he drove. Retrieving the medikit, Omega got out the painkillers and popped them, swallowing them dry with some difficulty.

"Four?! That must be some headache, Meg."

"Yeah. Woke up with it today. I thought my morning caffeine would kill it, but no such luck."

"Tension?" Echo took one hand off the wheel and squeezed her left shoulder lightly, shot her a glance, then carefully probed the back of her neck. "Damn, Meg, your shoulders are like rocks. No wonder you got the headache from hell. What's up?"

"It's this TRIP, Echo," the words burst out as if under pressure. "I just don't see—"

"Damn. I thought you'd gotten past that. This is really eating at you, isn't it?" Echo said, slightly startled, as he returned both hands to the wheel.

"Yes, but not for the reason—"

"Look, baby, if there was any way I could influence this to bring you along, I would, I swear I would," Echo told her, his earnestness obvious. "I know how much you want this. But I can't, Meg. It's not my call. It's not even Fox's call. You know that."

"Echo, it's not—"

"Meg, quit fighting it. Come on," he said, pulling the Corvette to the curb, "let's have a chat with Mack the Knife about Gordo's latest escapades. Maybe that'll get your mind off it. Romeo wants the info, anyway."

* * *

But it hadn't. Nor had the alien analgesics stopped her headache. Nor did a skilled neck rub from her partner. The painful throbbing in her temples had, in fact, increased, until by quitting time Echo had been concerned enough to outrightly cancel their gym workout—which had been postponed to the evening in order to accommodate another meeting with Fox that morning—in favor of giving her a chance to rest. Omega had taken down her French braid to allow her scalp to relax, before she stretched out on her couch and closed her eyes.

"Echo?" she murmured to her partner, who stood in the back door, watching, "would you mind...handling dinner tonight?"

"Are you even going to want dinner?"

"Not much," she admitted, and tried to zone out. She was evidently at least partly successful, because a few moments later, Omega felt a cool, moist compress laid across her closed eyes and forehead.

"Forget dinner," Echo's voice said quietly above her. "Get some rest."

"No argument. This is far and away the worst headache I've had since... since gettin' knocked upside the head by a telepathic two-by-four, I guess."

"You mean Slug?" Echo clarified.

"Yeah."

"Ouch."

"Eee-zackly," Omega responded wearily. "And that was our first—no, I guess it was the second—real mission as Alpha Line, so it's been a little while..."

"Are you sure you're not under attack again? I mean telepathically. Other species 'do' telepathy, you know."

"Yeah, I'm sure. There isn't that 'pressure from outside' feeling that I always got." She clenched her teeth against a sharp twinge. "Mmph."

"Meg, you gonna be okay?"

"Nnnnggh..." Her hands went to her head as the pain unexpectedly increased dramatically, and she doubled up in pain.

"MEG??"

"AaaAAAHHHHIII—" It was a shriek of pure agony. Abruptly the throbbing pain peaked, spiking at incredible levels, then diminished. It left Omega weak, lying on the couch and panting. "Ohhh...finally..."

Suddenly the compress across her eyes vanished, replaced by a flashlight.

"Ow!" she exclaimed, trying to push Echo's hand away. "Never do that to an astronomer!" She grinned shakily as Echo knelt beside her.

* * *

"Meg, look at me," Echo commanded. "I'm serious."

She obeyed, and remained quiet while Echo checked her eyes.

"Now smile," he said. She pasted a patently fake smile on her face, then started snickering. The corner of Echo's mouth curled up despite himself as he looked at her. "Come on, Meg. I mean it; I'm really serious. Now say something."

"Like what?"

"Mmm...'The stranger came early in February, one wintry day, through a biting wind and a driving snow.'"

"All right. 'The stranger came early in February, one wintry day, through a biting wind and a driving snow.' Opening line of H. G. Wells' *The Invisible Man*, right? What are you doing?" she asked, obviously perplexed by his actions. He watched her face intently as she spoke. Now he glanced down the length of her body, considering.

"Raise your right leg."

She lifted it.

"Now your left."

She complied.

"Flex your hands."

She did.

"How's the headache?"

"Gone at last," Omega said, gratified. Echo rocked back on his heels from a kneeling position beside the couch, and exhaled in relief.

"Okay, good. It doesn't appear to be anything bad. At this point, at least."

"What? What do you mean, 'bad'?" Omega asked, raising a puzzled eyebrow.

"I was checking you for a brain hemorrhage or something similar, Meg. That headache was...unusual. Isn't it almost time for your physical?"

"Mmm...yeah, I guess. Getting close, anyway. Still a couple months away, though."

"You might want to go ahead and schedule it just the same, baby. Let's make sure everything is okay before I go charging off across the galaxy and leave you here, alone."

"Aw! Do I gotta?"

"Meg," an earnest—and very worried—Echo knelt beside the couch again, "if you won't do it for yourself, will you at least do it for me? I'd feel a lot better going on an extended offworld mission if I know you're gonna be all right while I'm gone."

* * *

Omega blinked, and studied the solemn expression on Echo's face, seeing the hint of anxiety in the depths of the brown eyes, which were gazing into her own eyes so intently.

He...really wants to make sure everything is okay, she realized. *He's worried, and doesn't want to leave me alone if something's wrong. And maybe he's right. That headache WAS strange. I just...dammit, I HATE all the poking and prodding. But maybe, just maybe...* she considered. *If something's a bit off with me there, maybe it'll give us the excuse we need for him to stay here.*

"All right," she capitulated with a sigh. "I'll try to call Zebra in the next few days and set something up for before you leave."

"And if the headache comes back?" he urged. "You'll call the medlab immediately?"

"I'll call the medlab immediately." Omega nodded, agreeing.

"Good. Thanks, Meg. I appreciate it."

* * *

The rest of the evening passed quietly; while the headache was gone at last, Omega's appetite didn't return in its wake, and the duration of the headache had sapped her energy, leaving her listless. So she and Echo did little but lie around their respective apartments and putter or read. She threw in the towel and went to bed early, hoping to regain some of her energy by morning with an extra-long sleep; tomorrow looked like being yet another long day spent preparing for the arrival of the Cortian first-contact contingent.

Now Omega was trying to unwind in bed before turning out the light, sitting up in bed and reading from a collection of poetry she'd picked up at the Agency library the day before. Slowly she relaxed, sliding down sleepily in the bed, as she read through the rhythmic verse.

"Mmm...Walt Whitman. I always did love Whitman," she murmured absently, and lost herself in the verses.

* * *

Adieu, o soldier,
You of the rude campaigning, (which we shared,)
The rapid march, the life of the camp,
The hot contention of opposing fronts, the long maneuvre,

Red hot battles with their slaughter...

* * *

"Huh," she mumbled to herself with a slight smile, "that could almost be me...and...Echo..."

Abruptly, Omega pushed herself upright, eyes wide, head spinning as if reality had suddenly turned itself inside-out. Before her—and seeming real enough to touch—she saw, not her own dimly-lit bedroom, but a far more sinister vision, clear and unambiguous.

* * *

A struggling Echo was a helpless prisoner, bound immovably with unseen bonds, being carried away by uniformed aliens onto a large spacecraft, never to return.

* * *

She blinked, and the familiar room reappeared.

"What the hell was THAT?!" she whispered, shaken. After a moment in which the apparitions didn't recur, she flipped several pages over and settled back to reading. This time, it was Henry Wadsworth Longfellow.

* * *

...Just as the moon rose over the bay,
Where swinging wide at her moorings lay
The Somerset, *British man-of-war;*
A phantom ship, with each mast and spar
Across the moon like a prison bar,
And a huge black hulk, that was magnified
By its own reflection in the tide.

* * *

The room dissolved again, fading into another place and time...

* * *

Omega watched as an unfamiliar, hulking black spacecraft settled into the locks of a landing bay; its hatch opened into a yawning black hole. Near the hatch was an inscription in alien lettering; as Omega watched, the letters morphed into Roman letters spelling the word Trindak. *Without hesitation, Echo walked right up to the singularity...and was sucked in. His body ripped apart, shredding into gory, bloody bits, just before he disappeared through the event horizon.*

* * *

Closing her eyes, a horrified Omega shook her head in desperation. When she opened her eyes once more, she was back in her own bedroom.

Quickly she turned the page, this time to Elizabeth Barrett Browning. *That's better,* she decided. *A lover's poem ought not to trigger those...whatevers...*

* * *

Is it indeed so? If I lay here dead,
Wouldst thou miss any life in losing mine?
And would the sun for thee more coldly shine
Because of grave-damps falling round my head?
I marvelled, my Beloved, when I read
Thy thought so in the letter. I am thine—
But...so much to thee? Can I pour thy wine
While my hands tremble? Then my soul, instead
Of dreams of death, resumes life's lower range.
Then, love me, Love! look on me—breathe on me!
As brighter ladies do not count it strange,
For love, to give up acres and degree,
I yield the grave for thy sake, and exchange
My near sweet view of Heaven, for earth with thee!

* * *

To Omega's chagrin, the room vanished yet again.

* * *

This time, Omega, in black shirt and Suit, knelt weeping, heartbroken and alone, before a single tomb in the Crypt, the Agency's burial mausoleum underneath the Tomb of the Unknowns in Arlington National Cemetery.

On its endcap was inscribed a lone letter: E. Underneath that was inscribed Echo's birth date...and the scheduled date of departure of the Cortian envoy.

* * *

Moments later the room snapped back to normal.

"No, no, no! Forget this..." she exclaimed to the now-empty room, and flipped over several more pages, "let's try a kinsman." Randomly, she began reading Walter Scott.

* * *

'Tis at such a tide and hour,
Wizard, witch, and fiend have power,
And ghastly forms through mist and shower
Gleam on the gifted ken;
And then the affrighted prophet's ear
Drinks whispers strange of fate and fear
Among the sons of men...

* * *

This time, in swift succession, Omega saw a series of gruesome images, all keying off the same picture.

* * *

Echo was standing in the hatch of that same hulking, black spacecraft, surrounded by yellow-feather-crested, uniformed aliens. Several of the aliens grappled Echo, trying to take hin into their custody; he resisted. A fight began; Echo was overborne and beaten, then carried aboard the alien vessel, bound and chained.

* * *

The picture rewound.

* * *

Echo was standing in the hatch of that same hulking, black spacecraft, surrounded by the same crested, uniformed aliens. Once more, several of the aliens grappled Echo, trying to take hin into their custody; again he resisted, and a fight began. This time, the aliens pulled weapons and shot Echo at point-blank range where he stood; he crumpled to the deck, bleeding out.

* * *

The movie started again, with yet a different ending.

* * *

Echo was standing in the hatch of that same hulking, black spacecraft, surrounded by those crested, uniformed aliens. For the third time, several of the aliens grappled Echo, trying to take hin into their custody; once more he resisted, and a fight began.

Suddenly Echo was bowled over by a flying projectile, lying sprawled on the landing deck, even as the alien spacecraft launched. Immolation followed instantly, as Echo's body became a living torch under their engines' exhaust.

* * *

"AAHH!" Omega cried in horror. She closed her eyes and shook her head, slamming the book shut and flinging it onto the night table, heedless of small items that went flying. When she opened her eyes, the bedroom had returned once again.

"This is...getting really damn strange..." she murmured, badly shaken. "I almost think I could've...touched them..."

What IS this? she thought, struggling for control. *SIX images where Echo has gotten on a ship. In two he stays alive, but is taken prisoner; in four he gets killed. This makes no sense. It can't ALL happen. You can't kill somebody after you've killed 'em. The only common threads I can see are Echo and an alien spaceship...make that a malevolent alien spaceship. Why am I even seeing this??*

She mulled over the scenarios. Suddenly a thought jumped out at her.

You know, it's almost like...a worldline nexus in hyperdimensional physics. Maybe Echo's worldline is dependent on interactions with some other worldline, or worldlines. That would explain the different outcomes. 'Course, so would a brain tumor, she thought, wry. *Thank goodness for the Agency policy on physicals. It IS getting close to time for one anyway, and it might make us BOTH feel better at this point. Echo's right. I hate the idea, but I think maybe I better go ahead with it...these damn long Division shifts may finally be starting to get to me.*

Or maybe...damn. What if Slug's tinkering isn't stable? Maybe he only intended it to last long enough for me to take Echo out, and now things are breaking down...? Shit. I may be on the verge of falling apart at the seams... literally.

Omega sat for a few more minutes, then leaned over and switched off the lamp. She plumped the pillows and settled down, lying on her back, staring at the ceiling in the nigh-dark. But without the visual cues to distract, the ominous images which continued to unreel were even more vivid.

And even harder to ignore, she decided.

* * *

There was a soft click in the darkness, and the bedside lamp came back on.

Omega sat for a moment, debating, then got up and put her new favorite robe on over her pajama top; the robe was a luxurious black jacquard silk, and it had been a joint Christmas/Hannukah present from Fox and Zebra. It had arrived somewhat late, given the Lambda Andromedan diplomatic mission which occurred over those holidays, but it was a gift from the hearts of two Agents for whom she deeply cared, and it meant a great deal to her.

Eschewing slippers, she padded silently on bare feet out into the dark living area of her quarters and stood, looking around, then headed for her kitchen, clicking on the light.

* * *

She had poured a glass of milk and was rummaging in the fridge for something to go with it, when she heard a knock, followed by Echo's sleepy voice.

"Meg? You okay?"

"Yeah, Ace," she answered, coming out into the living area. Echo stood in the back door, clad only in his robe. He ran a hand through sleep-tousled hair, rumpling it even worse; in the back of her mind, Omega thought it was cute.

No way I'm telling him about those images I was seein', though. He really WILL think I'm losin' it. An' I'm not tellin' him he looks cute, either. Not only does it give away more about how I feel than I wanna give, I doubt he'd be happy with a descriptor so opposite the 'tough guy' image he wants to project.

"What's the matter?" he asked then. "Headache back? Do I need to get you to the medlab, or make an emergency call an' get them here?"

"No, no. It's not a headache." She shrugged and shook her head. "I just couldn't sleep. I'm kinda...restless. So I thought I'd get a snack, since I didn't eat dinner. Did you?"

"Did I...oh, have dinner? Sorry, not awake yet."

"'S okay. Yeah, did you eat?"

"No, I didn't even try. I was, uh, a little too worried about you to bother with eating, to be honest."

"Oh. Um, thanks. I...really appreciate the concern, hon. Want something to eat?"

"Sure." Echo followed her back into her kitchen. "What are we having?"

"Well, I was debating between a sandwich, or firing up the stove and making an omelet."

"You ARE awake, aren't you?" Echo wondered, tone conveying concern, as Omega got out a large sauté pan and turned on the stove. She dumped a lump of butter into the pan and watched it melt as she cracked several eggs into a bowl and whisked them.

"Yeah."

"That's not like you, Meg. You usually sleep like the dead. Unless... something's bothering you. What's up?" Echo asked, as he got out two plates and flatware, setting them on Omega's dining table.

She winced at his simile and shook her head without looking at him as she deftly coated the hot pan with the egg mixture and let it set, then grabbed the package of shredded cheese blend, and another package of sliced mushrooms, from the refrigerator. "No, put one plate back and gimme the other one," she told him.

"It's the Cortian thing again, isn't it?" he guessed shrewdly, as he followed her directions, then sat down at the table.

"Yeah." She sighed.

He was silent, watching and waiting, as she filled the omelet, let the cheese melt, and flipped it deftly onto the plate.

"Here. Half's yours. Want some milk?"

He nodded, and watched her in obvious disquiet as she poured it. Then she joined him at the table and they started eating.

"Echo," she said, around a mouthful of egg, cheese and mushroom, "I really wish you'd take me seriously about this first-contact thing. It's got nothing to do with me going into space."

"I'm listening." Echo sat back and looked at her.

"But I've already told you..."

"Meg, hunches won't cut it here. This is a diplomatic engagement. If you've got something solid, tell me."

Omega shrugged and shook her head.

"Then the subject is closed." Echo stood and deposited his flatware in his glass, and the lot in the sink, running water into them so the food remains wouldn't dry before they could be put in the dishwasher the next morning. Then he came back and crouched down by her chair. Resting a soothing hand on her forearm, he told her, "Meg, it's all right, baby. I know what I'm doing. It's not like I haven't handled first contacts before. Remember how I started as an Agent?"

"Yeah."

"And I've done it a lot since then. More times than I can count. So this is just routine, Meg." He worried the sleeve of her robe up high enough to expose bare skin, then gently rubbed her wrist with the pad of his thumb, apparently trying to settle her.

"Maybe that's the problem, Echo."

"What do you mean?" Echo looked startled. He withdrew his hand.

"Maybe it's gotten so routine that you're missing the little warning cues."

"Are you saying I'm overconfident?" He scowled; Omega shrugged.

"All I'm saying right now is that I think you're taking it much too lightly."

Echo stood abruptly.

"It's under control, Meg. Go back to bed. I'll see you in the morning." He headed for the back door.

"'Thanks for the omelet, Meg.' You're welcome, Echo," Omega muttered under her breath.

From the other side of the back door, Echo's voice drifted.

"Thanks for the omelet, Meg. G'night."

"You're welcome, Echo. Good night." Omega sighed, piled the rest of the dirty dishes in the sink, and went back to bed.

She stared at the ceiling most of the night.

* * *

The following day, with Echo's full permisson and approval, Omega scheduled her physical...for the very next morning.

"I hate it," she noted. "I don't really wanna do this."

"Baby, we all have to do it."

"Yeah, I know—but they do way more on me."

"I doubt it," Echo said, shrugging.

"Yeah? Then how come you were back from yours by first lunch last month, but they scheduled me for all damn day? Division day, at that?"

Echo didn't have an answer to that.

* * *

"Okay, girl," Zebra said, as Omega reported for her annual physical. "For you, we do the five-buck tour."

"Again? Or should I rather say, still?" Omega wondered with a sigh. "I hate this."

"I know, hon, but..." Zebra broke off. "I don't like to keep reminding you, but given what was done to you as a child, we need to stay on top of everything. We don't know that, as you get older, some of that genetic tinkering might not go unstable on us."

"On ME," Omega murmured. "No offense, Zebra, but the person who will bear the consequences of it is not a 'we.' It's ME. I kind of find the medical 'we' bothersome, if not outrightly objectionable, especially in this instance."

"Oh. Well, I'm sorry, Omega. I didn't mean to upset you. And you're absolutely right, every bit. But for what it's worth, I'm your primary care physician, and in case you haven't noticed, I've taken a liking to you. If... something happens, I swear I'm going to be right there beside you, just as much as Echo will."

"I guess," Omega replied, stifling another sigh. "Time for the usual drill?"

"Yeah. Strip and put on the paper gown thing."

"Dammit."

"I know. We can put you into a jumpsuit for part of it, but the MRI gets persnickety."

* * *

Omega's physical exam was extensive, and incorporated almost every kind of medical imaging known to the Agency, plus quite a few other types of testing.

This included an immense number of vials of blood drawn, which procedure Omega despised. The negative pressure sensation in the vein made her want to cringe, and the technician took fully a dozen of the big vials, handed them off to the lab, then came back for twelve more.

"How the hell much is that?" Omega wondered in astonishment.

"Um, the vials are ten milliliters apiece, so that'd be...lessee..." the lab tech thought for a moment. "Two hundred and forty milliliters, or about half a pint, give or take."

"More like take," Omega grumbled under her breath.

"Sorry. They got a lot of tests they need to run. The genetic sequencing alone takes about a third of that."

"I'll bet."

* * *

Next came the manual and pelvic exams, so after Zebra took all her vital signs, to include an EKG, Omega had the opportunity to be poked and prodded in places that nobody else even got to see. She said little, merely bit her lip, and waited for it all to end.

"Okay, let's get the x-rays and ultrasounds out of the way," Zebra said cheerfully, as Omega got up from the exam table.

"Tell me those don't include mammograms," she said.

"Of course they do."

"Do you mean to tell me you STILL don't have something more advanced than smushing my breasts between two plexiglas plates and zapping 'em?"

"Um...no, not yet. Workin' on it. There's tech out there, we just haven't gotten access to it. I keep pushing Fox to make it higher priority, but he keeps forgetting." Zebra gave her patient an evil grin. "I've been threatening to drag him down here and smash his privates between two glass plates so he can see how it feels. That might make him remember better."

Omega laughed, but it was rueful.

"Let me know if you want help with that," she told Zebra. "Hell, I'll hold him down. Especially if it means something more comfortable than a standard mammogram."

"Um, you do know that Fox doesn't spend ALL his time in the office, right?" Zebra commented, face turning a delicate shade of pink. "Granted, he's a good bit older than he looks, but he knows what the inside of the gym looks like, really well. He's got the physical prowess of a much younger man, and I think you might need Echo's help to hold him down. And maybe Alpha Two into the bargain. Especially if he gets pissed."

"And if anybody would know, it'd be you," Omega teased the other woman, who happened to be Fox's significant other. Zebra blushed deeper, but grinned.

"I suppose," she said. "'Bout like you'd know about Echo's physique."

"What?!" Omega exclaimed, startled. "What do you mean, Zebra?"

"Just what I said," Zebra noted, grin growing wider. "Don't think I've forgotten you telling me, back when we were trying to find ways to combat the gastropoid, that you 'loved him to pieces.' And it's been a good while since then, so even if you weren't to that point back at Halloween, I figure you've had plenty of time to get acquainted with each other's physiques by this time. Neither of you is exactly the shy wallflower type."

"Uh, yeah, but...but that's not really what it sounds like, comin' from a Southerner," Omega tried to explain, feeling her cheeks heat. "I love Romeo and India to pieces too, but I'm not, um, like, sleepin' with 'em or nothin'. Nor Echo either."

"Oh," Zebra said, apparently understanding; the grin disappeared, to be replaced by something that looked to Omega a lot like disappointment. "But...you're so close...even closer now than...aren't...then you and Echo aren't...?"

"No, no," Omega murmured, face red-hot. "We're close, yeah, but..." Omega drew in a deep breath, then let it out in a long sigh. "Look, hon. Stop and think. Why are you doing such an in-depth physical on me?"

"Easy. Because of what was done to you by that damned gastropoid."

"Right. And what 'that damned gastropoid' did to me was a kind of in vivo genetic recombination technique," Omega pointed out. "Last I looked at my genetic scans, y'all had figured there were multiple slices of genetic material from around ten or twelve different extraterrestrial species in there, right?"

"Um, we upped that to thirteen after your last exam at Christmas, when you got the Harrnakian flu," Zebra muttered admission. "Not all of which are...sentient, as I've pointed out before."

"Right." Omega winced despite herself. "And I can tell you that he took me apart and put me back together, 'cause I remember him doing it. Well, I did after Zz'r'p got done with things. And then he telepathically brainwashed and programmed me. To KILL Echo."

"Yeah, okay. We already knew all that."

"Right. So stop and think. Why in the HELL would Echo want to get... involved...with a thing like that?"

"I...I don't get..."

"Zebra, I know you disagree on some level, but let's face it—I'm not human any more. I haven't been in a long, long time. YOU, of all people, should know this. Twenty years ago, Megan McAllister died, and what was born in her place was an alien assassin, a 'species' all to herself, created solely to see Echo dead...one way or another. That assassin...was me. I'm a monster, Zebra, just as surely as the fictional creature that Victor Franken-stein created was a monster, and by the same definition. Why the hell would any man—but ESPECIALLY Echo—want to get romantically involved with that?" *No matter how much I wish he would,* Omega added mentally, discouraged, and glad there were no telepaths about.

Zebra stood there, blinking at her. Suddenly her gaze became focused on her patient's face, and Omega realized she hadn't guarded her expres-sions well enough.

"Uh-huh," Zebra muttered then. "So you DO love him."

"It doesn't matter, Zebra," Omega sighed, not bothering to deny it, but not confirming it, either. "It hasn't happened, and it isn't gonna. And you're not gonna say anything to anybody about it. Got that?"

"No, hon, of course I won't. Patient confidentiality," Zebra murmured. "But...I mean..." She shrugged. "He hasn't even...I dunno, put out feelers, or something?"

"No. Or, well, if he has, I haven't seen...no. Just...no. He's got his own personal history to deal with, anyway. I won't breach his confidence, except to say I have reason to know he's not interested."

"Damn."

"Yeah."

They were silent for a long moment.

* * *

"Well, we can either stand here and stare at each other," Zebra finally decided, "or we can go do your mammogram...OR we can go get Fox and smush his family jewels in the mammogram machine." She snickered, but watched her patient in concern without appearing to do so.

"I vote for number three," Omega said, a weak smile forming on her face.

"Okay, but if we're gonna do that, we really do need to go for reinforcements. The way he has his Suits tailored, you can't tell, but Fox is way beefier than he looks. Strong as hell, too. I mean, I like it, but...don't mess with him."

"Well, I'm not really that surprised," Omega said, grinning openly. "I was halfway joking about holding him down. But seriously, if it gets us better tech, I'll give it a go!"

"Nah. I think we better go with the mammogram, girl."

"Aw, shit."

"Hey, at least the ultrasound comes after your mammogram," Zebra pointed out. "I'll make sure the lab tech warms up the probe thing for you, too."

"And the gel bottle, please," Omega requested. "The last time, the gel hadn't been in the little heating-cup thing long enough. It hadn't warmed up properly, so then she squirted it all over my torso, and I swear I levitated off the table. It was ice-cold."

"Damn, girl! Yeah, I'll get on that."

* * *

Echo spent the day in the Alpha Line briefing and activities room off the Core, where Fox had provided a small office space for Alpha One—not that the pair were there much, singly or together. But there were a couple of desks, back to back in the rear of the room, one in each corner, with computer hookups, wifi, filing cabinets, and viewscreens—there was even a safe, and a VERY well-tricked-out first aid kit. The department had even been in discussions over the notion of installing a coffeemaker of some sort, likely a pod brewer, to provide caffeine for all of Alpha Line, in order to avoid the whole lot traipsing down to the break room before and after every departmental meeting.

Echo was used to occupying the office space with his partner more often than not, but he knew that Omega would be gone a good part of the day—essentially all day, truth be known—with medical tests. His partner's medical history was unusual, to say the least, and after the full scope of what Slug had done to her had been uncovered the previous summer, a rigorous testing schedule had been set up for her physicals, to keep an eye on things.

The full extent of that 'rigorous testing' only became apparent to him the day before; Omega's complaint regarding her physicals had caused him to make a couple of discreet inquiries. As Echo was also her departmental chief, the chief of staff, Zarnix, had explained to him the magnitude of what comprised Omega's standard physical. Echo had been shocked. To say it was comprehensive was putting it mildly. And under the circumstances, this exam was likely to be even more extensive than THAT.

He was concerned, but there was little he could do save wait to see if everything was all right. The headache she had had was particularly troublesome, in his mind, but he hoped there was some humdrum explanation for it.

Meanwhile, he looked over various items of paperwork; on an impromptu whim, Echo went ahead and submitted the requisition for the coffee pod brewer and supplies for it, deciding his department had earned it. He also studied his partner's rankings for the latest batch of Alpha Line applicants; Omega had proven skillful in setting up test sequences and training sessions suitable for screening potential candidates, to include a recent addition: detailed psych profiles. So now he checked out the priorities she had set among the current slate of candidates, and ascertained why she had ranked them as she had.

Hm. Not bad at all, he decided, studying her files. *Meg's got everything laid out logically and sequentially. I like this. And her criteria make damn good sense to me. Yeah. I can see these candidates being part of the department. That'll add...what? Okay, it depends what we use as a cutoff, and she's got two possible levels listed. The top ten percent gives us five new teams, plus that extra to fill out Alpha Eight; the top twelve percent gives us eight, plus the extra—that'd double the department. Mm. Maybe it's time to schedule some interviews, to see what I think of 'em personally. We need to really start growing the department, now that we've got things pretty much established. But I think I'll have the candidates interview with Alpha One, and not just me. I'm kinda interested in seeing what Meg's impressions are. She was sure helpful with deciding on the new recruits last fall.*

He glanced at the clock.

Shit. Five minutes later than the last time I looked. It's gonna be a damn long day.

* * *

Next came the full-body MRI. In some respects, this wasn't so bad, Omega decided, because all she had to do was lie there. She even tended to get sleepy. But there were two problems as far as she was concerned, and both of them prevented her being able to nap through the procedure—the fact that she had to remain as unmoving as humanly possible, for as long as it took the machine to scan her from crown to sole, and the fact that the machine made so much clacking racket in the doing that she had to wear a noise-canceling headset.

"No, it isn't broken," Zebra had pointed out. "And this IS the galactic tech. It's just that loud. I dunno why. I'm not 'mechanical,' so I've never tried to look at the guts of the thing."

* * *

The cerebral scan was run next, because it would take longer than most of the other tests to analyze, the human brain being what it was, and Omega's brain being something considerably different than the norms.

"And I wanna go ahead and get that done before we start running the markers into you," Zebra pointed out. "'Cause that'll be up next."

* * *

The CT and PET scans involved running various dye and radiation markers into Omega's bloodstream, so they could determine all kinds of details of her circulatory system and metabolic rates. Omega especially despised those because she could feel some of the markers in her system, and they made her itch all over.

"No, you're not allergic, and it makes sense," Zebra had noted, when Omega complained of the itching. "There's nothing WRONG with you, per se, even though none of my other patients can feel it. You aren't my other patients, and your system is more...mm, sensitive, I guess. Not in the 'allergic' way or anything. Just...by the time you...were made like you are, your sensory and nervous systems were ramped up, and you just NOTICE stuff that other people don't."

"Lucky me," a rueful Omega said.

* * *

Last but not least was the full endoscopy of her digestive tract, coupled with a quick 'scope of her bronchial tubes. This was done while Omega was under a mild general anesthesia, however. There was never any prep for the endoscope other than not eating since dinner the night before. However, that made for a full twenty-four hours prior to the exams, and there was plenty of time for Omega's system to mostly clear itself; she never asked about the rest of the 'mostly,' not especially wanting those particular questions answered.

It's humiliating enough to be examined in detail from top to bottom and inside out, she decided. *I really don't wanna know that, too.*

* * *

"Okay, girl, like usual, you're as healthy as a horse," Zebra declared at the end of the day, as Omega was getting dressed. "All my patients should be so good."

"What about the cerebral scan?" Omega wondered, tying her tie. "That's the thing Echo and I were the most worried about, after that headache."

"Well, I won't deny that there are some differences from the last few cerebral scans we gave you," Zebra admitted. "But I've looked over 'em and I got Zarnix to give 'em a good eyeball, too—he is an absolute genius

38

when it comes to the human neural system—and neither of us sees anything to be concerned about. His take on the differences is that...lessee, how do I explain this? He thinks that the whole incident with Slug—the mental contact, learning to erect the telepathic block, all that shit—triggered additional development in the, ah, 'enhancements' there, and that as a result, your brain is continuing to...grow, I guess is a good way to express it. Not in size, but in capability. And I'm in agreement." The second in command of Medical shrugged. "I don't see anything to be concerned about."

"But what about the headache?"

"It may well have been some sort of threshold being reached and transcended, that your brain hasn't yet learned to interpret in any other fashion than 'pain,'" Zebra explained. "I know you said you had some funny dream-things. Maybe you're starting to pick up on some 'transmissions.' Would you like for me to contact the Arcturan embassy up on the eighth floor and request some sessions to see?"

"No," Omega decided, thinking. "No, I'll take care of that myself. Zz'r'p knows me."

"Ah, right. Uh, I think I remember Fox saying he was at the Geneva office, mediating some negotiations for somebody."

"Oh. That's good to know. Thanks."

"You're welcome. Okay girl, you're done for another six months or so."

"But...the other agents only come in once a year."

"The other agents aren't you. See you in six months."

* * *

A worn-out Omega dressed, left the medlab, and went back to her quarters. Echo hadn't gotten off duty yet, so she dug a pot pie he'd made from her freezer and heated it—it was already cooked—and ate half of it without slowing down, then covered the remainder and put it back in the oven on WARM.

She left a sticky note for Echo on the back door.

* * *

Ace,

If I'm not turned wrong-side out and bled dry, I don't know why not.

39

There's half a pot pie still warm in my oven if you want it, and some of your favorite beer chilling in the fridge. I pretty much inhaled the other half of the pot pie just a bit ago, 'cause it's been a loooong time since they let me eat, and I'm gonna go to bed now. Try not to wake me if you don't mind. To be honest, I'm wiped. Okay, evidently, but wiped.

—Ω

* * *

Then, true to her word, she got ready and went to bed.

* * *

Echo came home about an hour later, and promptly headed for the back door. The lights were dimmed in Omega's den, but not out; her bedroom door was closed, with no sign of light under it.

He noticed the note beside his hand, where he leaned against the door. He yanked down the note and read it. Then he nodded to himself.

"Well, that's something," he decided, drawing a deep breath of relief. "There must have been an ordinary explanation for the headache, I guess. Thank God. I don't even wanna think if..." He broke off, and shook himself out of the morbid mood into which he had suddenly fallen.

And...she thought about my dinner, even after all that medical shit, he considered, feeling a certain warmth inside, as he tiptoed into her kitchen and fished his dinner out of Omega's oven.

* * *

"Echo?" Omega turned to her partner as they took the Corvette out on a routine patrol two days later. "Can I ask you...a favor?"

"Sure, Meg," Echo responded, as he steered the Corvette through traffic. "Whatcha need?"

"Well..." she paused, trying to figure out how to start. "We're partners..."

"Last time I checked," he deadpanned, concentrating on the traffic as he drove.

"Yeah, but...oh, blast it, there's no good way to say this..."

"Just say it."

Omega took a deep breath and plunged in head-first.

"All right. Echo, do you ever think about if something were to...happen...to one of us?"

Echo cut his eyes over at her, then focused back on the street.

"No."

"Never?"

"No."

"Uh-huh. Yeah," she said knowingly. "Anyway, I've been thinking. You know me: Never know when to quit. So I wanted you to know that...I'm counting on you to..." she searched for words, "let me know? That it's okay to...quit? If and when the time comes..."

Echo abruptly pulled the Corvette over to the curb, parking it, and turned to Omega with an expression in which was the barest hint of something that might have been anxiety, at least to her mind, as she looked at him.

"Meg, are you trying to tell me something? Your physical was the other day...I gathered from the note you left on the back door afterward that everything was okay, but..."

"No, no," she told him, "I'm fine. Nothing like that. What I'm trying to say is, if something SHOULD happen—sometime—I'll keep fighting just as long as I can. But when the time comes, I need to know that it's...okay to let go."

"Just what is it you're asking me to do?" Echo studied her, dark eyes troubled.

"Be there for me, backing me up, like partners—like buddies—do... and then tell me goodbye. That's all."

"That's all."

"Yeah."

Echo put the Corvette back in gear and pulled out into traffic.

"Will you do it for me, Echo?"

Echo continued driving, intent on steering.

"Echo?"

Echo tore his gaze from the road long enough to meet and hold Omega's eyes for a moment. There was something vaguely tortured about the expression in the brown eyes, but she also saw a kind of reluctant acquiescence there.

Omega nodded, satisfied, and the Corvette drove on through Manhattan.

* * *

"Yeah, Boss, you wanted to talk to me?" Echo said, as he entered Fox's office.

"Yes, Echo, sit down, please," Fox said, looking up from his paperwork and then putting it aside to focus his attention on his department chief. "And close the door."

Echo obeyed, then sat looking at Fox as the older man pondered him for a long moment.

"Have you said anything to Omega about her attitude?" Fox finally asked.

"Uh, what do you mean?" Echo wondered, surprised by the question.

"I mean her inattentiveness, her sharpness, her apparent willingness to question everything and everyone, including me, among others."

"Including you?! When did she do that??"

"Mm. Yes, I think you had stepped out to fetch a report or the like. She did so two days before her physical. Started asking—almost demanding to know—why this mission was even necessary. Why it couldn't be put off or even canceled outright. And didn't seem to want to accept my answers."

"Oh. That." *Interesting. That would have been the day she had her headache, I think,* Echo decided. "Yeah, I have, a little bit, but it's all pretty recent, that behavior of hers. Seems to revolve around my off-planet Cortian mission."

"I was afraid of that. She's letting bitterness eat at her, eh?"

"Maybe. I'm not sure. She keeps insisting she isn't, but hey."

"Yes. All right; it's your best judgement, but I don't want you to let this go on too long before you put a firm stop to it, alter khaver. Good she may be, but she's still a relatively 'young' Agent; she's as yet a few weeks short of a year's tenure with us, if memory serves. I don't want her getting it in her head that she can wrap her department chief around her finger, just because he happens to also be her partner."

"Fox! She's not wrapping me around her finger!"

"Isn't she?" Fox queried, an enigmatic look in his hazel eyes. "All

42

right, Echo. Just see that she doesn't, and that she doesn't give that impression to OTHERS."

Echo sighed, understanding what Fox wanted.

"All right, Fox," he murmured. "I'll...take care of it."

"Good. Dismissed."

* * *

Omega closeted herself in her study, door closed. Echo was out, preparing for his diplomatic mission, and she desperately needed to talk to someone else—without Echo hearing. And she had already ascertained that that someone else was not at Headquarters, so she couldn't pay him a friendly, innocent visit.

So she booted her laptop, then placed a vid call to Europe, to a particular envoy in the Geneva Office.

A familiar blue, fishlike face appeared on the screen as the other end answered.

"Omega!" it said in surprise. "What is wrong?"

"Zz'r'p," she told the telepathic Deltiri ambassador from the Arcturan system, "I REALLY need to talk to you..."

* * *

"...Omega, this is potentially very important," Zz'r'p told her ten minutes later, once the explanations were complete and the ambassador had asked a few pertinent questions. "Have you told anyone else this is happening?"

"No. I, um, well look—if I told any other human, Zz'r'p, they'd think I was nuts. And I'm not entirely sure I'm not," Omega admitted. Zz'r'p watched as her face fell.

"Meaning Echo?"

"Echo, Fox, India, Romeo..."

"Omega, I cannot come there. I cannot leave the negotiations. They are at a critical stage."

"I know. I'm not asking you to. I guess...I just wanted to know if you think I really AM going nuts, or if there might actually be something to this."

"I cannot yet say either way, my dear girl, though you certainly seem quite lucid to me," Zz'r'p decided. "Can you come here?"

"No." Omega shook her head. "We've got this first contact going down—the same thing that seems to be triggering all this stuff—and given Echo is their preferred contact, that makes Alpha One on tap for every-thing..."

"Ah, I see," Zz'r'p commented, realizing the difficulty. "Well...I should much prefer to be in the same room with you so that I might see any body language responses, but I CAN do a brief distance mental conversation, if you like. I have a little while now, and if we need to do so, we can com-municate more later..."

"That might be good," Omega agreed. "I've been trying to figure out how to tell you what-all I saw in more detail, but I think the best way is still gonna be to just SHOW you."

"My thoughts exactly," the Arcturan agreed. "Give me a moment to 'locate' you, and then we shall begin."

"Okay, I'm waiting."

Zz'r'p reached out mentally, searching for the electromagnetic patterns he knew to belong to Omega's unique brain. When he had located them, he spoke.

"All right, my dear. Are you ready?"

"As I'll ever be."

"Then let us begin."

* * *

Omega took the Arcturan telepath through the entire sequence of im-agery she'd seen. When she was finished, he was silent for long moments.

Well? she wondered.

Interesting, he said. *Would you object to my conducting an examina-tion of your mental state?*

Not at all, Omega told him, relieved by the request. *I was kinda hoping you would, to tell the truth. If I'm going crazy, then I need to notify Echo, take myself off active duty—any kind of duty—and turn myself in to the medlab for psychiatric evaluation and treatment.*

All right. Give me a moment.

Omega remained quiet, sensing the alien's gentle presence, nosing about in her mind.

Mm. So that is the way it is, eh? she heard Zz'r'p's soft mental voice say.

What? Way what is?

Between you and your partner. You care. Greatly.

Meh. Omega mentally shrugged. *Kind of a moot point any more.*

Meaning you believe he does not. At least, not in this fashion.

Of course not. Would you, in his shoes? The woman he loved rejected him to marry somebody else, then his old enemy kills her, THEN uses his PARTNER to try to kill HIM. By turning her into an inhuman thing. Now THERE'S a really attractive image, she pointed out, then gave a bleak mental laugh.

* * *

I have heard you make comments like that before, Omega. And when you are speaking, you can pass them off as jokes, exaggerations. Here, you cannot hide the truth from me. This is truly how you view yourself—an 'inhuman thing.'

She gave another mental shrug.

So? It's the truth.

No, it is not.

Of course it is. I'm a construct. I've got something like a dozen or more different gene sets in me. I'm not human any more, therefore I'm inhuman. I'm not any recognizable species, therefore I'm a thing.

Oh, my dear girl. Is there anything I can say to convince you otherwise?

No.

What if I—

Zz'r'p, no offense, but unless I'm going nuts, this isn't really about me. It's about determining if what I'm seeing is legitimate, and if it is, what to do about it. No matter what I am, you still read me right—I don't want anything to happen to Echo.

All right. How far are you willing to go with that determination, Omega?

Huh?

At what cost would you save him?

There was a long pause, and Zz'r'p felt Omega mentally steeling herself.

Any cost, came her answer, and he stifled his shock.

Even though he does not believe you?

What he believes is beside the point. If any of that shit I saw is gonna happen in real life, I'm gonna do my damnedest to stop it any way I can.

But if he does not love you, then why...?

Because that's not the way love works, Zz'r'p. I'd have thought you, of all people, would know that.

You would risk your life for a man who does not believe you, who does not love you?

Do you know he doesn't? Omega's mental voice was wistful. *'Cause you'd know, if anybody did...*

No, I do not know, my dear. I have not had occasion to consider the matter, and unless he was 'wearing his heart on his sleeve,' as you humans say—which he, of all Agents, does not—I am unlikely to 'see' it offhand, and I would never invade his privacy so. I only saw your feelings because they are so intimately tied into this situation. I did not go looking for them.

No, I knew, when I told you to check me out, that you'd probably find out. Omega sighed mentally. *It's okay. I just thought maybe...*

No, I do not have that information, Omega. I am sorry.

Okay. Then, based on what I've seen, he probably doesn't. And I don't blame him. Like I said, inhuman thing. Which also means that I don't RE-ALLY even belong here, in the Agency. I don't belong any place, really.

Dear Creator, child. You do not truly mean to say... Zz'r'p was horrified.

Sure I do, Zz'r'p. Out of everybody in this whole damn place. But especially with respect to Echo. And Fox too, I suppose. But yeah. Echo is the department chief, and the next Agency chief, top Agent and all that. Gotta keep him safe. Besides, you...might as well kill me...if anything happened to him.

Which means you consider yourself...

Expendable. Right.

But your friends...

Will get along fine without me. Romeo and India have each other. Fox has his work. And Zebra, I suppose. Echo...

...Is your best friend.

But I'm not his. The only time he's ever indicated that was during Slug's siege. He's never said it since. Not once. So the way I figure it, all things considered, he was just trying to keep me going.

Now, I am fairly certain THAT is not true.

Meh. Omega shrugged again. *He'll live. That's the important thing. He'll live, and be free, not a captive. So tell me if these vision things are real or not.*

* * *

If Zz'r'p's race had had hair, he would have been pulling his out at that point. Omega's mind was made up already, this he could tell without doubt, but her chain of inference was so sound that the telepath could not break it. Of everyone there of importance to her, all had other interests...except her. All had places they felt they belonged...except her.

And she has no one to go home to, were she to leave, the alien realized, *and no way to do so in any event. According to her categorizations and logic, she is indeed the most reasonable candidate to put at risk in attempting to stop whatever may be happening.*

But in all honesty, the telepath could not yet say for certain if what Omega had experienced as visions was legitimate or not. Such things were not unheard-of in the telepathic community, but they were rare enough that he needed to consider what she had presented him in detail before he could even garner an inkling as to the causation.

Certainly Slug's machinations will have something to do with it, whether they prove legitimate precognitive imagery or not, he decided. *But I must first determine a mechanism before I can begin to say they should be considered a risk.*

So he told Omega as much.

I cannot tell you yet, Omega, my dear girl. I have heard of such happening, certainly, but it is unusual. I need to consider everything you have given me to analyze, first. Do we have time for me to do this?

Yeah, we still got time. The Cortians haven't even made planetfall yet, and won't for a couple more days. And as far as I can tell, none of the possibilities would go down until they left, which would be several days of negotiations past first contact. So I estimate we got about five days or so. More, if they decide to delay to look over the planet in more detail.

Excellent. Do you object if I contact a personal mentor on my homeworld, to ask her advice and opinion?

Ooo. Um, can you...I mean, it's all so personal...

I will not reveal any more than is necessary for her understanding. I am highly experienced and well trained, but she is much older than I, with concomitant experience and knowledge. I seek to determine what she knows of precognition, which is not one of my study specialties.

Oh, I see. And she's not gonna talk to anybody else?

No, no. I can assure you of that.

Okay. Yeah, do that, then. And let me know what you find out.

As soon as I can, Omega, I swear to you.

All right.

Back 'outside.'

* * *

Returning to the vid comm, the Agent and the ambassador stared at each other for long moments, neither sure what to say next.

"Well, um, thanks, Zz'r'p," Omega finally murmured. "So I'm not crazy?"

"No, not at all," Zz'r'p replied softly. "All I need to ascertain is whether or not these...experiences...are legitimate precognition, or some sort of mental effect produced by...what was done to you as a youngling."

"Okay, well, that's good to know, I guess. At least for now; it could get nasty later on, if it started to affect my ability to perceive the real world, I expect..."

"That...is true."

"Shall I wait to hear from you?"

"Yes, please. I will contact you as soon as I can. It should not be more than a day or two at most. Is that soon enough?"

"Yeah, it'll be fine."

"Very good. Zz'r'p out."

"Omega out."

Chapter 2

"There you are!" Omega said, meeting Madrid, the head of the Weapons Lab, on the top floor of Headquarters, just outside the elevator. "Are you ready?"

"I rather think so, old girl," Madrid remarked with a smile, dropping in beside her as she turned for the stairs to the rooftop. "I appreciate your giving me this opportunity to look at your observatory. It should help me decide if I want to take your class next semester."

"Oh, I don't think you have anything to worry about, Madrid," Omega said, opening the door onto the roof and stepping into the sunshine. "You've got the science background, and I don't plan on this one being much more than a basic intro course. It's just that I'm trying to tailor it expressly to people working for PGLEIA."

"I can understand that," Madrid agreed, following her across the roof to an urban-camo-colored observatory dome. "And this is your observatory?"

"It is," Omega declared with a smile. "Thanks largely to Echo and Fox."

"How on earth do you manage to observe in the middle of the city? Isn't the light a problem?"

"Oh, that's not so hard to deal with, not with galactic tech. Adaptive optics on the 'scope and some special light-dampeners, arranged in a perimeter," Omega pointed out the devices ringing the little dome, "pretty much take care of it. C'mon in."

* * *

Inside, Omega proceeded to remove the cover from the big black telescope, as Madrid pulled out his cell phone and activated an app.

"Damn, old girl, that's a bloody big 'scope! That's corking, that is! So Echo gave you that for Christmas?"

"Yeah, that or he got Nicholas to bring it down, I'm not sure which.

Either way, he's responsible," Omega agreed, coming to Madrid's side. Madrid's phone beeped softly, and he looked at it.

"Ah. Everything is clear," he murmured. "No one is watching or listening, not in here. Evidently it was set up with the same specifications as the agent quarters, given that it is, effectively, something of a retreat for you. I show the same emergency capacity as is in our quarters—in that you can call for help and activate certain sensors to help Security determine the proper emergency response—but not active surveillance, not in here. So we're free to talk, though we probably still ought to keep it down, because there IS a security system on the roof as a whole. Now tell me what this is all about, and what you need."

"Well, I think I've got a potential situation developing, Madrid, and I need a little help, designing some special equipment," Omega breathed, extracting her own smart phone. "Here. Here's the specs." She tapped her phone gently to his to transfer the files.

"Good. And now you've got the surveillance detection app, too," Madrid said softly, opening up the files Omega had just passed to him. "Mm. Okay, I get it. I think this is really just a modification of that ring shield that Echo tested for us. We almost have that thing ready to start distributing to the field agents, anyway. Finally."

"Yeah, but this thing of mine is a little more complicated than that," Omega pointed out. "Look here at what I need it to be able to do..."

"Mm. Yes, I see that. A small, powerful force field completely encasing the person, easily concealed, capable of automatically detecting and extending to include a second person..."

"Right. And it needs to be proof against handheld projectiles, photonic or bosonic beam weapons, particle beam weapons, and brief plasma bursts."

"What kind of plasma? What temperature? What density?" Madrid peppered her with questions. "I'm gobsmacked. This is a damn tall order, Omega."

"Don't I know it," Omega sighed.

"What do you need it for? And why haven't you gone through Echo, or even Fox?"

"I'm...seeing stuff, in the...in the files," Omega hedged, twisting the truth a little. "Stuff I don't like at all, but I can't pin it down. It's this first contact thing."

"Oooo. But Echo and Fox?"

"They're kinda stuck," Omega admitted. "They got orders from higher up. But I don't like what I'm seeing, so I just..." She sighed, then shrugged. "I wanna be ready for anything, Madrid. DAMN, I hope I'm wrong, and I won't even have to use it. But just in case, I need that," she nodded at his cell phone.

"All right, I get it," he murmured. "I suppose you want me to keep this off the record?"

"Yes, I do."

"Do Fox or Echo even know about it?"

"Not...yet." *I hope they won't have to,* Omega thought. *'Cause chances are, the point at which they find out about it will be the point at which I have to use it. But I need to have it in my hip pocket—literally, I guess—just in case.*

"Very well. Now, I need to know about that plasma."

"I...got nothin.'" Omega shrugged. "I honestly just don't have those specs."

"I need SOMETHING to go on, Omega," Madrid pointed out. "According to your list of priorities, that's an important one."

"Yeah, I know."

"What's producing the plasma?"

"It's the exhaust from an alien spacecraft engine. But I don't have specs on that either, so..." She shrugged again. "Look, I guess...why don't you try to approximate using a wide-beam particle weapon? Or one of our big ion exhaust engines, if you can get access. That should do it, I think, either way."

"All right, my dear, so..." Madrid opened the file and made some modifications, "make the particle beam specs applicable for tight-beam or wide-field. And as high intensity as I can manage, I assume?"

"You assume right."

"Duration of activity?"

"Battle mode."

"Right. So...not THAT long. Good. How long have we got to build the bloody thing?"

"Well, I don't actually anticipate anything upon the arrival," Omega determined, drawing her brows together in thought. "If they were gonna do that, they'd be bringing an invasion force. And they wouldn't be giving us a heads-up about it. AND I doubt they're gonna pull anything until they've scoped us out and see what we got, first. No, I think we have until departure before something happens. So around five Division days, maybe six. And..." Omega pulled a face. "Maybe you better make sure you and your people can't be tied to this, Madrid. If a...'diplomatic incident' goes down, I'd rather be the only one to have to take the heat. I don't want to get the Weapons Lab in trouble."

"Very good. And thank you for that consideration, old girl. Don't worry; I'll handle this personally, and make sure there aren't any identifying characteristics. Now, perhaps you'd better give me a quick tour of your little observatory, so if anyone asks, I can answer their questions."

"Good point," Omega said, turning. "So the way I got this set up..."

* * *

Fox and the Alpha One team met the Cortian ship at the Chicago Station spaceport two days later. Nothing more had been said between Echo and Omega regarding the Cortian mission since the discussion over the midnight snack, and to all appearances everything was now normal—Echo knew Omega's Celtic ancestry made her quick-tempered despite her proper Southern upbringing, but her anger always vanished as swiftly as it arrived. So Echo had not had occasion to call her on it since Fox's heads-up several days before.

However, as Echo watched his partner out of the corner of his eye while the spacecraft landed, he recognized the signs of trouble brewing. The tight lips, the squared shoulders, the faint hint of a crease between her eyebrows, all told him that she was on edge. He also understood that she was making a valiant effort not to show it, however, as she realized he was watching and flashed him a quick smile that somehow never quite reached her bright blue eyes.

"Come on, Meg," he said quietly, as Fox started toward the opening hatch. "It'll be okay."

"Of course it will," Omega said in an overly-cheerful voice, dropping into step with him. "The Agency Director AND Alpha Line's chief are both good to go on this. Nothing to worry about. Rookie jitters."

"You've been with us almost a year now. You aren't a rookie anymore. I've told you that, multiple times. You're an experienced, trusted agent."

"Funny way you have of showing it," Omega murmured under her breath. Echo just caught the remark, and threw her a perturbed glance.

* * *

"Not now, Meg."

"Fine. Name the time."

"Just drop it." His low voice was firm. Her back stiffened and her eyes flared.

"Yes, SIR."

"Don't push it, Meg." Echo's eyes glinted.

* * *

"What? I'm only giving my department chief all due respect, sir."

"We WILL continue this conversation...LATER," Echo muttered as they arrived at the spacecraft's ramp behind Fox.

"Good," Omega murmured, immediately dropping all pretense of anger. "At least I got your attention this time."

Echo blinked in surprise, then turned that attention to the alien contingent descending the ramp as Fox gave them both a kind of 'children, behave—we have company' look.

* * *

The Cortians are an...intriguing-looking species, Omega thought, suddenly trying not to laugh as she watched them disembark. *They look like nothing I can think of so much as giant humanoid canaries in uniform! No wings, though. Wonder if they're related to the Ke!endarians somehow, way on back up the family tree. Big bruisers, to be a diplomatic contingent. Well, maybe those are the bodyguards. I hope so, anyway. Otherwise, we're in really big—* Suddenly she caught her breath in recognition. *Oh shit. Shit, shit, shit. Forget 'really big' trouble. Make that HUGE trouble.*

Echo stepped forward as an important-looking Cortian came down the ramp; the other Cortians deferred to him. Omega tensed subtly, watching.

"Ambassador B'ka?" Echo queried. The Cortian nodded, and Echo continued, glib, "N'cha al Earth, Padosh B'ka. Tle'e do Echo, ab Division One Agency. Tle'e kad'm te ab decort."

Despite her concern, Omega shot her partner an amused glance as the tongue-twisting language emanated smoothly from his mouth. *Wow, Ace. How long did it take you to learn THAT?* she wondered.

"BLT—Binary Language Transmission," a smiling Fox whispered to her, aside. "It's a math code. It enables a being to learn a language based on interstellar transmissions of that language without having formal instruction or a translator."

"Excellent, Agent Echo," Ambassador B'ka replied. "You have picked up Cortian very quickly. I am impressed."

"Thank you, sir. One of my degrees was in linguistics at Division One University. I've kept up my fluencies."

"You have served first contact duty before?"

"On...several occasions." Echo threw a wry glance at Fox. "May I present the Director of the Agency, Agent Fox."

"Director." The ambassador turned and raised his plumed crest in greeting.

"Ambassador." Fox bowed formally in reply.

"And this," Echo said, turning, "is my partner, Agent Omega."

"What?! A female? Why have you presented her before me?" B'ka scowled. His voice fairly dripped disgust.

"As I said, Ambassador, she is my partner."

"I take it Cortian society is...patriarchal," a rueful Omega ventured. B'ka ignored her statement.

"Your female has permission to accompany you as we tour our vessel. But she will remain here when we depart." The statement was directed at Echo.

Omega stiffened again, ever so slightly, and Echo and Fox unobtrusively watched her reaction, concerned lest diplomatic relations be compromised. She understood, and her jaw tightened almost imperceptibly, but otherwise Omega's face remained completely neutral. She looked up at

Echo, who met her eyes understandingly.

That's it, Meg. Don't let 'em get to you, he telegraphed to her, and she nodded almost imperceptibly, jaw tightening further.

Easy for you to say, she thought, incensed—but did NOT code to him. *You aren't a non-person to them.*

"We comprehend the conditions you have established," Fox told the ambassador then. "They will be followed."

"Very well. Come." B'ka led the way back into his ship.

* * *

A complete, or almost complete, tour of the Cortian vessel, the *Trindak*, ensued. The flight deck was fairly typical for a starship; Omega always thought of a *Star Trek* bridge whenever she saw one—which, so far, was not nearly often enough to suit her. The *Trindak* was powered by the standard Alcubierre warp hyperdrive, and used an ionic interplanetary propulsion system. Omega wandered over to study the helm, inspecting it with intense curiosity.

Wow. Awful lot of offensive and defensive armament for a diplomatic vessel, she considered, noting the alien language labeling the various controls. *On the...aw, dammit...the TRINDAK. This just gets worse and worse.*

"Agent Echo," B'ka said with annoyance, "please restrain your female. That is the helm control, and it would be dangerous for one so ignorant to tamper with it. We do not wish to repair damage she has caused."

"Ambassador," Echo said firmly, shooting a glance at both Fox and Omega, "let's get something straight up front. AGENT Omega does not in any way 'belong' to me. Nor is she a servant. She is my colleague, and my," Echo looked straight at her, "equal. And that includes her intelligence and skill. She is no more likely to cause 'damage' to your ship than I am."

Omega blinked her thanks to her partner. In turn, Echo firmed his jaw and let his brown eyes twinkle at her, just a little.

He's on my side, she thought, appreciative. *At least in this much.*

"I...see..." B'ka said thoughtfully. "Human females are...different, then. Perhaps...on our next...visit, we might...mm. Yes. Let us move on, and tour the rest of the ship."

* * *

As they moved through the spacecraft, Echo watched unobtrusively as Omega casually but thoroughly scanned her surroundings. As they came to a corridor intersection, Omega looked off to her right.

"What's down here?" she tossed out, curious.

"That is prohibited!" B'ka exclaimed, and the bodyguards moved in on Omega. She and Echo both tensed, and Echo moved immediately to her side, backing her up. Fox watched the unfolding scenario carefully, hand in one jacket pocket, ready to call in support—and provide it himself—if needed.

"Why so excited, Ambassador?" Echo asked, pointed. "And we'd appreciate it if your bodyguards would stand down. It was an innocent question." He shot Omega a meaningful glance.

* * *

"Of course, Agent Echo," B'ka said, studying Echo closely. He gestured to the guards, who backed off but continued to watch Echo, wary. They ignored Omega. "A...regrettable misunderstanding. You see...that is the way to the, ah...crew living quarters. Cortian custom dictates that such private areas are...taboo...to those not specifically invited in."

* * *

As Omega listened to B'ka's explanation, the alarms went off in her head again, even as Echo and Fox relaxed. Then her acute hearing caught a faint noise echoing down the corridor from behind and she cocked her head slightly.

Was that...a SCREAM? she wondered, shocked...but not surprised. *Nope. Not any more,* she thought. *Kinda hard to be surprised about things you've already seen.*

The sound wasn't repeated, and it had been too faint for her to be certain. So Omega followed Echo in some reluctance as the party moved on, deeper into the ship.

Omega noticed that the Cortians were extremely intent on her partner, almost to the detriment of diplomatic courtesy. B'ka had scarcely spoken two words to Fox, and his only interaction with Omega was to show irritation. But the Cortians almost fawned over Echo, quizzing him, studying him surreptitiously, testing his knowledge of ships' functions. It made her nervous for some reason. Echo caught her eye, and she realized he was aware of their scrutiny as well.

Don't you find all this a little unusual? She cocked an eyebrow.

No. Not really. Echo shrugged.

* * *

Shit, Echo thought, annoyed. *She's doin' it again. I was hoping she was over all this crap.*

Echo shot a quick glance at Fox, and realized that her behavior hadn't escaped him, either; the Director was watching Echo's partner with annoyance so carefully hidden that only another Original—or possibly his lover, Zebra—would have recognized it.

Just then, Fox glanced Echo's way. He caught the younger man's eye, then raised his eyebrow. Echo let out an irritated breath, quirked his lips in aggravation, then nodded.

Dammit. I really didn't want to have to do that, he considered, jaw hardening. *But Meg's left me no choice.*

* * *

At last the tour of the *Trindak* was over, and Fox led the party through the hangar.

"Ambassador B'ka, please allow me to return the favor and show you around some of our facilities," he offered.

"Excellent. I eagerly anticipate it," B'ka responded, and he and his cortège followed Fox through the hangar...after sealing the *Trindak.*

Echo hung back, and Omega moved to his side at a subtle gesture from him. B'ka turned.

"Agent Echo, you are coming, I hope?" B'ka asked.

"In a moment, Ambassador. My partner and I have a little...conversation to finish. Please continue and I'll catch up."

B'ka nodded as Fox shot the Alpha One team a concerned glance, and the contingent exited the hangar.

"Finally!" Omega began, relieved. "Echo—"

"AGENT Omega," Echo interrupted, face tight, voice hard, "you will consider yourself removed from this detail until further notice. Alpha Two will replace you."

"Echo?!" Omega exclaimed, shocked.

"You wanted to play hardball, didn't you? Be careful who you play it with."

"Echo, please listen..." She held out her right hand to him, palm up, imploring. Echo looked down at the hand she offered him, his gaze cool, then turned on his heel and walked away, leaving her standing there.

"Dismissed, Agent," he barked over his shoulder. The door closed behind him.

Omega stood alone in the hangar with only the sinister alien spacecraft for company.

* * *

A pained Omega stayed in her bedroom the next morning until Echo had left his quarters to meet Fox, starting his day rather earlier than usual; they were planning to hand over dealings with the Cortians to Agent Sugar—who was head of the Diplomatic department—until it was time for departure, but Echo needed to interact with the alien contingent a bit more in order to ensure that appearances were met. This was especially important, given that Echo was the chosen Agent—'exchange student' was how Omega thought of it—to go with the Cortians upon their departure. *Not, she thought, that they're leaving anybody behind to complete the exchange. Which is damn suspicious in itself, if you ask me.*

Once Echo left for the day, she came out of her bedroom, already dressed, and went to her study, placing a vid call to the Geneva Office, and Zz'r'p.

"Omega!" the Arcturan ambassador exclaimed in surprise. "What has happened?!"

"It's all gone to hell in a handbasket, Zz'r'p," Omega murmured, downcast. "I dunno if you've talked to your mentor or not, but I'm convinced now that you don't need to. It's happening, no doubt about it."

"I have; I simply had not had time to get back to you with her remarks. For that, I apologize. It seems I should have set it as my first priority. Why are you now so sure?"

"Remember when I showed you the memories of all the visions?"

"Yes? They are happening?"

"They sure as hell are. The only thing I don't know yet is which one of the endings is gonna happen."

"Which ones, so far?"

"Well, the Cortians are the spitting image of those giant yellow canary aliens I 'saw,' and the ship is identical to every version of it I saw in every vision that had it. And would you like to guess what its name is?"

"Do not tell me. It is the *Trindak*."

"Yup."

"Damnation."

"'Bout like, yeah." Omega sighed again. "What did your mentor say?"

"That it was most definitely possible. She wanted to 'meet' with you if you could find time, so that she might mentally 'feel you out' herself to see what she could determine, but it sounds as if you may have your hands full."

"Actually, if things hadn't gone the way they're going, I might have had time," Omega admitted. "But evidently I irritated Echo yesterday, when the Cortians arrived, and..."

"Oh no. What happened?"

"He got more pissed than I've ever seen him, at least at me, and...he removed me from the Cortian detail. Said he was replacing me with Alpha Two." She raked a hand through her platinum hair, which she had not yet braided for the day, throwing it into disarray. "To say last evening was kinda rough was putting it mildly."

"Why?"

"Normally Echo and I hang out together in the evenings, make dinner and eat it together, maybe watch a movie...or at least read books in the same room. We're pretty companionable. At least, we usually are. But last night was...'awkward' doesn't even begin to cut it, Zz'r'p. He stayed in his apartment the whole evening, fixed his own dinner, watched TV on his own. He barely spoke two words to me, the whole time. I thought..." She broke off and swallowed hard, before her voice could crack with the force of her emotions—anger, hurt, rejection, and a deep feeling of betrayal. Finally, when she thought she could control her tone, she resumed. "I thought he trusted me. I thought he believed in me. But he's so convinced of his own experience and ability that he's not even listening to me."

"He has been the top Agent in Division One for a very long time, Omega, and that unquestioned—by anyone, even in the Council. He has proven it, time and again. He has reason to be confident of his abilities."

"I know. But I thought he understood me better than to think I'd..."

"Yes, well. We all must learn. What are you going to do now?"

"Well, so now I gotta figure out how to save Echo, when I'm not even supposed to be at the spacecraft hangar."

Zz'r'p pondered her statement.

"What do you have in mind to do?" he asked.

* * *

The vid call came in to India's study a little later that morning, while Alpha Two was taking their time preparing for the day, and shortly after they had had breakfast. India wandered in and answered it.

"India here."

The screen flickered and came to life, depicting a blue, fish-like Deltiri face.

"Ambassador Zz'r'p here, India. I hope I do not call at an inopportune time."

"No, no, it's fine. We just finished breakfast and I was about to go put on my Suit jacket before we clocked in for the day."

"Excellent. May I have a few moments of your time? I have some important matters I think you may need to know about."

"Sure. What's on your mind?"

"Well, it pertains to your friend, Omega."

"Is something wrong with Meg?"

"No...and yes. Some interesting things have been happening, and I am concer—"

"Hey, India, baby," Romeo called from somewhere in the apartment, "heads up. We got a mission comin' in."

"Hold on a minute, Zz'r'p," India told the alien diplomat on the other end of the vid call. "I'm in here, Romeo. What was that?"

"I said we got a mission assignment," Romeo said as he came to the door, texting on his cell phone. "Whoops! I didn't know you were on th' phone too, babe."

"That's all right, hon. What's the assignment?"

"Well, I'm tryin' to figure that one out. Best I can tell, Echo's givin' us th' Cortian departure escort detail."

"But I thought Meg was doing that!"

"Not according to what she told me some fifteen minutes ago," Zz'r'p interjected, very quiet. "This is why I decided to contact you. There may well be more going on here than meets the eye, and you will need to know about it, if you are to take her place on the assignment."

"Well, shit," Romeo muttered. "Why's Meg not doin' it?"

"I dunno," India admitted. "Did you ask Echo?"

"I texted 'im back about it, yeah."

"What did he say?"

"Basically, 'None o' your damn business,'" Romeo noted, reading the text message sequence, "though he was a LITTLE bit more polite than that. Not a whole lot, but a little bit."

"What, precisely, did he say, Agent Romeo?" Zz'r'p queried. "If I might make so bold."

"I was gonna ask the same thing anyway," India said.

"Uhhh, lessee." Romeo scrolled through the messages. "I asked, 'Okay. But I thought Meg was doing that,' and he responded, 'Agent Omega is no longer on this assignment.' That right there is pretty damn tellin', if ya ask me."

"Yeah, it is," India agreed. "He's almost never that formal when talking about Meg, unless there's a reason to be formal. Which means something happened."

"Yeah. So then I asked what happened, an' he wrote, 'That is a matter between the department chief and his subordinate. Be at the hangar, blah blah.' An' that was th' end of it. I texted back for a little more info, but he ain't answerin' me now."

"Damn," India murmured.

"Yeah," Romeo agreed.

"Let me explain to you both what has happened, as best I understand it, and from Omega's point of view," Zz'r'p offered.

* * *

"...This doesn't sound good at all," India decided, when Zz'r'p had finished.

"No shit," Romeo agreed. "Man, I can't believe she an' Echo done got into it like that. An' you're sure Meg ain't losin' it?" he asked the Arcturan.

"I am certain of it," Zz'r'p averred. "I am not certain what IS happening with her...but without doubt she is lucid, coherent, and logical. She is also very, very concerned, and I cannot say I blame her, in the circumstances."

"Damn," Romeo muttered.

"Maybe we should talk to her?" India wondered.

"I think it might be better if only one of you talked to her," Zz'r'p recommended. "She is understandably uncomfortable about matters, and has already expressed to me her worry that none of you will believe her, that you will all believe that, as Agent Romeo just expressed it, 'she has lost it.' If you both meet with her, it is apt to subconsciously register with her as ganging up on her. In her current state of mind, that may not go over well."

"Good point," India murmured. "Romeo, why don't you go back in your quarters, and I'll give Meg a call and see if she'll come over for coffee and some girl talk. We've still got plenty of time before shift, and even if it goes past shift starting time, we can always use the excuse of handing over the assignment from the previous Agent."

"Works for me, hon," Romeo agreed.

"Excellent," Zz'r'p decided. "I recommend you go forward with this to Fox, once you have talked to Omega. It is my considered opinion that Fox needs to know. And he does not, as yet."

"Why not?" Romeo asked.

"I believe," Zz'r'p considered, "that, had Omega been able to convince Echo, they would have gone forward with it together to Fox. But, unable to get even her own partner to actually hear her out on the matter, she did not dare to go over his head, let alone to Fox."

"Shit," Romeo grumbled.

"Exactly. So...make sure you brief Fox; the Director MUST know what is happening. If you can involve Echo in the briefing as well, so much the better. I will back you up if needed."

"Good deal," India said, relieved.

"Call me if you need me," Zz'r'p said. "Good luck."

"Yeah, we gonna need it," Romeo agreed. "All of it, an' then some."

* * *

"...So what makes you think Echo would be in danger?" India asked over a cup of coffee at her dining room table. "He can handle himself."

"*I* don't know, India. It's like...like I can see it." She shrugged. "How do you KNOW you're walking into a trap when you enter a certain room during a search? I just...know. If Echo gets on that Cortian spaceship, he's NOT coming back. And he won't even listen to me." Omega was deeply troubled.

"Why won't he listen?"

"He seems to think that I want to get into space so bad...that I'm jealous of his assignment or something."

"And are you?"

"NO! Even if I was, I wouldn't be petty enough to try to hose Echo's mission on account of it! Look, let me show you something. Come in here." Omega led the way into India's study, and sat down at her laptop, which was already active. With a few keystrokes, Omega brought up an electronic request form. "See this? It's my request for pilot certification on a starhopper. I put it in several weeks ago, like right after the first of the year or so. Way BEFORE all this came up. Once I've got this certification, I can spend part of my off-duty time bopping around the solar neighborhood, as well as being better prepared for when I DO get my first offworld assignment. Why should I be jealous of Echo's mission??"

India looked from the screen to Omega's earnest face.

"All right. What do you want to do about it?"

"I...don't know yet. I met the Cortian contact party with Echo when they arrived the other morning, and I looked over their ship. I didn't see anything obvious...aside from the fact that women are complete nonentities to 'em, so be forewarned on that. But I think I'm more convinced now than ever that something's up."

"Meg..." India was thoughtful, "I know this is a sore point, but...could all of Slug's telepathic tinkering when he abducted you as a child have left you with some sort of...latent psi abilities? Precognition, or maybe passive telepathic flashes?"

* * *

Oh shit, Omega thought, anxious. *I don't exactly wanna tell her the whole story. Maybe I can get away with some more half-truths, so she and Romeo won't think I'm totally nuts.*

"Oh, that's just great." Omega sighed and slumped in the chair, pretending to be dismayed at the idea; it wasn't hard, and it wasn't much of a pretense, really. "But...that's what I suspect, yep. Something else weird to contend with, and for people to look funny at me about. Zz'r'p more than alluded to something similar, too. All I can say is, I sure hope not. But it would make sense, what with...certain things happening." Omega sighed again. "I guess we'll find out soon. Just...look, be ready for anything, okay?"

"You got it," India said.

* * *

After Omega had left, India called, "Romeo?"

"Yeah, hon. I'm over here..." Romeo answered from the other apartment.

"Got a minute?"

"F'r you? You know it." Romeo came into the room.

"Well...Meg and I just finished our little talk. And it's worse than we thought..."

* * *

"This ain't good," Romeo remarked when India had finished. "Damn, but I don't like the sound of that. 'Specially if Echo an' Meg are gonna start fightin' over it."

"I know what you mean. And it's not like them to fight. I don't know two better-matched agents—"

"Except us," Romeo grinned at his partner.

"—But I'm not sure what to do about this," India said.

The Alpha Two team paused in thought.

"Maybe we should take the direct, frontal approach," India finally said. "Like Zz'r'p suggested."

"Fox's office?" Romeo surmised.

"My thoughts exactly," India answered.

* * *

"Fox, you got a minute?" Echo stood in the open door of Fox's office.

"Come on in, Echo. What's on your mind?" Fox invited. Echo entered and sat down across the desk from Fox.

"I've had some little conversations with Meg in recent days, and they've been pretty intense ones. It continued yesterday morning in the hangar, after you and the Cortians left. And the more I think about it, the more I think I should mention it to you. The subject matter, I mean."

"Shoot, zun."

"Omega thought there was something fishy about the Cortians, sight unseen. And she's been telling me point-blank for days that I shouldn't go on this mission."

"I was wondering what was going on with you two yesterday. You don't normally fight."

"That's because we know each other," Echo nodded, "and normally, we think a lot alike. But not this time."

"All right. Is this the cause of her 'attitude problem' in recent days, too?"

"Oh, hell yes. It's the ONLY 'attitude problem' I've encountered."

"Very well, then. It isn't what I thought it was. So. What do YOU think?" Fox asked him.

"I blew it off. That's made her mad, I mean REALLY mad, AND she won't let it go, so I know she's damn serious. Yesterday, when we met the Cortian contingent, I kept an eye on her. Nobody but me would've noticed, but she scoped out everything about 'em."

"And?"

"*I* didn't notice anything particularly, and if Meg did, she didn't tell me. But I know it made her more concerned, not less."

"What did she say?"

"Nothing, really. It was the way she looked at me."

Fox nodded, trusting Echo's knowledge of his partner. "So—"

Another knock sounded. Romeo and India stood at the door.

"Sorry to interrupt," Romeo began, "but you're just the two guys we need to see."

"C'mon in and join the party," a sardonic Fox said, as Alpha Two entered. Romeo closed the door, and India got right to the point.

"Echo, why have you started blowing off Meg's hunches?"

Fox and Echo exchanged glances.

"That's why I'm here, India," Echo told her. "Because I'm NOT blowing it off. What's she doing coming to YOU about OUR disagreement, anyway?"

"Trying to save your hide, Echo," India retorted sharply.

"Did Omega put you up to this?" Fox asked.

"Nah, Fox," Romeo replied. "The girl don't even know we're here."

"Why is Omega reacting so strongly to a hunch?" Fox wondered, puzzled.

"India ain't so sure that's all it is," Romeo volunteered. Echo sat up straight.

"Explain," he barked.

"Well, the first thing you need to know is that SHE DIDN'T come to me; Zz'r'p did," India revealed. "It seems she's been consulting with him about some...things...that have been happening. To her, I mean. Personal things...of a sort where she'd NEED to contact a telepath for advice, if you get my drift. From what I gather, whatever the phenomenae are, they got a lot stronger after some horrible little migraine she had."

"Damnation," Echo cursed. Fox glanced at him.

"You know something about that?" the Director wondered.

"Yeah. She had what she calls a nastybad headache a while back. It halfway put me in mind of the one she had right before Slug's end game, last summer. Remember, when we were at Kennedy Space Center on a mission?"

"I remember," Fox noted. "The one you sent her for a CT scan over."

"Yeah. It seemed to me like it was a cross between that..." Echo waved his hands in the air, "and a stroke, or cerebral hemorrhage, or the like."

"Damn," India murmured. "Some headache."

"Yeah. It was pretty bad. At one point, I was prepared to pick up her ass and haul it to the medlab, it was so bad. It peaked, she let out a howl, then it went away, and she seemed okay after that. But late that night, she was really restless, and I woke up to find her in the kitchen, preparing to make a full-on meal, in the middle of sleep shift. So I joined her, 'cause neither of us ate dinner because of her headache, and we split an omelet, and we talked. About this Cortian mission...again."

"And?"

"Something had happened, but she wouldn't tell me what. She...there was a look in her eyes, though, like I've never seen there before. At the time, I took it to be anger, but it keeps coming back in my mind's eye, and I'm not so sure any more."

"What sorta look?" Romeo wondered.

"Like..." Echo hesitated, then glanced around the room at the others, and raked a hand through his hair. "The best I know how to interpret or describe it, is...it was like she was seeing me, but she was also seeing a lot more than just me. But I was the only other person there, and the lights were low..."

India drew a deep breath.

"That fits with what Zz'r'p said," she offered oblique reference. "Keep going, Echo. I'll explain more later...what I know, anyway."

"Okay. So I convinced her to go ahead and go in for her annual physical, and she did, but she didn't indicate anything came of it...except for a really morbid conversation we had a couple days after that, when she..." Echo broke off, as several puzzle pieces suddenly fell into place. *The headache, seeing more than just me there, the warnings against the mission. Shit. It isn't a complete picture,* he decided, *but what I'm seein' now is sure damn ugly...*

"Echo?" Fox murmured. "Everything okay?"

"I'm...not sure now, Fox," Echo admitted. "Maybe not. 'Cause Meg wanted to talk about what would happen if either of us was," he paused, then managed to choke out, "mortally wounded."

"Damn," Romeo whispered.

"What he said," India muttered.

"What happened next?" Fox wondered.

"Well, she wanted to make sure that...that if it was her...that, that got..." Echo was having more and more difficulty with this particular conversation, and his throat grew tight. He stopped and swallowed several times, then opened his mouth to resume, but nothing would come out.

"It's all right, zun," Fox said, gesturing at Romeo, who rose and fetched a cup of water from the small cooler in the corner of Fox's office and handed it to Echo. "We all know how much you two think of each other. But we need this information. Try to keep going, if you can."

Echo nodded, and sipped the water for a moment, as Romeo laid a light hand on his shoulder, then withdrew, returning to his own chair. The slight pressure helped; he suddenly knew the others understood, at least in some measure, though he suspected that only Fox grasped just how much his partner meant to him...and even then, he wasn't sure how much Fox knew. He drew a deep breath, and continued.

"She wanted to make sure that, if...if anything happened to her, I'd be there for her, to...to tell her...to let go," Echo said, managing to maintain a steady tone until the end, when his voice cracked a bit.

"Holy shit," India said, surprised. "This is even more serious than I thought."

"Yeah. She hadn't said anything more, though, until the other day at the hangar, when we were touring the Cortian ship. But I'd swear now, it happened again—she saw and heard more than Fox and me put together." He shook his head. "But again, my first 'read' on her expression was that she was angry or, or sullen, and I reacted appropriate to that sort of attitude."

"And now you wish you hadn't," Fox murmured.

"I'm sure reconsidering it," Echo admitted.

"And I didn't help by insisting you provide her with an attitude adjustment, I suppose. So tell us your part of the story, India." Fox turned to Alpha Two.

"Okay. So this morning, Zz'r'p contacted me via vid phone, and gave me a heads-up that Omega needed help. That was about the time that Romeo got the reassignment orders, for Alpha Two to pull the Cortian departure security duty, and Zz'r'p said it was partly about that, and explained a little bit. So I called Meg and indicated that I'd talked to the Arcturan ambassador, and was there something I needed to know? She immediately asked for my help, since you weren't listening, Echo," India told them. "She came over to my place, and we had a long talk over after-breakfast coffee. Then I told Romeo after she left, so we'd have backup."

"An' we decided we should appeal t' you two not t' ignore Meg's concern. Zz'r'p was in agreement on that, by th' way. At least let us take a few extra precautions, guys," Romeo added. "Meg's pretty serious 'bout this, judging from what India told me."

"But WHY?" Echo wondered, pained. "What's going on in that gray matter of hers, that I'm not seein', when I usually do?"

"Echo," India said, "she was bio-engineered to be the sleeper assassin of a telepath. She had extensive mental contact with that telepath. She was able to learn to block telepathic attacks. Now, what does that suggest to you about the state of HER extrasensory abilities?"

Echo's eyes narrowed in thought.

"Are you suggesting..."

"I'm not the one suggesting it. Zz'r'p is. But yes, that is exactly what we are suggesting. That Meg may now be some sort of latent psi. We—Zz'r'p and I—think it may only now be emerging."

"But India," Fox protested, "humans aren't telepaths."

"NORMAL humans aren't telepaths," India told him. "Much as I hate to say it, guys, Meg isn't...a normal human any more. Hasn't been since the alien abduction when she was a kid."

Echo's jaw tightened in objection, knowing what India was talking around, but he said nothing; there was really nothing he could say. *Like it or not, it's all true,* he thought. *My partner isn't...completely human. That bastard Slug made damn sure of that.*

"Have you mentioned it to her?" Fox asked, intrigued.

"Yes," India answered. "She positively hated the idea. But she admitted that it was possible. We don't really know everything Slug did to her. She was too young, and too untrained on the techniques being used at the time, to be able to recognize what each procedure was."

"I don't know about you, Fox," Echo turned to the Agency Director, "but...I think I'm going to take a cue from my partner after all, and conduct this encounter nice and slow."

"I'll have a talk with Omega myself." Fox nodded.

Glancing at Romeo and India, Echo told him, "Count us in when you do."

* * *

"There's just one thing we might wanna do before we talk to her, though," India pointed out.

"What's that?" Fox wondered.

"We might want to look at that new cerebral scan, maybe with Zebra's help, and compare it to her baseline. That should at least tell us if there's any anomalous brain activity going on in there," India said.

"Damn, skippy," Romeo muttered.

"What he said," Echo averred.

"Exactly," Fox agreed, and activated his video phone at the same time he opaqued the windows overlooking the Core. "Let me get hold of Zebra and see if she's free..."

* * *

"Oh hell, yes," Zebra said on the vid call. "Fox, I'm shipping you the file right now. Pop it up on one of your wall screens, and I'll explain what you're looking at."

"Got it, bubeleh," Fox murmured, working at the virtual keyboard in his desk top. "Annnd...there."

An image of a human brain appeared on one of the large wall screens in the Director's office. Like all cerebral scans, it wasn't a real image, but rather a simulation, depicting the activity patterns of that brain.

"There we are," Zebra said. "Now, I'll put the thing into a loop so we can watch it. There. You can see that we still have that extremely active, almost hyperactive, brain that we've known Omega had since her entry physical."

"Right," Echo said. "You can see all the bright yellow and white, pretty much all over."

"Exactly, Echo. But...Fox, hon, can you give me control of the display for a minute? I want to highlight the areas to look at."

"I see 'em," India said. "Parietal, insular, and occipital?"

"Yes, India. Point them out for me, would you?"

"Sure," India said, rising and moving to the screen. "The key places are in the top and back of the brain, guys. Look, right here in the back—this is the occipital lobe, usually responsible for most things to do with vision," India explained. "Then there's the parietal lobe, kind of on the top and running posterior. Now the parietal lobe is responsible for processing and correlating sensory information to spatial mapping. Down below that, and closer to the core of the brain where the thalamus and the brain stem are, is the insular lobe. And the insular lobe is believed to be responsible, among other things, for certain higher-order brain functions, including possibly our perception of consciousness."

"So we got sight, space, and higher-order consciousness," Fox murmured.

"Yeah, and they're all three lighting up like a damn Christmas tree," Echo observed.

"Yes, Echo, they are," Zebra said. "But not all of each lobe. Note that both the dorsal and ventral streams of the occipital lobe show high activity, denoting an extreme awareness of location and motion—which we can translate to space and time. And the lateral and ventral intraparietal regions, which interpret not only the visual inputs but all her other senses as well, but principally from a vision-centered reference frame, are wildly active. But the anterior insular cortex, the anterior cingulate cortex, and especially the claustrum, which helps govern consciousness, are all in or around the insular lobe, and they're just going crazy."

"So..." Echo put his hand to his chin and thought, "spacetime, her ability to SEE spacetime, and her conscious AWARENESS of it, have all been heightened."

* * *

"I can't say that for sure, Echo," Zebra noted. "There's a lot we still don't know about the human brain. But...given what we DO know, and I discussed it with Zarnix, who is much more expert even than I am...I can't say you're wrong, either." Zebra paused, and drew a deep breath. "Zarnix and I have been at a loss to know how to interpret it, but the one thing we can say for certain is that Omega's brain has indeed changed. It's subtle, but it's definitely there. And let me note that there are absolutely no signs of lesions or other pathological morbidities or abnormalities that either one of us sees. I don't know what you're looking for, but I'm placing an educated bet that it has to do with the 'enhancements' to which she was subjected?"

"Yes, Zebra," Fox admitted. "Depending on how things go, I may need to tell you later, so that it can go into Omega's medical record."

"Got it. I'll wait for your word, and won't ask any more questions." She shot him a smile, and he returned it.

"Thank you, bubeleh, for understanding my job," Fox murmured.

"Hey, honey, it works both ways," Zebra pointed out. "I got patient confidentiality to handle, too."

"So you do."

"Yeah. If you lot weren't who you are, I wouldn't be telling you jack-shit about her. But as it happens, she's listed all of you as...well, as family, with whom it's okay to share her info...at least, to a point. There's some things, obviously, that every lady wants to keep private," Zebra hedged, knowing exactly what Omega wanted left unsaid...and why. "But yeah, family."

"Really?" India murmured. "I'm...honored."

"Well, you're closest thing to a sis the girl got," Romeo pointed out. "Back over Christmas? I guess she wasn't jokin' when she called us her fam'ly."

"No, she wasn't," Echo agreed.

"Well, then," Fox said, voice soft. "Is there anything else you can tell us about...our girl's state of health?"

"Other than she's healthy as the proverbial horse, no. This was the only deviation from previous norms we found. And even that doesn't, to Medical, appear to be a BAD thing. Insofar as we can tell, it means she's more aware than she was. Which, I suppose," Zebra speculated, "makes her, at this point, one of the most aware humans that there's ever been."

The four Agents in the Director's office exchanged perceptive looks. Zebra noted them, and acted on the information.

"Okay, I'd say you guys need to talk something over," she said. "And I see that Omega isn't there, so...keep me posted on anything Medical needs to know, guys. Fox, I'll see you tonight when we get off duty?"

"At the usual time," Fox said. "Fox out."

"Zebra out."

* * *

As the wall screens went dark, the four sat in silence for long moments. Finally Romeo broke it.

"Damn," he said, voice very quiet. "My first reaction was t' think, 'Shit, I wish MY brain lit up like that.' But th' more I think about it, th' more I think I'm glad it doesn't."

"What he said," India agreed.

"Something's definitely going on in there," Echo decided, "and I'm betting that the headache Meg had was by way of being, kinda, 'growing pains' for her brain."

"I wouldn't want to argue against you," India acknowledged.

"Well, I don't think it changes anything we had determined," Fox concluded. "If anything, it supports Zz'r'p's theory, I believe. We all need to think about this, and then we need to sit down with Omega and see if she won't tell us, in detail, what has been happening."

"It's a plan, Fox," Echo agreed.

"All right. Come to me immediately, any of you, if you come up with anything that bears on the matter. Meanwhile, things will proceed on schedule," Fox ordered. "Echo, as Alpha Line chief, I'll leave the decision as to who attends your departure to you. Alpha Line—members present, at least—is dismissed."

* * *

"Echo, wait," Fox said, as the younger Agent prepared to accompany Alpha Two out of the room. "Come back. I just thought of something, and I believe I need you for it."

Echo returned and resumed his seat, as Romeo pulled the door closed behind himself and India.

"What's up, Fox?"

"It occurs to me that an extra set of eyes, scoping out the Cortians, might be useful in the circumstances. Do you think so?"

"Well, sure. It might confirm what Meg's been saying...although it sounds to me like it's already sufficiently confirmed in her mind, and maybe in Zz'r'p's, too."

"True. But I can't take that forward to the Council to request a delay, and it isn't enough to save my ass—or yours, or hers—if I decide to countervene orders. After all, she's baseline human, and humans don't do telepathy OR precognition."

"Yeah. What did you have in mind?"

"Follow my lead, here." Fox punched up a vid call. After a moment, the narrow, defined face of a man with short, blond hair and pale blue eyes appeared on the wall screen.

"Diplomacy. Sugar here."

"Sugar, this is Fox. Do you have a moment?"

"For the Director, of course," Sugar, the current head of the Diplomacy department, agreed instantly, in his cultured European English.

"What about the Cortians?"

"My deputy is currently showing them around the Atlantis Office, to include the duty-free shop, and the theme park," Sugar explained. "And he chose to take them in an all-medium shuttlecraft rather than a maglev, to give them the more scenic view, descending through the water. They will be gone several hours. I can afford the time, I assure you."

"Good. I'm invoking a Level 2 Security Classification."

"Planet-wide? This sounds serious," Sugar observed, raising an eyebrow.

"Potentially, it is," Fox agreed. "We have reason to suspect that the Cortians may not be all they're cracked up to be, or may have ulterior motives behind this visit. But what we don't have is evidence."

"And what you do have is orders from the Ennead," Sugar murmured, thoughtful.

"Exactly."

"So you probably need me to keep my eyes and ears open for anything that you can use to support your decision, should you need to go against those orders for the sake of Agency—no, make that planetary—security?"

"Bingo. Nailed it in one, Sugar."

"All right, Fox, this is not a problem. Echo, do you have anything to factor in?"

"Um, not really," Echo said, shooting a surreptitious glance at Fox. "Just that I...well, Omega and I...have had some really bad feelings about it. I think Meg may have some more specific ideas, but..." he hesitated for the briefest moment, "we...haven't had a...good chance...to talk about it in detail yet."

"Fair enough," Sugar agreed. "And I may not have a need to know in any event. Well, I shall debrief my second when he returns. I shall also keep an eye on things personally, in addition, and if I see anything unusual or outrightly worrisome, I will notify you immediately, Fox."

"Good man, Sugar."

"Anything else?"

"No, that should do it."

"Very good then. Let me go off and review my notes of interactions to this point, while they are gone, and I will get with you soon."

"Excellent. Fox and Echo out."

"Sugar out."

The Director and the Alpha Line chief looked at each other.

"That...will help," Echo decided. "Sugar is a sharp sort. Not field-trained, not like Alpha Line, but he knows his shit."

"He does," Fox agreed. "He better—I trained him in the job."

"Keep me posted on what you get from him?"

"Of course."

"Good. Need me for anything else?"

"No, not right now. And I know you have things you need to do, and so do I. I'll ping you if I hear anything, or if I need something."

"Okay, Fox. Later."

"Take it easy, old friend."

* * *

After Echo left, Fox sat in thought for long minutes. *Yes,* he finally decided, *I want to hear it first-hand.* He reactivated the virtual keyboard in his desktop and placed a vid call to a particular ambassador, currently mediating certain negotiations at the Geneva Office. As the blue, fish-like face appeared on a wall screen, Fox nodded a greeting.

"Zz'r'p here."

"Hi there, Zz'r'p. Hope it isn't too late for you over there."

"Salutations, Fox. No, I have been expecting a call from you at some point today. In fact, after Omega and I talked this morning, then I called Alpha Two and advised them to speak with you, I rearranged my schedule for the rest of the day, in order that I might await what I considered an inevitable call."

"You were that sure you'd hear from me?"

"I have known you for many years, Fox. I know what kind of man, what kind of leader, you are, and both are good. I was certain that you would want to be able to talk to me directly, to ask questions, and satisfy your own mind on matters."

"Well, thank you, Zz'r'p, on many levels. So...can you tell me your side of all this? What have you picked up?"

"Do you mean with regard to the Cortians?"

"Yes."

"For myself, nothing," Zz'r'p confessed.

"But I thought Omega told you..."

"She did. But I do not have a precognitive talent, nor does any Deltiri. So I cannot truly speak to her visions, though she has shown them to me. All I can tell you for certain is that I do not detect any adverse pathologies in her thought patterns. Insofar as I can tell, she is mentally and emotionally healthy, if stressed."

"Stressed? Why?"

"If you were seeing visions of potential future disasters, would you not feel stressed?"

"Good point. So she's that worried?"

"Immensely. Remember, Fox, she has nothing outside the Agency, and no longer feels she belongs anywhere else."

"Mm. And it sounds as if..." Fox broke off, thinking. "Zz'r'p, Omega thinks a great deal of Echo, doesn't she?"

"She does, Fox. That should be obvious to you."

"How MUCH does she think of him?"

"I cannot answer that question, my friend. It would violate her privacy, and as her counselor and advisor—not to mention teacher in matters of telepathy and such—I may not divulge personal confidences."

"Which tells me probably more than you meant it to. Do you think it's compromised her objectivity?"

"No, it has not. If anything, she is more aware than I have ever seen her. She is focused, laser-sharp...but she is also cognizant of everything going on. In a way that, frankly, I have yet to see very many humans do."

"So, what CAN you tell me, of what she has told—and shown—you...?"

"Let me think..."

* * *

"...Interesting, Zz'r'p," Fox decided after an extended conversation.

"Is it not, though?" Zz'r'p agreed.

"And you say she even claimed to nail the Cortian ship's name?"

"She need not claim, Fox—she DID. She told me herself, and mentally SHOWED me, before the Cortians even arrived." Zz'r'p's impassive face stared out of the screen at Fox. "Are you going to talk to her yourself?"

"Most definitely. But I've been gathering data beforehand."

"Understood. And are you going to go through with sending Echo off with the Cortians?"

"I don't know yet. Ennead orders, you know."

"Ah. That IS difficult."

"Exactly."

"But you are looking into it?"

"Oh, yes."

"Then, for now, I can ask no more."

* * *

Omega spent the day in her quarters; her removal from the Cortian security detail while Echo still worked the mission effectively left her without a task, though not confined to quarters. And no replacement assignment had been forthcoming, despite the fact that she kept her cell phone on her person, and her laptop active all day. It did not occur to her that that was because her removal from the detail was being second-guessed and debated.

So she made her own assignment—Omega pulled up the specs, design and layout of the Chicago spaceport, particularly as pertained to Hangar 16.

It took a bit of doing, and some aliasing to obscure her attempts, but after a few hours of truly inventive work, Omega even managed to hack in and access the security laid around the hangar in question. Given she was the Alpha Line executive assistant, it wasn't even inappropriate. Only Echo himself would know that he had not requested the information, and even then, if she was asked, she could say she intended to supply it to Alpha Two in order that they would be properly prepared to take her place.

And since I'm going to do just that, Omega thought, *it isn't even a lie. I want India and Romeo to have as much information as possible, 'cause I think they're gonna need it, one way or another.*

So by the time Echo came back to his quarters, Omega was deep into the virtual guts of the Chicago spaceport hangars. As soon as she heard his door open, however, she executed the procedure she had devised beforehand for Operation: Save Echo security—she quickly hid the spaceport files and brought up her notes on the astronomy class she was planning. Next to those, she also brought up the data she had obtained on her observing runs, so she could determine how to best utilize them. Then she focused on working out the lesson plans for the course.

"Hey, Meg, you here?" Echo called.

"Yes, Echo, I'm in my study," Omega replied, raising her voice sufficient for him to hear. *Damn it, that sounds stilted,* she thought, in vexation with herself and the whole situation, *but I can't help it. He's made such a big deal in the past out of how he trusts me. Then, when push comes to shove, he shows me just how much he DOESN'T trust me. So now I sound stilted and overly formal. If he can't figure that one out, I'll be happy to educate him.* She sighed, as she heard his footfalls pass through the back door en route to her study. *So much for any hope of him being interested, I guess. Not that there was ever a whole lotta hope. But, through this whole mess, I've gotten a whale of an introduction to exactly how NOT interested he is.*

"There you are!" Echo said with a smile, as he stepped into the room, right inside the door. "Whatcha up to?"

* * *

At the question, Omega stopped her work and just stared at him, jaw

78

slightly slack.

Uh-oh, Echo thought, trying not to facepalm. *Echo, you idiot. THINK before you toss something off, next time. I want to sit down and talk to her, discuss the situation and actually HEAR her this time, which means that first I need to try to make up with her somehow, make this work. But I know I've hurt her. Damn, this is gonna be harder than I thought.*

"I'm working on my class for the university," Omega said, enunciating unusually clearly, and he realized he had annoyed her. He could almost hear her thinking, *'But I'd be working on security for the Cortian visit...IF my best friend hadn't reprimanded me and pulled me off the assignment...then not bothered to give me a new one.'*

"Oh, okay," he tried again. "Um, how's it coming along?"

"All right, I suppose. Assuming I'm still here to teach next semester."

Zing. Damn, Meg, he thought, pained. What he said was, "Well, have you had dinner yet?"

"No." She turned back to her laptop.

"Wanna go out and get something?"

She stopped and gave him the same stare, and he imagined he heard the same mental voice. *'Why would I want to go out with you, when you obviously don't trust me?'* Just then, he saw her eyes shoot to one side, dilating slightly before she closed them momentarily. She shook her head almost imperceptibly, then opened her eyes again and met his gaze. But her eyes were still dilated, and once more she had that 'seeing ghosts' look in them. Finally she answered.

"No, I'd rather not take the time to have to go out and come back."

"Well, okay, that makes sense. Shall we, I dunno, slap something together in the kitchen, then?" Echo tried a third time. "I got a fresh six-pack of your favorite chocolate stout to go with dinner..."

"Maybe later, Echo. I'm not really hungry right now, and I need to get a little bit more done on this." Omega gestured at the laptop screen. "I know you're probably hungry, though, so go on ahead and eat. Don't wait on me. I'll grab something when I feel like it."

"...All right. You sure?"

"I'm sure."

Echo turned and headed back into his quarters, somewhat slower than he had left them.

* * *

Echo went into his kitchen and rummaged around for something to eat, but found his appetite, which had been substantial when he'd gotten home, had evaporated.

But I gotta eat, he thought, morose. *Alpha Line Agents stay way too busy; we can't afford to skip meals if we don't have to.* So he foraged in his kitchen, looking for anything that appealed; nothing did. The interaction with Omega had sufficiently disturbed him that he found it hard to think of anything else.

Eventually he settled on a bowl of cold cereal, and shoveled it in on autopilot. *Ieucch,* went through his mind. *Tastes like cardboard.* But he kept shoveling until it was gone, knowing he needed the fuel. And it wasn't as if the cereal provided to field agents was ordinary corn flakes, in any event—like their 'protein bars,' a single bowl provided a full meal's nutrients. *So at least it's healthy,* he decided.

After he got some calories inside himself, he wandered back into his den, automatically glancing through the back door. Omega's den was empty, the lights low, except for the glare of light that still came from her study door.

Well, I'll just keep an eye on things, and as soon as she comes out of her study, I'll try again, he decided.

With a sigh, he went and found his novel, which he had left on the nightstand that morning, and threw himself down on the couch, deliberately positioning himself so he could look through the back door and see if she came out of her study. Glancing up, he saw the framed image of the Orion Nebula she had made for him, and lost himself in it for long minutes, studying the delicate, intricate filaments of gas and dust.

An apology, he remembered. *A pretty one, too. One that I thought I'd accepted. I guess she decided I had a funny way of showing it. And she might be right. Wish I could figure out how to manage one as pretty.*

Then he opened his compendium of H. G. Wells stories and resumed reading where he'd left off last time.

* * *

In the study next door, once Echo left, Omega minimized the half-finished class syllabus and brought the Chicago spaceport documentation back onscreen.

After all, she thought, *it's moot if this doesn't work. It'll all go to hell in the proverbial handbasket, if I lose Echo. Although,* she sighed, *arguably, I guess I've lost him anyway, metaphorically speaking at least. But can you lose something you never really had?*

She studied the spaceport documents the rest of the evening.

* * *

Omega didn't come out of her study the remainder of the night, not even to eat. Food held no interest for her; she was too concerned over the possible ramifications of the Cortian business.

When bedtime arrived, Echo came back to her study door; she heard him coming, and once more hid the spaceport plans.

"Got to a stopping place yet?" he wondered.

"Um, not really. Why?" Omega wondered.

"'Cause it's getting late. It's past time for bed already. I figured you might have lost track of time, which is why I thought I'd pop back over to see about you." He offered her a slight smile. "Just tryin' to look out for you, baby."

"Yeah, well, it isn't like I have to get up early tomorrow," she murmured. "You go on to bed. I'm gonna work on this a little while longer, then go crash."

Echo sighed and headed for his bedroom.

* * *

The next morning, Echo knocked on the open door of Fox's office, and the Director looked up.

"You called me, Fox?" Echo asked.

"Yes, Echo. Are you alone?"

"...Yeah." Echo shrugged. "Meg...doesn't know yet that we...that I... am starting to seriously consider her concerns. So it was easy enough," he scrunched his face slightly, "to slip out to see you without her. She's been holed up in her study, doing some sort of personal online research for that university class she's gonna teach, ever since I relieved her of duty."

"How's she handling that, by the way?"

"Not great, but it's my own damn fault. From her point of view, I demonstrated to her that I don't trust her, and she's...well." Echo sighed. "Let's just say that we aren't talking much lately, and leave it at that."

"Mm. Come on in and sit down, zun. Close the door behind you. This is a friend to friend chat."

"Oh," Echo said, voice somewhat flat, as he followed instructions. "One of THOSE."

"Yeah. Look, are YOU handling this all right?"

"What do you mean?" a cagey Echo responded.

"Don't give me that, zun. I'm not blind, and I'm not stupid, and I've known you since you were a hormonal, teen-aged boy. Which you are not anywhere close to being now. You've become one of the finest men I've ever met, and I'm proud to know you, let alone call you friend."

Echo flushed, but said nothing. Fox suspected, with some fondness, that the other man was uncertain what to say.

"So," Fox continued, "I know you well enough to be pretty damn sure that you've fallen for your partner."

"I, uh, well Fox, it..."

"Don't 'well Fox' me, Echo," Fox said, allowing a hint of the stern Agency Director to enter his demeanor, "and don't try to lie to me. I remember the look on your face back during the Lambda Andromedan negotiations. Am I right, or am I not?"

Echo dropped his gaze to the floor, slumping in his chair with a sigh.

"Yes, I thought as much," Fox noted then. "So, I'll ask again—are you handling this all right?"

"I honestly don't know how to answer, Fox," Echo said, raking a distracted hand through his short black hair and standing it on end. "I'm... worried, yeah. On a lotta levels. Is Meg right? WHY is she right? Why is this happening at all? What's going on inside her? Is she gonna be okay? Are the Cortians really up to something? Am *I* gonna be okay? And...are WE—she and I, as partners—"

"As a couple," Fox amended.

"—As partners, gonna be okay?" Echo finished, reiterating the Alpha One partnership status. "Unfortunately, Fox, I don't have the answers to any of it. And now that I know that something really IS going on in her mind, I'm worried that, by the time I get the answers, it'll be too damn late. Because either it'll already have happened, or it'll BE happening right then and there."

"Go on."

"Huh?"

"There's something else you're not saying. I can hear it in your voice, and see it in your eyes."

Echo sighed again.

"Dammit, Fox, you're almost as perceptive as Meg. All right. Now that we know, I'm starting to feel like the guy in those space opera movies—I've got an awfully bad feeling about this."

"Bad how?"

"I dunno exactly." Echo shook his head. "Like...something bad is gonna happen. Only...I can't see what. Evidently Meg can, I guess."

"Could it be that her anxiety is transmitting to you?"

"Well, I can read her body language really damn well, so I suppose that subconsciously, I'm—"

"No, that's not what I mean, son. If she really is doing what Zz'r'p and India suspect, then she may be inadvertently, MENTALLY, transmitting her own feelings on the matter...to you. After all, she's not been trained on how to do any of this, except throw up a telepathic block. If she is transmitting to you, she may not even know it. And even if she does realize it, she may not know how to prevent it."

"Well...that's true..." Echo rubbed his chin in thought. "I guess it's certainly possible. Great, Fox. You just added another question to the list for which I got no answers."

"Sorry, son," Fox chuckled, rueful. "I didn't mean to. I just wanted to get your read on it."

"I sure can't say it's not happening," Echo allowed. "All I know is, now I have this sense of...of something hanging over us, big and dark and DAMN heavy, and it's about to drop. And I don't know who-all it's gonna drop on top of."

"And you're afraid it might drop on Omega."

"Damn straight. Or both of us. Or the whole lot of us. I just...don't know."

"Which one of those frightens you most?"

"Damn, Fox! That's kinda like asking the condemned man, 'Had you rather die by poison, hanging, electrocution, firing squad, burning at the stake'...! Some hurt worse than others, sure, but in the end, you're still dead."

A lone bark of laughter, decidedly black in humor, emerged from Fox.

"Fair enough," he murmured in agreement. "Next discussion point— what would you like me to do, to help?"

"Another question for which I don't have an answer, Fox." Echo paused, thinking. "I suppose...if you could consider blowing off some of the diplomatic requirements, it'd help. Maybe waiting to send me off with the Cortians until we've scoped 'em out a little more, or something."

"Unfortunately, that's the one thing I CAN'T do, Echo." It was Fox's turn to sigh. "I have my orders from the Council, and while I'm taking this seriously enough that I tried to contact Pulgey first thing this morning to talk to him about it, I haven't been able to reach him yet. So those orders are still in effect. The Cortians are touchy. If we put 'em off, we might lose the whole thing. And the analysts say the potential economic trade benefits from resources on Cort could be substantial."

"Or...they could be lying through their teeth, to get at something of ours."

"True. But we can't find out until we go through with the whole first-contact negotiations. And that involves sending you with them."

"Which is exactly what Meg doesn't want to happen. Because she apparently sees something that you and I don't. Something that you and I... CAN'T see."

"I know, Echo, I know. But I was thinking in terms of something more personal, to help. Like maybe sending your partner-slash-MATE along with you. I could always denote Alpha One as life partners. We still don't have any sort of marriage in our charter, and the Council keeps putting the amendment on the back burner in favor of other things they see as more urgent, so I can't do anything more. But I could do that. Does she feel the same about you?"

"I...have no idea."

"Have you still not acted on it, then?"

"Not...really," Echo admitted. "I've tried a couple of discreet little things, to try to determine whether she'd just laugh in my face or not..."

"I can't see her doing that, even if she wasn't interested."

"No. But you know what I'm trying to say."

"Yes, I do. Go on."

"Well, anyway, I've tried a couple of subtle..." Echo frowned. "I hate to call 'em 'come-ons,' but..."

"I get it. You've tried to feel out her emotions on the matter, without being blatant and revealing your own feelings as yet. Keep going."

"...But she doesn't even respond, Fox. Either way. I can't tell if she's not interested, or if she just didn't catch on to what I was doing. We go out, sure, all the time...but in so far as I can tell, she just views that as a couple of pals running around together in their off hours. It doesn't help at all that lately, she's been in a bad mood because I've been blowing off whatever it is she's been trying to warn me about." Echo bit his lip for a moment, thinking, then continued. "So no, I haven't made any sort of actual move, like asking her out or something—at least, no more than our usual hanging out together, like I said. And I..."

"Echo? It's not like you to be this tentative about the thing. You're a 'go get 'em' kind of mensch, so normally, I'd expect you to be pursuing her with some enthusiasm. There's something else eating at you about your relationship with her. What is it?"

"Well, it's like this, Fox. If she doesn't...appreciate my interest, it could wreck the partnership," Echo pointed out then. "And that would be a bad thing all the way around, and I know it. It breaks up the premier team in the Agency, let alone in Alpha Line, for one thing. Besides, I don't...it hurt bad enough when I realized that Chase had sidelined me. I'd rather not try something like that with Meg until I'm sure it isn't gonna destroy what we already have. If that's all she wants, I can deal with it, as long as we stay partners." He broke off and swallowed. "But if she despises the idea, if she ends up leaving, she's as dead to me as if..."

Fox watched as Echo slumped even farther into the visitor chair, and frowned, worried.

Echo's right. This is potentially serious, he realized. *Alpha One is the best team I have. Alpha Two is a close second, but I need 'em both—especially if something major goes down, like the Klydonian invasion. I hadn't even considered that complication, my own self, and I'm the Director. Farkakt. I need to think this over some more, taking it more seriously, and not treat it like I'm an amateur shadchan in my off-duty hours.*

"All right, Echo, zun," he murmured then, as gentle as he knew how to be; the man in front of him was indeed, in Fox's opinion, as much his own son as he had been X-ray's; non-genetic, certainly, but as close to a son as Fox was likely to get for a long time, if ever. And said adoptive son was obviously in some pain and distress, into the bargain. "I get the picture. Things haven't developed far enough to be able to go that route yet. I hope they will; I think the two of you are very well-matched, in every sense, and that a life partnership would make Alpha One damn near unstoppable. Let's think about this, you and me, and see if there isn't a good way to move forward, something that gives you a shot with her without breaking up the partnership. Meanwhile, we still need to talk to Omega about the more immediate issue and see how she reacts."

"Okay, Fox. Just let me know when."

"I will, alter khaver. I will."

* * *

"Here's what you asked for, Omega," Madrid said quietly later that day, as he discreetly handed her a small package in the Core. "I incorporated as many of the specs as I could in the time I had, old girl. It isn't perfect, but it isn't bad, either. It was a bit of a rush job, though."

"I understand, Madrid. And I appreciate it," Omega told the English agent, who was the Agency's top resident weapons expert. She slid the package into an inner jacket pocket. "It's just in time, too. The departure is late tomorrow. Let's keep this simple. What can it NOT do?"

"Actually, it can do everything you asked for except automatically include a second person; you'll have to manually toggle it off and on, to do that. It also won't completely stop a high-intensity particle beam, I'm afraid. I simply didn't have time to figure out how to boost the miniature power supply that much."

"Does that mean it will at least partially stop one?"

"Yes. But if it's just you in there, you're still dead meat. If you have someone else in there with you, whichever one of you is in the direct line of fire...won't..." Madrid's voice trailed away, and his eyebrows drew together in pain and anxiety.

Omega considered for a bit, lips pursed, then nodded.

"All right, those are just the parameters under which I'll have to operate, then. Thanks, Madrid. I really appreciate this. Keep it to yourself, okay?"

"Glad to do it, Omega. Mum's the word, old girl."

* * *

After Madrid had left, Omega stood looking around the Core, lost in thought.

I'm positive those Cortians are up to no good. They're after Echo; I don't know why, but I'm sure of it. The parts of their spacecraft we weren't allowed to tour...the 'living quarters,' they said...yeah, right. And I've got some swampland in Arizona for sale...cheap.

They were just a little too fixated on Echo, too, if you ask me—which nobody is, unfortunately. Even with Fox and me there, they were practically pawing him. They all but ignored the two of us. No, they couldn't be bothered with us for looking Echo over like they were... Oh no, oh damn, no... like...they...were...BUYING A HORSE...

The pieces fell into place.

"That's it," Omega murmured to herself. "It's gotta be. It's not a diplomatic emissary. They're slavers, picking up prize stock. It's gotta be. That, or I'm cracking up."

Well, if I AM right, I guess I'll know soon enough. And if the Cortians really are slave traders in disguise, India and me are gonna have a little surprise waiting for 'em. They won't get MY partner without a fight— whether he wants one or not. She furtively patted her jacket where Madrid's little package was hidden.

"Omega?" called a voice from behind her. She turned, and saw Fox standing in his office door. He waved her over.

* * *

As Omega entered Fox's office, she saw Echo sitting by the desk, an empty chair next to him. As she took it, she said, "What's up?"

"That's what we'd like you to tell us," Fox said, spotting India and Romeo entering the Core and signaling them. "Here comes Alpha Two."

"You told Fox?" Omega shot Echo a dirty look.

"Yes." Echo nodded firmly.

"So now Fox thinks I'm out to replace you on this mission too, huh?" she all but snarled. "Shall I consider myself on report now??"

"What?!" Fox asked, startled, as Echo looked away. Omega shrugged.

"It's what Echo seems to think. I thought he knew me better than that."

"Omega, Echo told me because he decided you might have a point," Fox informed her.

"Oh," Omega sighed, anger evaporated. "Highland hothead strikes again." She looked back at Echo. "Sorry?"

Echo nodded and shrugged.

"I'm...not thinking through this right, either," he admitted. "I know you wouldn't react like that without a reason. I just can't see what it is. And it's confusing the hell outta me."

"It's okay. Truth is," she told him, "my reaction has caught me off guard, too. But we've got to stop fighting about it." Echo nodded in agreement. Romeo and India entered then and sat down.

"Good. The gang's all here," Fox said. "Now, Omega, we know about your conversations with Echo and India..." India shot Omega an apologetic look. Omega put her head in her hands.

"Remind me never to tell y'all any of my really personal secrets..." she muttered.

Echo laid a hand on her shoulder, and when she looked up, met her eyes meaningfully. *You know they're always safe here,* he telegraphed, subtly putting one hand on his breastbone while rubbing his temple with the other hand, and she nodded.

Likewise, she responded in kind.

"Meg, you asked for my help," India said, a bit defensively.

"I know, India," Omega smiled crookedly, "and it seems to have worked. You got through."

"Like I told you, Omega, Echo had already begun to discuss your concerns with me," Fox reminded her. "India merely provided additional information in the form of your potential psi talent."

To their surprise, Omega abruptly stood and walked away from them, to the big bay window where she could survey the Core, her back partly turned to them all.

"It just won't go away, will it?" she murmured softly. "Every time I start thinking of myself as an ordinary human again..."

* * *

The room was silent for a moment. Finally the Alpha Line chief broke it.

"Meg," Echo asked quietly, watching her with anxious concern, "any more hunches?"

"Yeah. But I don't know if it'll make sense to you." Omega's face and voice were devoid of expression. Without turning, she began to chant softly.

"'...A phantom ship, with each mast and spar

Across the moon like a prison bar.

And a huge black hulk that was magnified

By its own reflection in the tide...'"

She paused for a moment, still looking out at the Core. "That's what I was reading when I first saw the *Trindak.*"

"Huh?" Romeo responded, confused.

"She's quoting a Longfellow poem," Echo told him, still watching Omega. "*Paul Revere's Ride.* It's the description of the *Somerset,* the British warship."

"You mean the one in the Boston harbor, to keep the American colonists under the British thumb?" India asked. Echo and Omega both nodded.

"An implied threat," a thoughtful Echo remarked. "But Meg, you said you were reading it when you saw the *Trindak.* You didn't have a book with you in the hangar. We were talking—arguing—when the ship landed."

"Yes, Echo. But that's...not the first time I saw the *Trindak*."

"What?!"

"Remember the other night when I couldn't sleep, and I fixed a midnight snack? After the headache?"

"Yes..." Echo's eyes narrowed in thought. *The same night you looked as if you were seeing...ghosts...*

"I couldn't get to sleep because...I kept having these..." she searched for the right word, "visions..."

"You were dreaming?" Echo verified.

"No. I was wide awake, reading."

Dammit, she really WAS seeing ghosts, Echo realized with a shock. *Or something not of this normal world.*

"What kind of visions, Meg?" India asked softly.

"It was like...they'd cue from the imagery of whatever I was reading, then go off from there. And they all revolved around Echo and the *Trindak*. They took him prisoner, they beat him, they...killed him..."

"Ugh. Kinda...sinister," remarked Romeo, and Omega nodded again without looking.

"And substantial enough that I started a couple of times to try touching them," she told them.

"Did you?" Echo asked, curious.

"No. I, uh, decided I...didn't wanna go there."

"But...what does it mean, Omega?" Fox asked.

"Echo...do YOU understand?" Omega turned to him. Echo nodded.

"Yeah. I do now. I get the idea, at any rate. Tell the others."

Omega turned back toward the Core and sighed.

"They're a race of slavers, guys. Echo is to be their first acquisition here, obtained via subterfuge. I'm next. Remember what the 'ambassador' said, Echo? 'Human females are different. Perhaps, on our next visit...'" Echo nodded grimly, fully comprehending her probable fate in the scenario she was outlining. "We'll become nothing but a resource, human cattle," she added.

"Slavers?!" Fox exclaimed. "What gives you that idea?"

"If nothing else, the way they checked Echo out the other day. Like he was...just another head of cattle. Like they were getting ready to negotiate a horse trade."

The four listening Agents exchanged glances.

"That true, Echo?" Fox wondered.

Echo nodded affirmation, hiding a slight guilty feeling; he HAD felt a little uncomfortable under the intense scrutiny of the aliens, though he hadn't admitted as much at the time, even when Omega had asked him.

"Do you have any other evidence to that effect, Omega?" Fox asked.

"Only the scream," Omega added.

"Scream?!" Fox and Echo both exclaimed. "What scream?"

"The one I heard from their 'living quarters' corridor, when they were giving us a tour of the ship," she replied. "It was distant, and it echoed, and it was a scream of pure, desperate pain. I take it, neither of you heard it?"

"No, but that doesn't mean it didn't happen," Echo noted. "I've known from the time you first set foot in Headquarters that you had damn sharp hearing."

"So you're saying, Omega," Fox tried to put it together, "that what they claimed was their personal quarters was in fact the area where they were holding slaves, and that THAT is the reason we weren't allowed to inspect it?"

"That was my immediate take, Fox," Omega averred. "But other than the one scream, I got no more proof. Just...what I've...'seen.'" She quirked her fingers around the word in air-quotes.

"Well, why don'tcha try readin' their minds directly, Meg?" Romeo suggested.

"HOW??" Omega turned and looked at him. "Even if the psi talent IS there, and I don't know that it is," she glanced around the room at them all, "it doesn't exactly come with a user's manual." She looked at the floor. "Or maybe I'm just...losin' it..."

"How can we be sure?" Fox asked. "Is Omega on the money, or is she having a psychotic break?"

"She's awfully lucid, Fox," India remarked, "and everything she says hangs together. I've talked to several people since finding out about all of this, and I have to say, it's the consensus of Zarnix, Zebra, and Whiskey that Omega is completely healthy, mentally as well as physically. And the whole psi notion was Zz'r'p's theory. Who also says that Meg is lucid and coherent. And he says to tell you he checked."

"Speaking of which, is Zz'r'p handy?" Echo asked. "After all, he IS the Agency's resident alien telepath."

"He's on-planet, but occupied. He's negotiating that conflict in Eastern Europe that the Dorians and the Krefons started," Fox told him. "I think he's at the Geneva Office, if memory serves."

"Yeah," Omega confirmed.

"Damn," Echo grumbled.

"I talked to him already," Omega admitted, "a couple times. And India's right; he AND his mentor say I'm not goin' crazy, though in some respects, I could almost wish I was. He was too distracted by the negotiations to actually do a remote mindlink in order to try to teach me, but he promised to do it when he got back. Assuming it isn't too late in general, by then."

Echo thought for a moment, then cocked his head toward Omega.

"Well, try this out, Meg. You can still set up a telepathic block, right? Zz'r'p taught you that to battle Slug last summer."

"Right..."

"It's kind of inside-out and ass-backwards to boot, but what if you... sort of reversed the block? Inverted it, kinda?"

"Oh! I see what you're saying. I'm just not sure if I..." Omega bit her lip, thinking. She moved back to her chair and sat down. "Hey, it's worth a try. Everybody hush for a few minutes and let me concentrate."

* * *

Echo stood and turned his chair sideways, then pulled Omega's chair, with her in it, around to face it.

"Put your feet up, lean back, and relax as much as you can. It should help," he told her. She complied, and closed her eyes. The room grew quiet as four pairs of eyes watched her closely.

"Stop staring at me, y'all," Omega said without opening her eyes. "I can't concentrate with everybody watching."

Fox, Echo, India, and Romeo all blinked in surprise at the command, given in the blind—at least, it appeared to them to be.

92

Three heads immediately averted their gazes. The fourth maintained position, its eyes trained on Omega.

"You too, Echo."

Echo raised an eyebrow and looked away, still keeping her in his peripheral vision. The others fairly gaped, furtive glances exchanged between the members of Alpha One.

"Echo, I SAID...oh, never mind..."

* * *

Fox caught Echo's eye, and sent him a gestured message, not bothering to hide it from Alpha Two: *Did your partner just do what I think she did?*

Echo looked at him, quirked his lips, shrugged, and shook his head. *I dunno, Fox. It sure looked like it to me.*

Hold on, signaled Romeo. *You tellin' me she just read us without even lookin' at us?*

Yes, Fox confirmed with a single nod.

Damn, skippy, Romeo mouthed.

India jerked her thumb at her partner and nodded. *What he said.*

Echo waved his hand at the others, then pointed at Omega. *Watch, guys. Let's see what happens.*

* * *

Omega rubbed her temple for a moment, then grew very still. Her breathing slowed dramatically, and she scarcely moved for over five minutes. Romeo finally shot the others a worried glance, and reached out slowly, intending to take Omega's shoulder and make sure she was okay.

"Don't touch me." It was a curt, immediate order. Instinctively, Romeo snatched his hand back before he could contact her.

But Omega's eyes never opened.

Four jaws dropped in shocked surprise: There could be no mistaking it this time—Omega had reacted to Romeo without ANY sensory cues whatsoever.

Omega shifted slightly, then became still again. Unexpectedly, she jerked upright with a little cry, eyes wide in dread. The other Agents rushed to surround her. Echo knelt beside her chair.

"What? What is it, Meg?" he asked. "What did you pick up?"

"I...I think, I mean I don't...I...no...no, nothing for sure...I, I'm not really certain...what I'm doing anyway..." Omega ran a distracted hand across her braided hair.

But Echo noted that the look—the 'I'm seeing ghosts' look—was back in her eyes. And he realized why he'd initially been thinking she was angry, or picking a fight. *Her brows are drawn together, almost as if in anger...or maybe pain...and she's frowning slightly,* he observed. The overall effect was that of disapproval, if one only gave her face a cursory glance. *But she's not. She's...scared. And worried. BAD worried.* He berated himself silently for having taken his partner so for granted that he hadn't caught the difference. *And that, even with how I feel about her. Dammit.*

This...is not good, he thought to himself. *She did get something just then, I'd stake my life on it. But now she's afraid to say what she picked up on, because I didn't initially believe her. And if I didn't believe her, she doesn't think anybody else will, either.*

He met her haunted gaze and sent her a coded message with a few blinks, nods, and subtle hand gestures. *Want to tell me in private? Just me?*

Omega met his eyes with a troubled gaze, then bit her lip, looked away, and shook her head.

Damn, he thought, and sighed.

* * *

Fox, Romeo, and India sighed as well, and began making contingency plans. Echo eyed Omega skeptically, and she averted her face.

He knows me entirely too well for my—or his—own good, I think, she decided. *But how can I tell him that, if Alpha One goes to the Cortian spacecraft's departure, one of us won't be walking away from it?*

Chapter 3

"All right, if they really are slave traders, they want Echo because he's one of our top, most experienced agents. The head of Alpha Line and the youngest of the Originals," Fox said, looking at Echo, who returned his solemn gaze. "Arguably, THE top Agent, at this point, no offense to the rest of you. The other candidates are all in this room at the moment, anyway."

"Makes sense," India agreed. "So what do we do?"

"Well, we can't be too overt," Fox said. "If Omega's wrong..."

"I'm not," Omega said quietly, subdued. "I only wish I was. But too much of it has already happened," she added, and Echo watched her with apprehension.

"But if you are, we'll have ruined an important diplomatic contact," Fox replied. "And our first from the Sagittarius Dwarf Galaxy."

"Look, Fox," Omega told him, "I might as well 'fess up to something. It may solve your problem." India gave her a worried glance, trying to signal her to abort her remarks, but Omega ignored her.

"What is it?" Fox asked.

"As you probably already know, Echo removed me from this detail the day the Cortians arrived, but..." she paused, and Echo glanced down so no one could see his expression, "I planned to be at the departure anyway. With...whatever it took to stop the Cortians." The others looked shocked, and Echo's head shot back up. "I'm convinced what's going down will come clear in the hangar just before launch."

"You were going to go rogue?!" Fox wondered in stunned amazement.

"Yes."

"You're that sure??" a pained Echo asked her. "To risk...everything? Just to keep me from boarding the *Trindak?*"

Omega turned to Echo and looked steadily at him, meeting his eyes. He nodded acknowledgement, tight-lipped at what he saw there in her gaze. She turned back to Fox.

"I'm offering...if...if it will help you out of a diplomatic bind, Fox... and keep Echo OFF THAT SHIP...consider me a deranged rogue agent, beginning now."

"Meg..." India whispered, horrified. An outwardly-calm Omega looked at her friend, cocked her head, and shrugged in resignation.

"If that's what it takes, India. You have a scapegoat, Fox. Plausible deniability."

Echo, however, noted the squared shoulders and the light trembling in Omega's hands, and realized exactly what this exchange was costing his partner. Knew, too, that she was well aware of the repercussions that would ensue from her actions...yet was still determined to go forward with her plan.

"Omega," Fox asked in all seriousness, "why are you so sure?"

"I DON'T KNOW!!" Omega threw up her hands in frustration and turned away, running now-visibly trembling fingers over her forehead. "Romeo—how did you and India KNOW you could trust each other, KNOW you could trust Echo? How did ANY of you know you could trust me after I nearly KILLED Echo? Echo, the night Slug attacked and almost tore me apart, how did you KNOW—BEFOREHAND—that you needed to leave the back door open to hear me scream for help?? HOW DID YOU KNOW??"

Echo, Fox, and the Alpha Two members watched Omega's flushed face as she pleaded passionately to be believed. She spun to face Echo.

"Echo, I'm asking you—trust me. Please. If I have to, I'll beg: DON'T GET ON THAT SHIP!" Her hands extended toward him in a wordless plea, and he remembered her pleading gesture in the hangar, amplified now by desperation, even as she went down on her knees before him. "You've told me you DO trust me. But if those were only empty words, tell me NOW...so I can request an immediate transfer." Her voice dropped to a whisper then, as her face contorted in agony. "So I don't have to see...what's coming."

"Damn, Meg," Echo responded, looking down at her, shocked by her drastic vehemence. Omega's shoulders slumped in defeat at his reaction, the burning light in her eyes died, and she rose to her feet and turned away from him.

* * *

"Fox..." she began, and choked.

Abruptly a strong hand rested firmly on her shoulder. She looked up into dark brown eyes; Echo stood before her, shoulders squared, jaw firm, expression resolute.

"Fox," Echo said quietly, still meeting his partner's gaze, "Agent Omega is back on the Cortian assignment. In charge of clandestine security. Alpha Two—and any and all other Alpha Line teams she deems necessary, to include candidates—will report to her. If she feels it is required, the entire department will receive temporary reassignment orders to the Cortian departure."

"Officially noted," Fox replied, and Romeo and India nodded. "Romeo, India, either of you got a problem with that?"

"Not at all, Fox," India declared, voice—and jaw—firm, amber gaze steely.

"We'll follow those two wherever they need us to go, Fox," a determined Romeo added. "Into hell itself, an' out the other side, 'f it comes to it. Family's family. Even if it ain't blood."

Omega hiccuped, and looked down to hide the unwelcome tears that had sprung, unbidden, to her eyes at her companions' confidence and faith in her. *Not now, not now,* she thought, biting her lip. *Be strong, girl. You might've won this battle—and thank God for that—but the war is still ahead.*

She felt Echo's hand tighten slightly, and knew he had seen her emotional reaction. With an effort of will, the strength of which those same companions would never realize, she sucked everything back inside, raised her head and, not yet trusting her voice, simply nodded acknowledgement.

"All right, Meg," Echo continued, "what do you want us to do?"

* * *

Omega's hours of planning now became invaluable; based on the strategy thus devised, she gave Alpha Two their orders and sent them out to start organizing the rest of the department—which was, indeed, being called in, at least those teams who were not in emergency situations of their own.

This meant that Echo's security now included teams Three, Five, and

Six. It also included Agent Monkey, who still did not yet have a partner, though Alpha One had been hoping to fix that in the next batch of applicants; Agent Kako, out of the Moscow Office, looked promising, and got along well with the quirky Firewall Team member. Monkey, Alpha One had decided, was coming along nicely in his rehabilitation, and looked like making a fine addition to the department. He had also become quite loyal to the Alpha Line department chief and its administrative assistant, initially out of gratitude, then out of true appreciation; he would be a very determined member of the security Omega was assembling around her partner.

Omega had also given Alpha Two orders to bring in the top thirteen candidates—which included Kako, the agent they had been considering to partner with Monkey—and brief them with the rest of the department. Echo, the department chief, approved the order.

More, Alpha One decided to go ahead and approve all candidates for Alpha Line admission, a decision which Fox also approved, raising the number of partnerships in the department to sixteen. This gave Alpha Line a total of eleven teams—twenty-two Agents—available for the departure.

"A fair contingent of highly-skilled Agents," Fox observed. "I should say Echo is much better protected now."

"Damn straight, skippy," Romeo declared at the orders. "Ain't no way we're lettin' our department chief go 'thout a fight."

"Amen to that," India agreed.

"It's still not enough," Omega pointed out. "There's a bunch more Cortians than that. There's way more of them than in all of Alpha Line. The *Trindak* is a damn big ship."

"True, but hopefully, we're better," Echo encouraged.

"Yeah," Omega agreed.

"Good," Fox commended. "Go ye forth and prepare, then."

"That," Omega said, waving her hand. "What he said."

Romeo and India headed out of Fox's office with determination etched on their faces, and purpose in their strides.

* * *

"Sugar, what have you got for us?" Fox asked the Division One diplomat on the vid call shortly thereafter.

"Not a great deal, Fox, I am afraid," Sugar replied. "We HAVE ascertained that they are lying—one of their lesser diplomats admitted, for example, that Cort has no great supply of diamonds, as they had said in their initial brief. They may not even have as much as Earth has."

"Dammit," Fox cursed. "I was hoping to put a kibosh on the blood diamond trade with that! How did you get the diplomat to talk?"

"It was not especially difficult, once we got a good fix on their comestibles," Sugar admitted with a shrug and a slight grin. "Gamma got him drunk."

Echo snorted softly, and Omega emitted a noise that sounded vaguely like, "Snrk." Fox grinned.

"Tell your assistant chief that I said, 'Good job,'" Fox said, still grinning. "Anything else?"

"From the same conversation, we determined that Cort's geology does not appear to be anything like what we were told," Sugar noted. "Titanium, tungsten, and cobalt in particular, the structural materials we were most interested in, appear to be far rarer than we were led to think. Again, possibly more so than on Earth."

"So they're lying through their teeth," Omega observed in satisfaction, "in order to look more appealing to us. Surprise, surprise."

"Emphasis on lying," Echo agreed. "Maybe not so much on surprise." He smiled at his partner, who smiled back.

"True, but that does not automatically condemn them," Sugar pointed out. "Such a tactic actually is not at all unusual in first contact negotiations. There are even some cultures who consider it a must, and are offended if you do not 'pad your résumé,' as it were. They view it as a sign of your eagerness to develop trade relations with them. A kind of backward compliment, if you will."

"Are the Cortians like that?" Echo wondered. "I didn't see any sign of it, myself..."

"It is a little too soon to be certain," Sugar decided.

"Then it's too soon to be sending Echo off with 'em," Omega declared. Echo smiled slightly, pleased at her protectiveness.

"Unfortunately, I can't stop it, Omega," Fox observed with a wry grimace. "Certainly this info is a red flag, rather large in the greater circumstances, but it's also not unusual, as Sugar said. It's not nearly enough for me to take to the Council to request some additional leeway in the orders, sufficient to scope out the Cortians a little more."

"Why didn't the Council do that before issuing the orders?" Echo asked.

"I don't have the background on it, Echo," Fox said, shaking his head. "They may have thought they knew enough. Some lower-level bureaucrat may have gotten lazy. I haven't got the answers to that question. I might know more once I've discussed it with Pulgey in some detail, but right now, I just can't answer that."

"Pulgey Entiyti of Emdali?" Echo verified. "I didn't think he was still on the Council."

"He's not. He retired from the PGLEIA about two years ago, Earth time," Fox confirmed. "But he still has a lot of influence, and he still knows all the ins and outs. And he and I go back a looong way, as you know, but Omega and Sugar may not."

"I've read the handbook, Fox, cover to cover," Omega murmured. "I was impressed as hell when I got to that part."

"Thank you, Omega," Fox said, smiling his gratitude. "So you know I do have a bit of experience at this drek."

"Meaning Echo still has to go?"

"Meaning Echo still has to go. I'm sorry. To both of you."

"Damn," Alpha One said in unison.

"Fox—may I ask what is going on?" Sugar inquired. "Or is that classified information?"

"Yes, Sugar, it IS classified, but I think as a department chief, especially one involved in the general diplomatic efforts for this contact, you're owed that information; stand by. I'll pop you the same classified brief I sent Pulgey."

"Standing by."

Fox sent the file in a ciphered blip, then they watched as Sugar opened and read it. Light blond brows drew together, then pale blue eyes widened in shock.

"Damnation!" he exclaimed. "Omega, are you all right?"

"Mostly," Omega replied, wry.

"Echo, do you believe it?"

"I do," Echo said, calm and confident. "We verified—actually Meg herself had it very thoroughly verified—that she's healthy and normal—"

"For me," Omega interjected. Echo winced.

"...And Zz'r'p and the medlab BOTH vouch for that," he finished.

"Verdammt noch mal!" Sugar cursed, lapsing into his native German briefly. "You realize that this raises a whole new line of inquiry."

"What do you mean?" Omega wondered.

"Well, if they really are slavers, as you suspect, it makes a certain sense now," Sugar pointed out. "And most likely, pirates, into the bargain."

"Because of the scarcity of natural resources on the homeworld?" a shrewd Fox wondered.

"Precisely, Fox. It makes a great deal of sense, in that context," Sugar observed. "Especially in terms of our findings. From all Gamma and I have been able to tell, they have little to nothing to trade; every inquiry we made regarding those aspects of their dossier came up grossly short. So I would estimate that their planet has few resources for even their own activities, and likely little left over for offworld commerce. Slavery and piracy—stealing other worlds' resources and people to sell as their own—would become their standard modus operandi, in order to finance their interstellar operations. Depending upon the internal politics in the home system, they may even trade in their own people."

"The scream I heard on their ship," Omega breathed in comprehension. Echo turned to stare at her, eyes narrowed in understanding. Fox merely nodded.

"Keep going, Sugar," Fox murmured. "I'm listening."

"Then consider this," Sugar said. "They have set up a scenario wherein their attentions are highly desired by us, such that we will do whatever it takes to establish formal relations with them. Then they have requested a one-person envoy, with so many restrictions upon that envoy that only one of our top agents meets their requirements. And given the qualifications testing the Agency uses, that puts Echo in the top fraction of a percent of humans on the entire planet."

"Right," Omega agreed without hesitation. Echo felt his face warm in a certain amount of embarrassment.

"And then," Echo added, "they express an interest in my PARTNER."

"Oh, verdammt," Sugar muttered, frowning. "They didn't."

"They did," Omega confirmed.

"Ah, that's right," Fox remembered. "And it fits the scenario. An enhanced human would go well with one of the top humans on the planet, I'd think. Especially if...certain other aspects are intended. Cattle, after all." He shot a glance at Echo, though only Echo recognized its meaning.

"Yeah, I guess so," Echo agreed, subdued. *Shit,* he thought in dismay. *THAT sure isn't the way I want it to go down. Not to mention they'd probably break us up as soon as they could, anyway. And...dear God, probably use us as breeding stock. Forcibly, when we proved unwilling. That's a little harder for me, given human male physiology, but Meg would just get gang-raped.*

A deeply concerned Sugar ran a hand through his hair.

"In that case, Fox, I have a request," the diplomat stated.

"Shoot."

"As you know, my team and I will be at the departure with you..."

"Yes?"

"I assume you have a backup plan, in case Omega's visions continue coming true."

"We do."

"Make us part of it. I want us armed and ready to assist."

"Omega is now in charge of clandestine security on this detail," Fox noted, "per Echo's orders and my confirmation and approval. Get with her, and do whatever she says."

"Omega?" Sugar asked. "May we—my team and I—assist?"

"I'll send you the plans, Sugar, as soon as we get done here," Omega promised. "I'll definitely accept having the extra firepower on hand. And thank you."

"Same here," Echo averred.

"Good. And you are both very welcome," Sugar added. "Aside from being a friend and fellow Agent, Echo saved my ass on one of my earliest assignments. He will always have my gratitude; I owe him."

Echo waved a dismissive hand.

"I've told you a thousand times, you don't owe me anything, Sugar," he murmured. "I wasn't gonna see a colleague get his bacon fried on my watch, if I could help it."

"I intend to repay it, nonetheless," Sugar pointed out. "If necessary and at all possible."

"And we appreciate it," Omega declared.

"Anything else, guys?" Fox wondered. When Echo, Omega and Sugar all shook their heads, he added, "Very good, then. Fox out."

"Sugar out."

* * *

The three in the Director's office were silent for a long moment.

"I gotta wonder, now, just exactly how much the Cortians are lying about," Echo admitted.

"Me, too," Omega agreed.

"Me three, to be honest," Fox confessed, and Alpha One stared at him. "What? I'm not stupid, you two. Something is going on here, and it looks like Omega may have a bead on it. Unfortunately, I don't really have ANY-THING I can take forward to the Council. They just aren't going to believe that a baseline human can do the things Omega is claiming."

"Even an enhanced human?" Omega wondered, voice very quiet. "Because I'm not exactly baseline."

Echo laid a light hand on her shoulder, squeezing, and cocking his head slightly. *It's okay, baby,* the gestures coded to his partner. *You were never 'baseline' to begin with.*

Omega glanced at his hand, then at him, and nodded once in acknowlededgement, her eyes warming. *Thanks,* was the simple message it telegraphed.

"Yes, even that, Omega," Fox averred. "There is something you have to realize, maydele. You see what was done to you; you're aware of it and see it in yourself. The rest of us, even those who know you best, not so much. You are yourself an impressive individual, and I dare say you would

103

be, even had Slug not...done what he did. So we have learned...or are, at least, learning...not to be surprised at what you can accomplish when you are determined enough. More—and this is something you may not know—you are developing a significant reputation in PGLEIA; even the Ennead has heard of you now. It is generally considered throughout the Pan-Galactic Administration that you are perfectly partnered with Echo, here, and that together, you are a team to be reckoned with."

* * *

Fox watched as Omega's jaw went slack in total surprise, her mouth popping open as a result, and she blinked in rank astonishment. Beside her, Echo's brown eyes developed an almost golden glow of pride, and he smiled, ever so slightly. Then, Fox noticed, Echo nudged her with an elbow, subtly and very gently, before allowing that elbow to remain in comforting contact with her torso. The Director hid a smile of his own.

"But even though they know what Slug did to you, to them you are still a human," Fox continued. "An exceptional human without doubt, but a human nonetheless. Which...is true."

"And humans don't do telepathy or precog," Echo added, before Omega could protest.

"Exactly," Fox agreed. "And precisely my point."

They were quiet again. Finally Omega broke it.

"But that still leaves us wondering just how far down the proverbial rabbit hole the Cortian deception goes," she noted.

"Yeah," Echo agreed. "Or black hole, or...something."

"I'm betting it goes all the way down," Omega declared, staunch. "After some of the...shit...I've 'seen' in the last few days," she quirked her fingers around the word, "ALL of which has been confirmed one way or another, I just don't trust 'em any farther than I can throw 'em."

"All well and good—or not; but my question to Echo is: If Omega turns out to be wrong, at this point, can you be objective enough to fulfill the diplomatic needs of your mission?" Fox wondered.

"I can, Fox...IF Meg turns out to be wrong. I'm a lot more worried about what happens if she turns out to be right," Echo pointed out. "And by the sound of it, so far she's batting a thousand."

"But she said herself that she saw many possible endings."

"None of which had a happy conclusion, Fox," Omega reminded him.

"...True."

A soft, deep tone, like a church bell, sounded a warning, and then Bravo's face popped up on one of the wall screens.

"Sorry to interrupt, Boss, but I thought you'd want to know. Pulgey Entiyti is on the line for you." Bravo glanced at Alpha One in an apologetic fashion. "And he wants to speak to you in private."

"Understood, Bravo," Fox murmured. "Stand by one. Alpha One, would you excuse me, please?"

"Sure thing, Fox," Echo said, as he and Omega rose and headed for the door. "Call us if you need us, or have anything that pertains to us, or the situation."

"Roger that, Echo."

* * *

A white, reptilian face, possessed of sleek black, back-swept horns, and flame-colored eyes with the vertical-slit pupils characteristic of his race, appeared on the screen, and Fox smiled.

"Pulgey!" he exclaimed. "It's been too long, alter khaver!"

"It has indeed, Franz—ah, Fox, rather; I forget myself!" the Draconan agreed, showing sharp white teeth as he smiled with his broad, lizard-like mouth. "You look quite well, my old friend."

"Yes, I'm doing fine, Pulgey," Fox said, offering a smile himself. "Thank you for returning my call."

"You saved my life the day we met. I shall never repay that debt. Returning a call is no recompense."

"As I recall, you turned right around and saved mine. Twice over. I'd say you repaid that debt with interest, long ago."

Entiyti waved his hand in a dismissive fashion.

"Forgive me that it took so long to call back; I have been busy with clan matters. What can I do for you today, Fra-Fox?" Entiyti wondered, correcting himself in mid-word.

"It's this Cortian thing, Pulgey," Fox elaborated. "Did you get that classified brief I sent you?"

"I did. I found it...most interesting. This is the human who was kidnapped by Slug and...modified?"

"It is. Agent Omega. If Echo is our top male agent, she is almost certainly our top female agent. And smarter than the proverbial whip. In fact—and you didn't hear this—Agency-wide, I'd say she's second only TO Echo, and that's largely because she's still a comparatively inexperienced Agent."

"A rookie?"

"No, Echo and I have discussed it many times, and we are both of the opinion that she's proven herself in the field sufficient to have left that category behind some months ago. With a little more experience under her belt, she's going to be every bit his equal as an Agent." Fox drew a deep, thoughtful breath. "And she is serious as hell about this. Echo believes her now, though he admits he misunderstood at first, and damn, Pulgey. Now I'M starting to wonder."

"Fair enough," Entiyti agreed. "Is there reason to think she might be right?"

"There is, and to spare," Fox averred, "though not as much hard evidence as any of us here would like."

"Tell me."

* * *

Fox sketched a quick outline of the clues Omega had given, as well as the latest information from Sugar, effectively laying his cards on the table before the former galactic leader.

"...And so I'm wondering what you know about the situation," he concluded the briefing.

"I know that the Ennead is keen on getting a representative of the Sagittarius Dwarf Galaxy on board," Entiyti said, frowning in thought. "It is, after all, largely a part of our own galaxy now, little more than a vertical, rather than horizontal, arm of the Great Spiral—and the Cortians are supposed to be from a system near what once was the core of that galaxy. The Ennead is pushing hard for this."

"So hard, we won't be allowed a little leeway for the sake of caution, and the safety of one of our own?" Fox pressed.

"What is it you and your team are wanting to do, Fox?" Entiyti wondered, what passed for reptilian brows drawn together; whether in concern, skepticism, or some other emotion, Fox could not be certain, despite his years of familiarity with the other male.

"We'd just like to slow down the timetable a little," Fox explained. "According to the original schedule, Echo would be leaving with 'em well inside a—oh hell, forget a Division week, the timeframe is inside an EARTH week—from their arrival; tomorrow, to be specific. That's pretty damn fast, Pulgey."

"Yes, it is."

"We're gradually starting to pick out information here and there, and we—myself and Alpha Line—would like to have the opportunity to verify that the Cortians really are who and what they say they are, before laying Echo's life on the line like that. And we'd also like the opportunity to make an appropriate response, should they turn out to be belligerent, malicious, or otherwise unfriendly."

"Because if Omega's...metaphysical, hyperphysical, ultraphysical, however you are terming it...impressions are correct, Echo would be killed—or enslaved, as soon as he was away from Earth," Entiyti verified. "If not before."

"Right. Now, if they draw first, all bets are off, and we WILL respond as appropriate. But if we find out what they're up to before they try it, I mean to PROVE it...we'd like to take action."

"Fox...damn, friend, I hate to ask this...is Alpha One being objective about this? What is their...relationship to each other? I know you have another Alpha Team that are life mates..."

"They're partners," Fox answered honestly. "And no, they aren't lovers, if that's what you're asking."

"But are they—what is the term you humans use? 'Wannabe' lovers?"

Fox put on his game face.

"Personal matters are not part of the job, and you know it, Pulgey. I'm not allowed to give out personal information, even if I knew all the answers."

"Meaning I should not have asked," Entiyti said, allowing a rueful, lopsided grin to show his fangs on one side. It would have been a frightening sight to most humans, but Fox had been Pulgey Entiyti's chief bodyguard—and, some said, best friend—for many years before joining the Agency, and knew the other male as well as anyone in the galaxy. "I'm asking anyway. I will tell no one, Franz. I am only trying to assess the situation."

Fox sighed.

"All right," he murmured. "I'm swearing you to secrecy, Pul."

A taloned, scaled hand appeared in the side of the image.

"I do swear on the name of the Maker," a solemn Entiyti declared.

"Okay. Yeah, Echo is interested in Omega. Pretty seriously, I'd say."

"But Omega is not interested in him?"

"We...haven't been able to figure that one out yet," Fox admitted. "I suspect she MIGHT be, but I'm not sure. She's as private and reserved as her partner. If I hadn't known Echo since he was a teenager, I wouldn't know he was in love with her. I doubt there's another member of the Agency who CAN tell. Well, maybe Zz'r'p."

"The Arcturan ambassador? The Deltiri?"

"Yep, the telepath. And Omega is just like Echo in that regard."

"So if she does not wish it known, you will not know."

"Exactly. Well...probably not," Fox amended. "I still read her pretty well, and if I can catch her off guard, I sometimes recognize things."

"But why would she not wish it?"

"I can think of a good fifty valid reasons, just off the top of my head," Fox pointed out. "Only one of which is the fact that she was programmed to assassinate him."

"Oh damnation—that's right. I'd forgotten that." Entiyti paused, thinking. "So how DOES she feel about him? At least, what you can tell?"

"They're close, no doubt about it," Fox said. "I've never heard her say it personally, but I have several reliable sources who have heard her state that he's her best friend. And I also know that she's gathered a kind of 'family' around herself, here in the Agency—the core member of which is Echo, but which also includes Alpha Two...and to a lesser extent, myself, I think."

"Ah. The father figure, perhaps?"

"In a manner of speaking, yes, I think so. My appearance is commensurate with her dead father's age, I'm certain. Never mind that I'm really old enough to be her GRANDfather, at least. Maybe GREAT-grandfather. Not that I feel like it," Fox decided.

"Especially when Zebra's around, eh?" Entiyti teased, and Fox felt his face grow warm.

"It certainly doesn't hurt," Fox shot back, and Entiyti laughed, a big, roaring, cheerful sound.

"Ah, my friend, my dear old friend...whenever you decide you have had enough of the bureaucracy and let Echo have your job, you have my word—if you wish it, I will happily give you your old job back, along with the bonus of another rejuvenating bath...and pay and quarters suitable to bring along a mate. I am certain a physician of Zebra's capabilities would be useful in my travels. And we might even have room for a small nursery, if matters...follow their natural course."

"I may just take you up on that, Pul," Fox grinned. "Not for a few more years yet, though, I think. Even if there weren't any other considerations, I want to give Echo time to get the field work out of his system, and as things stand with Omega as his partner, right now he's fairly reveling in it. In the meantime, what about the Cortians?"

"Are you certain that Alpha One is being objective about the matter?"

"If by that, do you mean that their feelings are involved, of course they are," Fox pointed out. "They care about each other, whether they're IN love or not. If you're asking if I think they're off the beam on things, no, I don't."

Entiyti was silent for long moments, rubbing his scaly chin—or what passed for it; his race, the Draconans of Draigon, known to them as Emdali, had prominent jaws, but little in the way of chins—in thought.

"Let me go see what I can find out," he decided. "Perhaps I can tug a few strings here and there, and sort out your tangle in a way best calculated to allow safety for your agents. ALL your agents."

"Now that," Fox declared in some relief, "would be greatly appreciated."

* * *

About an hour and a half later, another vid call came in from Pulgey Entiyti, and Fox dropped his paperwork and took it immediately.

"What did you find out, Pul?" Fox asked, as soon as Entiyti's image

109

had properly formed on the wall screen.

"That there is a disappointing bias in the Council against the notion that humans can be anything but ordinary human," Entiyti said in some disgust. "Especially in the higher echelons."

"Meaning they don't believe there's anything to Omega's visions," Fox interpreted with a sigh.

"No, they don't. More, and worse, the current head of the Council—"

"Dulziv? The Virmergin from HD 10442b?"

"The same. Dulziv is...what is that American indigenous term? Ah. 'Counting coup.' It has a positive fixation upon gathering contacts from around the Galaxy and as many of the satellite galaxies, let alone the Local Group, as it can manage. It seems to think that that will be a mark of how successful its term as Council Chair will be."

"Well, hell," Fox cursed.

"Exactly." Entiyti ran a clawed hand over his horns. "If the Cortian first contact goes south, I think Dulziv will be surprised at how right it will be."

"Ain't that the truth," Fox said, wry. "And not in the good way. So we didn't get an extension to scope 'em out better?"

"No, I'm afraid not, old friend. I did try, but Dulziv pointed out in no uncertain terms that I am retired and out of the loop."

"It dared?!"

"No, no, in that respect, it was entirely correct. That said, I did...shall we say, make some connections...in an effort to override it as Council Chair, but nothing is going to come to fruition in time to help your situation. But damn the being to the eighteenth level of the abyss, if we lose Echo in any sense of the word, I WILL have its job!"

"You'd go back into harness?"

"No, no. Well, if necessary, yes. But I meant I would see Dulziv ousted from the Council for it."

"Ah." Fox sighed. "So we're back to square one."

"Well, not quite. I did get approval for you to take whatever actions that turned out to be necessary, in the event things went...badly. And I managed to get Dulziv to word it broadly enough for you to interpret that as, 'whatever actions are necessary to ensure things do NOT go badly.' Stand by; I'll ping you the addendum to your orders. You'll be getting it via official channels soon, but I want you to have the heads-up and start making whatever preparations you deem necessary NOW."

"Standing by," Fox agreed, and waited for the alert to arrive on his desktop virtual display, promptly opening the file. "Okay, I've got it. Hm... you know, I'll bet gelt to gefilte fish that this is more open-ended than Dulziv intended it to be."

"And you'd be right. I wasn't head of the Ennead for a century without learning a thing or two about, ah, getting my own way when it was needful."

Fox laughed.

"Well, to be honest, Pul, we were planning to do a certain amount of 'ensuring things don't go badly' as it was. But this definitely helps. I won't have to play CYA quite so hard, this way. Thank you."

"I'm only sorry I couldn't get Dulziv to see reason. I'll be watching this, Franz. I remember Echo from the First Envoy to Earth, and I've kept an eye on him ever since. You, X-ray, and Oboe did a fine job with him."

"We had outstanding material there to work with. He was a good kid, with a great set of parents who raised him well, from the beginning."

"No doubt. Well, I have affairs to tend, and I'm certain the Agency has work for you to do, Franz. Keep me posted."

"I will, Pul. You'll be the first off-planet notification, after...whatever is gonna happen, happens."

"Let us hope to the Maker that Omega is wrong."

"Amein."

"Entiyti out."

"Fox out."

* * *

Fox and nearly all of Alpha Line, including the hand-selected candidates, accompanied by Sugar and a somewhat small but significant contingent from Diplomacy—Sugar had done a quick review of who was up on their weapons certifications, as well as how well they passed those certifications, and picked the top twenty percent—were the Division One Agency representatives in Hangar 16 of the Chicago Station spaceport for the de-

111

parture of the *Trindak*. This combination resulted in twenty-one teams of agents present; Fox passed it off by explaining to the Cortians that twenty-one was a significant number to humans, using a 'twenty-one gun salute' as an example.

It still wasn't enough to suit Omega—the *Trindak* crew complement was in the near vicinity of one hundred, by her estimate, more than twice her guard contingent—but the agents present were no slouches, and per her observations, were better honed and disciplined than the crew of the *Trindak*. Relative fighting skills remained to be seen.

Omega shot a discreetly questioning look at India, who nodded imperceptibly and lightly touched her hip as she glanced over her shoulder at the other twelve Alpha teams, standing at formal attention. Then India cut her eyes at Romeo, standing beside her. Romeo, too, nodded slightly, and rolled his left shoulder, as if stretching. Omega understood, and covertly flashed them both a grateful, if worried, smile. Then she looked at them, casually unbuttoned her jacket, and lightly, almost absentmindedly, fingered her belt buckle. They nodded again.

Omega looked across at Fox with a pleading look, but Fox returned the look firmly, uncompromising. She read that look clearly: *I tried, I can't, so don't ask me.* She sighed, looked at Echo, and blinked twice. Echo returned the signal, then stepped forward.

* * *

"Well, Meg," Echo said as he walked up to her, "hold down the fort while I'm gone, okay? I'll be back in a couple weeks, at most. Don't forget to water the flowers." He laid a gentle, confident hand on her shoulder, squeezing gently; it was obviously meant to be encouraging.

"Sure, Echo," Omega said in a normal tone, then dropped into a whisper intended for his ears alone. "Goodbye, Echo...take care of yourself—"

"Always do—sometimes with a little help from...my friends," he murmured softly, looking down at her with a gentle gaze, patently trying to reassure her. Then he turned and headed for the spaceship hatch.

Omega tensed as two uniformed Cortians met him at the base of the ramp to escort him aboard.

Here it comes, she thought, readying herself. *What happens next will tell me exactly which scenario I have to deal with.*

* * *

At the top of the ramp, just before he entered the hatch, one of the escorts lightly and stealthily touched a small metal rod to the base of Echo's skull. His entire voluntary nervous system locked up from the neck down, and he stiffened instantly. But he was able to call out the pre-arranged signal Omega had insisted upon, though it left him somewhat breathless.

"Meg! DANTE!! DANTE, baby!" Echo yelled, as loudly as he could. The Cortians grabbed him before he could finish, and began to manhandle him aboard their craft.

* * *

"ALPHA LINE! Commence Operation: Dante! GO!!" Omega's shouted command echoed through the hangar, and Romeo and India coordinated team actions as they began picking off Cortians with the stun-rays Fox had chosen in order to preserve diplomatic appearances. Even Sugar and his contingent joined in the action, to rather good effect, as the chief diplomat had insisted upon his hand-picked team being armed also, much to Omega's gratification. Even Fox pulled a hidden weapon and began firing, his dead-accurate aim mute testament to the fact that, even now, the Director was not merely a desk jockey.

But the head of clandestine security for the operation had a different part of the plan to execute, and the adrenaline which had been pumping through her system for days, with no outlet, now found release. She spun and broke into a hard sprint—straight for the *Trindak*.

Omega punched a hidden button on her belt buckle, and a dim yellow glow formed around her running figure as a personal force field materialized. She darted right at Echo as the Cortians produced projectile weapons and began firing back at the Division One agents. The little force field flared brightly each time a projectile glanced off it—which meant it was flaring a lot. Behind her, the Alpha Teams and Diplomatic agents dived for cover.

"HANG ON, ECHO! I'm coming!!" a determined Omega called, approaching swiftly from the side of the spacecraft. As Omega reached the ramp, she springboarded powerfully off the landing strut and leaped directly at Echo. In mid-air, Omega punched off the force field, tackled Echo—who remained vertical only by dint of his limbs being too stiff to crumple, due to the stun rod's effect—and re-established the field. The shimmering glow of the field formed around both of them as they flew through the air and landed in a heap on the hangar floor, some distance to the other side of the hatch.

"ICHOUB!" the Cortian 'ambassador' cried, just as a stun-ray from Alpha Five found its mark. B'ka crumpled to the ramp, and the Cortians, intent on recovering Echo, now diverted to assist their immobilized commander.

* * *

"N'deki yoh!" B'ka managed to call, his voice hoarse. Echo understood him.

"Quick, Meg!" he exclaimed, "They're preparing to launch! I still can't move. Get us out of here!"

"I'm...sorry, Echo," Omega said, looking down at him with a strange expression from where she lay sprawled awkwardly across him. Her breath was coming in little gasps of pain. "I can't. When I dropped the field to get you inside it, I took a shot in my leg...I think it's broken." She raised her head and looked around the hangar as the firefight raged on. "Everyone else is pinned down...we're on our own." Omega grimaced as she struggled around until she was directly atop him. "I'll do what I can..."

"Meg," Echo said urgently, "that ship has an interplanetary ion drive."

"I know." Omega's voice was subdued, low.

"Is our force field proof against particle beams?"

"Not completely. But it's enough that...you won't need much more... shielding. Hang on. This will be...rough..." Omega carefully folded Echo's now-limp arms across his chest, then pushed herself painfully down toward his feet, straightening his sprawled legs as she went, and extended her own folded arms upward until his paralyzed body was completely covered from head to toe.

"Meg, get out of here! What are you doing?!" Echo exclaimed.

"The same thing I've been doing all along. Making sure Alpha Line's chief—my partner and...and my best friend—makes it out of this. The only way I know how."

"But you're—"

114

"Expendable."

"No, you're not," he whispered, as he heard the hum of the propulsion units coming on-line. "Dear God, baby. You knew. All along, you knew...it would come to this."

"Yes. Take care of yourself, hon. Goodbye, Echo." Omega met Echo's horror-struck gaze, waiting, her lips moving in a silent prayer.

* * *

Fox and the rest of Alpha Line watched helplessly from across the hangar as the observation area's automatic force field activated in front of them, snapping on when the spacecraft took off. The Cortian vessel heedlessly abandoned and incinerated stunned or straggling crewmembers in its hasty flight.

The forms of the two Agents beneath it disappeared in the glow of the ion drive. The watching Agents averted their gaze as the sound of a lone human voice rose over the high whine of the departing vessel.

It was the only time they had ever heard Echo scream.

* * *

"*SHOOT IT DOWN!!*" a furious Fox yelled into his cell phone. "Dammit, I don't care if it's over the WHITE HOUSE! They just tried to kidnap Echo, and probably fried Echo AND Omega when they took off! I want them ON THE GROUND!! Preferably in PIECES!!"

Romeo and India stood staring at the aftermath in horror, as appalled Alpha Line teams milled about, beginning to secure the site; Diplomacy teams coordinated mop-up efforts under Sugar's direction. Carbonized Cortian bodies lay scattered across the hangar floor; the hangar doors were buckled outward from the craft's unexpected departure. Abruptly, Romeo pointed at a movement, and he and India ran over. Fox was close behind.

"They found 'em!" someone yelled just then. "They found Alpha One!"

All other activity in the hangar abruptly ceased.

The last flickers of the tiny force field faded and died as a finally-mobile Echo crawled out from under Omega's charred form. He sat beside her body on the hangar floor, his face white to the lips, horrified dark eyes wide in shock and stunned disbelief, as the Director and the Alpha Two team ran up.

"Oh, my—" India broke off, and paled. Fox grimaced in pain. Romeo surveyed the scene, then turned his head away and closed his eyes.

"The...the force field...wouldn't protect...both of us," Echo murmured in explanation, "so...so she...dear God...she..." Gently, he picked up his partner and turned over her body, holding her in his arms and pulling her ever so carefully into his lap.

The platinum mane was gone, the soft pale skin blackened and burned. Even her lips were blistered. Seared strips of scorched skin and flesh hung from her back, arms, and legs through the charred, tattered remnants of her Suit. One ear was missing. Bone showed through one shoulder. Her hands were black, skeletal.

"Oh, Meg..." Echo whispered. "Baby..."

A soft, gurgling sound cut through the stillness.

"Eh...Echo...?" Horror filled the faces of the assembled Agents as, impossibly, Omega's eyelids fluttered and opened. "Ech...Echo?"

"Oh, dear God..." Echo whispered, appalled. "I'm here, Meg. Right here. Can you see me?"

"Ye...yes." She blinked several times, evidently trying to clear her damaged vision. "You all...r-right?"

"Yes, Meg. I'm...fine."

"Hurt?"

"Got a few beta burns here and there. Nothing too serious. You...made a good shield..." Echo's voice grew rough.

"G-good. Tried...tried hard."

"Ssshh. Rest," Echo told her softly, then he looked up with agonized eyes at Fox, who was back on the cell phone, this time to Medical. When he disconnected the call, he met his department chief's tormented gaze.

"On their way, Echo. As fast as they can move."

* * *

A still-very-pale Echo sat on a gurney in the corner of the medlab as India and a medtech examined him and treated his burns. Across the room, his partner, hidden by a curtain, was being tended by half a dozen doctors, and more were arriving with every moment.

"In fact," India told him, "they put out an all-hands call for burn ex-

116

pertise across the entire Division One Medical staff, regardless of shift or Office assignment. We've got everybody who can help, either here already, or arriving soon. There's even a couple of offworld physicians coming in on emergency transports."

When India was finished with Echo, she released the medtech to assist the other doctors, and led Echo out to the waiting room. Fox and Romeo were there.

"Damn. Talk about déjà vu. Haven't we been through this once before?" Echo muttered. "Anybody heard anything?"

"The girl's...in bad shape, Echo..." Romeo began.

"Tell me something I don't already know, hot shot," Echo snapped. Then, as Romeo blinked at him, uncertain what to say next, he raked a lightly-trembling hand through his hair and said more quietly, "Sorry, pal. I just...watched it all happen, up close and personal."

India moved near Echo, and laid a sympathetic hand on his shoulder.

"You...watched her burn?"

"Yup." He nodded. "Watched it, heard it, felt it, smelled it...and couldn't move a muscle to stop it." He turned away. "Damn."

"Why couldn't she get you two outta the way?" Romeo asked. "That was the plan."

"She took a bullet in the thigh when she dropped the force field to pull me in. Damn thing broke the bone. It hurt so bad she could barely move it, and it wasn't goin' the right direction when she did manage to move it. Standing was outta the question, let alone picking me up, or dragging me... or much of anythiing, really. I don't think she could even crawl on it. From what I could tell by feel and a little peripheral vision, it wasn't just cracked, it was flat-out in two pieces." He flopped his hand in the air, bending it at the wrist to demonstrate.

"Do the doctors know about it?" Fox asked.

"Yeah. I told 'em," Echo replied tersely. "Along with the whole litany of other shit. It may be the only thing of the lot that they can fix."

"Why didn't MEG know about it?" Romeo asked. "She's the one called the whole thing, right down to th' damn timing."

"She did," Echo told him, bleak.

"Then why didn't she plan for it??" India demanded.

"I...don't think she knew how, with what time and resources she had left, after we—after *I*—"

"WE," Fox corrected, voice raw.

"...Took so long to convince." Echo shot a pained look at Fox, who returned it, then glanced away. "I don't know that any of the rest of us could've done any better under the circumstances, either. It just...came down to a choice..."

"And she chose to save you," India whispered. "How typically... Meg..."

Echo nodded wordlessly.

"Echo, we've brought everybody in we could reach, homeworld and offworld. We've even brought in some burn specialists from Mayo and some military radiation specialists," Fox told him quietly. Echo nodded again.

"Now we wait?"

"Yes."

* * *

After some half an hour, an agent entered the waiting room and approached Fox.

"Report on the renegade Cortian vessel, sir," she said, handing him a sheaf of papers.

"Thank you, Mary," Fox told her. "What's the gist of it?"

Mary shook her head with a frown. Fox sighed.

"All right, Mary. You can go. Thank you."

The agent nodded, but remained, though her manner was somewhat diffident. Fox looked up from the report.

"Something else, Mary?"

"Yes, sir...sir, I just came from the Core. There's a whole group of agents collected there, most of Alpha Line and a bunch of others too, just waiting for word. Diplomacy, Weapons, Science and Engineering, even representatives from several of the embassies, all...waiting. And we were wondering..."

"Yes, Mary?" Fox encouraged gently, suspecting what was coming.

118

"How is Omega doing, sir? And..." she glanced at Echo, "is Echo all right?"

Fox deferred to Echo with a look, but Echo shook his head.

"I'm fine, Fox."

"Echo is unhurt, except for a few mild beta burns, which have already been treated," Fox told Mary then. "Omega...is another story."

"We heard...what she did," Mary said, voice soft. "The Alpha Line Agents have been telling us, at least what they could. Not...not all of 'em could...could talk about it, you know? Monkey was especially broken up, I think. Um, sir? Do...you think she'll...make it?"

Fox glanced at India. Romeo, Echo, Fox, and Mary watched as India closed her eyes and shook her head wordlessly. Echo's wan face tightened, paling even further, and he turned away. Romeo swallowed and moved to stand beside India. Fox looked back at Mary, who nodded sadly.

"Thank you, sir. If it's all right, I'll...tell the others. They've been asking."

Fox nodded.

"That would...be helpful, Mary. Thank you."

"Agent Echo?" Mary said.

"Yes?" Echo responded without turning.

"I'm...sorry, sir. We all...thought she was special, too."

Echo nodded once, and the agent left quietly. Fox sat down to study the report in detail. Several minutes of silence later, his face contorted and he uttered a single harsh word into the silence.

"HELL."

Echo turned at Fox's exclamation.

"Whassup, Fox?" Romeo asked.

"Bad report?" India added.

"We didn't shoot down the Cortian ship," Fox answered them both. "Or even stop it."

"Aw, damn," Romeo said, disgusted.

Echo's eyes narrowed, and he grew very quiet. Fox watched his department chief with considerable anxiety; he knew that look.

"...And we've had the largest UFO sighting in all of North American history," Fox added, continuing to watch Echo, if surreptitiously. "Looks like almost all of Chicago saw the slave ship leave, as well as most of the Great Lakes states and part of Canada. Fortunately, the Chicago Office is handling matters. Between strategic brain bleaching, and substantial disinformation, that'll be all right, at least." He read a bit more. "PGLEIA authorities have been notified to watch for a craft fitting the *Trindak*'s description and apprehend it if possible, or take it out if surrender refused. Unfortunately, the damn craft appears to have vanished. Once it left our solar system, it seems PGLEIA lost track of it, for reasons unknown; nobody can find it."

Brown eyes glinted with a fierce bronze light, and facial muscles hardened into granite.

* * *

Without a word, Echo turned and walked over to the medlab door, cracking it to look through.

But Omega was completely surrounded by physicians and medical equipment, and he couldn't catch even a glimpse of her. He let the door swing shut.

* * *

"That does NOT look good," India murmured to Fox, motioning at Echo's straight, rigid back.

"It's not," Fox told Alpha Two in low tones. "As long as Echo's talking, everything is fine. But when he gets quiet—really quiet—well..." Fox sighed. "Heaven help the crew of the *Trindak* if Echo ever catches up to them, because he'll send 'em straight to hell."

* * *

"How about the cleanup?" Romeo asked.

"Massive control efforts are underway," Fox replied in a normal tone then, carefully watching Echo as he stood gazing coolly into space. Fox knew he was listening, despite the distant expression. "Every agent in the Midwest is being called in to Chicago to help. We're even sending a few in from Headquarters to help out. But like I said, some strategic memory rearrangements and some skillful disinformation—notably, that it's an Air Force experimental aircraft test that inadvertently got out of its designated airspace due to instrument malfunction—and we should get the upper hand on that phase of the whole mess."

"Shee-it," Romeo exclaimed. "You need me 'n India to go back, help with the sitch?"

"No, Romeo," Fox told him, still observing Alpha Line's chief, "I think I need you two right here."

* * *

India had been studying Echo intently as well, concerned, and wanting to offer supportive comfort. Now, being as quiet as she could to avoid startling him, she moved up behind him and laid a light, sympathetic hand on his arm.

It didn't work.

On alert, Echo spun in automatic, instinctive reaction to stare at her, brown eyes blazing with a dangerous light, and India involuntarily stepped back from the cold, bitter wrath she saw there. Echo said nothing, but he stared down at the hand still on his arm, and India quickly withdrew it, edging away.

Echo promptly resumed an intense contemplation of things only he could see.

* * *

"What happened?" Entiyti asked as soon as his scaly white face appeared on the video screen in Fox's office, a little while later; he didn't even bother to preface it with a greeting. His black horns, normally furled backward, close to his skull, were angled forward in a Draconan signal of anxiety. "Was it as bad as your Agent Omega expected?"

"Every bit, and more," Fox said, grim. "Worse, what she didn't tell anyone else...was that, in order to save Echo..." Fox broke off and looked away, shaking his head. "Pul, she had to sacrifice herself. And she did. Without hesitation."

"Oh, dear Maker," Entiyti breathed. "So you lost one of your two top agents anyway?"

"She's not dead quite yet," Fox murmured, refusing to look at his oldest friend; he was laboring to maintain a level of professionalism, but Entiyti had known the man now called Fox for over half a century, and it was proving far more difficult than he had expected. "But she might as well be; it's only a matter of time. By the Name, Pulgey! She was burned so badly under the Cortians' ion drive that parts of her are..." His face crumpled momentarily, despite his best efforts. "I...I can't...it's gone, Pul. Most of her back...it's just ash on the floor of the spacecraft hangar. Her ear, her hair, her spine...Elohim adirim, Pulgey, her hands—they're nothing but blackened bones! Her HANDS, Pul!"

"Hush, my friend," Entiyti whispered, patently aghast, yet endeavoring to calm his friend. "Were you there when it...happened?"

"Yes. But not close enough to actually help. I picked off a few Cortians with my stunner gun, and those bastards were among the ones incinerated. But...it just wasn't enough."

"For you, of all people, to be so deeply affected, it must have been horrific."

"It...was. Do you want to know the most horrific part?" Fox wondered. "What?"

"Not only is she still alive...she's still conscious and lucid."

"Maker have pity! She is talking?"

"Yes."

"And Echo?"

"Is all right...physically."

"What about emotionally and mentally?"

"That...remains to be seen," Fox sighed. "He's completely withdrawn. Doesn't want to talk, doesn't want to be touched, but—if I know him at all—he wants to kill something. Preferably some Cortians, but he probably wouldn't care at this point if he kamikazi'ed out in the process."

"Damnation. Tell me what happened, Franz, if you can."

"Pul, it was Omega's stun rod scenario. Right down to the last niqqud. The Cortians zapped him with one—at the base of his skull, it looked like—and Echo couldn't move a muscle except to talk a little. Omega got him away from the slavers, but they landed hard under the drive, and she took a projectile in the leg in the process. I've gathered from the physicians in Medical that the bullet essentially shattered the femur. She couldn't walk, she couldn't even crawl. Echo said her leg was sort of flopping around, it was so bad. There was no way she could get the pair of them out from under the Cortians' craft, not in that shape. Hell, she couldn't have gotten herself out from under. And those bastards were willing to—and did—torch some of their own crew to get away from the spaceport before we could apprehend them. So the sons of bitches didn't hesitate a nanosecond over the fact that both members of Alpha One were under their engine ports."

"What happened next?" Entiyti's voice was gentle. "Only if you can speak of it, my dear friend."

Fox nodded slowly.

"Insofar as I've been able to get out of Echo, who was badly in shock in the hangar, evidently the personal force field Omega was using was insufficient to completely shield them both from the plasma. And she KNEW it, Pulgey! And she knew what was going to happen, and she went in anyway! God help me, she knew it. So she...covered Echo...with her own body...to shield..."

"Oh, Maker, what a brave child," Entiyti whispered.

"But that...is part of why I'm concerned for Echo," Fox explained. "He experienced it all...and he loves her. He, he didn't actually admit to it—but I've known that boy his whole adult life. I KNOW him. I trust him...and I care for him as a son." Fox raked a distracted hand through his salt-and-pepper hair. "By HaShem, Pul! In all the years I've known him, I've never heard Echo even scream before, let alone...like THAT."

Entiyti was silent, uncertain what to say.

"He saw it all, experienced it all, I'm sure of it," Fox went on. "And couldn't lift a finger to help, or stop it...or anything else." He put his head in his hands. "And it's at least partly my fault."

"You had orders, Franz."

"DAMN the orders!" Fox shouted, slamming his fist onto his desk hard enough to bounce pens about. "I know my Agents! I should have trusted her! Even if it was only a hunch, I should have listened! Even Echo said... that he and I...share the blame."

"I could offer platitudes, my old friend, but I know all too well that they are worthless at a time like this. What...can I do to help?"

"Help us find that Cortian ship, the *Trindak*—damnation, she even got the ship's NAME right!—and take it out," Fox growled.

"WHAT?? It got away?!"

"Yes," the Agency director ground out through gritted teeth. "Evidently the sons of bitches are very highly experienced in planetary escapes. I've seen the video, and it was quite the tutorial in evasive maneuvers. And my people aren't exactly inexperienced themselves, not after the Klydonian invasion attempt. It's not surprising, I suppose, when you consider that, according to Omega, their entire culture is based upon piracy and the slave trade. Sugar, the head of my Diplomacy department, agrees with her; from what his people were able to ascertain, the home system is pretty damn piss-poor in resources, despite what their dossier said."

"Mm. Piracy too, eh? All right. Let alone what they did to your Agents, we don't need that lot wandering the galaxy. Send me a description and I'll see what I can do," Entiyti offered. "If nothing else, we can send out an all-systems bulletin to watch for them. And I, personally," he added, baring razor-edged teeth in anger, "will see to it that Dulziv is ousted as far from the Ennead as I can personally fling it. In fact, if I can send it to the Sagittarius Dwarf Galaxy to see for itself, it seems to me it would be...apropos. Preferably direct to Cort. In chains, if I can arrange for it."

"Thank you," Fox whispered. "That was to be my next request—get Dulziv off the Council. I don't care what you do with it, as long as it is never in a position to issue orders to me and mine again. And, as long as I'm its Director, I count the Agency and its people as MINE. In every sense of the term," he added.

"You need not make such a request at all, friend," Entiyti declared, anger fading into a kind of melancholy. "I have read the reports on your Omega. I had looked forward to meeting her one day. Now...it seems I never shall."

"No."

"How long do you think she has?"

"I...don't know. The doctors were still assessing when I came up here to take your call."

"I see."

"Would you like...to meet her, before...? I can make arrangements..."

Fox offered, struggling to pull himself back together. Entiyti pondered that for a few moments before answering.

"No, I think not," he decided. "In truth, Franz, I should like to, very much. But I fear it would only stress her, and might even hasten her demise, to meet with a stranger. Better she has those about her whom she considers friends...and family. Those she loves. That is a better way to pass from this life." Entiyti paused, then looked straight at Fox. "And speaking of family, should not the father figure be making his way back to the side of his adoptive son, and that son's dying chosen?"

"I suppose so," Fox sighed. "Damn, Pul. I've done many things...as a Mossad agent, as your bodyguard, and as an agent, then director, of Division One. But nothing I have done—or, I suspect, will ever do—will haunt me like this."

"For all your years, Franz, you are still young compared to me," Entiyti said. "But in despite of all my experience...I fear I have no wisdom to give you. You are a good man, with a good heart, and you have done your best to keep faith with all sides. It is your unfortunate lot to have been caught squarely between the sea whirl and the rock daemon. There was nothing you could do."

* * *

Some time later, when Fox had returned to the medlab waiting room, a team of doctors, both human and alien, came out of the lab and approached the waiting group. Echo immediately came out of his self-imposed mental exile.

"Director," Zarnix, the chief medic, formally acknowledged. "Agent Echo; Alpha Two."

"What's the word?" Echo cut to the chase.

The doctors all glanced at each other, then stared at the floor.

"Omega is dying, Echo," Zarnix said quietly, as Zebra, his second in command in the Medical department, moved to stand beside Fox, offering comfort by her close presence. "There's nothing we can do to stop that. We can prolong it, postpone it a little while. She'd be in tremendous pain. But we can't save her. Even her internal organs are..."

"...Parboiled," supplied another physician who, Echo recalled, was code-named Whiskey. No one said anything for a long moment.

"Does she know?" Echo asked then.

"Yes." Zarnix nodded.

"You told her?"

"No. We didn't have to. She...already knew."

The Alpha Line members exchanged meaningful, agonized glances.

"Have you considered alternatives? Cloning, maybe?" Echo pressed.

"Yes," the chief medic replied, "but she doesn't have enough time left for us to properly clone a new body. And done improperly...it would only make matters worse."

"How so?" Echo asked.

"Right now, Echo, her mind...her brain...is intact," Zebra answered for Zarnix. "Somehow. We don't know how. But it appears undamaged. We can't afford to risk transplanting..."

"I don't get it," Echo admitted.

"Echo," India explained, "transplanting a normal brain into an improperly cloned host body can cause severe neural feedback, resulting in massive brain damage. It would kill her as surely as her current injuries. Think about..." she shrugged. "Think about what the neural feedback from the Shell's death did to Slug, and you'll get some idea. And what they're saying is, right now, her brain is relatively healthy and functioning."

"Oh. Damn," Echo said, voice very quiet.

"But that intact mental state makes it worse for her now," Zebra added. "I've never seen anyone this badly injured still conscious, much less coherent and lucid." The other doctors nodded their agreement, pained expressions on every face. "It's like...she's not done yet...like she's waiting..."

Echo's eyes widened, then closed in tormented grief, his face trying to crumple into a grimace of agony despite his best efforts, as he remembered a promise he'd made only recently.

Damn. I didn't really believe I'd ever have to...but she already knew. That's why she asked.

* * *

A concerned Fox, seeing his reaction, put a hand on Echo's shoulder and felt those shoulders slump ever so slightly.

126

"Then...I'll give her what she's waiting for," Echo said softly.

"What's that, Echo?" Fox asked gently.

"I'll tell her...goodbye. Like I promised." His voice cracked and he fell silent, but Echo headed doggedly for the medlab door. The other Agents winced and looked away.

* * *

"One possibility there may be..." a thoughtful voice said unexpectedly.

Echo spun, and his attention focused on the cluster of medical personnel.

"Who said that??"

"This one Indak yclept is." A wizened little orange-skinned alien moved through the group of doctors to the front of the pack, to address Echo. "Wellbeing her, you yearn recovering? One opportunity possessing she has. Within Spur Orion of the Arm Sagittarius your system planetary residing is. Side opposite of the galaxy, to the Arm Outer, journey you requiring. A star old, Edeptis yclept, there discovering. A contact binary is it. The planet fourth of the system there, your destination is. The Doron healer legendary, there locating. Tissue he regenerate is capable. Examine her he necessitate, or she unavoidable expire."

"Do you know him?" Echo asked urgently.

"Yes, with him I associating am." The diminutive creature nodded.

"Can you contact him and tell him to come?" Fox demanded.

"Yes, yes, him I approaching can. Him to come I enjoining cannot. Between the systems planetary, people of Doron's traveling not."

"Can we stabilize Meg enough to get her there?" India asked the medical contingent. They conferred a moment, then shook their heads.

"We can stabilize her to a point, but not enough to do that. Omega just wouldn't survive the warp jump," Zarnix determined. "Not in her current condition."

"Then I'll bring Doron to Meg," Echo said, unhesitating. "Romeo, you and India take Indak to the communications hub. Have them send a message from him to this Doron. Then I want a map and coordinates. I want to know exactly where I'm going."

The three headed out quickly. Echo turned to the medics.

"How long can y'all...keep Meg going?"

"Two days before systems collapse sets in," one of the doctors replied.

"Earth or PGLEIA days?"

"Earth. No matter what the galactic government says, the human body's limits are always gonna be in terms of Earth days."

"All right. Do it."

The cluster of physicians immediately broke up and began a coordinated effort to stabilize their patient, and eke out whatever life force was left to her, for as long as it could be stretched. Echo watched them, pondering what they were doing.

Forty-eight hours. I have forty-eight hours to get across the galaxy, pick up an unknown physician, and get back before my partner dies. The one being in the entire damned universe whose death would kill me as surely as... He looked up.

"Fox, what's the fastest ship we've got immediate access to?"

"It's an experimental scout ship. Research & Development calls it the *RD-1,* but it's a one-man clipper."

"Can it carry two?"

"In a pinch."

"This is a tight pinch, Fox. Make it happen."

"You've got it, Echo."

* * *

Within minutes, everything was set. Romeo and India brought Indak back to the medlab to inform Echo that Doron would be waiting, and Indak went over the nav charts with him in detail.

"Echo, the *RD-1* is waiting for you at the Pennsylvania Station. They'll have your spacesuit waiting," Fox informed him, looking up from his cell phone. "Countdown has started."

"Penn Station. Countdown under way. Suit ready. Got it. Thanks, Fox. I'll catch the maglev at Grand Central downstairs in half a minute. I just want to go over this chart once more..."

"Echo?" Romeo tentatively approached his former partner, "You sure maybe India or I can't—?"

"I appreciate it, junior, but you're not test-pilot-rated, or trained in warp

128

navigation; I'm both. Plus, the *RD-1* will only hold two, and that's a tight fit. That means one seat is mine, and the other is Doron's." Echo turned and looked at the two worried Agents, and let his hard, businesslike demeanor soften a little. He laid his right hand on Romeo's shoulder, his left on India's. "Look, guys," he said, voice very quiet, "I'm counting on you two to take care of her for me until I get back. Make sure she's here for me to get back to. It means..." his voice grew rough, and he cleared his throat, "it means a lot. More than either of you know. Do that for me, okay?"

India blinked hard, and Romeo swallowed several times, but they both nodded.

"All right, then." Echo gathered up the nav charts and tucked them into his inside jacket pocket. "We're off to see the wizard."

A medtech emerged from the back. "Agent Echo?"

"Yes?" Echo said, already at the door of the waiting room.

"It's Agent Omega, sir. She's asking for you."

Agonized, torn between the need to save Omega and her request to see him, Echo looked at Fox, then at his watch.

"Fox...I've...got a countdown..." He glanced back at the medtech. "Did she say...?"

"Yes, sir. She said she just wanted to talk to you...one more time. To say goodbye."

Echo glanced upward in a silent, wordless plea, then closed his eyes and said, "Fox...tell her I'll be back soon. Tell her to hold on for me, okay? To keep fighting. We'll talk when I get back. I swear we will."

"Echo!" Fox exclaimed, as the determined Agent headed for the door. "You can't really expect me to tell a dying woman—"

Echo was gone.

Chapter 4

Grand Central Station had an emergency maglev transport ready and waiting, expressly for Echo. And it hauled ass. Less than five minutes after leaving the medlab, Echo was at the Agency's Pennsylvania Station space-port, suiting up. He would have preferred not to have to deal with an awk-ward spacesuit, but the *RD-1* was an EXPERIMENTAL clipper, and the suit was therefore required. At any rate, the suit's life-support functions would make the trip more comfortable.

Echo burst into the locker room and promptly stripped all the way down to bare skin, then began putting on the 'spaghetti suit,' the mesh un-dergarment that contained the vital signs sensors, life support, and body-temperature and -humidity systems. He pulled on the cowl containing the comm unit. Then he moved into the suit-up room, where two agents were waiting to help him into the pressure garment.

The white spacesuit was similar to the NASA EVA suits, but was far less bulky, being made out of more advanced materials, as well as possess-ing sophisticated body armor in places, notably the torso. It also had a clos-er fit, being less a pressurized suit and more a compression-type garment, making it somewhat easier to flex and maneuver. That said, areas of the suit were still lightly pressurized, particularly beneath the armor; it helped provide additional padding between the skin and said armor, in addition to allowing for a small emergency reservoir of breathable air.

Echo stepped into the bottom half of the suit, and he and the two agents assisting him worked the snug garment up his body to his waist. Then he moved over to a frame which held the upper half of the suit, suspended in the air.

On the right shoulder was a cryptic insignia: A circle divided into quar-ters, the universal symbol of Earth, was inscribed in black. Overlaid on that was a large red numeral 1, symbol of PGLEIA Division One. On the left shoulder was a variant on that theme—the black circle, cut by a single horizontal line, over which was laid a Greek capital letter lambda. Together, the lambda and horizontal bar also formed the overscribed Greek capital letter alpha; the logo of the Alpha Line. On the left breast was a single black letter, identifying the suit's occupant—E. The motifs were repeated around the lower sides of the helmet cowling.

Bending down, Echo slipped inside the suit top, worming his way up the inside, and as his hands and head emerged through their respective openings, the assistants lifted him by handles on the suit bottom, until the ring seals on bottom and top half made contact. There was a metallic clink, and the seals locked together automatically. The assistants removed the handles and lifted Echo off the frame, lowering him until his feet touched the floor.

Echo spun, sat down on the suit-up couch, and leaned back as the attendants slipped on his boots and gauntlets, sealed them, and began checkout of the suit systems. Echo willed them to hurry as he alternated between watching the countdown clock and the continuing suit checkout.

Meg would love this, the thought drifted through his mind. *She'd probably be able to tell me every difference between this suit and the NASA version.* He hoped he'd get the chance to hear it. *Preferably sooner than later,* he decided.

One of the attendants handed him the specs and nav charts he'd brought with him, and Echo stowed them in the thigh pocket of the spacesuit.

"Umbilical connected and functional, sir," the other attendant reported, putting on a headset. "Pressurization beginning."

Echo felt the suit partially inflate—which was almost as much as it was going to; the pressurization was more for his comfort than for any real survivability need. It was, however, connected to his helmet, thus providing for that small reserve in the event of his main oxygen supply being cut off.

"Suit comm check," the attendant continued, and abruptly, his voice came over Echo's headset. "How do you read? I give count: one, two, three, four, five..."

"I read you loud and clear," Echo said into the mic at his mouth.

"I read you five by five also," the agent reported. "Suit potable water reservoir is full and sufficient to last two full Division days under normal consumption." Echo adjusted the water straw's bite valve in the helmet ring so that it was within easy reach of his mouth, then the two attendants placed the helmet over his head and locked it. The suit inflated fully, and the compression layer responded by tightening, holding it relatively close to his body.

"Helmet fit?" Echo heard the attendant in his ears. He turned his head about, testing, then gave the agent a thumbs-up. Echo stood and moved around for a few moments to check the overall suit fit.

"Everything is a go," he told his attendants via the mic. He turned, picked up the portable umbilical pack—which would be replaced by a hookup directly into the spacecraft; this umbilical could be removed for short periods in the event of an extended EVA, during which the suit would run on internal power and scrubbed, recirculated air—and followed the attendants to his craft.

The black scout ship was indeed tiny, somewhere between the Corvette and the T-38 in size, a sleek blend of delta-wing and saucer, somewhat reminiscent of the Martian craft from the original 1950's film version of *War of the Worlds*, but much smaller, and without the head stalk. It was a snug two-seater; the attending agents had to practically fold Echo's tall figure into origami to fit him into the cockpit. Echo hoped this Doron being was smaller than he was himself, or it would be a damned uncomfortable ride home. Glancing into the rear seat, Echo saw the diminutive spacesuit provided for Doron, and breathed a sigh of relief.

Once his umbilical was plugged into the scout ship, Echo spoke again.

"*RD-1* to Launch Control. Comm check." The attendants began sealing the canopy hatch.

"Launch Control here, *Rubber Ducky One*—" Fox's voice replied.

"—What?!" Echo interrupted Fox. Fox chuckled, and Echo heard laughter in the background on Air-to-Ground, quickly stifled.

"Sorry, Echo, that's what the wags in Research & Development nick-named your little ship. I thought you knew. That's what *RD-1* stands for."

"That's...a negative, Launch Control. I wasn't informed. How about that comm check?"

"We read you loud and clear," Fox's voice said, amid quiet background telemetry checks from R & D.

"Copy. You are loud and clear as well. Tell the boys and girls in R & D that when I get back, this ship has a new name." The background chatter decreased.

"Which is?"

"The *Tour de Force*." There was a long pause.

"Copy that, *Tour de Force*. This ship has a few surprises, Echo; have you been briefed?"

"All the specs were waiting for me at the maglev, Fox. I'm on the curve." Echo flipped a switch, and the spaceship became white. "Just changed the liquid crystal skin to white for ascent. I'll change it back when I'm exo."

"Roger. You know it isn't outfitted with interstellar comm?"

"Affirmative. R & D just hasn't gotten there yet?"

"Affirm. We haven't taken it far enough out to need it, so far."

"That's encouraging...not. I'll have to make do, then. Commencing launch prep." Echo looked down at the flight console and did a slight double-take; someone had found a small ID-type photo of Omega and thoughtfully fastened it in a corner of the console. He looked down at her face, smiling up at him, the blue eyes seeming almost to twinkle, as if to say, *Hey, Ace, I'm right here with you.* Suddenly it blurred, and he blinked hard to clear his vision, biting his lip. He put up a gauntleted hand and looked at the photo for a moment longer, stoic, fingering it lightly. Then Echo started working his way down the checklist posted for him on the console next to the photo, flipping switches and testing systems. When it was complete, he keyed the mic and said, "Launch Control, *Tour de Force*. All systems are go."

"I show launch doors open, systems internal. You have a go for launch at your discretion, *Tour de Force*."

"Initiating ascent...now."

The scout ship shot into the air, accelerating smoothly at about 3 g's as it climbed through the atmosphere. Echo read off the parameters to the ground during ascent; he could hear the scientists and engineers from R & D in the background, monitoring his progress with satisfaction. The blue sky out the cockpit window gradually grew darker and darker as his altitude increased.

"Launch Control to *Tour de Force*."

"Go ahead, Launch Control."

"We have a request for a description, Echo. Stand by."

"*T-Tour de Force*, Launch C-Control. How do...do you read?" a gurgling, weak voice came over Air-to-Ground.

"Meg??" Echo whispered in surprise, then he continued in a normal voice. "Launch Control, I read you...loud and clear."

"Echo, w-would you...tell me...w-what it looks like up t-there?"

The R & D background chatter fell silent.

"The sky," Echo told her quietly, "is a deep shade of blue, Meg. It's that deep, rich shade of blue you like so much. The higher the *Tour de Force* ascends, the deeper blue it gets." He paused, waiting and watching, his hand on the joystick urging the little ship onward. "There. The blue just...faded... into black. Stand by one, and...okay. I'm in Earth's shadow now, and I can see thousands of stars..." He reached out with a gauntleted hand and flipped a switch as he heard a soft sigh on Air-to-Ground. "Liquid crystal skin to black. Ascending past one-five-oh nautical miles." Another switch. "Increasing acceleration to standard interplanetary." Quiet chatter resumed in the background. He pulled back on the stick. "Meg, I'm pulling out of the gravity well now; Earth is getting smaller and falling behind. I'm setting a bearing that will take me above the ecliptic and into the galactic plane."

"Echo...r-remember the...w-warp generator..." Omega's voice returned.

Echo was puzzled by the statement. *Is she getting confused from the pain?* he worried.

"Yes, Meg—I'm getting ready for the warp jump."

"NO," she responded clearly. "...Important...rememb-ber it...LATER..." Omega moaned softly in pain, and the microphone picked it up. Air-to-Ground became very still. Echo sighed inaudibly, forehead creasing with distress.

"All right, Meg; I'll remember, I promise. Ground Control, I am in position for warp jump. Setting initial coordinates," Echo said a few moments later. Fox's voice returned on Air-to-Ground.

"You are go for warp jump at your discretion, *Tour de Force*. Godspeed." At the benediction, Echo nodded once, and sent up a silent request.

"I copy. Go at my discretion. *Tour de Force* to Ground Control for Omega."

"Echo, O-omega. Go...'head..."

"I'll see you soon, Meg. Fight, baby. Fight for me."

"A-always do...G-goodbye, Echo..."

"NO. Hasta luego. See you later."

Silence.

"Say it, Meg."

"Has-hasta l-luego...oh, Echo, HURRY..."

Echo closed his eyes for just a moment, fighting down the heartache, and then scanned his readouts.

"Ground Control, *Tour de Force*. Initiating warp jump...NOW."

And in seconds, Echo had left Earth—and his dying partner—far behind.

* * *

The first leg of Echo's journey was progressing smoothly so far, with nothing off-nominal to report; two hours down and he was already around 10,000 light years away from home. The warp drive was functioning well, at maximum capability. The Edeptis system was some 90,000 light years from Earth on the extreme fringes of the Outer Arm, but unfortunately, the galactic center, with its 3.91-million-solar-mass black hole, Sagittarius A*, lay squarely between the two systems. So Echo had to detour, making a long, difficult journey even longer.

The route he had chosen was a single dogleg that cut it as close to the galactic center as he dared go, given the radiation levels and the resolution of available navigation charts—it did Omega no good for him to attempt to find this healer, if Echo didn't survive to return with him. Even so, Echo had a one-way journey of around 110,000 light years. At the *Tour de Force*'s maximum warp, the round-trip travel time alone would take him forty-four hours. That didn't include stopping over to locate and pick up the healer. And Omega only had forty-eight hours at the outside. So Echo was casting about in his mind for some way to boost his speed.

If only the damn black hole wasn't in the way...wait a minute. Maybe that's the answer. Or AN answer, anyway.

In recent weeks Echo, aware of Omega's starhopper certification request, had made it a point to brush up on his astrophysics, especially with regard to general relativity and field theory, as these pertained so strongly to galactic navigation. Omega, with her PhD in astrophysics, had been happy to work with him, enthusiastically expanding on topics that Agency references glossed over. She found him an apt student, being possessed of more than his own fair share of gray matter and already with some experience in the subject, given his PGLEIA-certified piloting skills. In turn, Echo, usually Omega's teacher, found her to be quite gifted at instruction, not that their intense discussions could really be categorized as formal teaching, most of the time—though she HAD broken out the whiteboard and markers once or twice. But she was able to simplify even the most abstruse of concepts into something that was immediately comprehensible and related to his interest.

Now he remembered the sessions they had spent discussing black holes and singularities. Echo had been principally concerned with them as navigation hazards, but Omega had told him that it was theoretically possible to use a black hole to boost one's spacecraft's kinetic energy significantly. Moreover, she had insisted he master the calculations for the Penrose process.

"No telling when you might need 'em," she'd said, "and you can't count on my always being there to run the calcs."

* * *

In retrospect, the statement hit him with the force of a sledgehammer blow.

Did she know even then? he wondered. *Or was it merely an offhand, coincidental remark? How long has this been happening? What if...* a sudden recollection hit, *maybe that whole 'Don't go chasing the Glu'g'ik without me' thing back at Halloween was...*

Well shit, an' hellfire damnation, to boot, he grumbled to himself. *Right in front o' me, an' I missed it. I'm gonna have to start paying a LOT more attention whenever she opens her mouth. And LISTENING, next time.*

* * *

At any rate, Omega had derived the macro-scale equations for the process, and they'd stepped through the calculations together, varying the parameters over and over, until Echo had gotten the hang of it. Now all he had to do was find a Kerr black hole somewhere along his course, and run the calculations. *Piece of cake,* he thought, sardonic. *Yeah, right. Well, if I can find one somewhere along the route, I can do this.* Echo brought up the onboard computers and pulled the nav charts from his spacesuit.

"Still, I sure wish you were here, Meg," he murmured to the photo as he scanned the charts. "You could probably run this in your head."

But she wasn't, and if Echo didn't get this right, she might not ever be. He bent over the charts, studying them intently.

There. He jabbed a fingertip into the chart. *A rotating black hole, only about twenty-four light years from my projected dogleg.*

Echo pulled the physical data for the Kerr singularity off the chart and input them into the computer. Then he began painstakingly working his way through the complex calculations.

An hour later, his computations were completed, checked, and double-checked.

Satisfied, he stretched as best he could in the confined space, and surveyed his instrumentation. It was 03:00 by the Mission Elapsed Time clock, or MET as Omega called it, and all was going well. Echo momentarily recalled Omega's Longfellow quotation. *Hmm...maybe I should've named the ship after Revere's horse,* he thought with black amusement. *Not that I know what its name actually WAS.* Echo made a slight midcourse correction that put him on a heading directly for the black hole, and tried to relax in the peacefulness of deep space.

* * *

Shortly thereafter, that peace was rudely interrupted by a proximity alarm. Echo sat up straight, cut off the klaxon blaring in his headset, and began scanning his sensors. Sure enough, a large vessel paced him several thousand miles to starboard and nudging closer, shields up and weapons armed. The universal translator snapped on as an incoming message arrived on interplanetary channels.

"Unidentified vessel, you are trespassing in Ganotian space. Identify yourself immediately or prepare to be destroyed."

137

"Friendly, imaginative types," Echo muttered sarcastically, before he pressed a momentary toggle to broadcast. "Ganotian ship, this is the *Tour de Force*, piloted by Agent Echo of the Pan-Galactic Law Enforcement and Immigration Administration, Division One, headquartered on Earth, Sol System. Per the Sydys Concordat, section six, paragraph two-one-one, I am on an errand of mercy."

"State the nature of this errand."

"My partner was seriously injured in an altercation with intergalactic slave traders. She is...dying." His voice cracked despite his best efforts, and he broke off momentarily, swallowing hard, before continuing. "I am searching for a legendary healer in the Edeptis system of the galactic Outer Arm who may be able to save her. I now have less than one PGLEIA-standard day to locate this healer and bring him to my homeworld if he is to have any chance of saving her. I apologize for trespassing in Ganotian space, but time is of the essence, and I take the shortest course between systems that is feasible for my ship."

There was a pregnant pause as the Ganotians assimilated the information. Echo prepared to power up what defensive and offensive armament the little scout ship had.

"*Tour de Force*, we believe we may have had...interaction...with the fugitives in question; this is why we are currently patrolling our boundaries with such care. I am Captain Yonat commanding the United Ganotian vessel *Ridiki*, and I am pleased to greet you."

"*Ridiki*, this is *Tour de Force*; thank you very much. If you would, please contact the nearest PGLEIA Office and report the interaction. We are attempting to apprehend the culprits; I fear the altercation was of such severity that their ship escaped us in the...carnage."

"Very well. We are familiar with your organization, and although not signatory to the Accords, Ganotia accepts them as galactic protocol. We will do as you request."

"Excellent," Echo answered, pleased, realizing that it could lead to the Cortians' capture. "Should you wish to join the PGLEIA, I would encourage you to contact Director Fox of Division One, on transmission band 55 of the standard galactic communications frequency bands. Offhand I don't know where I am with regard to the various division boundaries, because my map to Edeptis doesn't show 'em. But Fox will know, and can put you in contact with the proper personnel to get you signatory to the Concordat."

"Our thanks for the information; we will pass this knowledge along to our diplomatic corps at once. We have also heard of you, Agent Echo; you are a human of some renown in the galaxy. If this partner of yours possesses half of the daring and honor for which you are reputed, she is worth saving."

"She does, I can assure you. She obtained her injuries, functioning as a...living shield...to protect me, when I had been...incapacitated."

"I see. She is courageous and caring into the bargain. Very well. You have safe passage through Ganotian space, Agent Echo. Should you find yourself in difficulties within our space, contact me on this frequency and my vessel will come to your assistance at once. We are notifying our homeworld, as well as all patrolling units, of your mission. You may proceed at your best possible speed. Let your mission be successful."

"You have my thanks—and my partner's."

"No thanks are necessary. Creator go with you, and help your partner survive."

"Amen," Echo murmured.

* * *

After the encounter with the Ganotians, Echo prepared a digital recording for continuous-loop broadcast across all frequencies through the universal translator. The interplanetary comm didn't have the power to get far, but it would serve the purpose: Any spacecraft close enough to register the *Tour de Force* on its sensors would be able to receive his broadcast. He finished recording, and initiated the transmission.

"This is the interstellar clipper *Tour de Force*, piloted by Agent Echo of the Pan-Galactic Law Enforcement and Immigration Administration, Division One, headquartered on Earth, Sol System. I am on an errand of mercy to secure a healer to save my dying partner. She does not have much time. I claim the right of safe passage per the Sydys Concordat, section six, paragraph two-one-one.

"This is the interstellar clipper *Tour de Force*..."

139

* * *

When the Mission Elapsed Time clock showed 04:30, Echo began assessing his situation. The clipper's systems were all functioning nominally; R & D knew how to build 'em. At maximum warp, it was still another three and a half hours before he reached the black hole. But once he got past the black hole he would need to be as alert as possible; Echo doubted R & D had ever intended the little experimental craft to undergo what he intended to put it through.

With that in mind, Echo turned the *Tour de Force* over to the Digital Autopilot—the DAP, Omega called it—and set the systems and proximity-sensor alerts and alarms. The DAP would keep the scout ship on course, and alert him if anything off-nominal occurred. He set a timer to wake him at MET 07:30, leaned back, loosened the straps, closed his eyes, and tried to rest.

Instead, however, Echo found himself wondering what was happening back at Headquarters. He was glad he had rethought Omega's concerns and discussed them with Fox—especially when India and Romeo had brought their concerns, along with Zz'r'p's, to the table. The team had been halfway prepared for what ended up happening. But only halfway.

Maybe, if I'd listened sooner, dammit... he cursed himself. *But no, I assumed I knew Meg well enough not to bother, because I...care. All while having told her, all through last Christmas, not to assume she knew all there was to know about ME. Damn fool hypocrite.*

The Cortian slavers were smooth operators, with a lot of nerve, but evidently unused to having someone see through their charade. Echo was fortunate that Omega HAD seen through it, although no one was quite sure how, least of all Meg herself.

The theory which India and Zz'r'p put forward had some merit. *After all, if a telepath bio-engineered you to be the perfect Agent candidate, then programmed you to be a sleeper assassin in the organization, it stands to reason there would have to be some form of two-way communication between you and the telepath,* Echo decided. *Even if you didn't consciously know about it, at least initially.* And hadn't Omega herself once told him, after Slug was finally dead, that a telepathic link could be a two-way street?

Maybe Meg had abilities of which she herself was unaware...to this point, anyway.

That thought left Echo with mixed emotions. True, he and Omega were now so attuned to each other that in the field they seldom had to converse, although they not infrequently chose to at other times, often to their mutual enjoyment. And it was also true that having a telepathic partnership would make them a hell of a team to go up against, damn near unbeatable. But Echo was an intensely private man, and he found the idea of someone being able to tiptoe around in his head—even someone he trusted and cared for as much as Meg—more than a little disconcerting. He supposed, though, that if anyone had to go poking around in there on a regular basis, he'd rather it was Meg. She knew him well enough to guard his privacy as well as he could himself. And vice versa.

But there were secrets in that mind that Echo did not particularly want Omega finding out about. At least, not until he was ready to tell her himself, a thing which would only come to pass if he could be certain she wouldn't cast him aside in annoyance...or worse, disgust. Secrets that he had no idea how to hide from her, if she really WAS a budding telepath, like India had said.

And if she does find out, and she turns out to be offended by those secrets, he considered, a wave of morose indigo washing over him, *then it could be the end of the partnership, even if she lives.*

His tired mind drifted then to her condition. How was Omega making it, so very far away? She was in such pain. Echo could scarcely believe that she had remained conscious. *But Meg has promised me she WILL fight,* he reminded himself, *fight for me...and my baby always does...what she promises...*

Echo's head finally nodded lightly to one side, and his limp hands drifted slowly upward until they hung, weightless, in front of his helmet.

* * *

"India..." The whisper from the form in the hospital bed was barely audible, and India had to bend low to hear. Romeo moved nearer to the bed as Omega continued. "India, it h-hurts...really, really b-bad...p-please...Echo... wants me to...to f-fight...I-I can't do it...a-alone...n-not like-like this...I-I'm not th-that str-ong...is-is there an-anything..."

"Hang on, Meg," India soothed, "I'll go see about getting you some pain medication." She glanced meaningfully at Romeo as she left the room. Romeo nodded in response to the unspoken message, and moved next to Omega.

"Hey, Meg," he said softly. "It's gonna be okay, girlfriend. India's gone to getcha somethin' that'll make ya feel better. An' Echo'll be back 'fore you know it. Hang in there, girl. Jus' hang on."

"Yeh," the response was almost a pant, "I'm...hangin'. I...I jus'...jus' w-wish I could-coulda seen 'im one more t-time...be-before I..." Omega's voice tapered off as Romeo mentally finished her hopeless statement. "I...I wanted to...wanted to t-tell him..."

Romeo waited, but Omega didn't finish.

"Tell him what, Meg?" he asked softly. "Do you want us to get a message to 'im?"

"No. Does...doesn't mat-matter now. Nev-ver d-did matter, r-really."

A blackened claw crept out and nudged Romeo's hand where it rested on the rail as India came back in with a syringe. Romeo glanced over his shoulder at India for a moment, then looked back down at Omega and, very carefully, covered the mutilated hand with his own, comforting his colleague—his 'chosen sister,' he decided—as best he could.

"India's back, Meg, an' she's got meds for ya. You're gonna feel better soon. Just try to relax," he soothed as India injected the hypodermic's contents into the IV line.

"How's that, Meg? Any better?" India asked after a moment. Omega jerked, almost as if she'd been startled awake, and responded.

"Does-doesn't hurt...as-as much...b-but I...f-feel fun-ny..."

"Funny how?"

"B-body's made o'...o' lead...head's a...h-helium bal-balloon...float... away..." Her voice grew distant, then faded out.

"Romeo, get the medics! Meg, just try to take it easy," India said as Romeo sprinted out the door. "Everything is all right, but you might pass out. Your body's overreacting to the pain medication."

"How...how bad...?" Omega queried faintly.

"I don't know yet, honey," India replied honestly as Romeo came back with Whiskey, bearing two medical scanners. "I don't have my bio scanner with me. We'll know in a minute."

Whiskey handed the extra scanner to India, and the pair of medics checked Omega quickly with the handheld electronic vitals scanners, then Whiskey shook his head.

"Omega?" the medic asked.

No answer.

Whiskey touched her gently, then lightly shook her—his touch as delicate as he could make it, while still attempting to evoke a response. Omega remained unresponsive. Dr. Whiskey recalibrated the scanner and passed it back over his patient. Then he shook his head, and looked up at Alpha Two.

"Coma," he said succinctly. "Stable—or what passes for stable in her condition—for the moment. I'll see about getting monitors hooked back up. Probably we should've done it as soon as Echo left. We took 'em off when we thought..."

"I'm sorry," India murmured. "But she was in pain—SO much pain— and asking for medication to ease it, which she almost never does. So I checked the charts, and..."

"And you verified it with me, not five minutes ago," Whiskey noted, soothing his colleague. "And I approved it. Dose, drug, and all. It's not your fault, India. Omega is..." The physician shrugged. "She's a special case, in a very bad situation. I guess you know that, as least as well as anybody on the medical staff. She's not reacting at all like any of us in the medlab expect her to, to any stimuli. It's hard to judge how to help. Or what could harm."

"Anything we can do?" India asked.

"No. She should come out of the coma when the medication wears off. We won't give her any more. But I suspect the damage has been done. I fully expect that she'll be slipping in and out of the coma from now on until..." The doctor's voice tapered away. "Just...until."

"Well, at least she's outta pain," Romeo said, after a moment.

The Agency medic adjusted the medscanner's parameters, ran it back over Omega, and shook his head, meeting Romeo's eyes. His own gaze was grim.

"Nope. 'Fraid not," Whiskey told Alpha Two quietly.

* * *

Echo found himself back in the hangar on Earth. The hangar was empty now, the huge doors standing wide open. He stood just inside them, looking out across the tarmac at distant green hills, bright in the sunshine; there was no sign of a city anywhere in sight. He should have thought that odd, given that the spaceport was just outside Chicago and it was winter-time, but dreams seldom made sense, and even in the midst of one, Echo knew THAT much.

A soft, familiar voice sounded behind him.

"Echo?"

He turned, and Omega stood there a few feet away, smiling warmly at him, whole and beautiful. Her azure blue eyes reflected the sunlight coming through the hangar door. Her hair, long and luxurious and flowing loose over her shoulders, shone silver in the light. Her pale skin was flawless, and her soft lips flashed white teeth for a moment as she laughed gently at his surprised expression.

Omega held out her right hand to him again, just as she'd done before, and this time he slowly extended his left hand and laid it in hers. Her fingers wrapped around his, and she smiled. She moved close to him and slid her arms around his neck, leaning up as if to kiss him. He held his breath in anticipation, waiting for the touch of her lips on his own, the taste of her mouth in his.

But the instant her fingers touched the back of his head, his body stiffened in paralysis, and dread gripped him. The core of his being seemed to freeze, cold horror clutching his entrails, and he could only wait for the terror to begin...again.

Her long hair flared first, kindling into ash in seconds, like dry grass in a blowtorch, as it whipped about her face, flaming. Her fair skin blistered, then blackened, and the blue eyes filled with tears in a blur of pain as Echo heard an awful hissing, sizzling sound. She began to tremble, and her body made little spasmodic jerks of pain, thrashing lightly against his, even as she fought to remain as still as humanly possible. A faint haze of blue smoke rose from her body, and Echo's nostrils filled with the sickly sweet odor of roasting flesh. Little panting gasps escaped the raw sores that her lips had become. She twisted against him slightly, in agony, and Echo watched, immobile and helpless, as the delicate shell of one ear burned away. Her mouth opened in a soundless scream as the seared flesh slipped from the bones of her shoulder; the bones themselves began to scorch. Her hands had somehow moved from around his neck to cover his face and head, and he watched them shrivel and char, the ash dropping down on his cheek. Through it all, she never moved from her position shielding him.

Echo watched in stunned horror as her body continued to burn, slowly reducing to powder and ash. At last the blackened skeleton crumbled. His own emotions seemed to have burned away in the conflagration of his part-ner's body; numb, he looked down at the small pile of gray ash by his feet that was all that was left of his partner, the woman he had cherished. A soft, warm breeze came through the hangar door, caught up the ash, and swirled it into the now-dark sky, scattering it among the twinkling stars. As the breeze died away, he heard it sigh, in a familiar, feminine voice.

"...Goodbye, Echo...it hurts so much...I'm so tired...tired of fighting... tired of hurting...please...tell me goodbye and...let me go..."

"NO!!"

* * *

Echo snapped awake with a start, drenched in a cold sweat. His envi-ronment suit sensors registered his discomfort, and the undergarment began wicking away the excess moisture, thermostats clicking softly as the suit re-established a comfortable body temperature.

He turned his head slightly and sipped on the straw that led to his water supply, trying to moisten his dry mouth. Finally he leaned back in the pad-ded seat and took a deep breath.

The MET clock read 07:02.

Echo didn't sleep again the rest of the journey.

* * *

MET 08:46

The *Tour de Force* was now rapidly approaching the black hole Echo had located. Echo began inputting the parameters he had calculated earlier into the navigation computer. It would be a bumpy ride, but if it worked,

145

it would boost his speed immensely. If it didn't, it would end his trip immediately. And permanently.

According to Omega's explanation, a rotating singularity, known as a Kerr black hole, was possessed of two separate surfaces: the event horizon, and the static limit. The event horizon was spherical and the true boundary of the black hole—if Echo crossed it, he was lost. But the static limit was an outer surface generated by the rotation of the gravitational collapse, and it was a flattened ellipsoid. The roughly doughnut-shaped space between the static limit and the event horizon, Omega had told him, was the ergosphere. According to the Omega-Penrose process, if the *Tour de Force* hit the ergosphere just right, a virtual, possibly antimatter, duplicate of the little ship could be created and sucked into the singularity, while the original would be ejected—most likely via wormhole—at increased velocity.

So Echo had diligently calculated a hyperbolic trajectory that would take him past the black hole just inside the static limit. At superluminal velocity, provided by the warp drive, he expected a wormhole to open for him on the other side. There were two tricks the singularity could have up its sleeve for him, however.

Echo had no idea what effect the splitting of himself and his ship into a real/ virtual pair would have on either himself or the ship. It could kill him; it could drive him insane. It could break the ship apart. It could implode the warp pod. Or it could do nothing.

The other trick was controlling the wormhole. It did him no good to utilize this technique if the wormhole dumped him unceremoniously on the wrong side of the galaxy, or worse, into the middle of intergalactic space. But Omega and Echo had brainstormed this possibility, and had devised a simple plan that they thought would work.

In a way, Meg's helping me to save her life, Echo thought, glancing at her photo with a warm gaze in which was more than a hint of affection. *You're good, baby. I'll never argue that point. Just stay with me. That's all I ask. You don't have to feel the same way. Just put up with me, and don't leave. In any sense of the word.*

As he approached the black hole, Echo initiated a sensor scan of the singularity in order to quickly refine his computations. He linked the sensor data directly into the onboard computer, and it tweaked his calculations based on the additional information from the sensors, then passed the result to the navcomp, which automatically adjusted his velocity vector. Echo raised the shields, tightened his seat straps, and waited.

* * *

"Uunnh..." Omega groaned as she emerged from the coma, and Romeo and India came quickly to their feet, moving to the bedside.

"Meg?" India asked. "Meg, honey, can you hear me?"

"Mmm-hmm..."

"How are ya?" Romeo asked, concerned.

"...Sick..."

"Gonna lose your lunch?" he continued.

"No...n-no lunch...t-to lo-lose...feel...awful..."

"How?" India asked quietly.

"Like...I jus' went th-through it...all-all over 'gain...oh, God...help me, p-please..." The prayer was whispered.

"Did you dream about it?"

"Yeah. Think...I think so...'s awful, India...jus' a livin' hell. If I s-sleep, I re-relive it...'f I'm 'wake, I-I...oohh..." Omega moaned again, struggling to endure the torment of a raw, failing body. India and Romeo exchanged glances, eyes agonized and helpless. Omega continued. "It'd be...so easy... jus' to l-let go..."

"NO, Meg!!" India exclaimed. "Don't give up! We're counting on you! ECHO'S counting on you! Fight!"

A scant, lone tear trickled down a blackened, blistered cheek. Omega nodded.

"Fight..." she echoed.

* * *

Echo could feel the gravity well of the black hole intensely now; the differential pull across the length of his body was becoming painful. The little *Tour de Force* was beginning to shudder under the tidal forces. With some difficulty, Echo reached out and entered a command which tightened the shields close around the ship, reinforcing its structural integrity. Then he prayed it was enough.

Struggling to see through vision distorted by hyper-relativistic effects, Echo double-checked his angle of approach. Omega had derived that the approach was the critical factor in determining the wormhole heading. In a hyperbolic trajectory, she had told Echo, the wormhole should follow the asymptote. So the more accurate his trajectory on approach, the more accurate the wormhole terminus would be.

The foreboding, empty blackness of the event horizon loomed ahead, blotting out the stars.

The *Tour de Force* crossed the static limit.

Muscle became taut and inflexible with intense pain as the relentless gravitational force tore at Echo's body. He experienced a sudden wrenching, a rending, as if his body were being ripped asunder. His back arched in excruciating agony, and he cried out despite himself. Then a tremor rocked the spacecraft, and Echo opened his eyes—just when he had shut them, he didn't know—and saw the wormhole open in front of him. As the little craft entered the maw of the wormhole, Echo detected a movement to the side just as the proximity sensors registered a 'possible collision' alarm, and quickly turned his head.

Another small scout ship, a delta-winged saucer, moved away from his ship, from the vicinity of the wormhole, toward the event horizon...or was it the other ship's wormhole? A single being sat within, clad in a white spacesuit. Brown eyes met brown eyes in a brief moment of recognition. Then both pilots lifted a gauntleted hand in salute, and the other ship disappeared through the event horizon, as Echo's craft was sucked into the wormhole.

* * *

Within moments of entering the wormhole, he found that he had to switch off the proximity alerts. The environment of the wormhole so confused those sensor elements that the alarms went off continuously, and no sooner did he shut off the alarm than it triggered again. Given Echo's nerves were taut anyway, it took him less than two minutes to decide to kill the alert settings until after he exited the wormhole.

However, while celestial navigation inside the wormhole proved difficult, it was not impossible. Although distorted by the unique spacetime geometry, the starfields were recognizable to the navigation sensors, and

Echo was able to get a fix on his course and speed. To his relief and gratification, he found that he was on course to within a few ten-thousandths of a percent. Provided he didn't overshoot, he should exit the wormhole within a couple of light years of the Edeptis star system, if not closer. And his relative velocity had doubled. He would reach the Edeptis system in seven more hours.

If all went well at Edeptis IV, he could have Doron at Omega's side in about one and a half standard Earth days.

* * *

Mission Elapsed Time 12:03.

Omega's remaining life was one-quarter gone.

The *Tour de Force* raced down the wormhole, and Echo kept a close eye on the ship's readouts. He was pushing the little craft well beyond its specs, stretching the envelope to the limit. And as any test pilot knew, stretching the envelope was one thing; rupturing it was quite another. So he monitored his status intently.

Thus it was that Echo became aware that he had a shadow. He switched to an undetectable, long-range, passive sensor mode and scanned the object following him.

"Artificial construct...a ship, then, not an asteroid," he murmured, studying the data. "Makes sense; I'd have to be passing the asteroid, not leading it, 'cause it woulda been moving at sub-light speed when it got caught in the wormhole. So...ship. Multiple sentients...volume of...damn, it's bigger than I am, by a long shot."

Echo commanded the computer to assemble the sensor data into a schematic of the vessel which was trailing him. After a few minutes, a display came up on screen.

"Shit!" Echo exclaimed as he recognized the alien ship's configuration. It was Cortian. And judging by the pattern of scoring and damage on its hull, it was one with which he was all too familiar. Suddenly, Echo began flipping switches as fast as he could, killing the automated broadcast. "Damn it all to hell and back," Echo muttered to himself, "I might as well have hung out a sign saying, 'Here I am—come and get me.'"

Obviously the slavers aren't willing to give up on me quite yet. I won-

der how long they've been following me, and how they managed to get into the wormhole behind me without my knowing it. Well, it doesn't matter now, he thought. What mattered was that, if they caught him, not only was HIS future in doubt, but Omega's future would cease to be. And that was something that Echo simply was not going to allow, if he had any say in the matter at all—and if anyone could do something about it, he could. *And I plan to,* he thought, implacable. *Oh HELL yes, do I plan to.*

Brown eyes blazed momentarily, then became deadly cold.

Swifter than light, Echo analyzed his options. Utterly calm, he began shutting down or cutting back all systems he deemed nonessential, including some of the life support to his spacesuit. It would take a little while before the cold began to seep through the suit, and hopefully, by that time, the situation would be resolved. One way or another.

Next, he worked to fine-tune the efficiency of the warp generator, squeezing every erg out of it he could. Echo took all of the extra energy thus obtained and channeled it into the propulsion system. The *Tour de Force* lurched forward with a whine, as the wormhole's physics amplified the acceleration.

Echo put all of the offensive and defensive systems—including sensors—on full standby, and armed a couple of special switches, just in case. The shields, fortunately, were still up. Then he checked the sensors again.

Hm. Only Cortian lifesigns. Good. No slaves aboard...nobody but those damn bastards. No need to worry about rescue. Huh. I wonder what happened to the person Omega heard scream. He shook his head. *Probably either dead, or already sold. Or maybe it was one of their own people, enslaved to a crew member—most likely the damn captain. 'Ambassador' my ass, the sonovabitch.*

Well, he considered, *by my lights I'll be doing it a favor, and setting it free...one way or another.*

Just then, the *Trindak,* realizing it had been detected, put on a sudden burst of speed and began slowly closing the distance.

HERE we go, now... Echo thought, with vengeful anticipation. *Time for a proper engagement. And it WILL be...THIS time.*

Echo watched, sharp mind cool, dark eyes hard, as the larger craft bore down on him. Then, as his sensors registered tractor beam activation, he punched one of the special switches and grabbed the joystick.

The warp amplifier opened up, the little experimental craft's equivalent of a jet afterburner, and Echo executed a hard maneuver to port. He might be outmanned, outgunned, and outpowered by the bigger craft, but he'd be damned if he was going to be outmaneuvered. The little *Tour de Force* was far more agile within the restricted confines of the wormhole than the much larger Cortian vessel, and Echo intended to make the most of it.

The tractor beam shot past Echo's tiny ship to starboard, glowing slightly orange in the wormhole's unusual environment.

Hmm, Echo thought in intense satisfaction, *there's a useful little side effect, for a change. Seeing the beams makes it that much easier to avoid them. Speaking of which...*

Echo activated the liquid crystal skin in camouflage mode, hooking it into the main sensors. The computer pulled in optical data on the surrounding environment across multiple spectral regions, and the little ship suddenly became a chameleon as it took on the mottled, distorted appearance of spacetime as seen through the wormhole.

Echo cut the *Tour de Force* back across the wormhole, rolling 180 degrees to fly close down the opposite side of the wormhole. A green beam shot through the space he had occupied only moments prior. Before the Cortians could recover, locate and target him, he kicked his ship into a clockwise barrel roll, spiraling down the inside of the wormhole. Abruptly, he reversed the direction of the spiral to counterclockwise, just before a dim orange beam locked onto nothing, in the location where he would have been.

As he maneuvered, Echo was silently, intensively studying the sensor data on the *Trindak,* looking for weaknesses. He moved back to the center of the wormhole and began executing a series of random bobs and weaves which were, he fully expected, unpredictable enough to leave the Cortian weapons master with a headache. *Preferably a migraine, I hope,* he thought, in a kind of vindictive glee.

Spotting a hull weakness, Echo threw his little ship into a translation maneuver, returning to the edge of the wormhole at about one o'clock high, and kicked the prop units into full reverse at the same time as he yawed 180 degrees; this left him flying down the wormhole tail-first, facing the *Trindak*. The *Tour de Force*'s structure screamed in protest at the combination maneuver, but held fast.

Rapidly, he keyed a sequence into the targeting computer, and fired. Blue beams lanced from all three apexes of the *Tour de Force*, converging on the Cortian vessel. Atmosphere exited in huge puffs from several hull breaches in the slave ship as Echo pitched a negative 180 degrees and shifted back into forward-facing motion—'airplane mode,' as Omega liked to term it.

That's for trying to kidnap me for breeding stock, Echo thought with satisfaction, jaw tight, eyes glinting with a dangerous light.

Just then, the Cortian vessel tried a new tactic: It laid down an interwoven, combination pattern of tractor and disintegrator beams across the wormhole. Echo fought the stick as he wove in and out of the shifting green and orange beams, trying furiously to avoid getting tagged in this deadly game of chase. He had to keep moving, or the constantly changing pattern of the rays would catch Echo's tiny craft like a fish in a net, and one way or another, it would be all over.

As he dodged and spun silently, with almost preturnatural calm, eyes gleaming almost black in a perilous, cold rage, Echo used the visibility of the beam weapons in the wormhole environment to his advantage—he started targeting the Cortian beam projectors. He couldn't keep this up forever, and if he could lessen the odds against him, he stood a better chance of surviving.

But merely surviving wasn't what he had in mind. One at a time, he gradually, patiently picked off the disintegrator guns and tractor beams.

Unexpectedly, the *Tour de Force* shuddered violently as a green beam brushed the starboard 'wing,' locally overloading the shields, and alarms began to sound.

"Damn." The curse was little more than an exhalation. Echo shut off the alarms and initiated auto-repair sequences. It was time to try something different—if he lived long enough to do it.

Icy cool, Echo drove the little ship straight at the side of the wormhole, warp amplifier wide open...and disappeared.

* * *

The Cortian commander, B'ka, was gleeful as he studied his ship's viewscreen. The kreplact little ship had finally been damaged by his gunneryman. It was only a matter of time now before the human male was in his possession. The man was one of the top, if not THE top, operatives of the Division One Agency, and the Agency was among Earth's best. This male would bring a high fee. And the Cortian knew of more than one bounty hunter who would be interested in this one.

Perhaps an auction is in order, he decided. *After considerable breeding, of course. No sense letting the genes go to waste.*

Abruptly, the commander howled in frustration as the small scout ship on the screen rammed into the wall of the wormhole and apparently disintegrated.

"Iplik! Kidey on tach. Toluy moch."

"Ohchoy, tok."

Unexpectedly, the viewscreen went dark.

"Clo'y!"

"Tron clo'y, tok!"

"I'tley! Tan'ck ndo. KLE'E!"

* * *

Just before Echo impacted the side of the wormhole, he activated another of the *Tour de Force*'s little surprises—a sensor jammer. To the *Trindak*, the scout ship disappeared as if it had never been, and Echo cut his trajectory hard to avoid contacting the n-dimensional wall of the wormhole, then killed the warp amplifier. He cruised silently, paralleling the edge of the wormhole close enough to touch it, and watched coldly, ruthlessly, as the *Trindak* passed by his little vessel without becoming aware of him. When he was behind the other ship, Echo disengaged the jamming device, reset the field parameters, and re-engaged it.

But rather than wrapping back around the *Tour de Force* once more, the jamming field extended, surrounding the Cortian slaving vessel. But the *Trindak* didn't disappear from Echo's sensors. Instead, Echo had inverted the field, blinding the malicious pirate vessel. To the Cortians, the rest of the universe suddenly vanished, and they ran head-on into the side of the wormhole at full speed before they could react.

The *Trindak* imploded as the cosmic string effect of the wormhole created a singularity in the ship's matter. As an unsympathetic Echo watched the ship collapse in upon itself, he murmured, "...And THAT'S for Meg, you sons of bitches."

Then he shook himself out of his brown study.

"I guess I better get my ass in gear now, or I'm gonna lose it...AND Meg." Dropping the sensor jamming field, he punched the warp amplifier, shot over to the far side of the wormhole and down it. At the point where the pirate ship impacted the wormhole, the wormhole began to unravel, losing its integrity. In moments, the entire circumference of the wormhole had decayed, but by that time Echo was past, flitting down the wormhole toward the Edeptis system. Behind him, the wormhole structure continued to break down, the destruction speeding in each direction as the wormhole collapsed from the middle outward.

Now it was a race to see which arrived at Edeptis first, the *Tour de Force*, or the wormhole instability wave.

* * *

The MET clock showed 13:32, and Echo was racing for his own life now, as well as Omega's. Behind him, the instability wave, itself propagating at superluminal speeds, was collapsing the wormhole at a rapid rate. And although he had a head start, the instability wave was still propagating faster than the *Tour de Force* could traverse the wormhole, and it was gaining fast.

The warp amplifier helped...provided it held up. Echo knew the R & D people had intended it to be used like an afterburner, in short bursts, to provide additional speed in dogfight-type situations. But it had been running wide open almost continuously now for an hour and a half, and no one had yet determined the usage lifetime of the amplifier.

"Hmm...guess I'll find out for 'em," he decided, wry.

The cold was starting to seep into the spacesuit now—or rather, his body heat was starting to leach out, as Omega would have said while she explained the thermodynamics—but given the circumstances in which he found himself, Echo couldn't afford to boost power to the life-support systems. Instead, he powered off all remaining life support except for oxygen. He also powered down all the weapons systems, and reduced shield power to 50%. He shut down all the sensors except those used for navigation, and powered down all onboard computers except the master clock and navigation computers. Then he diverted the freed power into the prop units.

The *Tour de Force*'s speed increased marginally, and the juggernaut approach of the instability wave slowed noticeably. If Echo could hold this pace for—he glanced at the clock—about fifteen more minutes, with the increase in speed the warp amplifier gave him, he would be able to exit the wormhole before it collapsed, and proceed the last short leg of the journey to Edeptis under normal warp.

Six minutes later, Echo discovered the lifetime of the warp amplifier, as the *Tour de Force* lurched, staggered, and slowed. The instability wave bore down on him.

Echo killed all but the forward navigation shields and the last of the life support, and diverted all of THAT power to the prop.

There should be enough air left in the suit and umbilical to get me through nine more damn minutes, he thought, *but if there isn't, it won't matter anyway.*

He gripped the stick, navigating directly down the center of the wormhole, watching the clock and the navcomp readouts intently.

Seven minutes later, reality began setting in with a vengeance.

The air in the suit was getting stuffy. Echo realized he was having difficulty focusing on the readouts; Omega's picture was distorted when he glanced at it. His lungs were laboring, and nausea began to build in the pit of his stomach. He recognized THOSE symptoms; he'd had them before.

"D-damn," he muttered, "anox-anoxia set-setting in..."

Unexpectedly, the position alarm on the navcomp sounded. Echo glanced down at the readout, striving to focus, then dove for the warp drive control, killing it.

The wormhole truncated in front of him, and the *Tour de Force* shot clear, into normal space, and coasted for several million miles, as Echo yawed the stick 180 degrees to look back. The maneuver almost cost him his last meal, hours ago though it was, and as he watched the remains of the wormhole collapse, he quickly began re-establishing his life support.

Echo slumped in the seat of the scout ship, breathing heavily as fresh oxygen washed over him and the suit's heaters kicked in. He glanced at the chronometer on the console. 13:57 MET. He was three minutes early.

The wormhole collapsed and vanished.

"Sic transit gloria cavi vermis," Echo said drily, in a hoarse voice. "Sorry, Meg, but I can't go anywhere for a minute until the anoxia symptoms go away," he told the photograph.

Echo leaned back and closed his eyes for a moment...and saw anguished but understanding blue eyes staring back at him from the midst of a scorched, blistered—but nevertheless cherished—face.

His eyes snapped open, and he sipped some water from the suit reservoir, finding his mouth suddenly dry. Then he started surveying the area of space in which he found himself as he rested.

When his hands and feet were no longer numb with cold, and the oxygen deprivation symptoms had abated, Echo resumed normal statuses on ship functions. Next, he began rebroadcast of his errand-of-mercy message, and started comparing navcomp position readouts with the chart Indak had provided.

Once done, Echo slowly scanned the area around the ship again. Then he set a course for where he estimated Edeptis to be. According to Indak's map, he should be no more than a couple of light years away, and there was a double star in that direction that fit the description.

* * *

Omega's eyes fluttered open and she stirred, restless and in pain. Romeo sat up straight as India and Dr. Whiskey moved to Omega's side.

"Meg? Can you hear me? Are you awake?" India asked as the other medic scanned the monitors. Omega didn't answer, but put out a groping hand.

"Hm. This is interesting..." Whiskey murmured. "India, have a look at this."

"Wow," India said in surprise, leaning over to look.

"What?" Romeo inquired from behind them both, and India and Whiskey both turned.

"Well, according to the medscanners, Agent Omega is still in a coma," Whiskey explained. "But her eyes are open and she's moving about. It's like...she's here, but she's not here..."

Romeo and India looked at each other, gazes conveying worlds of information.

"Do you suppose..." began India. "Surely not."

"Nah," Romeo replied. "No way. If she couldn't read the Cortians when they were right here, how the hell is she gonna reach Echo onna other side o' the damn galaxy? Shit, girl. Get real."

"Yeah. You're right."

They were interrupted by a bubbling, rough sigh.

"S-sic trans...transit..."

"Damn!" Whiskey exclaimed, and he and India swiftly bent over Omega. "India! Talk to her! Get her attention!"

"Meg, sis, it's India. Come on, girlfriend! Fight, Meg! Fight, honey! You promised Echo! Fight!"

"What is it?! What's wrong? What'd she say??" Romeo asked, alarmed.

"Two Latin words," the grim male medic told Romeo, while India continued trying to gain Omega's attention. "*Sic transit.* They mean 'so passes.' She may be giving up." He left to ready the emergency life support team, on standby since Echo had departed Headquarters. Romeo knelt by the bedside in his place.

"C'mon, Meg," he encouraged. "Don't let Echo down. Hell, don't let US down. Echo made me 'n' India promise to look out for ya while he was gone, an' if anything happens to ya, he'll KILL us! C'mon, now, you wouldn' want that to happen, now wouldja?" Romeo joked with the unresponsive form, hoping against hope for a spark of amusement in the blue eyes. He was disappointed. "C'mon, Meg...aw, shit..." he pleaded softly, and looked up at India as Omega's eyes slowly closed again.

"Let's go, Romeo," India said quietly. "The medics are going to want room to work."

As Alpha Two left the room, Omega's eyes opened again. This time there was awareness in them. As she stared at the wall, soft blue eyes hazed in pain, she whispered, "So c-close...Echo—PLEASE h-hurry...for-r THEM, as we-well as..."

The blue eyes closed, and the empty room fell silent.

* * *

As Echo dropped out of warp, he saw it: A dull orange binary star system, so compact the two stars touched, sharing outer layers and forming what resembled nothing so much as a single peanut-shaped star. Initiating a sensor sweep, he searched for the fourth planet.

"Bingo," Echo said with satisfaction. "There it is."

As he approached the planetary system, however, the proximity alert suddenly sounded and the communications system activated with an incoming message that routed through the universal translator.

"WARNING! YOU ARE ENTERING THE EDEPTIS SYSTEM. UNAUTHORIZED TRESPASSERS WILL BE DESTROYED. PLEASE IDENTIFY YOURSELF AT ONCE."

The voice was artificial; the syntax, formal. *Probably a system computer,* Echo decided. He double-checked his automated message, nodded to himself and pushed onward.

Moments later, another message arrived.

"WARNING! UNIDENTIFIED INTRUDER! YOU ARE UNAUTHORIZED TO ENTER THIS STELLAR SYSTEM. DEFENSIVE CONSTELLATION ARMED."

"Aw, shit," Echo grumbled, punching the sensor suite to maximum, and verifying that the errand-of-mercy message was indeed broadcasting. "Why isn't it recognizing me?"

"UNIDENTIFIED INTRUDER! YOUR VESSEL DOES NOT MATCH ANY KNOWN PARAMETERS IN THIS NETWORK. YOUR COMMUNIQUE HAS BEEN LABELED AS SPAM. IDENTIFY YOURSELF OR BE DESTROYED IN FIVE...FOUR..."

"Shit shit SHIT!" Echo exclaimed, punching off the automated message. He scrambled to open an external channel on the correct frequency and get the universal translator switched over, already barking, "EDEPTIS SYSTEM! This is Agent Echo from Earth, Division One headquarters of the Pan-Galactic Law Enforcement and Immigration Administration! I'm here for the healer Doron! My partner's dying! I need help!"

"TWO...ONE."

Nothing happened.

"What the...?" Echo murmured. "Did I get it in there in time?"

Just then, the proximity sensor alert went off for the second time. A heads-up display showed a lone object only a few meters to starboard. But the shape was one that Echo recognized.

"Aw, dam—"

The space-based version of an explosive caltrop made no sound in the vacuum, but it lit up the darkness outside the small clipper ship. Seconds later the shock wave slammed into the tiny craft, rocking it violently and knocking it off course. The proximity sensor screamed multiple alarms, as the heads-up display plotted over a dozen more explosive caltrops to his port side; the blast was shoving him toward them.

"HELLFIRE DAMNATION!" Echo yelled, Texan accent in full sway, and grabbed the joystick with one hand, initiating high-acceleration avoidance maneuvers as he flipped the comm to continuous broadcast. "Edeptis system! This is PGLEIA Agent Echo from Earth! I am here to pick up Doron the healer! I am in an experimental spacecraft! You may know it as the *RD-1*, or the *Rubber-Ducky-1*! Please acknowledge!" *Dear God, I don't believe I just said that,* he thought absently.

Three more caltrops exploded. The little *Tour de Force* bucked and pitched...but held. *But if just one of 'em gets much closer, it won't,* a grim Echo considered.

Echo hit the interplanetary prop, accelerating forward. The heads-up display showed six out of fully ten remaining caltrops 'painting' his craft, then he felt a slight jostle as tractor beams locked onto the *Tour de Force*. The caltrops began to move, mirroring his evasive maneuvers even as they pulled themselves toward his ship.

Dammit. They've got a tractor lock, he realized. *And they're even smaller than I am. It'll pull 'em right into me.*

"EDEPTIS SYSTEM! PLEASE ACKNOWLEDGE! This is Agent Echo of Earth! I am here to fetch a healer for my partner Omega, before she DIES! ACKNOWLEDGE!"

Several insistent beeps drew his attention to a readout alongside the caltrop icon on his display, and he studied it briefly.

That'll work, he decided. *According to that readout, this defensive system is anything but state of the art. I'll bet if I...*

Echo expanded the radius on the proximity sensor, then swiftly studied the resulting readouts, before programming a series of high-speed maneuvers in all six axes of movement—x, y, and z axes, and pitch, yaw, and roll—into the navcomp. He leaned back, tightened his straps, and hit <INITIATE>.

The *Tour de Force* opened up with what Echo called his 'rotisserie mode,' a tight roll about the axis running from nose to tail, combined with an acceleration forward. This was then followed by a hard lateral translation to port, and a flat yaw spin about the craft's 'vertical' axis. This was in turn succeeded by a dead stop, a hard reverse, a double translation to starboard—one of which angled up at about 30 degrees—and a translation up combined with a 'cartwheel'—a multiple 360-degree pitch, nose down.

Simultaneously, the offensive armament automatically targeted all the caltrops in the area, picking them off by ones and twos.

The maneuver, which he'd used a couple of times before in space combat, was normally intended to prevent a target lock, but he hoped it would serve an additional function in this instance. He could only wait and see.

Echo's hands held tight to the internal 'shit handles' on each side of the pilot's seat; he forced himself deep into the seat, head on the back rest, and hung on for dear life.

All the while, he continued to speak into the mic near his lips.

"Edeptis system, this is Division One Agent Echo. I am here on an errand of mercy. My ship is an experimental spacecraft and will not be in your catalogues. My partner is dying. I have come to request that the healer Doron come back with me to Earth and endeavor to save her. Edeptis system, do you read? Please acknowledge."

Still no response, dammit, he thought. *I'm gonna puke if I have to go all the way to the damn planetary surface like THIS. And in a spacesuit, yet. THAT'LL be fun inside the helmet.*

Four of the six caltrops that had locked onto the clipper ship suddenly exploded, as the agéd beam projectors overheated; a fifth burned out without exploding, and slung off course, deorbiting and falling inward, toward the binary stars at the center of the system. The sixth was flung out of the system into interstellar space. *Intergalactic space, more probably,* Echo decided, briefly noting its trajectory. *After all, we're on the outside of the Outer Arm.* But twelve more caltrops 'painted' him and locked on.

"Edeptis, this is Agent Echo of Earth! If you don't call off your automated dogs soon, there won't BE an Agent Echo of Earth!"

Echo entered several more commands into the navcomp, enabling the *Tour de Force* to continue an indefinite series of largely randomly-generated maneuvers, yet still work his way, step-wise, toward Edeptis IV.

The current batch of caltrops met similar fates, save that two of them flung themselves through other clusters of the space mines, detonating several, and causing the rest of the mines in those clusters to lock onto each other.

Well, that takes care of THOSE, Echo concluded in some relief, seeing what had happened.

But not all of the caltrops lacked propulsion, it seemed, and the artificial intelligence governing the defensive system evidently figured out the pattern in the *Tour de Force*'s navcomp random number generator, because the mines began moving into the path of the little clipper ship.

So Echo took control of the joystick once more, tying the sensors into his movements in order to avoid accidentally maneuvering into one group while trying to outrun another. Loops followed spins followed jerky translations all over the sky, as he dodged and twirled, sending caltrops and debris flying in every direction, targeting as many as possible with what offensive beam weapons he had.

"What the HELL have I gotta do to prove I'm not a damn robot?!" he growled into the comm.

"UNIDENTIFIED SPACECRAFT, YOUR TRANSMISSION IS RECEIVED. PLEASE IDENTIFY YOURSELF."

"I'm Agent Echo of Division One, headquartered on Earth!"

"WHAT IS YOUR MISSION?"

"I'm here to pick up Doron the healer, to save my dying partner!"

"WHAT DOES YOUR PARTNER CALL YOU?"

"What the damn hell?!"

"WHAT DOES YOUR PARTNER CALL YOU?"

"You mean, like a nickname or something?"

"WHAT DOES YOUR PARTNER CALL YOU?"

"Omega calls me, 'Ace.'"

"IDENTIFICATION CONFIRMED. STANDING DOWN WEAPONS SYSTEMS."

Which was fine, Echo decided...except for the couple dozen explosive devices still hauling ass behind him.

Given how old the tech is, I wonder if it doesn't have a way to detach, or if they simply didn't get the stand-down signal, or what, Echo wondered. *All things considered, I don't especially want to find out the hard way, either.*

A few more tight maneuvers and well-placed beam cannon shots finally shook free the last of them, and the *Tour de Force* spun away, past the outermost planet of the Edeptis system, before coming to a gradual stop.

* * *

"What a pain in the ass," Echo grumbled, as he punched in a series of commands. The sensors located the fourth planet of the system for him—again—and he aimed for it. Punching up the interplanetary drive once more, he set the little two-seater back in motion as he opened up a communications channel.

"Edeptis IV, this is the Earth ship *Tour de Force*, piloted by Pan-Galactic Law Enforcement and Immigration Administration, Division One Agent Echo. Do you read? Edeptis IV, this is Division One Agent Echo."

After a moment the response came. And this time, there was a live body behind it.

"Agent Echo, this is Edeptis IV. Your arrival has been anticipated."

"Pardon the obscenity, but no shit."

"Excuse me?"

"I just had a fun time dodging your defensive system."

"Oh dear. It did not recognize you?"

"I'm afraid not. You might want to arrange to have some repairs and upgrades made, especially by the time I managed to get through it. Plus, I'm not sure I was entirely successful in taking out all the ones that are going to be falling into the system, so I can't guarantee you won't have any of 'em entering atmosphere."

"I...see. Your recommendations will be...uh, taken under advisement. Ah, um, we regret that our planet has no spaceport facilities for you, but that is our...custom. Please follow this transmission to planetfall."

"Copy that. Following transmission to planetfall. Incoming now."

"You may enter the atmosphere at your discretion."

Echo brought his ship down through the Edeptan atmosphere, a pink-tinged gaseous mix that reminded him somewhat of Mars during a dust storm, save that it was considerably denser...and cleaner. Near the terminus of the transmission, Echo found an open park waiting, and he nestled the *Tour de Force* down gently into the soft red grass. As Echo popped the hatch, a small reception committee emerged from the nearby government building.

"Welcome to Edeptis IV, Agent Echo," the scarlet-skinned, yellow-eyed leader said via a portable translator/headset. "You will find our atmosphere breathable, if slightly lower in oxygen than that to which you are accustomed. I am Teknon, and am what you would call the foreign minister for offworld affairs."

Echo removed his helmet and greeted the minister.

"Honored, Minister Teknon. I...suppose I'm a little surprised. I had understood that your people didn't do interstellar flight."

"We do not. That does not mean that we do not know how, Agent Echo," Teknon noted. "You may have noticed that the Edeptis system is, by dint of being on the outside edge of the Outer Arm, rather remote from other systems, so there was little in the way of incentive for us to develop interstellar travel. And our inclination is to direct our resources inward, to serve our own people."

"But you get some interstellar trade, I'd assume."

"A bit. Enough to warrant my ministry position, and to have required the installation of the defensive system you, ah, encountered. Though its installation was some hundred, or perhaps one hundred-fifty, of your years ago; I am as yet uncertain as to the conversion factors. You see, we believe we may have historic familiarity with the same race of slavers who so severely wounded your partner. What you call the Sagittarius Dwarf Galaxy, which you may or may not know is being cannibalized by our larger spiral..."

"Yes. My partner, Agent Omega, is an astronomer. She's filled me in on the whole orbital dynamics thing."

"Very good. The core is, oddly enough, not as far away from the singularity at the core of the Great Spiral as are we; but it is not in the plane of the Great Spiral." Teknon pointed up, and Echo took his meaning. "The Cortians come from the core of the Sagittarius Dwarf, which is on our side of the Great Spiral of our galaxy. It was their repugnant depredations upon our world which caused us to install the perimeter defense of the Edeptis system."

"Aha. So you have some sympathy to my mission."

"We do. We will do our best to help."

"Thanks; that's much appreciated."

"You are welcome. In turn, if we might make a request?"

Echo raised an eyebrow, suspicious.

"What?"

Teknon drew in a deep breath and let it out in a sigh.

"It appears that perhaps we need to update and upgrade our defensive perimeter. Perhaps—after your emergency has been resolved, of course—you and your organization might...help us?"

"I think that's a definite possibility," Echo decided, relaxing and smiling at the other being. "It would be easier, of course, if the Edeptis system joined PGLEIA..."

"Yes, we have been considering that."

"Um, okay; I can put you in touch with the right people...later." Echo bit his lip, doing his best to hide his antsiness. "Look, I know this is a first contact, but I hope you're not offended if we skip the formalities right now. I'll be happy to send a team from our diplomatic department to handle all that later, and do it right, and pretty quickly, all in all. But like I said, I have a partner dying on me back home, and I'd like to pick up Doron the healer and get back to her while there's still time."

"I...understand," Teknon replied hesitantly. "But there has been somewhat of a problem..."

Echo stiffened.

"Exactly...what kind of problem?" he asked, maintaining his patience with an effort.

"There is an outbreak of Vegan hemorrhagic fever on the northern continent. Doron is needed there. He refuses to move until the epidemic is contained."

* * *

Omega lay in the hospital bed, still unconscious. The medics had, some time previously, hooked life sign monitors to her comatose body, and now Romeo and India could both see the ravages taking place within her.

"What's all that stuff mean?" Romeo asked his partner quietly, waving a hand at the displays. India pointed at the readouts.

"Meg's undergoing slow circulatory collapse from all the burn damage, Romeo. As that happens, her heart is working harder and harder with fewer and fewer resources..."

"What? You mean she's bleedin' out?"

"More or less, yes. More like oozing, but...yes."

"But you got IVs an' shit goin'..."

"Once the damage reaches a certain point, we can't pump it in as fast as she's losing it, honey. Plus the blood vessels are becoming less viable. They're deteriorating."

"Oh..."

"Her respiration is rapid but shallow, and her blood is poorly oxygenated, because the back half of her lungs was partially seared by the ion drive. She's in renal failure—her kidneys...well, they really just aren't there anymore, Romeo. She's also paralyzed from the waist down..."

"Why?" Romeo asked, dreading the answer. India grimaced.

"Her spine...burned in two. Her liver's failing...Brain waves are starting to drop..."

"Damn. How is she even still alive?"

"That's just it, Romeo. We honestly don't know. She SHOULDN'T be.

It's kinda like..." India shrugged, throwing up her hands. "It's like her own willpower is all that's holding her together. But all of the pain, all of the bodily systems crashing...they're taking a toll on that willpower. And when it's gone, when she's too exhausted, with too few reserves left to support that will..."

"Shit."

"Yeah."

"Echo...better get here soon, huh?"

"Yes. Maybe he should've...spoken to her while he had the chance."

* * *

Echo settled the *Tour de Force* down onto hard-packed green clay next to Doron's emergency medical unit. Teknon had, upon request, provided very specific directions for finding Doron, and Echo had followed them to the letter. On the way, he had contacted Doron to let him know of his imminent arrival, and Doron had assured Echo that Vegan hemorrhagic fever was not a human contagion. He probably would have risked it anyway; Omega was in far more critical condition than any disease could possibly cause, he thought.

Upon removing his helmet and emerging from his ship, however, Echo was forced to reassess that opinion. The condition of the patients clustered around Doron's medical tent was horrific. Those in the worst shape bled from every bodily orifice, and tissue was breaking down at a great rate, rapidly creating new orifices.

Grim-faced, Echo stepped carefully over and around the disease's victims as he made his way toward the large tent at the center of the compound.

It's at least as bad as an ebola outbreak on Earth, he thought, watching a small child hold a bloodstained doll and rock silently beside dying parents. He scrapped his initial plan with an inaudible sigh—obviously these patients WOULDN'T wait until Doron could get back. And if Echo knew Omega—and if anybody in the universe did, he did—she'd never stand for it, anyway. Even if it meant her life.

"Doron?" Echo ventured as he reached the tent door. *Hope Fox's assistants sent him the BLT, or this is gonna be a short conversation.* A diminutive Edeptan looked up from a patient.

166

"Yes? Agent Echo? You are Agent Echo?"

"Yes, I am. It's pretty bad, isn't it?" Echo asked, waving his hands around.

"Not really, Agent Echo," Doron replied, to Echo's surprise. "I have the medication to make them well. It is the sheer numbers that prove overwhelming."

"Not enough medicine?"

"Not even that," Doron replied. "I have a synthesizer. I simply do not have a big enough generator to run at maximum capacity. And the locals cannot provide sufficient power. This is a very poor region of our planet."

"Is there anything I can do to help?" Echo volunteered, removing his gauntlets and clipping them on a D-ring at his waist.

"Can you administer medication?"

"I've had the full Agency field medical training, so...yeah."

"Excellent. I will have a nurse supply you with equipment. However, you did not come here to assist me with this epidemic."

"No. But the sooner it's under control, the sooner you can come with me to Earth."

"Your mate is critical?" Doron asked.

"Not mate—partner," Echo corrected him, somewhat surprised. *Mate?! What did somebody tell him? Did Fox say...?*

"Partner, mate. There is a difference?"

"...Yes." Echo felt relieved. *Aha. It's a semantics problem, rather than an indiscretion by somebody I trusted.*

"'Partner,' then. You can explain to me later. Come, let us get you fresh supplies from the synthesizer."

Doron led Echo to the machine and a curious Echo surveyed it. Something nagged at the back of his mind...

Echo...the warp generator...Ace, remember the warp generator...

Echo spun, instinctively looking for the familiar voice's treasured owner. No one was there.

Omega?? Echo stood still and reached out as best he knew how. *Is that you? Meg?! MEG!! Baby, answer me!* For a split-second, a familiar presence, warm, caring, concerned, was within him. He could almost reach out—or was that in?—and...

Echo...hurry... The presence faded, drifting away, leaving behind an odd, hollow sensation somewhere in the core of Echo's being.

Meg?? He opened completely, dropping his defenses, struggling to hold the fragile connection. *Baby, are you there? Where are you? What's going on?*

Silence.

Unexpectedly, Echo felt his legs give way, and he dropped to his knees on the hard ground, panting. His hands went to his suddenly-throbbing temples, and his heart pounded as he fought back a tsunami wave of nausea. Echo clenched his jaws, and simply waited. After a few minutes, the pain subsided, and he became aware of his surroundings once more...including a little Edeptan hovering close.

"What is it?" Doron asked, highly concerned, bending over him. "What is wrong? What happened?"

A wan Echo slowly got to his feet, feeling weak and drained. He sipped from his water reservoir and leaned against the synthesizer for a moment.

"...Nothing," Echo replied thoughtfully. "Nothing serious, anyway. I'm all right now. Had a little...glitch...with my spacecraft's life support system earlier. Probably some residual anoxia symptoms."

"Will you be all right? You turned very white..."

"Yeah, I'm okay. It's just...I just thought...I heard someone. Doron, I may be able to be of more use than merely doling out medicine. Show me the power leads for this thing..."

* * *

Fox entered the hospital room rapidly.

"What is it?! What's going on?"

"We don't know, Fox," India told him. "Something...happened." The medics, including Zebra, were setting up to replay the vitals data on the monitors for Zarnix, who had met Fox at the room's door, both headed in at speed. "Watch," India told them, pointing.

With the others, Fox watched the recording on the monitors as Omega's life signs slowly, inexorably dropped. Suddenly, the readings shot all over the screen, completely unpredictably. Then, unexplainably, they settled into

168

a normal rhythm.

"Interesting. These readings are those of a healthy, adult human," Zarnix, the chief medic, told Fox. "According to this, Omega should be up on her feet and talking to us. But you say she remained comatose throughout?" he asked India. The Agent nodded affirmation.

"There's more, Fox," Zebra, Zarnix's second in command and Fox's lover, added in a soft tone. "Those normal vitals? They AREN'T Omega's. But I know whose they ARE, 'cause I recognize 'em...from his last physical."

"Whose, then?" Fox pressed.

"Echo." Zebra met the Director's startled gaze. "They're Echo's vitals, right down to the cerebral readouts. I'd swear it on every degree I've got."

"Damn. What the hell...? How is she now?" Fox asked. The doctors shook their heads.

"Back to where she was before—whatever happened, happened. But not as far down the curve."

"How long did it last?"

"Two or three minutes," the medic on duty, whom Fox recognized as Whiskey, answered. "Now look at this." He pulled up Omega's encephalographic readings. "According to this, at the same time Omega's vital signs stabilized, she experienced a tremendous burst of brainwave activity, dropped into what Zebra is convinced was ECHO'S pattern, and then became COMPLETELY PAIN-FREE. Still in a coma...but without pain. For the moment."

"We think she...somehow...may have been unconsciously mimicking her partner, in order to buy herself a respite," Zebra said. "If, as India seems to think, she has some low-level psi abilities as a result of the, ah... modifications...that were performed on her when she was young, she might have subconsciously picked up on his readings over the approximate year they've been partnered now. Then, when she was in extremis, she tried to reproduce those same readings in her own body. And," she added with a shrug, "it seems to have worked, at least a little."

"And now?" Fox asked.

"She's hurtin' again, Fox," Romeo said in a very quiet voice, beside

India.

"Explanation?" Fox demanded.

"None, Fox," Zebra answered. "Somehow, Omega found the strength to rally for a few moments..."

"—It shouldn't have been possible," interjected Whiskey.

"...But it may have bought Echo the time he needs to get back here with Doron," India finished. "It seems to have slowed Meg's deterioration somewhat, at any rate."

Fox nodded, then glanced at the ceiling.

"Echo, old friend," he said quietly, "you'd better haul ass if you want to keep that promise to your partner..."

* * *

It took some tinkering—the connections weren't really compatible—but Echo finally got the *Tour de Force*'s warp generator hooked up to provide power to Doron's medical synthesizer.

A delighted Doron began producing the bacteriostat in massive quantities, and called in as many medical personnel as he could, from across the entire planet, to begin dispensing it. Within a few hours after that, the Vegan ebola epidemic was contained, and Echo disconnected the warp generator.

But Echo's Mission Elapsed Time was now 21:30. Omega's remaining time was almost half gone. Echo waited impatiently as Doron made arrangements for administration of medication to continue after his departure.

"Ready?" Echo said, when Doron was finally finished.

"Almost. Come over here," Doron told him, leading him to a special chamber in the back of the tent. "Get in."

"What's this?" Echo asked, suddenly suspicious.

"Decontamination," Doron replied.

"I thought you said the fever was non-communicable to humans." Echo drew his brows together in a scowl.

"That is correct. But do you work only with humans?"

"Oh. Duh. No..." The scowl morphed into a concerned frown.

"Then get in."

"Will it damage the spacesuit?" Echo asked before climbing into the chamber.

"No, Agent," Doron replied. "We also use it to...let me see, what is the medical term in your language...ah! autoclave our equipment and instrumentation. Your spacesuit must be decontaminated anyway, and this is by far the best way. I will decontaminate in another chamber, and I have sent some assistants to manually decontaminate your ship."

"Do they know how to handle a spacecraft?" Echo asked, suddenly worried, for no good reason that he could see.

"Oh, yes. Do not make the assumption that we are incapable of spaceflight technology, Agent Echo. We simply choose not to do so for cultural and religious reasons. We prefer to direct all our resources within our own planet, rather than waste it—as my people perceive it—on unneeded exploration of a vast space. I do not say we are correct, mind. Only that it is what our planet chose."

"Is there a problem in your coming with me, then?" Echo queried. *Not that it would stop me, at this point...*

"No, no. I am a healer. It is who and what I am, physically and metaphysically. You have come to me asking for help that cannot be obtained elsewhere, to save the life of one close to you. That supersedes all other concerns."

Echo nodded in mingled approval and relief, and prepared to enter the decon chamber as a technician entered the tent and approached Doron. They carried on a conversation in Edeptan for several minutes, then Doron turned to Echo.

"Does your ship live?"

"What?" Echo asked, not certain he'd understood the odd question correctly.

"Is your spaceship alive?"

"No, of course not."

"Does it have biological components?"

"No..."

Doron turned to the technician and they conversed in Edeptan for a few more moments, before Doron returned his attention to Echo.

"Are you certain, Agent Echo?" Doron asked with concern. "Anything—any component—biological in origin, or based on biological systems?"

"Well, the skin of the ship is a liquid crystal, hyperconducting neural net," Echo said, "'bout twenty years or so away from public use on Earth, but it isn't biological itself, just BASED on the human nervous system."

"How important is this...'skin'?"

"It provides visual camouflage if needed, and heat shielding during atmospheric passage," Echo told the Edeptan healer. "And it helps provide the interplanetary propulsion."

"What? How does the SKIN provide propulsion?"

"Well, like I said, it's a hyperconductor. Run an electric current through it, and you get a REALLY powerful magnetic field generated by the entire surface of the ship. The maglev effect—"

"Maglev?" Doron queried.

"Sorry. Magnetic levitation, shortened to just 'maglev' on my world. It helps generate lift and motive force relative to planetary magnetic fields. Once I'm out of the atmosphere, I can use it in local stellar fields the same way."

"Is this skin the only means of interplanetary propulsion?" Doron asked anxiously.

"No, but it sure helps a lot. The power draw is pretty steep otherwise," Echo told him. "Doron, what's this all about?"

Doron sighed and turned.

"You had better come with me, Agent," he said. "I have something important to show you."

Echo followed the physician with a strange sense of foreboding.

I wonder if this is how Meg felt, he thought, grim. *Dammit, I SO should have listened to her...*

* * *

Doron led Echo straight to the *Tour de Force*, and Echo stopped short, staring in dismay.

"What the hell...?"

The ship appeared to have had acid dumped all over it. The liquid crystal skin was completely missing in places, exposing bare alloy. In other areas, the skin had obviously degraded to black, rotting patches, mushy in

172

the middle but crusty around the edges, becoming useless.

"It is the Vegan fever, Agent Echo," Doron told him. "In some way, it has infected the skin of your ship, breaking it down. Evidently, its similarity to neurological systems left it...vulnerable."

"Shit!" Echo exclaimed. "How can we stop it?"

"The decontamination procedure has slowed it," Doron said. "I have ordered that your ship be coated in a thin film of the bacteriostat. We shall have to wait and see."

"Doron...I don't have TIME to wait."

A stern Doron looked at Echo.

"You do not have a choice."

* * *

Some time later, the technicians had completed the process of 'inoculating' the *Tour de Force*, and Echo and Doron inspected the little ship.

"Damn, what a mess," Echo muttered as he checked the vessel's coating. "Looks like the whole blasted thing's rotting away."

"That is essentially true." Doron nodded. "But the process of decay appears to have been halted by the bacteriostat."

"Well, that's something, I guess."

"Is your ship capable of flying in this condition?" Doron asked in considerable anxiety.

"Yeah, but we'll have a hell of a time getting off the ground. Once we jump into warp, I'd say off the top of my head we'd be fine, propulsion-wise, but I've got to get far enough away from the system that the local spacetime geometry won't be affected by the jump. And with the ship in this shape, that'll be damn slow going. Not to mention atmospheric reentry at Earth..."

"So the answer is 'not very well'?" Doron summarized, and Echo nodded. "What about fuel consumption?"

"Good point. I forgot about that. The spacecraft doesn't run on fuel, per se—um, as such," he corrected himself, realizing the little alien would not recognize the Latin phrase. "The ship doesn't run on fuel as such. Instead, the warp generator uses a miniature singularity. Virtual particle pairs get generated at the Schwarzchild radius, and that plasma is used in a cool

173

fusion reactor. Problem is, that removes mass from the singularity, which makes it 'evaporate.' The more power I have to draw, the faster the singularity evaporates. The singularity is also the source of the spacetime distortion that the warp system amplifies, so if we lose the singularity, the whole spacecraft dies."

"So without the skin to create lift..." Doron mused.

"Right. The singularity goes away fast."

"So you need either a new skin or a new singularity."

"Yep."

Doron mused for several minutes.

"Agent Echo, what do you need to create a new singularity?"

"Mmm...let's see. A quantum fluctuation amplifier, a Medusan laser array, a solid hydrogen nodule...and the strongest force fields you got on the planet. That oughta do it," Echo remarked, sardonic in the extreme. "You got handy access to any of that?"

"No..."

"Then we can't do it."

"Agent Echo?"

"Yes?" Echo was leaning over into the cockpit to check the status displays. "Nah—that's what I thought. Dammit..."

"It is perhaps my turn to be of use," Doron told him.

"How's that, Doron?"

"Do you know the structure of the skin on your vessel?"

"Not right off, but I've got the specs here somewhere..." Echo rummaged in the stowage pockets of his spacesuit, brought out a sheaf of papers, and began leafing through them. "Hmm...here they are."

"May I see them?"

"Sure. Here."

Doron studied the chemical structure for a moment, then turned and began scurrying back toward the medical tent.

"Agent Echo! How quickly can you hook your warp generator back to my synthesizer?" he called over his shoulder. Echo straightened with a start, suddenly realizing what the little red creature had in mind, and grabbed for the toolkit.

"How fast can a Qartonian cheetah do the hundred-meter?" he replied.

* * *

A short time later, the warp generator was powering the medical synthesizer again, as Doron struggled to precisely reproduce the structure of the neural net. Once finished with the generator, Echo put his head together with Doron's over the synthesizer, and they made several small experimental batches. None were exactly correct, but each batch was closer than the previous. So they kept doggedly at it, and Echo tried not to watch the clock too closely.

There's not a damn thing I can do about it anyway, he thought. *We've got to replace the skin or we'll run out of gas in the middle of the freeway. And it's a long way to hike to the nearest gas station.*

After a couple of hours' effort, Doron felt confident.

"We have the synthesizer correctly programmed now," he told Echo.

"Good," Echo told him with some relief. "Biochem isn't my strong suit."

"But your knowledge was extremely useful nevertheless," Doron told him. "Your experience with the physical behavior of the compound helped me determine more precisely the chemical properties."

* * *

"Now what?" Echo stood before the spacecraft and asked, glancing at the ship's MET clock. It read exactly 24:00.

One full Earth day. Meg is half gone. And that's at the outside. And I still gotta get Doron back to Earth. And THEN he has to assess and treat her.

"According to your documentation, and based on what I derive from the properties of the substance, we must remove the damaged portions of the skin and replace it with this," Doron explained, holding up the container with the new 'skin' material. "Then we must wait for it to cure and bond to the vehicle's surface."

"Hurry up and wait," Echo said, fighting the edgy instinct within that told him to simply grab the physician and head home to his waiting partner—never mind the fact that they wouldn't make it.

"I am afraid so," Doron replied with a sigh.

* * *

Echo set to, along with the other technicians, as they peeled away 'dead skin' on the fuselage of the spacecraft, preparing it to receive a new neural network. It was tedious work, but with enough of them on the job it went relatively quickly, for which Echo was thankful—something about the nature of the work left him with a deep sense of apprehension. Then it was finally time to apply the new skin.

"Here's a trick, Doron," Echo told the healer. "We need to get this spread as evenly as possible, or the magnetic field strength will vary too much for me to compensate for it."

"I...cannot help you there, Agent Echo. I do not know of any other method than simply painting it on. Will that do?"

"Mm. Probably not. It needs to be a lot more even."

"Then I do not know what to suggest."

"Hmm. I wonder," mused Echo, who quickly set about restoring normal function to the warp generator, detaching it from Doron's synthesizer. "There," he murmured to himself, climbing into the pilot's seat, "now let's try something..." He called, "Doron! Have the guys put a little of the hyperconductor on the starboard wingtip, please!"

"Starboard?"

"The right wing." Echo pointed.

"Very well. Ndk tl, brg drfl kck ngbh..." the healer called, and the other Edeptans responded, obeying Echo's request.

Once the Edeptans had spread a small amount of the liquid crystal on the Tour de Force's starboard apex, Echo waved them back, then powered up the little ship and activated the skin. The liquid material spread out under the influence of the electric current, depositing itself in a very thin film over the entire ship's surface. A satisfied smile spread over Echo's face as he watched, and he deactivated the skin.

"All right, Doron, tell your orderlies to dump the stuff on both of the wings!"

"Yes, Agent Echo! Kkdk tl, tttk kck ngbh jfmp! Ddrd kck!"

Within moments, Echo had a uniform coating of liquid crystal hyperconductor deposited across the entire surface of the scout ship. He carefully climbed out of the cockpit and leaped clear without touching the hull, leaving everything active until the outer layer solidified.

"There," he said, intensely satisfied, "that oughta do it."

* * *

Several hours of restless, enforced inactivity later, an uneasy Echo returned to the *Tour de Force* in the soft burgundy of an Edeptan twilight to check its condition. As soon as the outer layer of hyperconductor had formed a solid skim, Echo had deactivated the skin and Doron's team had spray-coated it with bacteriostat. Now Echo, with the help of an Edeptan phospho-lantern, did a visual inspection of the vessel's surface.

"Looks okay..." he murmured to himself. Gingerly he tapped the coating lightly with his fingertips, then guardedly ran a questing hand over the wing. "Feels okay, too...all right, let's do it."

He climbed back into the tiny cabin and activated the liquid crystal in camo mode. The scout ship promptly turned a mottled shade of dark reddish-green as it duplicated the appearance of the hard clay around it. Brown eyes gleamed in satisfaction, and Echo powered the prop, pulling back ever so slightly on the stick. The *Tour de Force* gently lifted off the ground and hovered about a meter in the air.

Echo settled the spacecraft back down, leaped out, and ran for the tent.

"Doron!" he called, bursting through the tent door. "Get into decon! There's a Southern belle waiting for us back home, and I'm not about to let her down. Let's go!"

* * *

After decontamination, Echo helped the diminutive little scarlet-skinned being into the spacesuit he'd brought. Doron was cooperative, but intensely curious, asking questions about every aspect of the suit-up until an impatient Echo was ready to break something. He restrained himself with an effort, however, wondering how it was that his reaction to another scientist could be so different. Omega was continually asking questions as well, but Echo never found they strained his patience as Doron's were doing.

Maybe I just know Meg, Echo mused. *No...no, it's more than that. Something to do with the attitude, I think. Meg knows there's a time and place to ask questions, for one thing,* Echo thought in intense, barely-controlled exasperation. *And Meg isn't merely satisfied to learn about something; she...delights in it. It's fun for her. And HER questions, unlike a lot of Doron's, aren't EVER trivial. Damn, when SHE opens her mouth, I better have my brain in gear,* Echo thought with a hidden, affectionate smile.

At last, Echo had Doron suited up and installed in the back seat of the *Tour de Force.* Echo unhooked his gauntlets from the D-ring at his waist, donned them, hooked his umbilical back into the ship, and ran an abbreviated suit check. Then he pulled his helmet from the pilot's seat, donned it, and with some effort, folded himself back into the little ship, sealing the hatch as he went.

"Systems check A-OK," Echo muttered to himself as he ran back through the launch checklist. "Ready, Doron?"

"I am ready."

"Ever been off-planet before?"

"Twice."

"Good. This won't seem too strange to you, then." Echo initiated the launch sequence, and the *Tour de Force* smoothly departed Edeptis IV.

Chapter 5

By the time the *Tour de Force* had left the Edeptis system behind and jumped into warp, the MET clock read 30:13.

"Hang on, Omega," Echo told the photo. "I'm on the way, baby. I'll make up the time somehow."

"Is that the woman I am to treat?" Doron's voice said over the headset.

"Yes, it is."

"May I see?"

"Yes, Doron," Echo replied, removing the photo from the console and passing it back over his shoulder. The little Edeptan took the picture and studied it.

"This is good. It is important that I know what she is like, so that I may properly assess her condition when I arrive. She is, by Terran standards, beautiful, is she not?" Doron asked.

"She doesn't look like that now," Echo said quietly. "Not after..."

"Is appearance the only form of beauty?" a calm Doron queried, sage.

"...No."

"Is it HER only form of beauty? I think not, or you would not be willing to travel across the galaxy to rescue her. Nor would your superiors be willing to let you. Let alone assist you in the doing."

Doron handed the image back to Echo, who replaced it on the console as he tried to think of a reply, unaware that his fingers caressed the image before returning to the spacecraft controls. He remembered the caring and concern he had sensed earlier, a concern focused, not inward, but outward, and he simply nodded once.

"I'm...not sure they could have stopped me, to be honest," Echo admitted then. "But yeah, they did help. Nobody wants to see her..." He broke off, unwilling to finish the sentence. ·

"Tell me what happened to your mate," Doron continued. Echo shook his head, stifling a sigh of mingled annoyance...and intense regret.

"I told you, Doron, Omega is my partner, not my mate."

"Oh, yes, so you did. But I do not understand. In Edeptan, they are the same. We do not even have different words. Please explain to me the difference, then."

Oh, great, Echo thought, aggravation returning. *Cultural exchange. Just what I need right now.* He sighed. "All right, I'll give it a shot. You obviously understand the concept of mate."

"Yes," Doron replied promptly. "An emotional and biological companion. One with whom a being may procreate."

"Right. Now, among Terrans, the use of just the word 'partner' usually means a working relationship, not a personal one. Not always, 'cause there are those who choose not to formalize a romantic relationship, and they sometimes use the term for that relationship. But in this case, we're an Agency team—the first in the Alpha Line partnerships, actually."

"All right. So your relationship to this Omega is purely business, and you do not take notice of her as a person. You seek only to preserve a useful agent," Doron stated.

"No, of course not!" Echo replied, taken aback by the coldness of the assessment. "I...care...about her..."

"But you would do this for any of the other agents in your organization."

"Well...I suppose. I hadn't thought about it," Echo admitted. "Normally, partners look out for partners. Under ordinary circumstances, I wouldn't have to."

"'Look out for'...?"

"Uh, let's see...take care of?" Echo suggested.

"Mmm..." Doron responded. "I see..."

"Good."

"You work together. You 'take care of' each other. You have an emotional bond. You are willing to traverse the Great Spiral for her in order to save her, but not necessarily for another agent—"

"Waitaminnit. I didn't say..."

"—But you are partners, not mates. I see...no...I do NOT see...please, continue your explanation?"

Echo gave up in exasperation.

We really need to work on that BLT, Echo decided. *Besides, I'm not entirely sure he's not right. And she ISN'T just a working partner to me. I just...don't know if it goes the other way, too. And I don't wanna jeopardize the partnership, if it doesn't. Time to change the subject.*

"You wanted to know what happened to her," Echo tried the diversion.

"Yes, please."

"A Cortian slaver ship, disguised as a first-contact embassage, tried to kidnap me. Meg figured it out and, with some help from Romeo and India—friends and fellow Agents—and several Agency departments working under those three, stopped them from getting me. But in the process, Meg broke her leg and...couldn't get us out from under the ion drive when the slaver ship performed an emergency liftoff to escape."

"Why did not you do so?"

"The Cortians used a stun rod on me."

"What is a 'stun rod'?"

"It's a device that short-circuits all the neural synapses of the voluntary nervous system below the point of contact. The victim maintains regular breathing, heartbeat, and all that, but otherwise...can't move a muscle. I could talk, but that was about it. And I had to try to regulate my breath just to do that."

"Ah. But you do not appear harmed from the ion drive."

"...No." Echo paused, instantaneously reliving the agonized moment when Omega had burned on top of him. "No, she had a personal force field around us both, and that helped. It probably kept us both alive. But I'm...not just her partner, I guess; I'm the department chief, and she was determined to protect me..." *I just wish I thought it was because I was more to her than the department chief.*

"She shielded you with her own body, then?" Doron intuitively grasped where Echo was headed.

"Yes. Meg's very..." Echo searched for the right word, "tenacious. And selfless. If she can help, she does. That's just...Meg."

"Her injuries must be principally on one side, then, rather than all over?"

"Yes. Her back is..." Echo shrugged, "gone." He managed to keep his voice even, and tried to act unconcerned. But his squared shoulders and the back of his head were, by deliberate choice, all that Doron was allowed to see.

"Her internal organs?"

"The Agency medics called 'em...'parboiled.'"

"'Parboiled'?"

"...Cooked," Echo simplified, fighting not to grimace. Doron was silent for a time, evidently pondering this information. Echo could only hope that he hadn't painted too grim a picture, and that the little healer really could save her.

* * *

Doron was not as naïve as he appeared, and this was by choice; sitting behind the Division One Agent, he observed carefully—Echo's body language, his movements, his voice. Even the lack of movement told the diminutive physician a great deal, for this was not the first human Doron had encountered. Long ago, Doron had met the chief bodyguard of Pulgey Entiyti of Emdali, the then-head of the Pan-Galactic Council of Nine. The bodyguard in question had been one Franz Levy, whom he had initially treated at Entiyti's request, for several near-fatal conditions; afterward, during Levy's recuperation, the two had had several long conversations, though Doron had no idea where the man had gotten to after their encounter. But the Edeptan had learned much from the human, ABOUT humans—not all of it intentionally shared by the relatively-young Levy—and the little alien put it to use now.

He is very strong, this one, this Echo, Doron considered, extrapolating from his observations of the Agent, and his knowledge of humans derived from an astute Levy. *Strong...but also caring. A good man. And that very caring, in this instance, gives away that he is not at all unemotional, where she is concerned. The touch he gave her image...had he caressed her real face, it could not have been more tender. But he will not admit to it.*

Doron pondered in silence for several moments before deriving additional information from his observations.

Therefore, either she does not know how he feels and he is afraid she

182

will find out, for some reason I cannot divine; or she knows and foolishly does not wish his attentions—for no man would be more worthy of a mate. He has traversed the Great Spiral for her! To a place of which he had no knowledge before! No. As caring as she appears to be, as she MUST be to willingly sacrifice herself for his sake, I cannot imagine this is the way of it. It MUST be because he has not told her, for some reason of his own.

Doron nodded to himself, reaching a conclusion.

So. Unless and until I ascertain the reason for his maintaining this distance from the woman he obviously loves, I must keep his secret, for his sake.

* * *

"And she is still alive? Your partner?" Doron finally asked quietly. Echo nodded.

"Conscious and coherent when I left. We talked over the comm just before I jumped into warp."

"She is strong-willed, this one."

"Yes."

"As much so as you."

Echo chuckled. It was a rueful sound, even to his own ears.

"Others have said as much, yeah." He shook his head. "I think that's part of the reason she's in this condition, to be honest."

"Oh? Her strong will, or yours?"

"...Both. At odds," he added, hiding the grimace of pain.

"How so?"

"Meg is...different from most humans," Echo tried to tap-dance around the matter, "and, well, she picked up on what the Cortians really were. The rest of us thought it was a legitimate first-contact embassage, and she realized they were slavers and pirates, who were after the top agents in our organization. Nobody else believed her, at least not initially...not even me."

"You say it as if you should have been expected to do so."

"I should have!" Echo exclaimed. "I know her as well as I know my-self! Better than I've ever known anyone else in my life! I trust her with my life! But, dammit, I didn't trust her on THIS. And by the time I figured it out..." He shook his head in disgust and despair at the confession. "It was way the hell too late to really do anything more than...what happened."

"I see. And the damage to her was...severe."

"Very. I'm...not even sure why she's still alive, and I don't think any-body else is, either, to tell the truth. The physicians on Earth are doing everything they can to keep her going until I can get you to her. And I've been hoping and praying that she's not so bad off that you can't..." Echo broke off, unable to voice his biggest fear: that not even Doron's advanced techniques could save her.

"...I understand. How long do we have?" Doron asked, voice soft.

Echo glanced at the MET clock. It read 30:14.

"SHIT! Dammit to hell and back...!"

"What is wrong??" Doron exclaimed, alarmed, as Echo started shut-ting down the warp drive and checking his readouts.

"The clock's frozen. According to the main computer, we took a cos-mic ray burst in the master clock. Multiple-event upsets crashed the clock computer."

"This is serious?"

"Very," Echo replied. "Without it, the navigational computer won't kick us out of warp. And without it, I don't know when to do so manually. I'm gonna have to drop out of warp and try to determine not only where we are, but when."

* * *

"Ind-dia?" Omega murmured, stirring slightly. "India? A-are you there?"

Slumped in one of the visitor chairs, India jerked out of her semi-con-scious state and sat up as Romeo stretched in the next chair.

"Oh, sorry, Meg; I must have dozed off for a few minutes. It's good to have you awake again. How do you feel, honey?"

"The...s-same."

"Whatcha need, Meg?" Romeo asked his friend gently.

"Y'all...p-please...help me st-stay aw-wake?"

India and Romeo glanced at each other.

"Why, Meg?" India asked.

"Ev'ry time I...g-go out...I-I re-relive..."

Alpha Two nodded in unison.

"We'll try," India told her. "Bear with us, and we'll bear with you, honey."

"O-okay..."

"Lemme tell ya a joke I heard the other day..." Romeo began.

* * *

The *Tour de Force* sat stationary in interstellar space, as Echo checked his nav charts against his surroundings. Doron mercifully, Echo thought, remained silent. Finally Echo looked over his shoulder.

"All right. Now I know where we are. But I still don't know WHEN. And unless I can reboot the master clock with the correct time, we can't calculate the hyper-relativistic time distortion effects for another warp jump."

"Can you not calculate them yourself?"

"Sure, but not in my lifetime. There's a reason why this bird uses a megaCray Black Storm 2.1 micro petacomputer. Maybe Meg or one of the guys in Astronav could, but...you can't hit the ball if you can't get to it. Or can I...?"

"What is a 'megaCray'? What is a petacomputer? What is 'Astronav'...? Why do you call your partner 'Meg' ? Is not her name actually Omega...?"

Echo thought for a minute, trying to ignore Doron. Finally he'd had enough.

"Doron, I need you to be quiet for a few minutes. I'm gonna try a long shot," he said then.

* * *

"What is a 'long shot' ?" Doron asked.

Echo suddenly twisted in his seat to glare over his shoulder at the small physician, who blinked disconcerted yellow eyes. The little alien had no clue what the Yellowstone supervolcano was, so had anyone explained that he had just been the recipient of Echo's 'Yellowstone glare,' he would not have understood. Nevertheless, the look conveyed intense annoyance, and implied imminent threat sufficiently well, that Doron found his native curiosity effectively and immediately quenched.

"...All right," Doron acquiesced. "I will be hushed."

He was very relieved when Echo turned back around and leaned back.

I must remember, he is under a great deal of stress, Doron reminded himself. *Perhaps now is not the time for questions, no matter how friendly he seems.*

* * *

Echo leaned back in the seat, concentrating on Omega's picture, then he closed his eyes, opened up, and tried to reach out.

Meg? Meg, it's Echo. Are you there? Can you hear me? Are you there, baby? I got a problem, and I need your help, kinda bad. I need you to do something for me.

Echo paused, listening fixedly, his whole being on alert.

Meg, it would be really good if you answered me, about now...

Silence.

It figures, Echo thought to himself with an inaudible sigh. *The one time I WANT a telepath in my head, and nobody answers.* Then a thought occurred to him, and his gut clenched into a sickening, hard little knot. *What if she's already...No. Not that.* He sent out a plea. *Meg...hang on. Just a little longer, baby, please. Hold on for me. Just a little longer. I'm coming, as fast as I can.*

"Okay," he murmured aloud, putting the worry aside for the time. "Looks like we're on our own. Let's see..."

* * *

Echo spent some time searching for another ship in the area with which to communicate; it was by far the simplest way of updating the master clock. Unfortunately, his shortest-distance course to the outer rim had taken the *Tour de Force* well away from the usual interstellar shipping lanes.

"Alone in the middle of nowhere, with no idea what time it is," an exhausted Echo grumbled. "Damn. I'd give an arm to have Omega, or maybe Travis, here right now. The Kirakallans are some of the best organic computers in the universe, and..." Echo stumbled to a stop, then grabbed the nav charts and searched them intensively.

"Damnation!" he exclaimed in disgust. "Where has my brain been? I ought to be able to see the galactic clock from here! All I have to do is find it..." he adjusted sensor parameters. "It won't be naked-eye, that's for sure,

186

not from here..."

"What is the 'galactic clock'?" Doron resumed his questioning. But it was a pertinent question, so Echo didn't mind answering.

"It's a short-period, extremely regular Cepheid variable called ZV Centauri. Should be..." Echo scanned the sky off the port wing, "mmm... Magellanic Clouds are there...so star-hop...to...there! Over in that section of sky." Echo gestured, waving a gauntleted hand at a region of sky, and was suddenly very glad Omega had taken him to visit the Cerro Tololo observatory last month during that South American mission.

"...What is a 'Cepheid variable'?"

"There!" Echo exclaimed, as the sensor readout popped up the variable star in crosshairs. "Now..." Echo began inputting requests to the computer, "absolute magnitude...mm, okay...plot it on the light curve...I know we're past maximum phase, because an MET of 30:14 would be Galactic Mean Time of..." Echo worked feverishly with the computer for a few more minutes. "All right, Doron," he said at last, "it's moment of truth time."

"And 'moment of truth time' is...?"

"In this case, time to reboot. I have to bring all the computers down to get 'em in synch with the master clock."

"And if they do not...'get in synch'?"

"Then we're stuck here until someone finds us, or our air runs out, whichever comes first. And Meg...is dead."

Echo brought all the little ship's computers down, then started bringing them back on-line in a specific sequence—master clock, main computer, warp computer, navigation computer, sensor array.

"All systems on-line!" Echo told Doron with satisfaction. The MET clock updated, and Echo glanced at it, then froze, staring in horror. "Oh, damn..." he whispered, losing some of the color in his face as his head spun and a chill of dread ran through his being.

"What is wrong, Agent?"

"I've been gone from Earth a total of thirty-eight hours and twenty-seven minutes. Omega only had forty-eight hours at most. And we still have about 68,000 light years to go, give or take."

"And this means?"

"It means, Doron...we're not gonna make it in time."

* * *

"What do you intend to do, Agent Echo?" Doron asked, as an intense Echo ran a frenzied sensor scan on local space, then reset the *Tour de Force* to detour slightly closer to the galactic center.

"I'll be damned if I'm going to just give up and let Meg die," Echo replied, vehement. "Doron, how dedicated are you to your profession?"

"I am a healer," Doron replied simply. "I do what is necessary to heal."

"Are you willing to risk your life?"

"A healer who goes into plague-ridden areas, as I do, is constantly risking its life, Agent Echo. We must do it, or give up being healers. So, to save the life of your...what was it...partner? Yes, I am willing."

"You don't know her—you've never met her."

"That is unimportant," Doron told him. "In any event, I have met you, Agent Echo. I judge you to be a man of honor, a man of heart as well as intellect. If you value your partner highly enough to risk your life, I can do no less."

Echo nodded in grudging respect.

The little alien dude might be annoying as hell at times, Echo thought, *but he's got guts. If he has the skill to go along with it...Meg might just have a chance.*

"All right, then. It's only fair that you know what we're gonna try. Do you know what a cosmic string is?"

"No."

"How 'bout a black hole?"

"Yes."

"Okay, that's a start. It's a lot more complicated than this, but imagine if you grabbed a black hole and stretched it out in a line, and it stayed stretched. That'd be like a cosmic string, sort of."

Doron paused for a moment, apparently wrapping his mind around the concept.

"Very well. Continue," he said then.

"I managed to create a wormhole to speed things up on my way to pick you up, but a battle—with that same Cortian slaver ship that nearly killed

Meg and was trying to catch me a second time—collapsed it. The collapse should've left behind a cosmic string."

"A...wormhole?"

"A tunnel in spacetime. A short cut."

"Ah. All right, Agent Echo. I understand you so far. What will a cosmic string do?"

"It isn't what it will do. It's what we're gonna do TO it."

"Which would be?"

"We're going to jettison the entire warp pod into it right after we kill the warp regulator. The warp pod will run wild, and when it hits the cosmic string, there'll be a huge warp in Minkowski space."

"Min...Minkowski...?" Doron echoed.

"Minkowski space. Spacetime."

"Oh. But is not the warp pod..."

"Our main propulsion system. Right," Echo finished for him. "Which means, if this doesn't work, we're stuck here...and we'll die. If it DOES work, we'll have a split-second to cross the warp and try to hit the Sol system."

"Agent, I have a question," Doron asked Echo.

Just one? That's a switch, he thought. What he said was, "Um, okay. Shoot."

"...I...do not have a weapon..."

"I meant ask your question," Echo sighed. *I have GOT to talk to Fox about updating the English BLT...*

"Oh. Well, if you created a wormhole going one way, why do you not create one the other way?"

"Well, Doron, maybe I could. But the *Tour de Force* took a lot of punishment going through the wormhole the first time, not to mention the dogfight with the Cortians. I've been looking at the ship's status, and I don't think it would make the distance through another wormhole, assuming I could even generate another one. At least this way, Meg has a chance."

"All right, Agent Echo. What is the Terran expression? Ah, yes—'I'm with you.'"

"Let's do it, then."

* * *

"Doron, we're in position," Echo told the alien physician a little while later. He set the DAP to stationkeeping, then made sure all the loose items in the cabin were stowed, tethered, or otherwise fastened down. "I'm going EVA to arm the jettison mechanism. Make sure you're strapped in." He clipped a suit tether to the anchor at his right hand. "Do you see the tether reel at your waist?"

"Yes, Agent. What is 'EVA'?"

"'Extra-Vehicular Activity'—a spacewalk," Echo added quickly as he saw Doron's mouth open again."Hook the tether to the titanium anchor ring on your right, and tighten your seat straps. I'm about to pop the canopy."

"...I have done so. What is 'pop the canopy'?"

"You're gonna find out right now. Here goes." Echo released the canopy latches, and the cabin outgassed into space as the canopy hatch smoothly tilted upward. Then Echo unstrapped from the seat and floated free. Working his way slowly out of the cockpit cabin, unfolding his tall form as he went, Echo began moving aft, hand-over-hand along the starboard side of the *Tour de Force*, using the built-in hand grips. The tether at his waist automatically unreeled as he progressed.

"All right, I'm here." Echo maneuvered around until he could reach the jettison arming panel, then clipped a short, fixed-length tether to an anchor on the spacecraft's side to hold himself in place. With some effort, he worked the toes of his boots into the attached foot restraints on the fuselage. "There. Now..." he pulled the EVA toolkit from its stowage location on a velcro patch on his left thigh and hooked it to a D-ring at the suit's waist. Opening the kit, he removed an electronic screwdriver; it automatically tethered itself to his gauntlet, and he set to work removing the jettison arming panel on the warp pod.

"Agent Echo?"

"What is it now, Doron?"

"Why can you not jettison the warp pod from within the cabin?"

"I can, and I will. But I have to disconnect it from the interplanetary prop system first, or we'll be dead in space. This is an experimental spacecraft, so the regular jettison assumes an emergency in the entire prop system, and dumps the whole damn thing."

By now, Echo's gauntleted hands were deep in the guts of the *Tour de Force*. Carefully, he rerouted systems, working delicately to disconnect the pyrotechnic bolts surrounding the interplanetary drive—one wrong move could trigger the explosive devices.

But before he was even close to removing the pyro from the loop, a soft *beep!* sounded in his headset. Multiple tiny red lights began illuminating all around the periphery of the drive unit, and a heads-up display popped up in his helmet visor.

"Aw, shit," Echo grumbled, as he read the display. "What the hell were they thinkin'?"

"What is wrong, Agent?"

"The dudes in R & D miswired this thing. When I tried to disconnect the explosive bolts, they armed instead. And I don't see a way to undo that, that won't take way longer to do than we really have time to fool with. I'm gonna have to do this with the pyro armed, and hope I don't blow myself to Kingdom Come in the process."

"That...is not good."

"Not by a long shot. Pun intended. Doron, if you believe in a deity, you might wanna start praying, 'cause I'm gonna need it."

"Understood. I think that I—"

"And I really need you to stay as quiet as you can, so I can concentrate. One wrong move and I'm dead immediately. But you'll sit here alone for a couple of days...until your oxygen runs out."

Doron silenced instantly.

As he spoke, Echo had been studying the overall layout of the pyro bolts relative to the interplanetary drive. *I'm gonna have to be awful damn careful, or it really IS gonna be a bad day,* he thought. *If just one of those goes, it could take my arm off. Or a leg, or my head. And then I'll be meeting Meg's parents, I suppose, regardless of which it turned out to be. Then again, I wouldn't have to wait very long for her to show up and introduce us.* The thought brought him up short. *I guess I'll be seeing her soon, either way.* A certain comfort washed through him at that notion, and the knot in his gut relaxed, just a little. *Okay, let's do this. I'd rather not take Doron with us if it comes to that, anyway.*

A cautious Echo reached into the propulsion unit and resumed work, disconnecting some wires and reattaching them elsewhere, and clipping others outright. *I gotta be careful not to touch the wrong leads, though,* he realized, *or I really WILL go to meet Meg and her folks awful quick...and leave Doron stranded, permanently...and terminally. And other people need that little guy besides us.*

Oddly, the thought—which would have set another man trembling—made Echo's hands rock-steady, his mind clear and sure. And while the pyro-arming complication made an otherwise long task even longer and more grueling, Echo simply concentrated on one connection at a time. Occasionally he absently sipped from the water mouthpiece at his chin, and a couple of times he heard the suit's cooling mechanism kick into a higher mode, but in general he ignored these distractions.

And for a wonder, Doron kept quiet, though from time to time and in the back of his mind, Echo registered the soft sounds of breath in his headset, breath that was not his own.

One at a time, he told himself over and over as he concentrated on his task. *One at a time.* Somehow he also managed to force himself not to look at the clock on his heads-up display. Doggedly Echo continued work, and finally had all of the pyrotechnic bolts around the interplanetary prop unwired or otherwise deactivated, and the prop itself disconnected from the interstellar propulsion system.

Then he specifically ensured that all of the pyro bolts anchoring the warp pod in place were still wired into the circuit and armed, before he carefully replaced the panel on the side of the ship's fuselage. Once that was complete, he put away his tools and sighed in relief.

"I'm done, Doron," he told the little alien then, as he untethered from the rear of the craft and started the slow trip back to the cabin. "I'm on my way back to the cockpit."

* * *

"How is she?" a worried Fox whispered to Alpha Two, as he entered the darkened room in the medlab. India and Romeo looked up.

"Fading, Fox," India murmured, glancing aside at the bed which contained Omega, and seeing the ravaged form still and quiet. A quick look at the vitals displays easily confirmed India's diagnosis, even to Fox's less-knowledgeable eye. "She's out again."

"Back into th' coma?" Romeo wondered. India studied the vitals display in more detail.

"Yeah, Romeo, she is. Even despite your jokes. Or maybe because of." She threw her partner and lover a grin that attempted to be humorous, but somehow still failed. He returned it in kind, then sighed.

Fox watched in sorrow as the weary couple's countenances immediately fell.

I could readily view her as my own daughter, he thought, mournful. *And was starting to, especially given how Echo feels about her...and how I suspect she might feel about him. And India and Romeo are already dealing with the grief right now, being forced to sit and watch her deteriorate. It's written all over their faces. This is going to hurt all of us. Tsu aldi rukhes. Time to do what I came here to do.*

He waved them out of the room into the corridor, closing the door behind him. Omega had sharp hearing, even with the shell of one ear gone, and he did NOT want her to hear the conversation that was about to ensue, should she wake. Then he turned to Alpha Two.

"She's not going to make it, is she?" he queried, sick at heart.

"Not without a miracle, Fox," India replied, amber eyes glimmering more than normal. "And unless Echo gets back with this Doron soon, and Doron's medical tools include a magic wand, I don't see one coming. At least, not in time."

"Damn," Fox mumbled, guilt layering on top of grief. *And it's partly my fault. I should have told the Ennead to go to hell, and acted on my Agents' knowledge and gut reactions.*

"No, Fox, don't go there, man," Romeo murmured. "I see that expression. Saw it on Echo's face, too. Y'all gotta do whatcha gotta do. She understood that. Ain't none of us knew how t' handle this. Ain't no human ever been able t' do what Meg did. Leastways, not th' way she did it."

"I know, Romeo, but..." Fox sighed, and dismissed the topic of conversation. "Never mind, son. My conscience is neither here nor there, for the purposes of this discussion. I came to get a status report, and figure out what to tell Echo when he comes out of warp in-system."

"You heard from him?" India asked, straightening up.

"No, the experimental ship he's in doesn't have interstellar communications," Fox explained. "Until Echo commandeered it, it hadn't been far enough out of the system to need it, and it would have meant additional equipment and power draw that R & D didn't want to fool with yet. But Indak contacted Doron's homeworld about half an hour ago, and got word that Doron left with Echo around twelve hours back. So I'm expecting Echo to arrive in Sol system in about three or four more hours."

"Cuttin' it close, man," Romeo decided.

"Probably too close," India agreed. "And speaking of close, I dunno how Echo is going to react if he's on approach and gets word Meg...didn't make it."

"I've been wondering the same thing," Fox affirmed. "I'm thinking maybe I shouldn't give him any information on Air-to-Ground, just tell him to bring it on home."

"I think that's a good plan, Fox," India decided.

"Me, too," Romeo added. "I mean, we all know those two 're thick as thieves. Y' almost never see one without th' other these days."

"I know," India said, smiling softly. "I've teased 'em about being conjoined twins more than once."

"Really? How do they react?" Fox wondered, curious. *At least maybe I can provide Echo some closure on how Omega felt about him,* he thought. *Then maybe I'll give him some counseling followed by extended leave time, to get over her...if he can.*

"Meg jus' grins, an' Echo snorts," Romeo answered, grinning himself. Then he sobered. "Well...they did. I don't guess they'll be doin' that any more, huh?"

Nobody said anything to that.

* * *

Halfway back to the cockpit, Echo discovered a legacy the Cortians had left for him, as a hand hold, evidently damaged in battle, broke away in his hand as he gripped it.

194

"Aw, hell," Echo muttered in intense disgust as he drifted away from the *Tour de Force.* "That's just great. The way my luck's been running, the damn tether will probably snap, next."

But it didn't, and as an anxious Doron watched from the the rear seat of the cabin, Echo braked the tether reel, coming to a gradual stop. Then he slowly reeled himself back in, toward the cockpit.

Once there, he gingerly folded himself back into the cabin, being especially careful not to catch the suit on anything. *A suit rupture would REALLY make my damn day,* he thought, sardonic. *And not do Meg any favors either, for that matter. Meeting her in the hereafter is one thing. But I'd much rather us both live a while longer and get some serious work done together. Not to mention just enjoying being together, whether we ever become lovers or not.*

Back in the pilot's seat, Echo strapped in, sealed the hatch, and untethered. Only then did he allow himself a moment to catch his breath.

"I'd forgotten just how much I hate EVAs," he muttered to himself. Then he allowed himself to look at the MET clock.

MET 42:51. His spacewalk had lasted almost four and a half hours. Omega was nearly gone. And that was assuming the doctors had been able to keep her going the full two Earth days while he had traveled to pick up Doron and bring him to Earth.

"Hang on..." Echo whispered again, looking at the small photo in the corner of his control panel. *Do you hear me, Meg? Don't let go. Don't you dare let go. Just hang on and wait for me, baby. I'll be there soon. One way or another.*

"Time to do it, Doron," he continued in a normal voice. "Ready?"

"If you say we are ready, then *I* am ready," Doron replied, game.

"Let's do this thing, then. First things first. I gotta kill the warp regulator..."

Echo entered a passworded command into the master computer, and watched in satisfaction as gauges all over the cockpit control panel began to redline. The master alarm went off, and he promptly silenced it. A countdown clock started in one corner of the computer display.

"There we go. Now to jettison the warp pod..."

He keyed in several more commands, then flipped up a small plexiglas cover in the far corner of the control panel and depressed the red button underneath. A deep *WHUMP* shook the *Tour de Force* as the pyro bolts detonated, and the runaway warp pod cleared the ship's aft.

Echo used maneuvering thrusters to temporarily increase the distance between the scout ship and the warp pod, then yawed until he was facing the cosmic string. It was visible only as a distortion of the background stars, but Echo wasn't worried about the warp pod missing it. The string's self-gravitation would pull the pod unerringly into itself.

Echo put the ship's sensors on maximum range, full scan, and instructed the sensor array to search for the Sol neighborhood. He tied the sensors into the navcomp with a command to initiate interplanetary drive at maximum velocity on a direct course for Earth as soon as the system was detected.

Echo gradually edged his little ship nearer the cosmic string, following the warp pod in, as the timer on the screen counted down.

At 00:00:02 seconds, the warp pod disappeared into the cosmic string.

"Hang on, Doron. Here we go..." Echo punched the drive, and they dove toward the cosmic string.

The clock tripped 00:00:00.

The *Tour de Force*'s navcomp engaged, and the little ship veered to port as it shot forward.

The universe turned wrong-side out.

* * *

They were everywhere, and nowhere. As the cosmic string wrapped in on itself, the *Tour de Force* plunged headlong into the massive Minkowski space warp, disappearing from regular spacetime at the same time its n-dimensional projection appeared throughout spacetime.

Echo saw his partner lying in a medical bed at Agency HQ at the same time he saw Doron's homeworld, now free of Vegan ebola; at the same time he saw the political machinations in the Va'du'sha'ān capitol; at the same time he saw the negotiations between the Caltorians and the Ulyffon Allance; at the same time...he heard Omega's moan of pain, the Edeptan children at play, the negotiators' arguments...

Echo's eyes glazed; he withdrew mentally, and felt himself losing his grip on reality.

Sensory overload, he thought, dazed and disoriented. *I'm about to go insane—literally.* Instinctively, he shut his eyes, trying to block out the images, the sounds, smells, tastes, touches. *Need to focus...just one thing... block everything else out...*

Omega.

She was the whole point of this exercise in astrophysical insanity. If he was her lifeline, SHE would be his anchor. He concentrated, blocking everything else out of his mind but the thought of his partner. She needed him...needed Doron.

DORON...

"Doron!!" Echo cried. "You okay?"

"I...I..."

"Pick one thing and focus on it!! Block everything else out! You'll go crazy if you don't!"

"Focus...on WHAT?! There is...EVERYthing..."

"I dunno! Something you like! Wait! Make that, 'The thing—or being—you love most in your life.' And CLOSE YOUR EYES!"

"Oh! I...yes...yes...that...that is...better..."

"Hang on, Doron!" *You too, Meg,* he thought. *I'm coming!* Echo thought of her laughing with him a few days before, over one of Romeo's jokes; of the spark in her eyes when he had made light of her fears regarding the Cortians. He forced himself to remember the nightmare that had been her agonized, burning body lying on top of his, shielding him in the spacecraft hangar.

That recollection very effectively blotted out all other sensory input, he found. He also discovered that the memory was still just as vivid as the events themselves had been, and showed no indication of ever fading. His face twisted in a grimace of helpless pain as the full scenario played itself out again on the screen of his mind.

The navcomp alarm sounded and Echo jerked to alertness, opening his eyes and surveying the region around the ship.

Normal space, he realized. They were out of the warp...but where? *And just as important...when?*

"Doron, we're through. You can relax...for now."

"Where are we?" the little physician asked.

"I'm checking that right now," Echo told him. Then he saw a familiar sight—a gas giant planet with one leering, bloodshot eye, surrounded by a myriad of satellites. Echo scanned the sky. "Constellations look right, too," he murmured. "Thanks, Meg; you're a damn fine teacher, babe. Navcomp shows..." He checked the readouts, then nodded. "Well, only one way to know for sure." He keyed the external broadcast mic. "Division One Agency Ground Control, this is the *Tour de Force*. Do you copy?"

Static.

"Division One Agency Ground Control, this is Alpha Line Chief Agent Echo, on board the *Tour de Force*. Do you read?"

More static. Nothing but static. An invisible, cold hand reached into Echo's belly and grabbed a fistful of his entrails, sending a wave of dismay and dread flooding his being.

Wrong time? he wondered. *If we came out in the wrong era, if this is Earth before radio comm, we're hosed. And my baby's dead.*

"Division One Agency Ground Control," he tried again. "This is Echo aboard the *Tour de Force*. Please come in."

"*Tour de Force*, this is Agency Ground Control. Welcome home, Echo," Fox's voice abruptly sounded in his headset, and Echo drew a deep, shuddering breath of relief. "You're early."

"Yeah, we busted ass, and then some. Fox—how's Meg?"

"...Bring it on in, Echo. You're authorized to return to launch site."

"Penn Station? Wilco. But, Fox, what about..." A thought struck him. "Fox, verify my Mission Elapsed Time..." Echo tensed, waiting.

"Well, Echo, we just had a helluva spacetime distortion wave come through, and we don't have all the clocks recalibrated yet. But I'm showing you've been gone something like one-point-eight work shifts. Call it... forty-three and a half hours, give or take a little."

"All right; that squares with my calculations. Now, Fox, tell me—"

"Did you make it back with the doctor?"

"Affirmative. I've got Doron right here, in the back seat." Echo's lips tightened as Fox evaded his questions. "Fox, answer me—"

"Great. Come on home, Echo. Good to have you back."

"...Roger. Tell the R & D folks that the *Tour de Force* is a little worse for the wear. Incoming."

A grim Echo set a course for Earth at maximum interplanetary speed.

* * *

Once on the ground and out of the tiny spacecraft, Echo moved out at speed; Doron had to jog to keep up, thankful that he stayed in shape.

But the swift pace covered ground rapidly, and within scant minutes the pair was in an emergency maglev; moments after that, they were in Headquarters.

Echo made a beeline for Medical.

* * *

Without even slowing down, Echo led Doron, both still in spacesuits, into the Agency medlab, where they met Fox in the ICU waiting room.

Fox spotted the diminutive physician behind Echo, and stopped dead in surprised recognition. Doron ran forward several steps, yellow eyes wide.

"Levy?" Doron queried, shocked. "Franz Levy? Is that you?"

"Doron!" Fox exclaimed. "I knew I recognized your name when Indak recommended you! I just couldn't pull the memory up with it! It's been a long time."

"It has! You are no longer with Lord Entiyti?"

"No, when Earth entered the PGLEIA, Pul decided I needed to come back and aid that situation."

"And now you head the division."

"Right. Good to see you again!"

"And you, though I could wish it were under different circumstances."

"Ain't that the truth."

"Fox?" Echo interrupted; the Agent had stood back in respect while his Director greeted the physician, but now he required information. "Where is—?"

"Oh! Sorry. Room twenty-one, Echo." Fox waved him past.

"Got it," Echo said.

"Doron, the medics are waiting for you to brief them in Lab B," Fox added. "I'll take you to them."

"Um, Fox?" Echo queried again, seeming slightly hesitant, but urgent for all that. "I hate to bother you with this, being the Director and all, but..."

"What do you need, zun?"

"Would you mind getting someone to drop by with a change of clothes for me and something that'll fit Doron? So we can get outta these space-suits?"

"Ah, of course. On it, Echo," Fox said, pulling his cell phone.

* * *

When Echo entered Omega's room, he saw a hospital bed with one side against the far wall of the room. Omega lay on it, face down, IV established, tubes and monitors everywhere, a white sheet tented over her so as not to contact her badly-damaged form. Soft clicks, whirs, beeps, and hums floated through the air, as the various pieces of medical equipment performed their intended functions.

India sat in a chair near Omega's head; Romeo leaned against the right-hand wall near her feet. Both of them had their arms folded and their heads bowed. They looked up silently with tired, haggard expressions as he entered. He nodded briefly to Alpha Two in acknowledgement and greeting, but Echo moved directly to the bedside.

"Meg?" he said softly. She gave no answer. "Meg, it's Echo. I'm back."

Still she made no response. He looked questioningly at India, feeling the blood drain from his face, even as that same cold, spectral hand gripped another fistful of his guts.

"Am I too la...?"

"She's been slipping in and out of a coma for the last thirty-six hours or so." India shook her head. "It's been touch and go, Echo."

"Can she hear me?"

"I don't know—"

"Y-yes, Echo..." the whisper came from the bed. "I...h-hear..."

Echo moved to the head of the bed and crouched down to look Omega in the eyes.

"I'm back," he said quietly. "And I brought Doron." He nodded at the alien healer, who had just entered in regular Earth clothing and now began a delicate examination of Omega's injuries. Romeo moved around to sit in the chair beside India's, in deference to Omega's modesty.

"Wel-welcome h-home, hon."

"Thanks, baby. How are you?" Echo continued as a medtech brought in his Suit, placing the clothes hangar on a hook on the wall. Echo nodded at the medtech in thanks, and the tech nodded once and departed.

"'Bout as well as...c'n be 'spected...of a ch-charcoal briq-uette," Omega said, trying to smile. Her lip cracked and started to bleed.

Without a word, India handed Echo a square of gauze, and he very delicately blotted the blood away, his touch as gentle as he could make it. Omega still winced.

* * *

"Y'know," Omega added, "considerin' all th' n-nerve endings are...s'posed t' be b-burned aw-way...not t' mention m' sp-spine...I sure...h-hurt like bl-blazes..." She saw Echo's lopsided grin. "What?" Omega mentally replayed her statement, then groaned. "Oooh...th-that was t-terrible. S-sor-ry."

"Always with the situational-appropriate descriptors, baby," he murmured.

"I kn-know. Somet-times...I p-plan 'em, just t' s-see your re-a-action. Not-not this t-time, though."

"Do you need more pain medication?" Echo asked, still in the same soft tone.

"Echo," India interjected, "she's not on any pain medication."

* * *

"What?!" Echo stood up and looked at India in shock and anger. "Why the hell aren't y'all treating her pain?! I told you and Romeo to look after her, not let her lie here and suffer!"

"Echo, you don't understand! We have been! Analgesics are...worthless for this. Local anesthesia would irritate the damaged tissue. And general anesthesia and narcotics...in her condition...Look, we tried already. That's what put her in a coma, Echo. We could've lost her. We almost DID. It's why we STOPPED the pain medication." Doron listened quietly, then stepped out. Echo shook his head, then dropped his gaze to the floor in an apologetic fashion.

"All right," he murmured, anger evaporated. "Sorry I lost my temper, there. But...damn."

"Don't worry, hon; I totally get it, believe me. It was that same feeling you've got now that drove me to give her the dose that brought on the coma," India added.

"Sh-she's been w-worried," Omega noted, "'at it was g-gonna d-do me in b-b'fore you c-could get ba-ack."

"Aw shit," India muttered in consternation, and Echo glanced between the two, disturbed. "I thought I hid it better than that."

"'S o-ka-ay," Omega murmured. "I-I know h-how it wo-orks, h-hon."

"Well, it didn't," Echo soothed. "I'm back, I brought Doron, and everything will be okay now."

"H-hope so," Omega panted.

"Hey, look Echo, go ahead and change. I'll leave for a moment," India added, heading for the door.

"Thanks, India. I'm afraid a spacesuit's not too comfortable on the ground," Echo said, as she exited.

With an obviously painful effort, rendered worse by the extensive damage to the back of her neck, Omega turned her face to the wall to give Echo privacy as he shed the spacesuit—not that he minded, in the circumstances; it was Meg, after all.

Sooner or later, he thought absently, as he watched her while peeling off the spaghetti suit, *I'd kinda LIKE for her to get a look. More than, to tell the truth. Er.* He broke off that thought, realizing where he was and who was nearby. *Pay attention to what you're doin', Echo, boy,* he told himself, throwing a sidelong glance at Romeo to see if he'd noticed Echo's abstraction. *Now is NOT a good time to go THERE. You're buck naked at the moment.*

Romeo hadn't noticed Echo's distraction, or much of anything else, being busy getting the Suit garments ready for Echo to don in their logical sequence. So he focused on getting himself properly attired. Romeo handed him items of clothing as he quickly dressed. Echo looked back at Romeo as he adjusted his tie.

"No painkillers? The whole time?"

"Almost the whole time," Romeo responded with a nod. "Jus' the once. Like India said, 's what put her in a coma in the first place. India said she was too sensitive to it, especially in her condition."

"B-been goin'...in an' out...ev-ever since," Omega added.

Echo turned back to his partner and instinctively reached out to lay a compassionate hand on her exposed shoulder, then froze, as he thought better of the contact with the dreadfully mutilated area. His hand hovered over her for a long moment, as he debated. Then he knelt back down as Romeo went to get India.

"Meg, I was gonna put my hand on your shoulder, but..."

"No! Not...a g-good p-plan. I feel like...t-that archaeolog-gist in th' mo-movie...that got beat u-up...'n when 'is gir-girlfriend asked...w-where it d-didn't hurt...he p-pointed to...his elb-bow." Omega glanced at her arms with a dry sob. "...I d-don't ev-even...have elbows-s..."

"Is there anywhere it isn't painful to touch you?"

"Yeah...one 'r two...b-but if mah daddy was s-still al-ive...he'd take a sh-shotgun to ya f'r tryin'..." Omega's eyes twinkled at her partner even through a haze of pain, and Echo smiled back at her as shadowed brown eyes darkened almost to black.

Romeo, India, Doron, and two Agency doctors that Echo didn't recognize entered the room just then. One of the Agency medics came to stand beside Echo.

"Omega, it's time to prep you," the medic said quietly.

Omega shut her eyes then, all trace of levity gone, and to Echo's shock, started trembling. He just made out her nearly-inaudible whisper.

"God, please...Ah'm so t-tired...h-help me g-get through this...or-or else t-take me out now...h-how much mo-more...?"

"Meg?? Baby, what's wrong? They're gonna get you ready to get well, babe. Why is that upsetting you like this?"

"You d-d-don't unders-stand, hon. Look, j-just go, Echo," Omega whispered hoarsely. "You've al-ready seen...and d-done...enough. India, get him 'n Romeo...an' y'all g-get outta h-here..." India waved Romeo back toward the door and took Echo's arm, leading—all but dragging—him out the door.

* * *

Out in the corridor, Echo turned to Alpha Two.

"India? What's happening? What was that all about? Meg looked... actually SCARED."

"C'mon, Echo," India said, heading down the hall at a fast clip. "You too, Romeo."

Halfway down the hallway, all three Agents instinctively wheeled around at the sound of an agonized cry.

"That was Meg!" Romeo exclaimed, starting to run back to the room.

"NO, Romeo!" India cried, grabbing Romeo's arm and body-checking Echo into the corridor wall with all her strength. "There's nothing you can do. They're being as gentle as they can."

"What in God's name are they doing?" Echo demanded, appalled, as another cry was wrenched out.

"They're prepping her," India answered, looking at Echo with anguished eyes. "Indak briefed us medics—and Meg—while you were gone. According to Doron's procedure, in a case like this, before new, healthy tissue can grow...they have to remove as much of the damaged and dead tissue as possible. It's called debridement."

The two men stood immobile, staring dumbfounded at India, as the full implication of her statement hit them, and Echo recalled his own sense of foreboding as he had helped 'prep' his spacecraft back on Edeptis, cutting and pulling away the rotting strips of coating after the Vegan ebola devastated its surface. Then Echo spun on his heel and headed back toward Omega's room.

"Echo! No! Stop—you don't know what you're walking into!"

"Right the opposite, India. I know just as much as Meg did in the hangar," Echo threw over his shoulder, and kept going.

* * *

When Echo appeared in the door, the tented sheet was gone, revealing the full extent of the damage to Omega's nude, ravaged body. The medics had temporarily stopped their work and were supporting Omega's head and shoulders as she dry-retched from pain-induced nausea. A pan rested on a shelf beneath her head, in the extremely unlikely instance of there being anything in her to come up. An IV bag of lavender solution dripped directly into the jugular vein in her neck; her arms were too badly damaged to have blood vessels viable for such use.

The medics looked up with tortured eyes and saw him, then nodded. Echo silently walked over and changed places with the doctor at Omega's head.

Struggling to remain impassive even as his heart threatened to shatter, Echo surveyed the ruined body of his partner—the body he had tenderly put to bed once before, privately admiring its beauty, even in the emaciated wake of an insane telepath's machinations—and the progress the doctors had made in their procedure. Then, wordlessly, he knelt before Omega.

"Echo...?!" Omega gasped. "I th-thought I...told y-you to...go..."

"I did. I came back."

"You c-can't...AAAH!...d-do anyth-thing..." The doctors had resumed their grisly task.

She sickened again, and Echo lightly sponged her face with a cool compress that Doron handed him. Then Omega tried to look back over her shoulder to see what the doctors were doing. Echo cupped a compassionate hand around her cheek, blocking her view, and gently turned her head back around to face him.

'Be there for me, backing me up...like partners do...' Yeah. I can do that.

"Sure I can do something. I seem to recall a postponed conversation..." Echo told her quietly.

Chapter 6

By the time it was over nearly two hours later, Omega had mercifully lapsed back into unconsciousness.

Doron quickly had the Agency medics hook up another bag of the peculiar lavender solution to her IV, then soak a sheet in the same solution to drape over the raw lump of flesh that now was Omega's body, keeping the tissues moist and viable.

Then he called Romeo, India, and Fox in to join Echo and Omega.

* * *

Soft muffled sobs rose from the pillow on the bed as Omega slowly regained consciousness. The raw, quivering form under the solution-soaked sheet was vaguely humanoid, but its contours otherwise now bore little resemblance to the Omega they had known.

Romeo and India were both swallowing hard, unable to watch the maimed figure in the bed.

Fox's lips tightened as he glanced at a very pale Echo, standing protectively over his partner, his hand resting, feather-light, on the denuded back of her head—the part that still had scalp, at any rate—as his fingers caressed, offering gentle, wordless comfort. Echo returned Fox's look remotely, dispassionately, as if he viewed them from a great distance.

"Well?" asked Fox, turning to Doron then. "Can you help her? Like you did me, once upon a time?"

"Oh, yes," Doron answered, confident. "This too is well within Edeptan medical technology. We will help her body to regenerate its own tissue. We must move her into the regeneration chamber very soon now, to begin the new tissue growth while the exposed tissue is still viable."

"Good," Fox declared.

"But," Doron continued, "I need to know how far to take the process. Are you aware Omega has been restructured, relative to normal Terran physiology?"

"Yes, we know about it. She was abducted as a child by a psychopathic gastropoid named Slug," Fox nodded, "and altered to be...more than she was before...in a revenge plot directed against..." he shot a quick glance at Echo, who stared back in inscrutable silence, "the Agency."

"Aha." Doron moved to stand beside Echo, and addressed the injured Agent in a soft voice. "Omega? Perhaps you would like to return COMPLETELY to normal, to the genetic configuration with which you were born? Without all of the artificial manipulation?"

The room became a babel of voices. Doron calmed everyone down and explained.

"The regeneration bath being prepared in the neighboring laboratory can be adjusted, within limits, to accommodate the healing needs of the patient. If Omega so desires, not only can the burned tissue be replaced, but her body can be restructured to its original...parameters. The effects of the alterations would be removed."

Echo knelt by Omega's bed, and spoke for the first time since Fox had entered the room. His voice was soft and encouraging.

"How about it, Meg? It's your call, baby."

* * *

An expressionless Omega looked at Echo, retreated far within herself. It had been the only way she could endure the procedure so recently concluded. But it left her reluctant to open up once more—her wounds now had raw tissue with exposed nerve endings, and were, if anything, more painful than they had been.

"You could go back to the astronaut corps, if you wanted to," India said softly over Echo's shoulder, and Omega blinked at that, still looking at Echo. She studied the faint hints of expression on his dear, familiar face for several long moments.

"Echo," she said at last, daring to reach out to him, at least, "w-would you m-mind...t-taking the others 'n...go-going outs-side? I need...need to talk to D-Doron...alone..."

* * *

Very soon thereafter, Omega's mutilated form lay completely submerged, floating—neutrally buoyant—in that same pale lavender fluid filling the inside of a horizontal cylindrical pod, a cannibalized hyperbaric chamber, in one of the medlabs. An observing window in the top of the pod enabled Romeo, India, and Echo to look down and see her nude head and shoulders as she drifted in the middle of the liquid. Her eyes were closed.

"She looks like she's comfortable, at least," Echo observed. "Her face is relaxed."

"Yes. No pain, according to the low-resolution cerebral scans," India agreed. "That's a relief. And she's stabilized, too. No more deterioration. She's going to survive." India hesitated. "I'm still not sure how well this is going to work, though. It seems...well, even for the Agency, this seems like only one step removed from a miracle."

"You're trying to warn us, aren't you, India?" Echo commented, turning to look at her. "Trying to warn ME."

"Well...yes. If it works as advertised, Meg will come out of it fine. Her old self, probably in more ways than one. But..." India shook her head. "If, for some reason, it doesn't go as planned...she could come out a cripple, or disfigured, or..." She shrugged. "Alive, true. But...not unscathed."

The three Agents were silent for long moments, pondering the possibilities.

"She not gonna drown in there, is she?" Romeo asked, concerned. "She's...like, breathin' that purple stuff, right?"

"Yes, Romeo, she's breathing it, but she won't drown," India soothed. "Meg's lungs can't tell the regeneration fluid isn't air; it's carefully oxygenated to optimize healing, in addition to providing nutrients and medications to her body to help support healing more directly. And when they take her out, the doctors will drain her lungs quickly, keeping them inflated, and with her next breath, the remaining fluid will volatilize and be exhaled. She'll resume breathing normally again."

"So, soon we'll have our 'pretty lady' back, huh?" Romeo grinned.

"She never left, hot shot," Echo said, mildly enigmatic but wholly philosophical, looking down into the pod. "No matter what happens. Our 'pretty lady' is still right here with us."

* * *

Late on the next shift, having spent the night in the medlab waiting room in case he was needed to decide something on his partner's behalf, a tired Echo sat alone at his desk in the Alpha Line room. It was the first time either of the Alpha One partnership had been in the office in several days—since before the Cortians arrived—and the paperwork had stacked up. Echo was determined to get through it all as fast as possible before heading back to the medlab to check on Omega.

So he sorted it into categories and prioritized the stacks as best he could, then decided the request-and-requisition stack was the most urgent, and the rest could wait. He was processing the departmental requests, when he got a form requesting a half-shift off for Alpha Two. Puzzled, he pulled his cell phone and called them in.

"What's up, guys?" he wondered, as they took desk chairs in front of him. "Not that I have a problem with it, but tomorrow isn't your usual day off, and you're only asking for HALF a day..."

"Wow, he really has been up to his nose," India murmured with a gentle smile.

"Well, yeah, India," Romeo agreed. "Meg, an' flyin' across th' galaxy, an' all. Y' can't expect him to remember shit like that, when there's way th' hell more important stuff goin' down."

"What am I missing here?" Echo asked, puzzled.

"Check the date, man," Romeo offered with a slight grin. Echo noted there was more than a hint of mischief in that grin.

So he pulled his cell phone and opened the calendar app.

"Okay," he noted. "Today's February 13th."

"An' tomorrow is?" Romeo pressed, as India smiled.

"February 14th, obviously— aw, shit," Echo said, smearing a hand down his face. "It's Valentine's Day. And you two..."

"Would like a little extra time off to celebrate," India verified, still smiling. "Not much. Just enough time to fix and eat a nice, candlelight meal for two, and spend the evening together. We'll still be in Headquarters if an emergency comes up, or you need us for something else, like Meg or some such."

"Yeah," Romeo agreed. "India an' I talked it over, an' we didn' wanna head out someplace for a night out, not with ev'rything that's been goin' down. We wanted t' stay close by f'r you an' Meg. So we thought we'd stay home, fix a gourmet meal, enjoy some cuddle time, a little satin an' lace..."

"Shut up now," India said, elbowing him. "Echo does NOT want an earful of TMI."

"Shuttin' up," Romeo said with another grin.

Echo snorted despite himself. Then he ticked a box on the electronic form.

"Request approved," he said, smiling. "Enjoy yourselves, guys. And hey..."

"Yeah?" Romeo said, pausing as he and India headed for the door.

"Thanks, guys. From me AND Meg. For...everything."

"It's what family does, Echo," India observed.

And they were gone.

* * *

Well, damn, Echo thought, morose, after Alpha Two departed. *It'll be Omega's first Valentine's Day in the Agency, AND as my partner. Never mind as the woman I've fallen for, though SHE doesn't know that. At least I don't think she does. And I can't even take Meg to a movie or some such thing. I don't even think she's conscious yet.* Then he paused. *I don't even know if she WILL be conscious. But she might be, even if she doesn't LOOK conscious. So if I do something for Valentine's Day for her, it has to be kinda innocuous, since I still don't know how she feels about me. And damn, but now is NOT the time to lay something like that on her. I want her to heal, not get upset over what she's supposed to feel or not feel. And by now I know her well enough to know—if I blindside her with it, she WILL get upset.*

Echo stared out the door of the Alpha Line room, absently watching various aliens walk through the Core outside, as he considered his personal conundrum.

"I gotta think about this," he murmured. "Maybe I can run out and get some stuff when I'm done here, before I head back to the medlab..."

* * *

The next day, Echo came into the medlab bright and early, carrying several items. The lights were still dimmed for what passed as an evening shift, so he waited in the shadows until there was no one around the door

210

to Lab B, the regeneration pod room, and no one visible inside. Then he slipped in, unseen.

"Okay, baby," he told the silent form inside the pod. "If you're awake in there, you probably don't have a clue what today is, all things considered, but I do. Happy Valentine's Day from your partner, the guy who cares enough about you to fly across the galaxy and back to keep you going at his side. Here."

The sides of the pod were rounded, but the top and bottom were flat-surfaced, creating a kind of lenticular shape in cross-section, and Echo now set a bud vase on that flat surface, just below the observation window. Inside the vase was a single, long-stemmed red rosebud. The positioning was just such that, should Omega manage to open her eyes, she could see the rose from inside the pod and know that someone had thought of her.

Then he pulled a small, oddly-shaped and brightly colored slip of heavy stock paper, almost cardboard, from a pocket, and tucked it into the frame of the observing window, facing down, into the pod, where Omega could likewise read it if she awoke.

Echo cast a quick glance around Lab B, being especially careful to check the corridor outside and ascertain that no one could see into the room, through the porthole in the room's door. Then he dragged his sleeve across his mouth to remove any skin oils or untoward moisture, bent, and gently deposited a kiss on the pod's observing window.

"Best I can do, baby," he whispered to the still, quiet form inside. Then he straightened and told his unconscious partner, "I got work to do, Meg, but I'll come back when I get off shift and have dinner with you. It won't be anything but me eating take-out of some sort, but I'll be here. I swear to you."

Echo turned and slipped out the way he came.

* * *

Fox and Zebra stood beside the regeneration pod in the medlab, surveying the recent additions to the decor. Zebra handed Fox the small piece of colored card stock. It was a Valentine's Day card, of the sort that elementary school children might give each other, and depicted two teddy bears, one male, one female, on a background of purple and pink hearts.

211

The brown male teddy was handing a red heart to the blonde female teddy, and the printed caption read, 'To My Valentine.'

A hand-written addition read,

Miss you, baby. Hurry and get well.

It's a Happy Valentine's Day because we're both still here.

~E.

"And the rose has to be from him." Zebra pointed at the flower. "It and the card appeared this morning at the same time."

"It would seem so," Fox agreed.

"But what on earth...?" Zebra wondered, confused. "Why a kid's card? A strapping, handsome guy like Echo?"

"If you were uncertain of how matters stood between us, or even whether or not I was interested, how serious a card would you give me?" Fox asked. "Especially if you grasped that, should I take it ill, it might destroy the wonderful friendship, the unparalleled working relationship, we already had?"

Zebra's mouth popped open in astonished understanding, and she stared at Fox, round-eyed.

"So," Fox wondered with a wide smile, "are you gonna help me play shadchan for these two yet, or not?"

"Play matchmaker? Um, hell yeah," Zebra agreed, smiling back. "Assuming this whole regen thing goes good, I'm more than game, now." She shrugged. "What do we DO?"

"Is she conscious yet? Does she know he left 'em?" Fox wanted to know.

"Oh no. She's not conscious, and may not be, until she's decanted."

"But you don't KNOW she won't wake up."

"Well, no..."

"All right. Here's what I want you to do, then."

"I'm listening, hon."

"Put the card back, and leave everything just the way he left it for a couple days," Fox instructed. "Until the rose juuust starts to wilt. That way, if she does wake up and opens her eyes, she'll see 'em and can maybe read the card."

"Okay..."

"Then, once the rose starts to wilt, come in here and get it and the card. Pay attention, because Echo might spirit 'em off before you can, and we don't want that. Preserve the rose somehow—dry and press it, or put it in a resin tchotchke, or whatever. YOU know what another woman would like; do that. Put it and the card in with her personal effects, so she gets it all once she gets out. She might not see 'em right away, but eventually she'll find 'em and realize what Echo did. And that might just give her a nudge, at some point, to pay attention to her partner."

"Oh, she pays attention," Zebra noted, tucking the card back into position on the observing window. "She just doesn't know how to..."

"What?"

"Ugh! I dunno if I'm breaching patient confidences," Zebra groaned. Fox rubbed his chin, staring at her in thought, for a long moment.

"I'm the Director, her ultimate supervisor," he pointed out. "If I have a sufficiently important need to know, you'd be justified in telling me, yes?"

"Well, yes, at least to a point," Zebra affirmed. "There's some things she'd never let me tell you or ANYbody, but others I can."

"I'm not asking about those," Fox said with a grin. "It's coming up on first lunch. Will you have time to join me in my office for a bite and a 'medical chat,' if I send Lima or Bravo for Chinese for two? I know you already have something planned for us for tonight..."

"Yeah, I think I can get away."

"Good. Let me run back to my office and see about getting lunch brought in, then, and I'll see you there in a bit. That ought to give me enough time to come up with a reason for you to tell me what's holding her back."

"Not all of it," Zebra warned. "She gave me express instructions."

"And I've probably already deduced about what," Fox said, sobering. "At least, to some degree. If I'm anywhere close to right, I can't say I blame her. But it wouldn't affect this, would it?" He waved a hand at the rose.

"If you mean what I think you do, no, I don't think it would," Zebra said, starting to smile again. "All right. I'll see you in your office in about half an hour."

"Done, bubeleh," he said, leaning over and depositing a kiss on her cheek, before heading out of the medlab.

* * *

Zebra made a point of informing the medics, including Doron, to say NOTHING about the flower and card that had been left on the regeneration pod in Lab B.

"Because they've both gone through hell and back on this one," she observed, "and I dunno about you guys, but I think they've earned the opportunity to say, 'I care,' regardless of HOW. But if you lot go sounding off about it, or worse, TEASING him about it, it'll all disappear before she even has a chance to see it."

"That is true," Doron agreed. "I gathered, during the flight here, that he was quite upset over what had happened, and possibly even blames himself. But he tried very hard to be...what is the word? Circumspect?"

"That's the word," Whiskey averred. "And yeah, that sounds just like Echo. He's got a reputation for being tough, but he looks out for the people around him, too. Especially her. They make a damn fine team, from all I've seen and heard."

"Indeed," Zarnix agreed. "Our tough Agent cares; he just prefers to keep it close to his vest."

"But why?" one of the other medics wondered. "Why does he have to pretend to be such a tough guy?"

"Oh, I got this one," Zebra noted. "I've talked to Omega about this very thing, and Fox agrees. Guys, we aren't field agents. We've never had to face down a perp that has inhuman abilities an' shit. Those guys, they face all kinds of drek, and have to not only come out still standing, they have to bring the bad guys into custody. You can't just pretend that you're tough, you have to really BE tough—and they are, especially those two. There's no pretense there, believe me. Echo IS tough. But he cultivates a reputation for it, because having a tough reputation means that criminals who've heard about that reputation will be more intimidated than they might otherwise be. It makes it just a wee bit easier to take 'em down and bring 'em in."

"Ooo," the medic murmured, and Whiskey whistled. "That makes sense."

"It certainly does," Zarnix averred. "Very well, Zebra. You have made several excellent points today. As Madrid likes to say in our department chief meetings, 'Mum's the word, old girl.'"

"Is that an order, sir?" Zebra asked with a smile.

"Consider it so, yes," an amiable Zarnix said, cheerful.

Nods went all around the room.

* * *

Zebra disappeared into Fox's office for first lunch, and Fox opaqued the bay windows overlooking the Core.

But this was not unusual when there were important and confidential medical matters to discuss, and everyone knew that Omega was in the med-lab, and that it had been touch-and-go with her. So no one thought anything of it.

When Zebra emerged, she was smiling, a mischievous expression. Fox followed her to the door.

"It isn't gonna be easy, ya know," she told him.

"No, it isn't. And it won't be quick, either. Especially given who—and what—they are. But nothing worthwhile ever is. This little mission we've set for ourselves is going to take a while." Fox waved her off. "Back to work with you, bubeleh. We will bide our time."

"Watch and wait?"

"Watch and wait. Get on, now."

"I'm goin', hon. See you tonight."

"I'm looking forward to it."

At the bottom of the ramp, she glanced back up, to see Fox standing on the balcony watching her with the same impish grin she still wore. She gave him a thumbs-up, and he returned it.

Then he went back into his office, as she headed back to the medlab.

* * *

Echo was true to his word: As soon as he got off shift, he left Head-quarters long enough to walk to the deli down the street and get a submarine sandwich and a little individual-serving bottle of wine; upon explaining that his lady friend was 'in the hospital' unconscious, and thus could not celebrate the day with him, the deli owner tucked a plastic disposable wineglass into the bag containing Echo's dinner.

"Dere," the man said, with a gentle smile. "Dat way, it will taste a little better dan from a styrofoam cup, or da bottle. And youse kin look at her over da top as ya drink, and it will taste even better."

* * *

Echo came straight back to the medlab in Headquarters, carrying his take-out dinner directly to Lab B. *It isn't champagne and candlelight,* he thought, stifling a sigh as he dragged a chair up to the side of the regen chamber, *let alone Romeo's 'satin and lace,' but it'll have to do in the situation.*

"Hey, baby," he told Omega's inert form. "I'm back for dinner with you, like I promised. It isn't much, but that's okay, because we're both here and safe, and we're both gonna be all right, you and me..."

He pulled out his sandwich, opened the tiny bottle of wine and poured it into the plastic goblet, then held the glass up, bobbing it in Omega's general direction.

"To Alpha One," he intoned. "Us two...always."

Then he drank.

Omega floated quietly in the regeneration pod, unresponsive.

Echo sighed quietly.

* * *

Three days afterward, the Valentine's card and the red rose, which—despite the water in the bud vase miraculously changing twice a day, a detail which escaped Echo's usually eagle eyes—had 'blown' and was starting to droop, disappeared.

Echo noticed their disappearance, but said nothing.

Damn, he thought, disappointed. *And she's still not conscious.*

* * *

A few days later, Echo walked into the medlab and immediately encountered Doron.

"How is she?" he asked without preamble.

"Ah...greetings, Agent Echo," Doron said, apparently startled by the blunt question sans even a salutation. "You are here to visit your...partner, again?"

"Yes. How is she doing?"

"Truthfully...I am concerned." The little healer frowned.

"What's wrong?" Echo's response was swift, as his intestines abruptly tied themselves into a tight knot.

* * *

"The...manipulations...her body has previously undergone seem to be affecting the tissue regeneration," Doron explained.

"What do you mean? You mean what Slug did to her? The 'enhancements,' she calls 'em?" Echo asked.

"Yes, that."

"Explain."

"Very well, I shall try," Doron said, steepling all eight fingers and letting his yellow eyes go distant as he pondered how to explain to Echo. "Mm. You could, perhaps, think of it as a battle between her artificial genetics and the regeneration biochemistry...each is struggling to overcome the other."

* * *

"Is she in danger?" Echo raked a worried hand through his dark hair, disarranging it.

"No, Agent Echo, I do not believe her life is in danger," Doron soothed. "It is only the complete success of the regeneration over which I am concerned. I did not anticipate...interference."

Echo was silent for a long moment, remembering India's warning.

"So you mean...she'll live, but...she'll be crippled?" he asked finally.

* * *

"...Possibly." Doron scrunched his face in displeasure; it was not something he wanted to admit, but he had also not expected to find the genetic manipulation to be so extensive, let alone so determined to control his patient's body.

"Is there anything I...anything YOU...?"

"I have just come from readjusting the composition of the fluid in the chamber," Doron replied, as comforting as he knew how to be, remembering just how much this Agent secretly cared for his partner, as well as the card and the flower which had appeared on what was, apparently, a special lovers' holiday on Earth. "I believe this will compensate. I will, as you humans say, 'tweak' it over the next few hours, and monitor the changes, and matters should resolve in our favor."

"But you're not sure."

"Not yet."

"How much longer?"

"What do you mean?" The terseness of the question puzzled the alien healer, and he was unsure what Echo was asking.

"How long will it take before you know if what you did will compensate?" Echo asked, more patient than he had been on their journey to Earth....but not by a lot, Doron decided.

Then again, were my desired mate—had I one—in such condition, I might have little patience, too, a compassionate Doron admitted to himself, before answering Echo. "We will know the outcome in...about two Earth days. Ehm, that is one of your Agency's days."

"So when I come by tomorrow, like usual...?" Echo queried.

"I will be able to tell you...one way or the other." Doron nodded. "But go ahead and visit her now."

* * *

I wonder if I SHOULD visit her now... Echo mused, as he entered Lab B, where Omega lay quietly in the regeneration pod. *If she's reading me, she'll know about the problem with her genetics, and that things might not turn out quite as well as we'd all hoped. Dammit.* Then he shrugged. *Hell. If she's reading me, she probably knows already.* He moved over to the chamber and looked down, into the window.

"Hi, Meg. I'm back, baby."

Omega's form drifted silently in the pod.

"Everything's going...fine, Meg." His face tightened slightly as he spoke the comforting lie, and he was glad her eyes were closed; she would've known without doubt that he was lying, otherwise. *Unless you're reading me...but if you are, you understand.* "Doron told me yesterday you'll be in here about a week or so more, but no longer than two more weeks. Then they'll take you out, and...it'll be time to get back to work, partner."

Omega's lips curled upward for just a second, and Echo instantly bent low over the observing window. He rested a hand on each side of the portal, leaned in close, and stared down at her face, watching its every nuance of expression as intently as if he were expecting an alien perp to produce a weapon.

"Meg? Can you hear me?"

He studied his partner's silent form.

"Meg, if you CAN hear me, let me know..."

Her eyelids fluttered momentarily, and Echo nodded.

"That's my girl. Hang in there, Meg." He pulled a chair over to the regen chamber and sat down close enough to allow him to peer directly into the window, his right thigh pressed hard against the side of the tank; if he could have gotten even closer, he would have, if only to provide her the comfort of his nearness. "I'm right here, baby. Wanna know what's happening out here while you're in there?"

Omega floated quietly. But Echo thought he saw a quiver of newly-regrown eyelashes against pale cheeks.

"Well, Fox has got me doing ALL the departmental paperwork while you're in here, basic Alpha Line bureaucratic stuff. Takes me half the damn day just to sort through it all and organize it, and the other half to work my way through it. It's what I get for agreeing to head up the department, I guess. I suppose I didn't really realize before how much of that shit YOU were helping with. I, um, I just wanted to thank you for all of that help, 'assistant to the department chief.' And, uh, to tell you that I'll be damn glad when you're out of here and back with me, working and junk."

Eyelids fluttered briefly, and the corners of Omega's mouth quirked.

"Yeah, I thought you'd get a kick outta that. I mean it, though, I appreciate all of it. Especially...well, saving my ass. I paid it back, in part—the Cortians came after me again, on my way to get Doron, and I took 'em out. For BOTH of us. I was madder than hell."

Eyelids quivered again. Suddenly her face seemed to contort briefly, and she looked for a split-second like she might cry. The readings on the bank of monitors nearby jumped to elevated levels.

"No, no, baby!" Echo exclaimed in alarm, standing up and leaning over the pod, bracing an arm on either side of the viewing window. "Don't cry, Meg. I'm sorry. I shouldn't have said anything. I just…I'm trying to tell you how much I appreciate you. That's all."

The door burst open and Doron, Zarnix AND Zebra entered at speed. A worried Echo pushed up from the pod, straightened, and turned to meet them.

"What's happening?" Zebra demanded. "Is she okay? Did you see anything?"

"Um," Echo said, feeling his face flush, "yeah. Meg and I were talking…"

"She cannot talk, Agent Echo," Doron pointed out. "She is in the regeneration chamber."

"You don't know me and my partner, Doron," Echo said with a slight, rueful smile. "Meg and I can talk all day long and not SAY a word. We got codes and gestures and shit, for when we're on a field assignment."

"Are you saying she is awake, and you were communicating with her?" Zarnix wondered, surprised.

"That's exactly what I'm saying, Zarnix."

"But I thought the healing would take up the energy…I expected she would be unconscious…" a thoughtful Zarnix murmured. "Doron, is it possible?"

"Given the unusual nature of Agent Echo's partner, I should say yes," Doron decided after a moment to consider the matter.

"Prove it," Zebra demanded. "And why did her vitals spike?"

"Uh, well, like I said, we were talking," Echo said, feeling sheepish and somewhat ashamed. "And I was telling her about my day, and how much I realized she did for the Alpha Line department—right, Meg?"

The three physicians and one field Agent watched as delicate eyelids flickered again.

"No," Zebra declared. "That was just coincidence, Echo. A reflex reaction to some internal stimulus."

"Baby," Echo addressed the woman in the pod, "gimme a grin, would ya, Meg?"

The corners of Omega's lips curled up for a few moments. It was subtle, but noticeable to the watching physicians.

"Now say yes."

Her eyelids quivered again.

"Do you believe me yet?" Echo wanted to know.

"Damn," Zebra murmured in surprise. "Omega, this is Zebra. Can you hear me?"

Eyelids trembled a yes.

"Can you give me a no response, just so I know you can do it?"

Still-peeling lips puckered slightly.

"Whoa," Echo muttered. "We hadn't gotten to any 'no' answers yet. That's good to know."

"Is this the first time she's done it?" Zebra wondered.

"Yeah. I just saw her react today. Just a bit ago, in fact. I had to get her to show me again, too, just to make sure I wasn't imagining it."

"That is...very good," Doron decided. "Please continue your explanation, Agent Echo. Why did her vital signs spike so alarmingly?"

"Oh. That," Echo said, and his voice sounded flat even to his own ears. "I, uh, well, like I said, I'd realized how much Meg does for me, helping run the department and all, and I was trying to thank her, and...well, I mentioned, um, the incident that put her in here, and how I, uh, took out the Cortian spacecraft on the way to fetch Doron..."

"Ah," Zarnix sighed. "That would do it."

"Yeah," Zebra agreed. "India and Whiskey both reported she was having flashbacks off and on, the whole time you were gone."

"Well, damn," Echo grumbled, annoyed and even more worried. "Nobody told me that, or I'd have thought before I inserted a size twelve-and-a-half foot into my wide-open mouth."

Just then, a soft *bloop-bloop* sound drew their attention, and they glanced at the pod's window in time to see several bubbles rising from Omega's curled, slightly parted lips, just as the vital signs telemetry spiked briefly.

"Well, damn, would ya look at that," Zebra said with a grin. "Echo, I think you made her laugh."

Echo drew a deep breath, raked his hand through his hair, and sat back down, rather harder than he had intended to do. Instantly the attention of the physicians focused on him.

"Echo, are YOU all right?" Zarnix asked in a soft voice.

"Yeah, I'm fine," Echo sighed, not realizing just how tired he looked to the doctors, nor knowing that they had been made aware—by Fox, and by Alpha Two, who were keeping several watchful eyes on him—of the irregular sleep cycle he was currently keeping. "I'm just...I've been..." He broke off, then jabbed a finger at the pod, and mouthed, *'I've been kind of worried. I wasn't sure she was gonna make it.'* Then he added aloud, "When her vitals jumped, she also looked for a minute like she was gonna cry, and I...was worried I'd messed things up."

"No, no, Agent Echo," Doron murmured in a soothing tone, laying a light hand on the Agent's shoulder. "Everything is fine. We simply did not know she had regained consciousness."

"Yeah, and that brings up a whole new consideration," Zebra pointed out. "We might want to get something in here, such as a television or the like, for when she doesn't have visitors, so she has something to focus on, to keep her mind occupied whenever she's awake."

"But her eyes aren't open," Echo pointed out.

"Yet," Zarnix added. "That may or may not change. But Zebra has a point. And she can at least HEAR, in any event. We must also see about arranging a sensor to respond to her eyelid movements and such so that she can adjust volume or channels as she wishes. It will be simple enough to do, I think. But I will call someone with electronics expertise..."

"He isn't quite in the same area as you're talking about, but Meg and Madrid, over in the Weapons Lab, are buddies, and he's pretty damn inventive. I'm sure he'd be happy to help you gin something up for her," Echo suggested.

"Good idea," Zarnix agreed. "Would you like that, Omega?"

Eyelids once more denoted a yes.

"Consider it done, dear," Zebra said with a smile. "Now, if you're feeling all right..."

They waited for the *yes* to come from her eyelids, and got it.

"Good. Then I think we lot of doctors should clear out and let you spend some private time with Echo. You like that idea?"

Her eyelids fluttered, and the corners of her lips twitched.

"She likes that idea a lot," Zebra said, grinning. "Let's go, guys."

As the three physicians departed, Echo leaned back over the pod and looked into the window, observing the sculpted planes of his partner's face in a way he seldom had occasion to see.

Yeah, he thought, studying the bone structure of the face before him. *Romeo's right—and so is Doron. She IS a 'pretty lady'—regardless of how you view it.*

"Okay, where were we, baby?" he said aloud. "Oh yeah. Romeo and India are off to the West Coast on an assignment..."

* * *

As soon as Fox saw the originator of the incoming vid call, he opaqued the windows in his office and took it. Pulgey Entiyti's scaly white, serious face formed on the wall screen.

"How is she, Franz?" were the first words out of the Draconan's mouth.

"She's going to live, Pulgey," Fox said with a slight smile. "Just as surely as I did, after you brought Doron in for me."

"Excellent! I knew, when I heard who you were sending Echo to get, that he could help...if Echo could only bring him in time. Keep going."

"Oh. Well, we don't really know much past that; I gather she may be awake now, though still pretty weak, as you can imagine. Echo informed me a bit ago that the, uh, the 'altered genetics' are fighting the regeneration." Fox broke off. "I'm not sure what this says about the things Omega is having Doron do, though. I'm inclined to think she's having her genetic material reverted back to pure human, by the sound of it. Doron offered to do so, and said he could accomplish it. And I know in her shoes, I probably would."

"Mm. Interesting. I am glad she will survive...but if she is pure human once more, what do you think she will do after she is medically released?" Entiyti asked.

"What do you mean, Pul?" Fox wondered, puzzled.

"There are several possibilities, Franz," Entiyti explained. "She may be as capable as ever she was, and for her sake and yours, I hope she is. But

223

she may not be. She could lose her speed and strength, mental agility, even some of her intellect. Certainly she will lose her budding psionic abilities. Depending on the degree of loss of these various capabilities, she may be unable to continue as an Alpha Line Agent. She may even be unable to continue in the field at all."

"Oh. Now that's an aspect I hadn't gotten around to considering," Fox murmured in dismay.

"After all, we don't know what her baseline WAS. She has no living family, does she?"

"Well, according to Echo, she has one—a very distant cousin, who happens to be a writer. But the ancestral distance is so great that we probably couldn't get any sort of accurate reading, even there."

"So we have no way of knowing how far she would 'regress' to return to her nominal human baseline." Entiyti quirked taloned fingers around the word, a gesture he had learned once upon a time from the very man to whom he now spoke.

"No, that's true."

"Or..." Entiyti added, then broke off.

"Or?"

"Or she may decide to retire from the Agency and go back to her first love—NASA."

"Aw, damnation," Fox said bitterly. "Then I've lost one of my top Agents anyway."

"And may lose another, a department chief into the bargain," Entiyti pointed out. "If she retires from the Agency, and Echo truly loves her as much as you have suspicioned, he may ask to accompany her."

"Well...FARKAKT." Fox rubbed his hand over his face. "You really know how to blow a good mood, Pulgey, alter khaver."

"Sorry, Franz," Pulgey apologized with a sigh. "But I suspected you had not yet had the opportunity to think through it all. I just wanted you to be prepared for the possibilities."

"Yes, I know. And you're right, I hadn't, and I thank you for that. But now I have a whole new batch of problems. Where the hell am I going to find anyone as qualified as those two, to run Alpha Line? Romeo might work—if he wasn't so young. I just don't think he has quite enough maturity yet, to run an entire department. And India has more of a healer's mindset than a warrior's...that's good for our current purposes, though, because it means that Alpha Line has a medic on staff." Fox shook his head. "The Alpha Three Enigma Team is too specialized to put in that position. Seven and what passes for Eight still haven't proven themselves to me after the whole infiltrator debacle over the holidays. The rest are much too new to the Agency, let alone the department." He shook his head. "I'll either have to take it over myself, or bring in somebody from outside. And given how dedicated the Alpha Line is to their chief, let alone his assistant, that'll be a hard row to hoe for anyone external, stepping into the position."

"I fear I do not have an answer for you, Franz," Entiyti said, frowning. "I'm sorry. I can, however, try to help you with the selections in a more official capacity, should it come to that."

"Huh? What do you mean?"

"I mean," Entiyti said, sitting back and exhaling, "that I am once more back in harness. By the time I was done with the Ennead—'done' in the sense of 'fowl being cooked,' I might add, for I thoroughly roasted them on a spit, metaphorically speaking—Dulziv was not only no longer the Council Chair, it is not even on the extended cabinet in any fashion, not even as a representative in the elected parliamentary body. It was recalled to its homeworld—in some degree of displeasure, let me note."

"Good enough for it," Fox practically snarled. "That political-gaming imbecile."

"Yes, and I agree with you totally; but that left a vacancy on the Ennead," Entiyti said. "So, based on my extensive past experience, the other members requested that I come out of retirement, at least temporarily, to serve as Chair until the various factions and parties can try to form coalitions capable of being voted upon by the Concordat signatory worlds. The Emdali ruling body concurred, as did the current representative in the Council body at large."

"And you agreed," Fox finished for him with a smile.

"Well, it was that or watch the least-experienced member try to do it," Entiyti said with a shrug. "It was obvious the more experienced ministers didn't want to try—especially once I was done with Dulziv. And I didn't figure anyone wanted to see a repetition of what your Agency just went through..."

"Oh HELL no," Fox proclaimed.

"...So I accepted." Entiyti sighed. "I cannot say that I am especially pleased; I was enjoying my retirement. But necessity demands when the adversary compels, as the saying is."

"Down here, it goes, 'needs must, when the devil drives,'" Fox said, hiding a smile, "but it's the same difference."

"Exactly. So if I may help you in any fashion, I shall, old friend. I am eminently positioned to do so, once more."

"Thank you, Pul. In that case, I think I am going to pop you the formal request that was submitted to me a day or so ago. Based on the considerations you've just now given me, it may end up being overcome by events, or it may not. But I was sitting on it until I saw how matters fell out with the Ennead. You'll understand why when you see it. Hang on a second and you can read it right now."

"Standing by, Franz."

Fox punched a few keys on his desk's virtual keyboard, then waited while Entiyti pulled up the file he had just transmitted to the Interim Chair of the Ennead. When the Draconan began to smile, then to grin, Fox sat back in satisfaction.

"Good idea, huh?" he asked.

"An excellent notion, provided, as you say, coming events do not supersede it," Entiyti agreed. "I will see what I can do. When in hell did he find time to submit this? And how is he doing?"

"Well, what with everything currently going on, he's had plenty of time to do paperwork...and to think. I've kept an eye on him, and...well, things aren't going as well there as he'd hoped, I believe. Or as I'd hoped, for that matter."

"What do you mean?"

"I'm afraid Echo is suffering from a bit of PTSD, Pul," Fox explained. "Post-Traumatic Stress Disorder. After all, Omega was literally lying on top of him as she burned, and him unable to move a muscle..."

"Oh, damnation."

"Exactly. I'm watching him personally, inasmuch as I can—mostly when he's in the Alpha Line room, though I did manage to convince him to join me for a brew a couple days ago, in between work and heading for the medlab—and I've given Alpha Two and Zebra a heads-up to do the same, in their respective capacities and interactions."

"And?"

"Among other things, it's my understanding that he's had a flashback or two, judging by some offhand comments he made over beer with me. But the main issue has been nightmares, according to Romeo, who managed to get him to open up a bit the other day."

"Ai! He is reliving the experience?"

"In spades, I'd say. But he's not stupid, and he's doing what needs doing, including talking to one of our counselors—and HE took the initiative on that; nobody had to nudge him. Zebra told me the counselor believes it's helping. So the work is getting done, done well, and he's thinking about the future and drawing some interesting conclusions. And in this particular case especially, I happen to agree wholeheartedly with his conclusions."

"It makes sense," Entiyti agreed. "A great deal of sense, actually. And, provided all goes well with the rest, will solve some of your dilemmas."

"It certainly will."

"I think I can get this approved pretty readily, Franz," Entiyti said with a smile. "All the i's are dotted and the t's crossed, as you like to say."

"Then have a look at this one, too." Fox hit another couple of keystrokes. Entiyti pulled up the new file and, seconds later, burst into laughter.

"AH!" he exclaimed, "it could not be any more perfect! Yes, yes! You have my approval! Go forward with it!"

"I'll be happy to obey THOSE orders, Pulgey!"

"Yes, I suspect so! And speaking of such matters, I suppose I need to get off this call and do a few briefings to bring me up to speed on the two Earth years since I was last in this job."

"Yeah, I got things I need to do, too, I guess. Nice break from paperwork, though. Listen, Pul...I seldom say things like this, but...you were always one of my best friends, even if I DID work for you. I miss seeing you like we used to do."

"I know, Franz. It is entirely too long between these little chats of ours, and even then, they are usually only occasioned by unpleasant events, such as this whole Cortian incident. I swear upon my wings, when you retire from the Agency, your old job awaits. With as many—or as few—attendant beings as you wish to bring along."

"Thanks, Pul. Hold onto that, please. As soon as I see Echo settled, I'll know better where I stand."

"Right. Keep me posted...on EVERYTHING, Franz."

"I will."

"Pulgey out."

"Fox out."

* * *

Promptly one full Division day later, to the minute, Echo arrived at the medlab. Doron was just exiting Lab B.

"Well?" Echo asked without preamble.

"Yes?" Doron responded.

"What's happening?"

"Ah. Well, the, um, 'television' I believe it is called, is installed, complete with galactic broadcasts, and your agent Madrid was able to develop a small optical device to detect Omega's eye movements, so..."

"How IS she, Doron?" an impatient Echo elaborated.

"Ah. Yes, I remember now. You wish to know the resolution of the biochemical problem."

"Yes!"

"Very well. I believe we were quite successful in reformulating the fluid to combat the interference."

"That means Meg's going to be all right?"

"Yes, it does."

"Good." Echo felt his entire body relax, though it would have been almost imperceptible to anyone else—*except Meg,* he thought absently—and he nodded. He knew what it would have meant to her to come out of the procedure and still be impaired.

"Yes," Doron continued, "she will be whole, and will regain full function of all of her faculties and limbs. I am persistent about such matters, and I was determined not to let the other thing beat me...and her...for her sake. But YOU must be patient."

"Huh? Me? Why?"

"I do not mean to eavesdrop, but I overheard some of your conversation with her yesterday, as I came and went to check on matters, and obtain the data sufficient to adjust the fluid formulation to my satisfaction. And I found what I heard to be a bit...troublesome. You see, Agent Echo, she will not be able to exit the chamber and immediately return to working with you, as much as you both may wish it, and I do not want you to, as you humans say, 'get your hopes up' in that regard...or to get hers up, either. There was considerable damage, and even a substantial part of her nervous system had to be regenerated."

"Her spine."

"Among other things, yes. So we must re-train that nervous system in order to retrieve her coordination and skills..."

"Oh. Physical therapy. I get it. Meg's gotta go through PT before you'll release her."

"Correct. I do not think it will take long. Your partner is rather...mm, what is the word...determined?"

"That's one way of putting it," Echo remarked, dry as dust. He let his lips quirk slightly.

"She greatly reminds me of you, actually," Doron observed, thoughtful, and Echo threw the alien healer a startled glance. "You are both very determined individuals."

"Most people just call it 'stubborn.'"

"There is that, too—though the two are not quite the same thing. And I should know, for I am, as well. But do not worry. She will be fine and back at your side very soon. Just be patient."

"All right, I'll make sure she knows about the physical therapy. It was really only to give her something to look forward to, anyway; I kinda figured she wouldn't bounce out of the pod and hit the streets with me. And I doubt she expects that, either. She's pretty practical when she needs to be."

"Ah, very good then." He hesitated, then asked, "Agent Echo...may I ask you something? It has puzzled me a bit..."

"Sure, Doron, whatcha need?"

"Oh, I need nothing," the little healer said with a smile. "I was just wondering...why do you sometimes call Omega 'baby'? She is a fully-adult human female..."

"Oh, that," Echo said with a grin. "That's a nickname I gave her, back when she was a rookie. See, some of the more experienced agents refer to rookies as 'baby agents,' because, well, you gotta learn to crawl before you can walk, and walk before you can run, so there's a parallel in learning to be an agent." He shrugged. "Meg is rightfully proud of her abilities and skills, and...she got kind of offended at the 'rookie' designation one day. So I sat her down and explained some stuff to her, about how it wasn't an insult, just a stage, and then it was all good. After that, I started teasing her, calling her 'baby agent' and junk, which pretty quickly got shortened to just 'baby.' And it stuck," he admitted. "I got in the habit of calling her that as a nickname. I did check to make sure she was okay with it when I realized I was still doing it even after she left rookie status, though. And she was. She told me once that she actually kinda liked it, because it reminded her of home—in the part of the planet we're from, family and friends call each other 'baby,' or 'honey,' or 'sugar,' see."

"Oh, that is interesting."

"Yeah. She calls me 'Ace' the same way, and for similar reasons—the first time I took her up in an aircraft, she was impressed with my flying skills, and 'ace' is an old military designation for a good flyer." He simplified the explanation, not wanting to have to delve into the whole history of World War I with the little alien. "Anyway, 'baby' and 'Ace' are our nicknames for each other. It's to the point now where, if she hears me call her 'Agent Omega,' she knows that either it's a formal diplomatic situation, or I'm pissed off at somebody."

"Um...'pissed off'?"

"Oh—mad at somebody."

"Ah, I see." Doron nodded, smiling. "It is a mark of affection between dear friends."

"Exactly."

"Very well. Thank you for that explanation, Agent Echo; it makes much more sense now. Let me leave, so that you may proceed with your visit."

"Doron?" Echo queried as the alien physician headed for the door. "Before you go..."

"Yes, Agent Echo?"

"What about Meg's...mental condition? After what she's gone through..."

Doron sighed.

"That is something I cannot tell you, Agent Echo. It is not my specialty. And she has been through much trauma, it is certain. But if she is indeed as...'stubborn' as she appears, and if you and your friends continue to provide her with your strength and devotion—no, that is not quite the right word; perhaps affection? What I am trying to say in my imperfect English is, if you and your friends are there to support her, emotionally as well as physically and mentally, I think she will be fine in time."

"Are you sure?" Echo wondered. *'Be there for me, like partners do,'* he remembered. *I can, and I will. As long as she WANTS me there. But...what if I'm a reminder...?*

"I am sure." Doron nodded an almost vehement affirmative. "She has a large, caring heart, and she does not begrudge what she went through to save you."

"How do you know?" a skeptical Echo asked, deeply pained.

"She told me," Doron said simply, and Echo felt the second tsunami of relief wash through him inside five minutes. "Now go see her."

* * *

Echo stepped just inside the door of Lab B and automatically scanned the room, seeing the bank of monitors depicting his partner's more or less normal vital signs; then he moved to the pod and looked inside.

The gaping wound in Omega's shoulder was knitting closed. A ridge of cartilage showed where her missing ear was regenerating. The blistered skin of her face and lips was gradually smoothing away. Her upper chest and shoulders rose and fell rhythmically, without any of the painful spasms that brought about the gurgling and gasping which had marked her respiration previously. A short, fine silver-blonde halo curled around her forehead

231

and ear.

"Hi, Meg. It's Echo. Can you hear me?"

Omega's head drifted to one side. Echo had the impression she had turned her face toward him.

"Good. Romeo and India said to tell you hi, by the way. They checked in today. Their mission's going well; Mack will be coming back with 'em in a few days, and they said they'd be by to see you when they get home."

Soft lips curled; they were almost smooth again, Echo noticed.

"Oh, while I'm thinking about it, did Doron talk to you about doing physical therapy after you get out of this regen pod?"

Omega's eyelids quivered gently.

"Okay, good. If it turns out you could use some help with stuff, an extra pair of hands or something, tell the docs to call me, all right?"

She smiled slightly.

"Now, once we get you back into your quarters, it'll be a lot easier for me to help out, 'cause I expect you'll still be a little stiff for a while. But we'll work all that stuff out when we get to that point. Fox and I will probably want to keep you on leave for maybe as much as a week or so after the medlab releases you, just to give you time to get back up to speed with daily activities. And even then, we'll still take it slow, and not do any strenuous missions for a little while; we'll give those to Alpha Two, or maybe Four or Five, if anything comes up. Now, quit that frowning. Everything is fine. You and I will just take care of the business of running Alpha Line, and maybe do a few routine patrols, at first. You know, kinda ease back into things. It'll all come back in time; just be patient."

He watched as the scowl continued for a few more moments. Then Omega's lips quirked to one side, and finally she fluttered her eyelids in what he had come to recognize as her *yes* response. He smiled to himself. *That was the most begrudging, 'Okay, if I gotta,' response I think I've ever seen,* he decided. *And that, without her ever vocalizing a word.*

"Yeah, you gotta," he replied, and watched as her lips curled upward.

The medlab was quiet except for the sound of Echo's voice, and a few soft electronic beeps coming from various pieces of equipment. He pulled a small book from an inside jacket pocket.

"I stuck my head into your quarters this morning to see if there was anything that needed doing, Meg, and found the collection of poetry you'd been reading, lying on your nightstand. I thought it might make a good break from me just talking, you know, monologuing all the time, so I brought it with me. Want me to pick up where you left off, or had you rather I read something else? I can download something to my cell phone from the electronic library if you'd rather."

Eyelids fluttered, then she puckered her lips. Echo smeared his hand down his face.

"Damn, I'm sorry, baby. I gotta remember, yes or no questions," he said with a wry grin. "Do you want me to read from your book of poetry?"

Lashes trembled again. *Yes.*

"Where you left off?"

Her lips pursed. *No.*

"No. Okay. You want me to pick another place in the book, then?"

There was a pause, then she pursed her lips again. *No.*

"Wait. Do you want me to read the book of poetry, or not?"

Her eyelids flickered in confirmation, and this time Echo thought he saw a flash of blue between them; he smiled at that. *Maybe soon she can look at me, and we can code a bit more,* he thought. *That'll improve communications a little.*

"Okay, so what we're trying to figure out is where to pick up reading, right?" he tried again.

This time a sliver of blue showed between her eyelids.

"But you're not sure if you want me to pick up where you left off?"

Her eyes didn't quite open that time, but Echo was pretty sure she at least got a glimpse of him, because her lips curved a little.

"We're playin' a damn game of Twenty Questions today, baby, you and me! But that's all right. Are you just afraid of what you'll see if I start where you left the bookmark?"

The eyelids quivered, and her lips curved downward in a brief frown this time.

"The danger should be over now, Meg. Anything you see ought to be good stuff at this point. I mean, unless some Big Bad Ugly is headed our way, I guess. Which I doubt. 'Cause Fox would have heard something out-ta GALINT, otherwise. That man has connections like you can't believe, Meg. I only hope I've got half that many when I have to do that job. But so...yeah, if you have any visions this time, either they'll be good stuff, or they oughta be far enough out that we can—and WILL—work with 'em, next time, I swear."

She didn't move for a few moments, evidently thinking over what he'd said; then finally, slowly, she batted her lashes at him.

"So start at the bookmark?"

This time it was the nearest she had come yet to a full blink, and a pleased Echo realized she was getting stronger as she healed.

So Echo opened the book to the indicated place and began reading Elizabeth Barrett Browning softly, thoughtfully, as he remembered her visions.

"'Is it indeed so? If I lay here dead,

Wouldst thou miss any life in losing mine?

And would the sun for thee more coldly shine...'"

* * *

The next time all three of the top Alpha Line Agents on active duty were able to visit Omega's pod together, a total of ten Division days had elapsed. Omega was asleep, according to Echo. When Alpha Two had asked how he knew, he merely pointed at the dark television.

"Huh?" Romeo responded.

"They got her that TV set up, so that when she's alone, she has something to pay attention to," Echo explained. "It's rigged to respond to small movements in her face, so she can turn it on and off, change the channels, adjust the volume, and crap like that. But it's off, and she hasn't responded to us, so chances are, she decided to take a nap. This isn't my usual time, so she didn't know to expect visitors."

"Oh, I see," India said, raising an eyebrow. "Nice. Good idea, and well observed, Echo. Which means we should be kinda quiet."

"Right," Echo agreed.

"Damn, th' pretty lady is startin' to look like her old self again," Romeo exclaimed with a pleased grin as he looked at the unconscious form.

"Hush, Romeo! I only just said to be quiet! But look at her hair," India said, pointing to the platinum cloud that now floated around Omega's head. "It's almost back down to her shoulders again. And she HAS shoulders again."

"Yeah. Every day she's a little more improved," Echo agreed. "Doron says we can take her out in about three more days, if everything keeps going as well as it is now. 'Decant' her, the docs call it." He shook his head, then chuckled. "Like she's a bottle of wine or something."

"You been by every day, man?" Romeo asked him.

"Yeah, as often as I can get away, for as long as I can. I'm not always sure how aware she is in there, see. 'Cause sometimes she falls asleep and the TV is still on, and sometimes she signals to me, and other times she doesn't. Once the medics realized she was awake, Doron thought she might open her eyes at some point, but she hasn't quite, so...I dunno. They only added the television after she'd been in there a few days—at least a week, I guess, now that I reckon it up—so initially it was just me. I know when she started responding to me, but we got no clue how long she might have been awake before that, only she was still too weak to react. And that thing she's in is a lot like a sensory deprivation tank. Ever been in one?"

"No. Heard of 'em, though," Romeo said.

"If you stay in one too long, you start to lose touch with reality. Dreams, hallucinations," Echo told him, still gazing into the pod thoughtfully. "After everything else that's happened, I didn't figure she needed that on top of it."

"So you stopped by periodically to—what?—talk to her?" India surmised, and Echo nodded.

"I'm pretty sure she could hear me. She's responded enough that I could kinda carry on the odd conversation once in a while. It was a little bit one-sided, though. Zebra thought I was imagining it, until I got Meg to respond in front of her. We got yes and no down pat. Not much else, but that, we've got."

"Or maybe she sensed your presence, like Romeo in Fox's office that day she tried to read the Cortians," India guessed. "And then responded to that."

"Whatever." Echo shrugged, unconcerned about the distinction. "Either way, she responded."

"What are you gonna do when she goes back to NASA, Echo?" Romeo asked him. Echo looked up, startled.

"What makes you think she will?"

"C'mon, man, the girl's been through nuthin' but hell as an Agent. An' she STILL ain't managed t' get inta space. You said yourself back when you were trainin' her that her life dream was t' be an astronaut. You KNOW she told Doron to undo alla Slug's shit so she c'n go back to it."

Echo thought over Romeo's statement for a moment, as he realized with a shock that he had had no further sense of Omega's...presence...since she'd been put in the chamber. *And why else would the genetics fight the regen,* he wondered, *except because the regen was trying to undo 'em. Hell.*

"I...think Romeo's right, Echo," India agreed, downcast. "I hate to say it, but...I think you're going to need a new partner pretty soon."

Damnation, Echo thought, as something inside wrenched. *I busted ass to save her, and I'm still gonna lose her. Unless...but I'm not sure if I'm ready for that, not this time. I'm not sure she'd want it, either. If I don't even know if she feels like that, how am I gonna decide?*

* * *

India and Romeo were off on assignment again, but Echo was staunch at his partner's side when Doron and the Agency medics came to remove Omega from the regeneration pod.

Earlier they had placed a sedative into her regen fluid to ensure she was knocked out when they came to get her; Doron had indicated that the sensation involved in draining the lungs could be distressing for lucid patients. And Zarnix and his team wanted to ensure that, if some other medical issue came up, Omega would not be aware of what was happening while they sought to resolve it. It was the considered consensus that she had been through hell enough in the last several weeks, so they wanted to make this process as easy as they could for her. And this decision, Echo understood, had been with her full knowledge and consent.

More, he had himself also approved it, as being the voice for his partner when she was unable to speak—just as she would be for him, were he in a similar situation. Which had been another reason he had spent so much time in the medlab, during her recuperation. *I'm glad we talked it over and put in that little bit of paperwork after I got shot at Christmas,* he realized. *It means each of us can advocate for the other, regardless of the other's condition.*

"Is she asleep yet?" Zebra wondered, coming to Echo's side.

"Yeah, I'd say she drifted off about ten minutes ago," Echo noted. "The vitals dropped a little about then, too."

"Yup, good sign she's asleep, then," Whiskey decided. "I think we can do this, don't you, Doron?"

"Indeed," Doron said with a nod. "She is ready."

"Echo, are you and Meg close enough that you want to help, or...?" Zebra wondered.

"Um, well, I probably could, and she wouldn't mind, but she'd be really embarrassed if she found out," Echo admitted. "Especially since everybody else would know."

"Okay, then why don't you stand over there in the doorway while we do this?"

So Echo remained discreetly by the door while the doctors raised the unconscious form from the fluid and swiftly drained her lungs. They examined her rapidly from head to toe, then wrapped her naked body in a sheet to avoid chilling her. As soon as she was cocooned, Echo moved over beside the pod.

"How is she?" he asked.

"See for yourself," Whiskey said quietly, and gently deposited the somnolent figure into Echo's arms.

Echo looked down at the silent body resting against him and studied its features with care. The skin was smooth and slightly flushed; the platinum hair was long and shining again, although still damp against his shoulder. Her delicately convoluted ears lay flat against her head, just as they should. Her bare arms and shoulders, outside the wrappings, were once again firm and muscular, the renewed flesh a glowing pink. And Echo could feel the re-formed muscle in her back and legs where his arms and hands supported her. Her respiration was slow, regular, and easy; a pulse beat lightly and steadily in the hollow of her throat.

Just then, she drew a slight breath, sighed, and turned her face into his chest; her feet flexed, one after the other, as if she were dreaming of walking at her partner's side.

He nodded, satisfied, and followed the doctors to the prepared hospital room with his fragile, treasured burden.

* * *

Echo saw Omega put to rights in a proper hospital room, then departed for Fox's office. There, he met the waiting Director along with Alpha Two, which latter had swung by Headquarters just long enough to get the word on Omega before they had to head out again. He reported to Fox, and notified Romeo and India, on Omega's condition and status in one scant five-minute debrief; all three were gladdened by the news. Then he came straight back to the medlab afterward.

When he glanced through the partly-open hospital room door, he found that Omega was awake, and experimentally, if somewhat diffidently, checking out her regenerated tissues. She studied her hands, flexing the fingers slowly, then ran those same fingers cautiously over her bare shoulders, probing, apparently not entirely sure what she'd find.

Echo watched as she slipped her hands up into her hair, fanning it out with her fingers and indulgently letting it fall across her shoulders and face, obviously relishing the sensation; he smiled to himself, affection filling him. *She does have pretty hair,* he thought. *I'm glad she enjoys it like that.* As he continued to watch, she picked up a lock of the platinum strands and stared at it closely.

But when she started pulling back the sheet to examine one leg, Echo quickly knocked on the door; evidently no one had yet come by to dress her in a medlab jumpsuit, and she was still naked beneath the bed covers.

So I either gotta let her know I'm here, or risk an accusation of being a voyeur, he decided. *And I don't wanna blow her opinion of me, at this stage, by a misunderstanding.*

"Meg? Hey, there."

"Oh! Come on in, Echo," she answered, quickly flipping the covers back into place.

"How are you feeling?" he asked as he entered and moved to sit on the bedside.

"Pretty good, all things considered," she said, averting her face, letting her long, loose hair cascade down to hide her expression. Echo saw the motion, and raised his eyebrows, concerned.

"What's wrong? Is something upsetting you?" he asked. Then, in a lower voice, "Are you angry? If I'd listened when you first warned me, we could've been more prepared...this wouldn't have happened..."

"No, Echo," Omega said quietly. "I'm not angry. I'm just glad you're okay." Her face was still turned to the wall, partly cloaked by that platinum mane.

"If you're not, you oughta be."

"And just how the hell were you supposed to know it wasn't some harebrained notion of mine? YOU'RE not a mind-reader."

"No. But I can read my partner. Instead, I jumped to conclusions."

"Echo, don't. Please. It's all right. Really."

"Then what IS wrong? Why do you just keep staring at the wall?"

"Oh, um, well, it's nothing important, really, it's actually kinda stupid...it, uh, it's just..." Omega ran her hands nervously over her averted face, the hint of an embarrassed blush creeping up along her jawline and throat, "see, they haven't let me near a mirror, or any sort of a reflective surface, since...the incident. And I know what kinda shape the REST of me was in." She gestured the length of her body. "So I know...it was...bad. And there's still...no mirror. I was," she explained, "trying to gauge how well things had healed when you knocked on the door, but I haven't gotten much of a good look at everything yet, so..."

Echo understood then.

"You don't know what you look like after...everything."

"Yes." Her head drooped miserably, and she continued in a low voice, "Is it...very...is the scarring..."

* * *

Echo put a finger under Omega's chin, and gently but firmly turned her face toward him, brooking no resistance, studying her facial features with intensity in the bright room lighting. Omega kept her eyes cast down, unwilling to observe his reaction, afraid of glimpsing even the slightest flash of revulsion in his handsome features; it would have crushed her to see such a reaction in him. Echo tilted her face from side to side, examining it from all angles, and Omega closed her eyes in tormented suspense, waiting.

"There's no scarring, Meg. Your face healed perfectly," Echo murmured.

Omega snapped her eyes open in some surprise, and studied Echo's face, only inches from her own, searching his eyes keenly. His gaze seemed oddly warm...and for some reason, fixed on her mouth.

* * *

"Echo...don't tell me what you think I want to hear." Her expression was tense.

"You know ME better than that," he told her.

"Yeah...I do." Her face relaxed.

"Want a mirror?" Echo dropped his hand and leaned back. "I'm sure they just haven't thought to put one in here yet. I'll go get one for you, and you can see for yourself."

"No...not now. If you say it's okay, I'm good." Omega sank into the pillows and sighed in relief. A cheerful Doron came bustling in just then, carrying a black medical jumpsuit for Omega. A female nurse followed him, prepared to help Omega don the garment.

"How is the patient? Ready to begin therapy?" Doron asked. Omega smiled.

"Better than I've been in several days," she declared. "But damn. Now I know what the entrée at a barbecue feels like." She shot her partner a mischievous glance, and Echo grinned.

"What is a barbecue?" a curious Doron asked.

Omega laughed, and Echo and Doron both smiled to hear the sound.

"Echo, do you want to tackle the cultural exchange, or shall I?" she wondered.

"I think I'll let you handle it this time," Echo said, characteristically enigmatic.

Chapter 7

Fox, Echo, Romeo, and India stood outside the closed door of Omega's hospital room.

"Now you're sure about this?" Fox asked his three Agents.

"You know the lady been miserable about what Slug did to her," Romeo declared, nodding. "An' it's been killin' her to get into space. I say we give the girl back her dream."

"I can't imagine that she wouldn't have taken Doron up on his offer," India added her agreement. "When she and I were discussing her hunches and I suggested Slug might've made her a psi...if you had seen her expression, Fox..."

"So the brain bleacher will work on her now," Fox stated, and India nodded.

But Fox noticed Echo's opinion was conspicuous by its absence. And that worried the Director. He turned to face him.

"Echo? She's your partner, zun. Are you...ready to do this?"

"No. But I'll do it anyway, if necessary." Echo's face was inscrutable.

"All right, then." Fox sighed, realizing he was going to have to find a way to patch up his department chief in despite of Omega's positive outcome. *And that patching up may include sending him after her,* he thought, stifling another sigh. "Let's go."

* * *

The four silent Agents slipped into the hospital room where their friend and colleague lay in the partially-reclined hospital bed, sound asleep. Omega was exhausted after all of the physical therapy, but she was almost ready to be released. The Agents watched her for a few more moments, hesitating. Then Fox resolutely slipped on his goggle-glasses, and the others followed suit.

Echo took a deep breath, steeling himself, despite the fact that something inside was breaking; he moved to the edge of the bed and sat down,

241

just looking at her for long moments—hoping to make the memory last for the rest of his life.

Because I can't go with her, he thought, despondent. *No matter how much I want to. 'Cause there's nothing, no story we can give, to tie us together outside the Agency other than as a mate, a spouse, and I don't know if she wants me like that...or not. And it's way the hell too late to find out now.* Gently he reached out and touched her shoulder, the one that had been so horribly wounded, rubbing it lightly. *For the last time,* he realized, and somehow managed not to groan in pain.

"Meg, wake up, baby. It's me. It's Echo. Wake up, sleepyhead."

"Mmmh." Omega stirred, stretched slightly, and pushed herself up in bed as she opened drowsy blue eyes. "Echo? Wha's up?"

"...Goodbye, Meg. I'll...really miss you, baby..." He raised his pre-set brain bleacher and activated it. Multicolored flickers reflected off the walls of the room as its mnemonic reprogramming function activated.

Fox, India, and Romeo slowly removed their goggle-glasses. Echo sat, unmoving, just watching the woman that had been his partner, the woman for whom he had flown across the galaxy and back, risking everything to save her—just as she had risked everything to save him. His jaw tightened, and he swallowed once. He watched...until he saw her vision return.

They all steeled themselves then, waiting to hear the inevitable question, "Where am I?" She blinked, and opened her mouth to speak.

"Y'all could've at least given me a pair of goggle-glasses, dammit! You KNOW I'll be seein' spots for the next ten minutes! I woulda thought by now, at least, the lot o' y'all could remember that. Helluva way to wake a body up!"

Three jaws dropped. One jaw tightened still further, the lips curving up in a slight smile. Echo removed his goggle-glasses and tucked them into his jacket pocket.

* * *

"Meg...but...well, we thought..." India began, patently dumbfounded.

"You thought I got Doron to undo Slug's tinkering?" Omega finished for her.

India nodded.

"We jus' wanted to give you back your life," Romeo murmured. Omega glanced down, deeply touched, then looked back up and smiled.

"Thanks," she said softly. "I appreciate that. But I have a life. Right here."

"Why didn't you...?" India asked hesitantly.

"It WAS...tempting."

"But you coulda been an astronaut," Romeo protested.

"Actually, Romeo, I figure probably not," Omega told him. "I thought through the whole thing very carefully, believe me. See, NASA wanted me for the advanced drive project, not the regular corps. So I decided that, without my...enhancements, I might well wash out of that department of the corps in my freshman year. And my only other shot at getting 'out there' is right here...with my 'family.'" She looked around at them. "And in THIS job, I'll take every edge I can get." Omega smiled and nudged Echo where he still sat on the bedside. "You're not gettin' rid of me that easy, Ace." He grinned.

"Good," was all he said.

"You know," she continued, "I've been thinking. I've had a damn lot of time for that lately—especially in the regen pod. Yes, Echo, I was aware in there, and I really looked forward to your visits and our little chats—not that I could communicate a lot, but I tried; thanks for bein' willing to yak away at me despite that. It...helped a lot, just to...to know that somebody I cared about was there, looking out for me." She looked around at the others. "I know all of you were there, at various times, 'cause I could hear you, and I...really appreciated it."

"Good," Fox murmured, sounding very gruff.

"Anyway, I've decided that whatever has happened to me in the past, strange or not, painful or not, has gone into making me who I am now, human or...not. Same as with y'all, or anybody else. Just a little weirder, I guess." She grinned. "And I think I've decided that I'm mostly glad of it. Because if it hadn't been for that, this guy here," she tapped Echo on the chest, "might be..."

"A slave in the trigonium mines of the Large Magellanic Cloud," Echo finished for her.

"Or dead," India remarked.

"Or worse," Fox added.

"Anyway, I've decided I'm...well, maybe not happy, exactly; more like satisfied, I think is a good word...with what I am, who I am, and," Omega laid a hand on Echo's shoulder, "where I am. I hope...y'all can say the same about me. Psi potential and all."

Smiles spread around the room. Then Echo made a stern addendum.

"But if I EVER hear the word 'expendable' cross your lips again, I'll—"

"You'll what? Breathe fire? Been there, done that," Omega teased. Then she sobered, glancing down. "And it wasn't fun at all." Omega looked back up and saw the same shadow in Echo's eyes that she knew was in her own. *After all,* she realized, *he was right there, too.*

"Expendable?!" Fox said, in shock. "Who the hell in Alpha Line is expendable?"

"Nobody," Echo said firmly. "But especially, nobody in this room."

* * *

"But they did not ask me," Doron noted, as Omega told him about the brain-bleaching attempt over one of her very last formal physical therapy sessions with the little physician. "I would have told them. As you requested, before I ever put you in the chamber. And I intended to do so; I simply had not the chance."

Omega smiled.

"They didn't ask me, either," she pointed out, performing shoulder flys with dumbbells to strengthen the musculature that had burned away and been regrown. "I think, because of the way my altered genetics fought the regeneration process, they assumed that you were undoing those alterations."

"Well, that does make sense, I suppose," Doron agreed, taking one of the dumbbells as she finished her set. "That was very well done, Omega. Your strength is returning right along. I am pleased...as you should be."

"I'm still not as strong as I was...before," she murmured, studying her upper body in the wall mirror.

"It will come, it will come," Doron replied. "Just be patient. Now, keep that dumbbell and let me show you a new exercise to do with it..."

* * *

"Yes, that's right, Pulgey," Fox told the galactic leader on the vid call. "Omega made it through everything just fine, and she deliberately chose to leave the modifications alone. I still have my Alpha Line agent." He paused, then added, "And my friend. Both of 'em, actually. Omega AND Echo."

"That is wonderful news, Franz," a delighted Entiyti told his old friend. "I am very glad to hear it. Is she handling it well...mentally?"

"Seems to be," Fox decided. "I gathered there was a little bit of angst initially, when she didn't know whether there was any residual scarring, but since there wasn't, that was okay. I can't imagine how she's handling the memories, though. Then again, I don't know how she handles the memories from Slug's abduction and...vivisection, from what I've gathered from Zz'r'p...either."

"How do you handle the memories of the Nazi concentration camp, old friend?" Entiyti asked the Socratic question. "Of seeing your family wiped out?"

"Ah. Well, yes, I guess you do have a point," Fox noted. "We all have our personal horrors to deal with, I suppose."

"Indeed. And it may be that, BECAUSE OF those enhancements, she is mentally stronger—strong enough to deal with the memories of their acquisition, and more."

"True. I hadn't thought of that, but that makes a lot of sense. Surely Slug had to know they'd come out at some point, and he needed her to stay sane enough to fulfill his mission if they came out before his end game."

"Exactly," Entiyti agreed. "I gather she herself does not talk about it?"

"No. Not any more than she has to. And even then, she refuses to share any details, even with Echo—maybe ESPECIALLY with Echo. She says it's not something others should have in their heads to deal with."

They were quiet for a time, considering the ramifications of that.

"So when will she be released from the medlab?" Entiyti asked.

"Tomorrow. Zebra and Echo corroborate each other on that."

"Excellent. Listen, Franz, I have a favor to ask. And I think it's one you might like..."

245

"Shoot, my friend," Fox said immediately.

"It's like this..."

* * *

Omega had just been released from medical care; Echo had met her at the lab—metaphorically picking her up—and had taken her to have her regenerated hand and foot prints removed. So now she and Echo were headed back to their adjoining quarters, walking side by side in a companionable silence. Unobtrusively, she studied his features as they walked.

"Echo?" she finally asked.

"Hm?"

"You...saw it all, didn't you?"

Echo glanced at her for a split second, dark eyes dilated, then looked away. "Yes."

"Total sensory experience, huh?"

"Damn, Meg, don't..." He stopped dead, and turned away for a moment. "Let it drop." After another moment, he asked her without looking, "Are you in my head now?"

"I...don't think so." She blinked in surprise at the question.

"How'd you know, then?"

"Body language," she told him.

"What?"

"You tuned out for a minute."

Echo nodded. He turned back and they continued walking, but slower.

"You know, I envy you," Omega said.

"How so?"

"Brain bleach doesn't work on me. I have no choice but to remember it. Have you set up a session yet?" she asked Echo casually.

"No."

"When, then?"

"I'm not."

"Echo! It was traumatic for both of us. Get rid of the memory. At least the details."

"No."

"Why not?" Omega asked quietly.

"It would be...disrespectful...to my partner, to eliminate the memory of what she went through to save my life. Besides, she can't forget. Why should I?" Echo said, equally quietly.

"I'd say that trip to get Doron and bring him back makes us even, hon. Fox showed me the video log from the little clipper. You did a really good job on the Penrose calculations, by the way. Couldn't have done better myself, if I'd been there. And the cosmic string...dangerous, but a great idea. I don't think I'd have come up with that."

* * *

"That reminds me," Echo said thoughtfully. "When I was on Edeptis IV, I...thought I...heard you... Did you—?"

It was Omega's turn to stop dead. She paled.

"Were you...in a tent? With a lot of...terribly sick people? Blood everywhere. The poor child...and not enough power for the medical equipment..."

Echo nodded.

"Then it wasn't a dream..." she whispered. "Oh, no."

"You were asleep?" Echo asked.

"I was comatose," Omega responded, face drawn in anxiety. "I thought it was a coma-induced hallucination of some sort. Oh, man. Oh wow. I'm...sorry, Echo. I'm so sorry."

"For what?" he asked, puzzled. "What you told me worked."

"Yes, but..." she hesitated. "Did...anything else happen? When we—spoke—in the tent? How did you...feel, for instance?"

"Actually," Echo said, thinking back, "not too well, come to think of it. I got a sudden splitting headache. Like a migraine, I guess, though I've never had one. I almost passed out at one point. I had to pick myself up off the ground." Omega was turning paler and paler as she listened, but she said nothing. "I just figured it was a combination of needing some sleep, some residual effects of anoxia after channeling everything into the prop to get out of the collapsing wormhole, and not being used to my partner talking in my head."

By this time Omega was white to the lips; her blue eyes were wide and horrified.

247

"No...oh, no...no, no, no." She swayed, badly shaken and still somewhat weak, and Echo caught her, easing her to the floor before she could fall. "Oh, Echo...I'm so, so sorry..."

"MEG?? You okay, baby? Do I need to get you back to the medlab?"

"No—it's not that. I—" Omega took a deep breath and looked up at her partner, who knelt beside her. "I'm okay now, I think. Help me get up." Echo offered her a hand, and as she stood slowly, still a bit stiff, she started to explain.

"It's...this is not good, hon. Evidently I'm invading your head and don't even know it, Ace. And I can't think of anyone—except me—who'd resent that kind of intrusion more than you must."

"Well..." Echo let his voice trail off. "That doesn't explain why you nearly fainted on me just now."

"Maybe not, but I bet this will. At the same time you and I were 'making contact,'" Omega told him, "the medics recorded my deteriorating vital signs unexpectedly stabilizing—at normal levels. AND it seems Zebra swears up and down that my cerebral scan pattern briefly duplicated YOUR norms. But I was still in a coma. They had no explanation for where I'd suddenly gotten the strength to rally. Meanwhile, across the whole damn galaxy, you—"

"Nearly pass out," Echo finished for her, nodding. "I get it. You needed strength, so you pulled from me." *'If I lay here dead, wouldst thou miss any life in losing mine...'* he reflected. *Literally.*

"I didn't MEAN to!" It was almost a wail. "I just wanted to help you... all those sick people..."

"Shush," he said. "Did it help YOU?"

"India said...I probably wouldn't have been here when you got back, otherwise."

"Good." He nodded.

"Echo...were there any other times—?"

Echo leaned against the wall and furrowed his brow as he tried to recall.

"Yeah, I think...there were a couple of times when you seemed especially...nearby. Usually when I was resting...or...asleep..."

Brown eyes met blue for a moment, both startled, both remembering a certain dream-state embrace, and wondering privately if the other had experienced it, too—or had even wanted to. Then they each looked away.

"...In other words, relaxed," Omega finished for him after a moment.

"Yeah. The only time I consciously tried to reach you, I couldn't."

"When was that?"

"Um, a couple hours before we actually arrived. Maybe a bit more than that, actually, say four, four and a half hours. When the master clock died. I'd thought maybe you could help me with the reset. Hell, I figured, if nothing else, you could ask somebody for the correct galactic time, then relay it to me."

"Oh. Let's see. That woulda been what time...? Um, yeah. I would've been conscious then, too...I think..." She shook her head. "This is...it's bad, Echo. Dangerous. What if..." Omega's voice dropped to a whisper. "Echo... what if the contact on Edeptis IV hadn't been broken when it did? And WHY did it break? I could've...oh, dear Lord." Omega turned and started back down the corridor the way they'd come, at the fastest clip she could yet muster.

"Wait! Where are you going?" Echo asked, turning to follow her.

"To find Fox. He's got to get Zz'r'p back here immediately, to teach me how to control this thing. Barring that...maybe Doron isn't finished with me after all."

Echo caught her arm.

"Hold up, baby. I thought you were okay with things as is."

"It doesn't matter." Omega shook her head, vehement. "It doesn't give me the right to violate your...being...like this. I might've killed you, Echo. Sucked you dry. And never known it."

"So you're gonna ask Doron to put you back in the tank, get rid of the psi?"

She shook her head again.

"No. It doesn't work like that. The 'tweaks' go down to the genetic level, according to Doron. I can't pick and choose. That's why I didn't have it done in the first place. It's all or nothing."

"So if you go back into the regeneration bath, you'll lose ALL the 'enhancements'?"

"Yes," Omega said quietly. "So maybe you'll be needing a new partner after all, Echo. I don't know if I'd be able to...keep up with you without them." She sighed. "I can't imagine what it's going to feel like, being unable to understand my own doctoral dissertation."

"*I* understood it."

"Yes, that's true," Omega acknowledged. "But could you visualize it?"

"No—not the way you can." They paused for a long moment, considering. "Meg, stop and think this through, baby. Are you really ready to do this?"

"No. But I'll do it anyway, if necessary," she said, and Echo heard the reflection of his own voice in hers. "I won't do this to you, Ace."

* * *

"You're kneejerking, Meg," Echo told her then. "Slow down. Come on, let's go home. Sleep on it. It's a major thing you're considering."

"But...what if, while I'm asleep..."

"First off, relax. Slug's been in my mind, remember? And based on recent experience, you're a helluva lot more...benign." Echo still held her arm. Now he pulled on it gently, and headed back toward their quarters, a reluctant Omega allowing herself to be towed along behind him. "Come on. Let's get some dinner started, and we can talk about it." He grinned. "The truth is, I'd just as soon not have to train another new agent any time in the foreseeable future. You and Romeo have been more than enough."

"If you say so," she muttered, not sure whether to laugh or whack him on the shoulder.

"I say so," Echo replied. Only then did she spot the mischievous glint in the brown eyes, and know he was teasing her. Finally Omega nodded, then remembered a particular item she had meant to bring up with him.

"Oh, I've got a little something for you," she told him, trying suddenly to keep a straight face.

* * *

"Oh? What?" Echo asked, curious, studying her expression and realizing something was up her sleeve.

"Call it a thank-you, or maybe a...memento," she said, unable to keep the twinkle out of her own eyes. "I had R & D whip it up for me."

Omega pulled a small black object out of her pocket and squeezed it as she tossed it at Echo. It squeaked as he caught it, and he looked down at the object in his hands. It was a little black rubber ducky, with *RD-1* neatly stenciled in red on its back.

Omega burst out laughing, and Echo calmly tucked the toy duck into his Suit pocket as he punched the elevator button. The door opened, and they got in the elevator.

Echo's eyes glinted in impish glee as he retaliated.

"How about barbecue for dinner?"

She hit him.

* * *

Fox and Arcturan Ambassador Zz'r'p joined Alpha One and Two in a small, private conference room off the Core; it was one Fox often used for such matters, and as such, it was generally considered 'the Director's conference room.' Echo and Omega had just finished explaining the contact Meg had made while Echo was on Edeptis IV. Romeo whistled, and the other Agents looked dumbfounded.

"Damn, skippy," Romeo mumbled.

"So that's where it came from," India realized, and Echo and Omega nodded. Zz'r'p also nodded in agreement.

"It is significant that Agent Omega was comatose when the contact occurred," the tall blue alien declared.

"Meaning?" Omega pressed.

"I think it likely that the unusual mental state produced by your comatose condition may have been what made the contact possible," Zz'r'p told her in his politely formal way. "Such a link, created under such conditions, would be a total, wide-open bond. The initiator, however—in this case, Agent Omega—has essentially no control of the link. Whatever one member of the bond thinks or experiences, the other can 'hear'. If one of the bonded beings has a need, it will be drawn from the reserves of the other."

Echo and Omega, brows furrowed, stole swift, confused glances at each other, unobserved by the others, each still wondering how much—and what—the other had experienced, then quickly returned their attention to

251

Zz'r'p.

"Why wasn't I more aware of what was happening to Meg here at Headquarters, then?" Echo asked.

"Did you consciously try to listen?" Zz'r'p replied in a rhetorical fashion. "Or were you too busy piloting your vessel?"

Echo nodded. "Too busy, mostly," he admitted.

"That is the reason," Zz'r'p told him. "Had you had the opportunity to concentrate, you most likely could have done so."

"But why Echo?" Omega asked. "He was on the other side of the galaxy. Why not somebody closer? Romeo, or India, for instance?"

"You must learn not to think in three-dimensional terms, if you are to become a skilled telepath," Zz'r'p told her. "Think as the astrophysicist you are. There is more to the universe than a mere three or four dimensions, as you of all people are aware. Physical distance matters little in a full telepathic link. Who is the being in this room that you are the most like? The person for whom the psychic distance is the least? The one you are 'closest to,' as you humans would say?"

Omega automatically looked directly at Echo, and the others nodded.

"Exactly," Zz'r'p said. "Your partner. THAT is the reason you contacted him, and not the others. Given your body's limited resources, it was actually easier for you to reach him than anyone else, despite the physical distance."

"What about the precog?" India asked.

"That is another matter," Zz'r'p admitted. "I have seen the cerebral scans from your last physical, and it has given me a few ideas. Let us begin a different sort of examination. Are you ready, Agent Omega?"

* * *

She nodded, and moved to stand in front of the tall blue alien, looking up into his piercing black eyes, trusting. A tremor went through her, then her body grew very still.

"That looks familiar," Romeo remarked quietly to the other Agents. "Jus' like in Fox's office, right before that whole Cortian shit went down." Fox and India nodded.

"Yeah," Echo murmured, remembering. "Yeah, it does..."

252

After about five minutes, Zz'r'p turned away from Omega's immobile form and spoke.

"I have placed her into a 'lucid dream' state. She is aware, but in a sleeping brain state. This is somewhere between her comatose state and the mental state of a normal, functioning telepath. If she is able to telepathically communicate in this state, I can train her to do so consciously, while in an active state. Now I would like each of you to step into her field of view and speak to her. Let us know if you get a non-verbal response. Director?" Zz'r'p moved aside, and Fox stepped into the spot Zz'r'p had just vacated.

"Omega? Do you hear me, tekhter?" Fox studied the agent with narrowed eyes, waiting, then looked at Zz'r'p and shook his head.

"Touch her," Zz'r'p instructed. The Alpha Line members watched closely as Fox laid a gentle hand on her shoulder, paused, then shook his head again.

"Very well. Agent Romeo?"

Romeo replaced Fox.

"Hey, pretty lady. Whassup? Your bro's here." No response. Romeo stepped forward and hugged Omega lightly as the others watched, then he leaned back and looked into the wide, unblinking blue eyes. "Nuthin'. Your turn, India."

"Hi, Meg," India said softly, as she stepped in front of her friend. "Sister by another mother, here! Talk to me, girlfriend." India reached out after a moment and brushed a stray wisp of hair off Omega's forehead, letting her fingers touch Omega's face, then looked at the others and also shook her head, moving back to Romeo's side.

"Agent Echo?" Zz'r'p invited, and Echo moved to stand before his partner.

"Now this oughta be interesting," Romeo murmured, and India and Fox nodded.

* * *

"Meg, close your eyes," Echo told her, and Omega's eyelids drifted shut.

"Why did you do that?" India asked quietly.

"She can already read my movements and expressions just by looking at me. If we're gonna work as telepathic partners, she has to be able to 'read' me when she can't see me."

Echo turned back to Omega and wordlessly held out his open right hand, palm up. Omega stirred slightly, but otherwise didn't respond.

"She senses you have requested her to act rather than speak, but she is uncertain what action you want," Zz'r'p told Echo. "Touch her."

Echo's eyes narrowed as he studied Omega, considering, then he raised his left hand and laid the palm firmly against her cheek, cupping it gently in his hand. His right hand remained outstretched, palm up.

"Good," Zz'r'p murmured at Echo's choice. "Direct contact. Skin to skin."

Omega's forehead slowly creased as she concentrated, and her left hand gradually floated upward, fingers splayed, then stopped. The frown deepened. Suddenly Zz'r'p stepped forward.

"No," Zz'r'p said to her. "You strive too hard. Easily...relax..." He lightly touched Omega's temple and her frown smoothed away. "Let me show you."

* * *

Omega's hand suddenly extended outward and laid itself in Echo's palm. Echo's eyes defocused as he abruptly sensed a warm, familiar presence gently touch his mind, and his attention turned inward.

Meg??

Hi, Echo. Ooooh, I got a headache.

Mmh...I can tell. He winced. A gentle laugh resounded in Echo's head.

Sorry, she told him in a soundless voice. *Note to self: telepathic headaches are contagious.*

* * *

Echo winced, then grinned, and the other Agents watched, curious, aware that a silent conversation was occurring.

"Interesting," Fox murmured, keeping his voice very low, so as not to disturb whatever was happening with Alpha One. "We may be witnessing a completely new kind of partnership for the Agency."

"History?" India wondered.

"Quite possibly in the making," Fox agreed.

* * *

Are you too uncomfortable with this, Ace? Omega continued.

No, I'm fine, baby. It's not quite what I'd expected. But then, you're not a psychotic alien telepath, either. Speaking of which, Meg...how do YOU think this compares to contact with Slug? Echo asked.

Well, you aren't trying to rip me apart, for one thing, a wry Omega told him, and Echo sensed her smile. *But it's hard. Slug was the one who always held the link. I don't know if I could hold this link if Zz'r'p weren't helping.*

So...you're not a nominal telepath. Echo's emotions were decidedly mixed; Omega sensed them, but was uncertain how to interpret them.

Zz'r'p interjected then. *There are in fact some weak telepathic abilities now resident in her neural pathways; they were not inborn. But she is correct; under current conditions she almost certainly cannot maintain this link independently. Nor can she adequately control it. However, neither is she operating as a 'nominal telepath' would.*

How so? Echo queried.

Typical telepathic contact is accomplished by the reading of the electromagnetic signals emitted by a sentient nervous system, Zz'r'p explained. *A 'transmitter/receiver' system, if you will. It varies among telepathic races, but there are various mechanisms enabling telepaths to communicate across vast distances, in despite of the relative slowness of said signals.*

What do you mean? Echo wondered.

We Deltiri, for example, having once met the subject, can communicate in this fashion via a variation of quantum entanglement with that subject, Zz'r'p elaborated. *The 'closer' the two beings in communication, the greater the entanglement, and the easier the communication. Gastropoids are much more limited in range, and must be within a reasonable reception distance of the subject. Other factors can affect them, as you already know—interference from other minds, and such like. But among those species capable of these more long-range methods, galactic distances are not a factor.*

But that's not what I'm doing, is it? Omega said.

No, it is not, Zz'r'p answered.

Well, what the hell IS she doing, then? Echo wondered.

She appears to be accessing higher-order dimensions in some fashion, Agent Echo, Zz'r'p told him. *This is especially how the precognition seems to function. It is as if she is viewing alternate realities stemming from current or upcoming events.*

Then I was right! Omega exclaimed.

What do you mean? Zz'r'p asked, surprised. *Did you have an inkling of this, Omega?*

Yes, I sure did. When it first started happening, the images were like one of those interactive video games where you start out at the same place, but each ending is different, depending on some choice that's made. I thought about it for a while, and then I had the idea of worldlines extending from a nexus.

Like we discussed in astrophysics? Echo asked.

Exactly, Omega told him. *Your historical worldline is fixed, but your future worldline has yet to be determined. A nexus is—or would be—where your worldline intersected someone or something else's worldline. That would open up multiple potential futures, depending on all the possible permutations of your decisions versus those of the other worldline...*

I get it, Echo told her. *If I choose A, and you choose A, or B, or C...*

Right, Omega said. *You get worldlines AA, AB, AC. Or BA, BB, BC, if you had chosen B instead. Whatever.*

Yes, Zz'r'p rejoined. *This makes sense, based on what I derive from your current mental capacities.*

But how do I tell which potential worldline is correct? Omega asked.

You cannot, Zz'r'p replied, *because there is no right or wrong worldline. There are only possibilities, and you can only see the options. You must then use your intellect and reason to determine the probabilities and attempt to alter them if necessary, to produce the desired effect or outcome.*

Oh, great, Omega responded, irony heavy. *That's a lotta help—not.*

Do not be discouraged, Omega. You were successful this time in intersecting your own worldline with your partner's to alter his future.

Yes, Zz'r'p, Echo said, *but she almost ended her own. Is there any way she can fine-tune this a little?*

I do not think she can control when it happens, or what she sees, any more than you can selectively view only parts of what is set before you, Echo. It may never happen again, if the n-dimensional physical conditions do not recur. But if it should, you and your colleagues can assist her by helping her sort through the scenarios she observes.

* * *

Gotcha, Echo answered. *But worldlines don't explain how Meg...talked to me.*

That also appears to be n-dimensional, Zz'r'p said. Perhaps like a warp.

A warp? How? Omega asked.

Oh, I see, responded Echo. *Meg, if you'd been on the* Tour de Force *when we came through the cosmic string warp, you'd catch on right away. Look...*and he showed her his memory of n-space.

* * *

Ooooh. Omega was impressed. *So, Zz'r'p, you're saying Echo and I... overlapped, sort of?*

Partially, Zz'r'p answered. *It is as good a metaphor as any, I suppose. Echo, let me ask you—when Omega made contact, was it extroverted or introverted?*

What? I don't get it. What do you mean?

Was your sense of her internal or external to your own being?

There was a pause, and Zz'r'p and Omega both picked up flashes of sensation and memory as Echo considered.

A little of both, I think, Zz'r'p, Echo finally replied. *First I heard her. I turned around to see who was there.*

External, Zz'r'p remarked.

Yes. But then I...felt her... and Omega sensed her own presence reflected back at her, overlaid on—or IN, it was hard to tell—Echo's presence. It was disconcerting. Echo registered her confusion, and suppressed the memory.

And then internal. Yes, that is what I would expect, Zz'r'p confirmed. And this was almost surely made possible by the opening of subconscious blocks—neural circuitbreakers, if you will—during the comatose state.

The mental conversation paused.

* * *

Well...now what? Omega asked.

Zz'r'p, Echo's voice sounded in Omega's head, and she felt his concern, *how is Meg doing...mentally...after being burned? Is she handling it okay?* She sensed Echo moving instinctively toward the vivid memory, still so near the surface of her mind.

NO, Echo! Don't! Omega told him, trying frantically to mentally shield that memory from him. She wasn't entirely successful. Searing agony exploded in two minds simultaneously as Echo contacted the memory.

Mmnh...nngh...Meg, is this—? Damn...ngh...it was hell, baby...How in God's name...rrggh...did you stand...

* * *

Both members of Alpha One suddenly convulsed in pain, as Fox and Alpha Two watched.

"What the hell?!" Fox wondered, shocked.

"That's not good," India declared in dismay.

"SHIT!" Romeo exclaimed, alarmed. "Somethin' bad done happenin' in there! We gotta stop it!"

He lunged forward, but before he could reach either member of Alpha One, Zz'r'p held up a restraining hand, and Romeo found himself unable to move forward any farther.

STOP, the Arcturan gave the mental command to the three watching Agents. *This is under control.*

"What the hell is going on?" Fox demanded.

One moment, please, Director, Zz'r'p replied. *I must see to this first.*

* * *

Zz'r'p, HELP ME! Desperately, Omega mentally shoved Echo away, as she struggled to regain control of her flashback. *What do I do?!*

But before Zz'r'p could respond, Echo answered.

Meg!! Uhng...Circuit...circuitbreaker! Pop it!

Wha—? OH!!

Immediately, a block erected itself around her memory of the ordeal, and Echo's mental distress faded.

Fascinating, Zz'r'p observed in surprise. *Echo, how did you know she could...?*

Easy, Zz'r'p. I know Meg, Echo responded, still panting a bit, both physically and mentally. *She cares about the people around her. And I'm her PARTNER. She won't willingly hurt me—she's told me so, many times, and proved it repeatedly, into the bargain. She just needed a nudge in the right direction.*

But that means, when I started draining you on Edeptis IV... Omega mused.

Right, Echo told her. *The contact wasn't severed, it was switched off. YOU switched it off.*

Of course! Zz'r'p exclaimed. *The connection that drained you was Agent Omega's autonomic nervous system response to physiological stimuli. An UNconscious response. But when her subconscious mind realized what she was doing to you, she broke the connection.*

So there's nothing to worry about, Meg, Echo said, reassuring. *You couldn't have killed me, because you wouldn't have allowed it.*

* * *

The watching Agents saw Omega's shuddering sigh of relief even as Echo and Zz'r'p experienced it. Zz'r'p directed a brief explanation at the small audience.

Agent Echo, in his concern for his partner, inadvertently contacted the memory of Omega's experience under the ion drive, he told them. *It caused Omega to experience a flashback, which Echo was then forced to share, because he was linked to her, and to the memory.*

"Damn, skippy," Romeo murmured again, appalled.

"What he said," an astounded Fox agreed.

"Are they okay now?" India wondered, concerned.

They are, Zz'r'p confirmed. *Stand by.*

* * *

Thank God, Omega said fervently. *I was having nightmares of becoming some sort of...of psychic vampire-thing,* she said with a shaky laugh. Omega felt a comforting 'touch,' and realized that Echo was trying to set her at ease. She flashed him an appreciative mental smile, then said, *Well... so what do we do next?*

Release the link, Zz'r'p told Omega.

Okay, just a sec. Are you all right, Echo? The mental contact was gentle, concerned. *I'm SO sorry I zapped you.*

It's fine, Meg. I'm...okay. But you are one damn strong person, baby. I... knew it was bad, but...I had no idea.

Yeah, well...I'd intended to keep it that way, Omega pointed out. *Nobody else needs to experience that. I never meant for you to, of all people. You got enough of it as it was.*

It's okay, baby, I swear. You and Zz'r'p, between you, actually blocked the worst of it, I think. But...if I didn't already respect the hell outta you, which I do, I would, after that.

Aw.

It's cool, Meg. See you on the outside.

All right.

* * *

Fox and Alpha Two watched as Zz'r'p stepped back from Alpha One, Omega's eyes flickered open, and Echo's body relaxed.

Hands still unconsciously joined, like mirror images, Echo and Omega simultaneously rubbed at one temple and murmured in unison, "Mmh. Anybody got an aspirin?"

* * *

"So, the upshot is," India summarized later in Fox's office, after Zz'r'p had departed to resume negotiations in Geneva, "Meg's a weak, intermittent precog because somehow her brain's been rewired, not just to visualize, like we'd thought, but to actually process more than three dimensions."

"Right," Echo said. "Though I don't quite think Slug intended for THAT to happen. The precog and stuff, I mean. But like Zebra suspected, Meg's brain has continued to develop, especially after Slug's end game attacks. Factor in her natural deductive and inductive reasoning, and Meg's 'hunches' are definitely worth hearing." He looked at his partner, and Omega didn't need to be a psi to know what he was thinking: *And I'll listen from now on.* She smiled at him as he continued. "And technically, she's a telepath, for the same reason."

"But practically, I don't seem to be strong enough to connect with anyone, even Echo, under normal circumstances," Omega added. "Evidently,

260

the brainwave state produced by a coma changes the parameters substantially, because then I could easily, practically effortlessly, reach across the galaxy. But..."

"Yeah," Romeo agreed. "What good is a comatose telepathic partner?"

* * *

"...As a partner...none," Omega said in a strange tone of voice. "It would actually be dangerous to the other partner. But to the Agency..."

"Huh?" Romeo wondered, and Fox and India both frowned, confused.

"Whoa, wait just a damn minute there, Meg." Echo turned to her. "You're not really considering that, are you? Not seriously?"

"You've got to admit, Echo, it would make one hell of an early-warning system..."

"NO. Absolutely not," Echo declared, unequivocal, as Alpha Two's jaws dropped, and Fox frowned. "The Agency does not render their own comatose in order to function as...sensor equipment." His face twisted in distaste and mild disgust at the idea.

"Echo's right, Omega," Fox agreed, equally decisive. "That would make us no better than the criminals we're supposed to police."

"All right. You won't get an argument from me," a good-natured Omega responded, shrugging. "I just wanted you to know of the potential."

"And we're apprised," Fox averred. "Now, why don't you two go home and get some rest, after that whole flashback thing? With your permission, Echo, I have a few things I'd like for Alpha Two to do for me..."

"Yeah, that's fine, Fox," Echo agreed. "I've set them up as the team to fill in for Alpha One until we're able to go back in the field. And by the look of her face, that little telepathic session tired Meg just a bit, anyhow."

"Well, it did," Omega admitted. "And I could still use an aspirin."

"We'll go by Medical and get something," Echo decided. "I think we could both use something a tad bit stronger than just aspirin."

"Go, then," India said, as Romeo nodded. "Romeo and I've got this."

"Yes," Fox said. "Alpha One is dismissed."

"Let's go, baby," Echo said, heading for the door. "I dunno about you, but I feel like pizza tonight."

"Sounds good, Ace. Wanna go out, or have Trifle send something over...?"

* * *

Fox rose and moved to the bay window to watch his top team head across the Core. Alpha Two joined him.

"There go two of the toughest people I've ever met, or am ever likely to meet," India remarked.

"What she said," Romeo agreed. "An' I've known some damn tough people in my time."

"I'm sure you have, Romeo," Fox said. "But I've known more, because I've lived a lot longer. And I still agree with India. And," he appended, "they're 'family.'"

"We're family," India amended his statement.

"Yes, India," Fox asserted. "Yes, we are. Damn strange family, I suppose. But family nevertheless. Now, let's get to work, shall we?"

* * *

"What's up?" Omega wondered several days later, as she and Echo headed for Fox's office.

"No idea," Echo said, cutting across the Core toward the ramp; around them, the lighting between the matte black floor and wall tiles gleamed a soft bronze—Alpha One was being summoned, but it was not the urgent, flashing deep red of an emergency notification. "I just got a cell call from Fox, asking if you were okay, while I was tying my tie this morning. And when I said yes, then he told me that Alpha One needed to report to his office at once, or as soon as we could decently get there—he knew he called me early, and we weren't on duty yet."

"Huh."

"Yeah. If it's a big emergency, I'm gonna insist he assign Alpha Two— and as many other Alpha teams as he thinks are warranted—to handle it. It's too soon for you to go on a really strenuous mission quite yet. You only just started back to doing desk work a couple-three days ago."

"If it's a big emergency, why isn't the floor lighting red? And I'm fine, Ace."

"You are, and it's probably not—but you still need another couple days to get acclimated. And that's not only me saying that. Doron, Zarnix, Zebra, and even Whiskey are a united medical front on this, baby. Alpha Line's resident medic India threw her weight in with them, too. So don't even try to question it. Under the right circumstances, they can even overrule Fox. And this is one of those circumstances. If it was a system-wide emergency, then MAYBE they'd let you go. If it was the entire Division, or the Galaxy, then they'd have to let you go, of course. But at this point, not even a planet-wide disaster looming is gonna get you off the reserve status until they say you're ready."

"Oh." Omega's shoulders drooped; she was already starting to get a little tired of only doing departmental paperwork and the odd city patrol. *After all,* she thought, *I was in that damn tank for two or three weeks easy, PGLEIA time—I really need to look at a calendar and figure out, 'cause I lost all track of time in there. It saved my life, no question, but it sure did get boring in that dinky little pod.*

* * *

Echo noticed her downcast expression and posture, read it accurately, and bit his lip to keep from grinning.

Never mind what I've got planned for us as soon as they release you for active duty, baby, he thought. *Just hang in there.*

* * *

The door to Fox's office was closed, and the bay windows dark. Echo knocked on it a couple of times, but instead of the expected and usual, "Come in," Alpha One heard Fox ask, "Who is it?"

Echo and Omega shot puzzled glances at each other.

That's different, she signaled.

No shit, came his response in kind.

"It's Alpha One, Fox," Echo replied to the Agency chief. "You rang, we answered."

"Both of you?"

"Yeah, boss."

"And JUST Alpha One, right?"

"Uh...right..."

"Come on in, then, but close the door behind you."

Echo opened the door, ushering Omega through in front of him before

263

entering himself and closing the door as requested. He looked up just as Omega gasped.

* * *

The wall screens were off, and the bay windows overlooking the Core had been opaqued. Instead of being seated behind his desk, Fox was standing in the middle of the room with another being. Omega gaped as she looked up at the nine-foot-tall reptilian being.

In addition to being so tall, it was quite well-muscled, and apparently covered from crown to sole in white scales, which glistened almost silver in the office lighting. It was clad in a knee-length velvet-like tunic of a soft rust color. Its shoulders held what Omega at first took to be a plush gray cape...until the being flexed slightly and they unfurled a bit.

Wings, she thought in astonishment. *It's got big bat wings. Like a dragon or something!*

The creature's eyes were reddish-orange, and seemed almost to glow like living flames; the effect was enhanced by the characteristic vertical-slit pupils. Two black, sleek horns adorned the top of its head, and were, at that moment, lying neatly along the contours of the skull, though they seemed to move slightly with the being's facial expressions. The head itself was broad, rather flat, and somewhat lizard-shaped; the nose consisted of two nostril-slits, and the mouth was essentially lipless and wide.

The overall effect put the female Agent in mind of a 'horned toad' lizard; this set her at ease, as she had had a semi-tamed lizard in the area of West Texas where she used to do weekend observing runs—when it saw her setting up, it would always come to her, and she always had tidbits—insects and such—to feed it. *He looks kinda like a big, intelligent one of those things,* she decided. *Maybe everything's okay.* The thought settled her somewhat jumpy nerves—until the being smiled at her. She gulped.

'My, what big teeth you have, Grandma,' ran through her head. *Holy shit, ain't THAT the truth. Sharp, too, by the look. Who the hell IS this?*

* * *

Echo looked up and promptly recognized the being standing beside Fox in the middle of the room. He immediately bowed.

"Lord Entiyti," he murmured. "This is an unexpected surprise."

Omega shot her partner a querying glance, her eyebrows rising; then she, too, bowed.

"Um, yes," she agreed. "Forgive me, I...didn't recognize you, um..."

"Nor did I expect you to," Entiyti said, smile growing wider. "Echo, I am pleased that you do remember me so readily; it has been a while."

"It has, sir."

"But please stop all this 'sir' and 'lord' nonsense," Entiyti added. "As long as we have known one another, I would have thought you would simply call me Pulgey, as Fox, here, does."

Echo stood up and smiled back at the being, tapping Omega's shoulder to let her know it was okay to rise from her bowed position.

"Mah momma an' daddy raised me to be polite to mah elders," he informed Entiyti, letting considerably more than usual of his native Texan dialect slip through. Entiyti roared a laugh.

"And several centuries is more than enough to rank me as an elder, eh?" the reptilian replied with another smile.

"Ah reckon so," Echo said, his own smile morphing into a grin. "But seriously, if you are inviting me to do so, I'd be honored."

"I am, son."

"Then, thank you...Pulgey. May I present my partner, Agent Omega."

"Pleased, sir," Omega murmured, bowing again.

"Stand, child, please. Yes, I have heard much about this one. It is I who am pleased to meet you, Omega. In fact, it is why I have come to Earth this time."

* * *

"Wh-what?" Omega exclaimed, startled. "You came here...just to meet ME?"

"Of course. Are you not the hero of the hour? Or perhaps that is heroine; I never quite got the hang of that particular declension..."

"Heroine usually denotes female," Fox noted softly. "But these days, hero can work for a generic term. You did fine, Pulgey."

"Ah, I see. Yes, my dear, Fox has kept me 'in the loop,' as you humans say, from the time your precognitive visions of the Cortians were reported to him, until the day you were released from the medlab to resume light

265

duty." Entiyti held out a taloned hand, the claws carefully curled into his own palm. Omega blinked, then threw a questioning glance at Echo and Fox. Echo understood first...because he'd been there, himself, once upon a time.

"Shake his hand, baby," Echo explained. "He's got his claws curled under so he won't scratch you. That's why it looks different."

"Ah! That explains it," Entiyti said, as Omega grasped his hand and they shook. "You have never encountered a Draconan before, have you?"

"Not until just now, sir," Omega replied, feeling her face flush. "Sorry if I seem a little, uh, confused."

"Dear Maker, little one!" Entiyti exclaimed. "I am surprised that that is ALL you are experiencing, after what you have done, what you have been through!" He turned to the Director. "Fr-ah, Fox, might we sit down and talk? I think it may put Omega more at ease if we are less formal."

"Great idea, Pul," Fox agreed, dragging his desk chair around the desk. "Echo, pull those visitor chairs around in a circle, here, and we'll have a nice chat. No, Omega, no lifting until the doctors give the go-ahead; Echo and I will handle the chairs. Pul, take my chair; it's more comfortable, and will probably accomodate your wings a little better."

"Thank you, Fra-damn it, FOX. Your code name is Fox. I must remember to use it," Entiyti said in some frustration. "As long as you have been 'Fox,' I should recall it by now."

"You knew him a lot longer as Franz, I'll bet," Omega said, taking the seat that Echo held for her, before sitting himself.

"Well, he has been a PGLEIA agent for some time, now," Entiyti admitted. "Very nearly as long as he worked with and for me. Still, I suppose we were closer when he was my chief bodyguard. How is it that you know about this, Omega?"

"There's a synopsis of the story in the historical section of the Agent's Handbook. I've read the thing cover to cover a couple times, and that section several extra times. I'm fascinated by the history of the Division."

Entiyti turned to Fox.

"So your background is known to the Agency?"

"Not exactly," Fox explained. "What Omega may not realize is that the particular section of the handbook SHE got is heavily redacted for non-Alpha Line agents."

"Ooo," Omega said, clapping a hand on her mouth. "I'm so glad I never had occasion to talk to anybody about it, then!" she said, voice muffled through her fingers.

They all laughed.

"Given that all of the rest of the Alpha Line Agents were recruited from within the Agency," Echo noted, "and already had the more redacted handbooks, I'd be willing to bet that Meg's the only one to have read it, Fox. The others probably haven't even noticed it's different."

"Most likely," Fox agreed, shooting a smile at Omega. "One thing for which your partner has never given me cause to complain is her thoroughness. Her intense curiosity, occasionally, but in an intellect like hers, it's to be expected, I think. And since we make as full use of that intellect as we know how, I'm more than willing to make allowances."

Omega's cheeks got hotter. Fox clapped his hands together in enthusiasm.

"So, Omega, Pulgey here wanted to meet you, especially after hearing about..." Fox sobered, "well, about this latest exploit."

"Oh," Omega said, voice going flat. "Um, are you, uh, wanting a debrief or something, sir? I, uhm, if it's all the same, I'd rather...not...yet..." her voice died away.

"No, no, Omega, not that," Entiyti said, leaning forward and laying a hand lightly on her shoulder. "No, Fox has told me all I need to know. I simply wanted to meet you. That's all."

"I don't blame you, Lor-er, Pulgey," Echo noted, correcting his mode of address in mid-word. "My partner is pretty damn special, if I do say so."

"Aw, you just wanna take the credit for finding me, 'cause you an' your perp ran over me—literally," Omega teased, grinning at Echo.

"That, too," Echo allowed, returning her grin. "And there's the sense of humor, back in full," he added. "Finally. Welcome back, baby."

"Indeed," Entiyti concurred.

"What they said," Fox agreed.

Omega smiled slightly and nodded.

* * *

"So tell me something about yourself," Entiyti queried, settling into Fox's cushy office chair. "Something I should not find in the PGLEIA records about you. I want to get to know you."

"Um, well, but...what about Echo?" Omega wondered.

"Oh, he knows me, baby," Echo demurred. "He was there the day I went looking to see what the hell kinda illegal alien shit was goin' on at the ranch...and got drafted. Both him and Fox."

"Yes," Fox chuckled. "Alien was the operative word that day. But they were all legal."

"They were, that," Echo agreed. "Anyway, Lord Entiyti—um, Pulgey—and I go back...well, not nearly as far as Fox and him, but pretty damn far. Of everybody in this room, the only one he doesn't know well is you, Meg. It's okay. He just wants to get to know you, like he said."

"Omega...after what happened with the Cortians...are you possibly uncomfortable with a non-human?" Entiyti wondered.

"No, it isn't that at all," Omega protested. "It's more like I'm suddenly the focus of attention, and I'm...not used to it." *And not comfortable with it,* she added mentally. *I just know it's all gonna end up revolving around what Slug did to me, and what these new 'abilities' are, and what I can do with 'em. And...while I was honest with Echo and the others—I AM satisfied with who and what I am—I just wish others would see me the same way. Just...me.*

"'Not like this,' is what you are thinking, isn't it?" Entiyti discerned, cocking his head to the side. "You want to be thought of as you, not merely for what you can do."

Omega blinked in surprise. *Is this guy a telepath too?* she wondered.

"Uh-huh. All right," a shrewd Entiyti said, eyeing her. "Then let us play a game that Franz taught me years ago, called 'Twenty Questions,'" the Draconan suggested.

Echo and Omega both burst into prolonged laughter. Fox and Pulgey exchanged amused glances, but said nothing, waiting for the explosion of hilarity to subside.

"Oh geez, like we didn't play THAT enough when I was in the regen pod, Ace," Omega eventually managed to get out, wiping tears of mirth from her eyes.

"Oh HELL yes!" Echo agreed, laughter finally subsiding to chuckles. "I think he's gonna go in a different direction with it, though."

"Indeed, I should think so," Entiyti offered mildly. "Tell me of your favorite foods and drinks, to start."

"Oh. Well, lessee," Omega murmured, thinking. "I guess my favorite non-alcoholic drink would be a chocolate malt."

"I didn't know that, but I'm not surprised," Echo decided. "Chocolate seems to be a theme with you."

"Yeah," Omega agreed. "I'm also kinda fond of chocolate stout, and, well, chocolate anything, really. We don't do a lotta fast food, and I don't usually keep the malt powder in the kitchen 'cause the Supplies people don't stock it, so it's been a while since I've had one."

"We'll fix that, the next time we go out on a street patrol," Echo noted.

"And I'll contact Supplies about the malt powder," Fox decided. "I'm rather fond of a malted from time to time, myself."

"Okay, that sounds good, guys. Thanks. So, um, I like pizza, and Echo's pot pies an' casseroles, and the way my mom cooked green beans fresh from the garden with new potatoes in the same pot..."

"What are green beans...?" Entiyti wondered.

* * *

"Well, that should do nicely, then," Fox decided an hour later, when the friendly chat lagged a bit, and the others—even Echo—had learned a few little details about Omega that they didn't know. "As soon as I knew Pulgey was coming, I checked with Zebra, and since today is her day off, she's been arranging a private little dinner party in my quarters, for around 26:00 Division time tonight. We—she and I—had hoped to have both Alpha One and Pulgey as our guests. And I already know Pulgey is coming. I had invited Doron as well, but it seems he is busy sharing medical technology with a substantial portion of the entire Division One Medical Department—rather enthusiastically, according to Zebra, who is just as excited about it—and since he's at the London Office right now, moving on to Geneva in the morning, he sent his regrets and the desire to meet with us all another day.

So it'll just be us tonight. Nothing fancy at all; I'm the one who introduced Echo to Trifle's Pizzeria, so we're ordering pizza, and Zebra is making some other courses to go along with it, salad and dessert and whatnot. So what about it, Omega, Echo? Can you come?"

"I certainly hope you can," Entiyti enjoined. "I am looking forward to a relaxed evening with more chat over food and drink. It is a custom of my people, and one I enjoy sharing."

Omega shot Echo a querying glance, and he realized that she was asking him as department chief if it was all right...as well as whether or not he had a personal or scheduling problem with it. He hid a smile, realizing that his partner had just made friends with a very powerful galactic personage.

"Sure, Fox, that sounds great," he answered for them both. "Meg, you're okay with that, right?"

"Sounds good to me, Ace," she agreed without hesitation.

"Good. Echo, if you and Omega have enough to go around, perhaps you wouldn't mind bringing the chocolate stout? I'm fond of a good dark beer anyway, and I know Pulgey likes Earth beers..."

"Indeed I do!" Entiyti agreed.

"Yeah, we can do that, Fox," Echo vouched. "I think maybe we oughta do a quick run down to the corner store, though, and get an extra couple packs, don't you, Meg?"

"Well, we have enough to go around," Omega decided, "but just barely. So...yeah, let's go down to the deli for lunch today—first lunch or second, I don't care which—and stop by the store on the way back. Then we can bring the stout tonight, and have plenty for everyone to have as much as he or she wants."

"It's a plan," Echo averred.

"Excellent!" Fox said.

"And I look forward to even more chat and getting to know each other, in an even more relaxed environment," Entiyti added.

"Me, too," Omega said with a shrug and a smile. "I have to admit, I never expected to be making friends with a guy who is, for all intents and purposes, a dragon!"

Entiyti let out one of his roaring laughs.

"Ah, child—if I may call you that, for compared to me, you and your partner are both children, and even Franz here is but a young adult—you are every whit what I expected, and more."

"I, um, I dunno what you expected," Omega said, reverting to a slightly shy response. "I'm just me."

"And I kinda like your 'me,'" Echo reassured her, quirking his fingers around the pronoun. "So 'me' is good."

"Yes, it is," Entiyti affirmed. "You should know—since I returned to the Ennead as interim chair, until a successor to that fool Dulziv can be determined—the Ennead is looking into a proper recognition for you, Omega. For both you and your partner, actually."

"Huh? What do you mean?" Omega asked, startled.

"Omega," Fox explained gently, "you very nearly gave everything to save Echo. Then he turned around and risked it all to get your only chance at survival—the healer, Doron—and bring him home to you."

"Fox," Echo protested. "Pulgey. That's not necessary. Not for me, anyway. You know why I did it." The two human males exchanged a knowing glance, and Echo knew Fox was aware of the dual meaning of the statement. "Besides, I'd be a damn sorry excuse for a person, let alone an Agent, if I didn't do everything within my power to keep Meg alive, especially after what she did for me." He looked down at his partner. "Now Meg deserves something. Something special. She went into all of it, KNOWING what was coming—and did it anyway. That warrants something really momentous. A medal, or a, a knighthood, or whatever. I didn't know PGLEIA had anything like that."

"We don't," Entiyti said. "That's why we're looking into it. We want to establish something, some special designation that means a being behaved with exceptional valor and principle. And I'm looking at two prime examples now."

"Hold on a second. Look, guys," Omega said, and her voice was very quiet; nevertheless, it caught the attention of all three men in the room. "I didn't do it for an award. I didn't do it for fame, or recognition, or honors. Those things are nice, I suppose. But...well, it's like this." She swallowed, then sighed, and Echo realized matters were about to turn serious.

"By the time Slug got done killing my family, stripping away my humanity, and showing me just how easy it was for him to commandeer my body, my mind...inserting me into an organization I didn't even know existed, and scotching my personal dreams to do it..." She dropped her gaze to the floor and swallowed again. "I don't have a whole lot left, guys. But I'll be DAMNED," she looked up at them, azure gaze suddenly flaming blue in raw fury, body seeming to expand in size as the muscles flexed and the magnitude of the personality within fully revealed itself, "if I'm gonna let a buncha thieving, pirating, slaver BASTARDS destroy what I got left!"

She rose to her feet in anger.

"There are a few people in this place that are the closest thing I have to a family left in this universe," she continued, fists moving to her hipbones. "Two of 'em are in this room, along with somebody I'm starting to think of as a 'friend of the family,' kinda. I work close alongside two more...and another one helps take care of me medically. If the Cortians had gotten Echo, whether they enslaved or killed him, it's a lead-pipe cinch I'd have never seen him again! And don't think for one nanosecond they wouldn't have come back for the rest of us, if they could have found a way—and believe me, they'd be trying!" She shook her head, vehement, as she scowled. "If I had it to do again, I would—no matter the pain. If I could take out a few more of 'em in the process, so much the better. If I knew that next time, I'd DIE, I'd STILL do it."

The room was silent for a long, respectful moment, no one else daring to speak in the face of the furious avenging angel before them.

"Meg...I've never thought to ask," Echo murmured at last. "Did...you know you'd survive, along with everything else?"

Omega turned to face him, the anger ebbing from her expression.

"No, Ace, I didn't," she said in a low tone. "In the scenario that actually took place, I never saw anything past us lying on the hangar floor, getting torched as the *Trindak* took off. Of that scenario, I saw two endings: both of us burning...or just me." She shrugged. "I...figured I'd do what I could to ensure that at least ONE of us made it."

"So you went into it expecting to die," Fox said, and she turned to him.

"Yes," was all she said. But it was enough. Echo closed his eyes to hide the pain in them.

"Damnation," he heard Entiyti say.

Dear God, Echo thought, bleak. *And if it hadn't been for Indak telling us of Doron and his healing techniques, and about a thousand things that went right for me on the trip to get him and bring him back, she would have.* He thrust his jaw forward, determined. *She cares. It may not be romantic love, but she cares about me. Maybe I can nudge it in that direction, and maybe I can't. But I'll stick by this woman for as long as she'll let me.*

* * *

Omega saw the thrust jaw, and understood...at least in part.

He cares, she thought, laying a hand on his shoulder, and watching as he opened his eyes and glanced up into her face. *Maybe not the way I do, but he's determined to see that nothing like that happens again. And with the kind of guts and determination he's got, not to mention his sense of honor and decency and general RIGHT, he'll do it, too. So if he wants me to help him—tinkered-to-hell genetics and all—I'll stand beside him and fight to my dying breath.*

* * *

Fox and Entiyti watched the look that Alpha One exchanged then, and suddenly both knew: This was no ordinary partnership, and it never would be. It was something special, and both members of that partnership knew it.

Although, Fox decided, continuing to watch, *I don't think either one knows how the other one feels. Not really. This...could get interesting. In the fun sort of way. I just need to play the cards right. And with Zebra helping...*

"I agree with you," Entiyti breathed over Fox's shoulder, knowing him well enough to have read his thoughts from his slight hints of expression.

"I don't doubt it," Fox agreed in kind. "You always did get a kick out of that sort of thing."

"Can I help?"

"Quite possibly, alter khaver. We'll see."

* * *

"So no, Mr. Chairman," Omega said then, flashing Entiyti a brief grin, "it isn't necessary to award us anything, except understanding, trust—"

"And the best damn equipment you can outfit us with," Echo finished for her.

"That," she agreed. "Lotsa that."

"What if the Ennead decides to do it anyway?" Fox wondered.

"IF you can find time for us to go to the awards ceremony," Omega pointed out, a mischievous twinkle forming in her eyes.

"You'll have to hog-tie me to get me to some big, fancy, formal thing like that," Echo grumbled. Entiyti laughed.

"Well, well, we shall see," the Draconan said. "Now, I am sure that Alpha One has things to take care of, and we have a dinner party tonight to look forward to, in any event. Fox, you said something about a tour of the facilities, too."

"I did," Fox said, standing. "Omega, Echo, you're welcome to come along on that tour, if you like. It's going to be very informal, in any event; Pul's just curious to see what we've done with the place."

"No, Fox, Pulgey's right. I've got stuff to do," Echo said with a regretful sigh. "Meg and I have been working on some more new applicants for Alpha Line, and I think I've about got it narrowed down to who I want to test—we finally got all of the new members we used in the whole Cortian mess into the system as Alpha Line, only yesterday...JUST as a brand-new, monster batch of applications came in. So even though I've been doing nothing BUT paperwork since Meg went into the regen tank, I'm still behind the curve. Meg, you can go, if you want to."

"I thought you wanted me to HELP you screen that new batch of applications," Omega pointed out. "I mean, yeah, I'd enjoy talking to Pulgey and Fox some more, but I don't wanna skip out on you, or on the work that needs doing."

"Go," Fox said with a benevolent smile. "You have work, and we still have dinner tonight, and all evening to talk. And Pul isn't leaving for a few days, so there's still some time...and future evenings we can plan, into the bargain."

Alpha One departed the Agency Director's office side by side, shoulders squared, heads held high.

The Director of the Division One Agency and the Chairbeing of the Ennead moved to the bay window—which Fox had adjusted to one-way glass—and watched them go.

Then they turned to each other, smiled, and nodded.

"C'mon, Pul," Fox said then. "Let's go poke around Headquarters and see what trouble we can get ourselves into."

"Lead on, my old friend," Entiyti declared. "Just like old times."

* * *

When Echo and Omega arrived at the deli for first lunch, the owner was waiting on the takeout customers again, and waved them over to the counter as they came through the front door.

"Ah, dere ya are, son," he said to Echo, in a friendly fashion. "Back again! Hold on a sec an' I'll take youse t' a table myself. And is this your purty little lady friend who was in da hospital over Valentine's Day?"

Omega blinked in surprise, and behind her, an alarmed Echo drew his hand across his throat in the classic 'cut it off' gesture.

"Um, yeah, that was me," she admitted, seeming a bit shy. "How'd you know?"

"Oh, Echo here—dat's your name, right?" the owner broke off.

"Uh, nickname, yeah," Echo affirmed.

"Right. Dat's what I've heard da guys call ya whenever youse was in—anyways, Echo here came in for a takeout dinner, so he could go spend da evening wit'chu in da hospital," the deli owner explained, eyeing Echo in a fashion which told the Agent that the other man would be discreet. "I gathered youse was still unconscious, an' he was missin' you somethin' awful, judgin' by how down in da mouth he was."

"Aw," Omega said, casting an appreciative glance at Echo before leaning into him with affection.

Echo smiled at her and shifted his stance, allowing him to counter her weight and lean into her as well. The watching deli owner tucked his chin and tilted his head, raising his eyebrows and giving Echo a glance that translated as, 'Okay, so I get that she doesn't know yet, but it looks to me like it's headed in the right direction, bro.'

"Anyhow," the owner added, "it was Valentine's Day, I remember, 'cause of all da people comin' in for, well, stuff for romantic dinners an' shit." He met Echo's gaze. "Didja toast 'er health wi' dat little bottle o' wine

I sent along, like I toldja?"

"I did," Echo averred, then shrugged. "Though she wasn't conscious to know it."

Omega stared at him, looking thoughtful.

"What?" Echo wondered.

"Was it..." She broke off and rubbed her forehead with the heel of her hand for a moment, seeming to concentrate. "Little single-serve bottle of..." she shook her head. "It was red wine, I think. Shiraz, maybe? I can't, um, I couldn't see the label too well...an' a sub sandwich..."

Echo raised both eyebrows and looked at the deli owner, who did likewise.

"Yeah, baby, it was, to both," he confirmed. "So maybe you were drifting in and out?"

"...Or something," she agreed, shooting him a guarded look, then darting her eyes sideways, toward the deli owner. Echo promptly sent her a message with one of their subtlest codes.

Were you 'seeing' without looking, then? he asked.

I'm not sure, she admitted in similar fashion. *Either it was the whole 'overlap' bit...or I actually was semi-conscious. But I don't really remember enough to be able to tell you which; I was too drugged up at that point.*

Right, Echo replied, then asked aloud, "Do you remember anything else about it?"

"Yeah, but I can't quite pull it all out," Omega said, frowning and rubbing her fingertips against her forehead. "Something red, sitting next to your sandwich, and...maybe a card, or something?"

"Uh-huh," Echo confessed. "When I remembered it was Valentine's Day, I thought about...well, everything..." he shrugged, "and I brought flowers and a card. It wasn't any big deal," he added hastily, seeing her eyebrows rising precipitately, "just a cute little card with bears, an' a flower. I wanted to kinda observe your first Valentine's Day here, what with...everything. They disappeared out of the La— uh, your room, a couple days later, so I guess the medics ditched 'em before you could wake up good. Sorry about that."

"It's okay," Omega said, laying a gentle hand on his forearm. "Just knowing you did, means a lot." She smiled. "I'll get with Zebra, and ask if they threw out the flower and card, or if maybe they kept 'em someplace for me."

"That'd be...good," Echo told her. "I think I'd like that."

"Awright, let's get youse guys seated at a nice table in da corner," the deli owner said, beaming. "Tell ya's what—da little lady here gets anything she wants on da menu, gratis on da house, on 'counta she's outta da damn hospital!"

"Oh, you don't have to do that," Omega protested.

"If he doesn't, I'm pickin' up the tab," Echo warned. "After all, you were IN there because of me."

"What's dat, den?" the deli owner wanted to know.

"She saved my life," Echo explained, modifying the story to something a casual listener would understand. "She...got me out of the way of, of a car that, uh, ran a red light...but she didn't get out of the way in time, herself. She, uh, suffered some internal injuries."

"Wow," the owner said, wide-eyed. "An' youse okay now?"

"Oh yeah, I'm fine now," Omega averred."The docs got me patched up pretty good. Well," she confessed then, "I'm still kinda stiff an' all, I guess. But that's gettin' better."

"So we's got ourselves a bona-fide heroine here, huh?"

"No no, now y'all cut this out," Omega declared. "I already said this once today: I did what I needed to do. Don't go makin' a big deal out of it."

"Say what you like, baby, it WAS a big deal. To me, anyway," Echo pointed out. "Because I wouldn't be here now, otherwise. Sir, we're going to have a couple of glasses of the wine with our lunch, if you don't mind. And it goes on my tab."

"An' I got 'er lunch," the deli owner grinned. "Youse kin take her t' a fancy-shmancy dinner all on your own."

"I will, that," Echo agreed.

* * *

When their simple but delicious meal arrived shortly thereafter, accompanied by two glasses of a rich red wine—which was rather more sumptuous than the little single bottle he'd had on Valentine's Day, though

277

the deli owner charged no extra for it—Echo lifted his glass to his partner. Omega followed his cue and lifted her own glass.

"As I said that night, 'To Alpha One. Us two...always,'" he murmured. Omega's face crumpled into a touched smile, her lips wobbling a bit.

"Amen," she breathed, and they drank.

* * *

"Does this look okay, honey?" Zebra wondered, as she set the dining table for a very unique kind of 'family' dinner, later that evening. "I know we're only having pizza and stuff. But I just wanted to put a small floral centerpiece there, to dress it up a little bit and make it kinda special, but I also know Draconans have some sensitivity restrictions. I THINK I got everything all right, but I wanted to make sure..."

Fox scanned the table with a critical eye, paying particular attention to the flowers in the center.

"That looks fine, bubeleh," he determined. "I don't see anything that might cause a problem. And that used to be something I did regularly for him, so I think we're good."

"Is there anything else I need to watch out for?"

"Well, roses and anything in the rose family," Fox said. "He's particularly sensitive to those. No human-edible flowers of any sort in the food, or for garnish. And whatever you do, do NOT put peanuts or peanut butter on the menu in any form."

"Oh! Is he allergic?"

"No, that one's a personal preference."

"Aw. Not even my special Oriental peanut salad dressing? I was gonna use that on the salad..."

"No, not even that. He can't stand the smell, let alone the taste, any more. Pul has never let me forget that particular little practical joke, and believe me, I paid for it in spades."

"What?! Why not?" Zebra wondered. "What's the problem?"

"Draconans—and reptoids, for that matter, since they're all distant kin—love the smell and taste of peanut butter when they're first introduced to it," Fox explained, "but once it gets into their mouths, it globs up and sticks to the roof of the mouth, which is highly arched, and ridged into the

278

bargain, and their tongues aren't shaped right to be able to get it out very readily..."

"Oh no," Zebra said, staring at her significant other. "You didn't."

"I did," Fox said with a reminiscent grin. "I was relatively young, and we were—and are, still—the best of friends, Pul and I, even if I WAS his employee. I didn't really believe it would work, though; I thought it was mostly folklore. I found out—it isn't." He shook his head, still grinning. "I swear, every time I saw him for the next three days, he had this distant look on his face, and his jaw was constantly moving from where he was trying to fish that farkakt peanut butter out of the crevices. He got sick to death of the taste, pretty quickly. I think in the end, he had to see his oral hygenist to get the last of it out..."

"That was NOT good for his oral and dental health, Fox!"

"Well no, but I didn't know that at the time." Fox shrugged, and the grin grew wider. "Of course, that meant he had to retaliate, at some point..."

"Oh NO!" Zebra exclaimed, fascinated. "What did he DO?!"

"I'll tell you later," Fox said, a devilish twinkle appearing in his eyes. "We need to finish getting the dinner ready for our guests; they'll be here soon."

"You aren't gonna tell me, are you?" Zebra demanded.

"...Eventually," Fox said, slipping past her and delivering an affectionate pat to her backside. "Just not now."

"Well...damn," Zebra said, mildly annoyed. "I'll just have to ask Lord Entiyti during dinner, then."

"Oh, I wouldn't do that," Fox advised in all seriousness. "Not unless you want to revive the practical joke war...and find yourself in the middle of it. And that war went on—and escalated!—for fully five Earth years before everybody on board Pul's personal flagship got sick of it. The captain—who had known Pul from childhood, or he wouldn't have dared—finally sat us both down and told us to stop; he understood we were the best of friends, but it had gone more than far enough. And, given the, ah, recent incident with the stink bomb and the interplanetary drive, we decided he was correct."

"Um, oh," Zebra mumbled, wide-eyed. "Al-all right."

"Good choice, dear," Fox murmured, and kissed her.

* * *

Dinner that evening was simple but filling; for the first course, Zebra made a huge salad—with BALSAMIC dressing—and a New York-style cheesecake for dessert. Fox ordered delivery from Trifle's Pizzeria as promised, thereby ensuring for himself that at least one of the pies was kosher, and Alpha One brought three six-packs of the chocolate stout. After dessert, they all retired to Fox's den with fresh stout, and sat chatting; Fox took his recliner, Zebra perching comfortably—and obviously familiarly—on its arm. Alpha One had the sofa, and Entiyti sank his large form into the oversized armchair beside Fox's recliner with a comfortable sigh.

"Oh, by the way, I'm sure you'd all like to know that Edeptis IV contacted me about how to join PGLEIA," Fox said. "For that matter, so did some race that Echo ran into en route to get Doron."

"Oh, the Ganotians?" Echo wondered. "That's good. Offhand I didn't have a clue what division they were in, but I knew you would, and could put them in touch with the right people."

"I do, and I did," Fox said with a grin, taking a sip from the bottle of stout. "It's in work already."

"Yes, I received the notifications of application late this afternoon, on my outboard brain," Entiyti observed.

"Outboard brain?!" Omega exclaimed, grinning, as she raised her stout bottle to her lips.

"Yes, that's what Pul always calls his principal hand-held device," Fox explained with a matching grin. "He's done it for years. And if you think about it, it makes a certain amount of sense, for those of us with a lot to keep up with. The things do serve as kind of an adjunct brain."

Echo snorted, and Omega and Zebra giggled.

"Yes, well, at any rate," Entiyti harrumphed. "I told the diplomatic service to expedite both memberships, and get a signatory addendum added to the Sydys Concordat as soon as possible."

"Great," Echo decided. "I think the Edeptans are rather glad to form the alliance; all the way out there on the edge of the Outer Arm, they were hanging out to dry—especially whenever the Cortians decided to raid."

"We will see that the Edeptans are properly protected, never fear. And we WILL take care of that particular planet of miscreants, I promise you," Entiyti observed, growing grim. "What they've done is against so many galactic regulations and laws, I don't even want to count them. But our legal teams do—and are, already."

"Good," Omega muttered, settling deeper into the couch. She knocked back a healthy slug of the stout.

"Easy, baby," Echo urged. "I know you enjoy the stuff, and so do I. But I expect your system may still be a little sensitive after...everything."

"He's right, Omega," Zebra confirmed. "I've got DeTox tabs if we need 'em, but I still wouldn't advise you getting too blitzed."

"Well, I wasn't planning on it," Omega noted. "But okay."

"Then why did you just belt your beer?" Echo asked, in mildly-amused puzzlement.

"Oh, that. Um, that was kinda by way of emphasis, I guess you could say," she offered with a rueful grin. "They've caused us—me, specifically, all things considered, if y'all don't mind me being selfish for a second— more than enough trouble. I'd like to see them get into some trouble, for a change."

"Hear, hear," Fox affirmed. "Though I rather think Echo took care of the lot that gave us such fits."

"With extreme prejudice," Echo added, scowling. "Damn sons o' bitches nearly killed Meg."

"And woulda killed—or enslaved—you," Omega pointed out. "You were the one in danger. I just got my own ass fried 'cause I stuck my nose into it."

"NO," Entiyti declared, vehement; it was nearly a bellow of rage, and the room fell silent. "No, little one. I will not hear it. I will not stand for you attempting to blame yourself for what those ssllsshhthh did! Any of it!"

"Yeah," Echo said, growing morose. He took a long pull from his own bottle. "Especially when, if I'd listened to you sooner..."

"Echo, you stop right there, too," Entiyti ordered, as Fox opened his mouth to speak. "No, Franz, old friend, don't even start. I fully understand that you both feel responsible for what happened. But as soon as you realized what was truly occurring, you both TRIED your damnedest to back Omega up. It is NOT the fault of anyone in this room that the Cortians were bold, experienced pirates and slavers of a like which even I have never seen. Nor yet is it the fault of anyone here that the political-gaming fool excuse of a Council Chairbeing we had at the time refused to even consider anything out of the ordinary, especially when dealing with extraordinary persons. And I am speaking of both members of Alpha One," Entiyti added.

"*I* think that was wisely said, Lord Entiyti," Zebra declared. "And something that three people in this room sorely needed to hear. So I thank you—professionally, and personally."

The room was silent again for a few more moments; Zebra and Entiyti watched Fox and Alpha One. But Echo and Fox watched Omega, as she leaned back, staring at the ceiling in thought.

"Yeah, you're right, Pulgey," she finally murmured. "Because there were no visions where we got out clean. I've been sitting here thinking, trying to remember, and the only options I ever saw were—A: I got hurt or killed, I couldn't tell the difference at the time; B: Echo got killed outright, in one of several different ways; or C: Echo got imprisoned and carted away as a slave."

"Which means that, if you and Zz'r'p are right about the whole world line thing," Echo extrapolated, "then there weren't any other world lines possible."

"Right," Omega confirmed. "So somebody in Alpha One was gonna get hurt, no matter WHAT any of us did."

"Were there any scenarios where both of you...failed to survive?" Fox wondered, a bit tentative. "Didn't you mention one this morning?"

"Yeah, there were kinda two possible terminations on what really ended up happening," Omega noted, voice quiet. "The one that actually happened, and another one where the force field failed outright and we both got torched. There was a variant on it where Echo got knocked under the drive alone and killed, but that one branched off earlier. Near as I could figure from what I saw, that one had an initial condition where I wasn't there at all. Which is why," she added, "I made sure, one way or another, that I would be."

"How did you know which one it would be?" Zebra asked.

"I didn't, entirely," Omega admitted. "But I made a point of getting Mad— uhm, my armorer to be especially rigorous in testing my design. Then I just had to hope it was enough, given the short time he had to work it up."

"No one who helped you is going to get into any trouble, Omega, I swear to you," Fox murmured. "Given what you told me you had planned, I fully expect that Madrid didn't know any more than you could get away with telling him, anyway."

"And you'd be right." Omega nodded. "I figured if I had to go rogue to do this thing, I wasn't gonna drag anybody else down with me, if I could help it."

"Honor, and to spare," Entiyti rumbled to himself. "Now, let us move on to more cheerful topics, please. Omega, Fox has been telling me about the small observatory dome you now have on the roof. Might we possibly have a tour of it later?"

"Oh, I'd love to," Omega said, flashing the Draconan a smile. "I've been working on a bit of an intro astronomy class to teach at Division One University next semester, and I obtained the observing data I'm going to use for the student projects in that little dome. Between Echo and Fox helping me get equipment, and Fox seeing to it the dome got built—with passive camo tech, and light-blocker shielding, I might add—it's a really sweet setup."

"Oh, excellent," Entiyti said. "What can you tell me about the optics?"

"Well, when Echo gave it to me for Christmas, I thought it was just like the one that got busted, the night he and I met," Omega said. "But it turns out, it's a lot more sophisticated. It's got adaptive optics, a REALLY nice worm gear clock drive, the latest hi-rez CCD imaging system, and an optical data drive. I requisitioned some attachments through the University, and now I'm set up to do astrophotography, polarimetry, photometry..."

Echo looked over at Fox and Zebra, and grinned.

"It's gonna be a late night," Fox decided.

"You knew that when you set the evening up," Zebra teased, nudging him with her elbow. "And I wanna see the observatory, too."

"Okay," Omega said, checking her wrist chronometer. "Give it about two more hours, and the moon willl be down, then I'll give y'all a tour of the sky from the point of view of the Headquarters roof. I might even," she shot a mischievous glance at Echo, "get my star pupil to give me a hand."

"I'll help with the equipment, Meg, but you'll have to do the talking," Echo said, waving a hand. "You're better at explaining."

"Not from what Doron told me."

"Pssht. I honestly have no idea what I told the guy. He asked more questions than all the kids at the toy store last Christmas put together. All with me trying to concentrate to work through the hit to the master clock, NOT blow my head off, and get us back safe to patch you up."

* * *

Zebra tapped Fox on the shoulder as she stood, and the Director rose and followed her into the kitchen. There, they prepared snack trays of chips, crudités, and various kinds of dip.

"Why does this feel like a family gathering of sorts?" she wondered to her paramour.

"Because it is," Fox answered with a knowing smile, and kissed her.

* * *

Late that night after hours of delightful chat and an enthusiastic little tour of her observatory, Omega found herself back in her quarters. Having had a quick, private word with Zebra in her kitchen before the gathering broke up, Omega went into her bedroom and closed the door. There, she fished out the plastic bag containing the few items of her personal effects that had survived her misadventure in the Chicago Station hangar, and which she had placed in the corner of her closet until she was mentally ready to sort through them.

Then she gingerly dug through its contents, looking for two specific things.

After several minutes, she came up with a small children's Valentine and a pink-tinged, transparent cube of resin, inside which was a single rose blossom, carefully preserved; the preservation didn't surprise her, because Zebra had told her she'd done it.

* * *

"...Because, under the circumstances, I thought you might like it as a keepsake," the medic had said. "Your first Valentine's Day in the Agency with your partner, and all."

"You thought right," Omega told her with a smile. "I was kinda surprised to find out he remembered a holiday like that, but evidently he did."

"Well, I agree with you," Zebra told her, "'cause Echo has such a tough-guy reputation, I didn't expect him to acknowledge it—not even to you. So I did a bit of sleuthing, and India told me that he DID almost forget, what with everything that happened, and you so injured and all. I mean, I think he didn't even hardly know what day it was, you know? Which isn't surprising in the least."

"Oh, hell no."

"Yeah. But he realized the dates when Alpha Two put in for a half-shift off...and then he acted on it, I guess."

"I guess so."

"I think he really cares a lot about you, dear," the medic had told her, leaning close to murmur it in her ear so no one else would overhear. "And I already know how you feel. I honestly think there's potential there. Don't give up hope, honey."

* * *

And sitting on the bedside, looking at the adorable card with its handwritten note, and the rose Echo had brought and Zebra had so carefully preserved, Omega found that her heart did indeed lighten.

Whether he ever does love me like that or not, she determined, *I'm still somebody special to him. Special enough for him to fly clear across the galaxy and back, risking his own neck to try to save me. And that means the universe to me.*

Then she pressed warm lips to the card, opened the drawer of her bedside table, and laid it carefully within, hidden under the photo of her birth family which Echo had seen at Christmas. She closed the drawer quietly, then picked up the block of resin, turning it this way and that for long minutes, in order to look at the rose inside, trying to memorize its shape and the delicate colors within it. She gently kissed the block, laying it on the top of the nightstand beside her deceased father's Bible...and a certain library book of collected poetry; the bookmark in said book was now very near the back cover, thanks in part to Echo bringing it each day to the medlab and reading to her.

She sat and looked at the preserved flower for another long moment. A soft smile etched itself on her features; sapphire-blue eyes shone happily.

Then Omega rose, tossed the effects bag with its remaining contents back into the corner of the closet, and headed for her den, calling, "Hey, Echo! You want a snack before bedtime?"

"Maybe a little something," came the distant response. "What have you got in mind?"

"Well, I baked a fresh batch of shortbread the other day, and there's milk, or maybe coffee..."

"YUM! That'll do!"

* * *

Several days passed, during which life at Headquarters got more or less back to normal. Lord Pulgey Entiyti took the opportunity to tour Earth's PGLEIA facilities both formally and informally, now that he was the Ennead Chairbeing once more. Sometimes Fox was at his side, sometimes not; occasionally one or both members of Alpha One escorted him, and twice Sugar and Gamma were his escorts.

But evenings always found them gathered back at Headquarters, in one Agent's quarters or another, sharing dinner. After that first night, said evening gatherings usually included Alpha Two, if they were not on assignment; twice it included Doron, as well.

Medical gradually allowed Omega to do more and more, into the bargain. The day they let her back into the gym with Echo, he was worried she might hurt herself, she was so enthusiastic.

"...But you still need to take it easy, baby," he protested, as she bumped up the weight stack on the leg press from where he'd set it for her. "You are NOT back at full steam QUITE yet."

"No, but damn, Ace, you have no idea how GOOD this feels!"

"It won't feel nearly as good if you tear something," he countered, knocking the weight stack back to where he'd had it. "I am NOT having Zebra rip me a new one because they let you back in the gym and I promptly let you hurt yourself. Now, don't go over that weight for this set, or I swear I'm throwing you outta the gym, bodily."

Omega sighed and obeyed.

* * *

It was sometime in the middle of March before Omega was finally approved to return to full duty status. The night she got that news, she and Echo had the entire lot—Entiyti, Fox, Zebra, Alpha Two, and Doron—over to their joint quarters for a small celebratory dinner.

The others all insisted on bringing something to contribute, so it turned into a rather LARGE dinner, somewhat reminiscent of a pot-luck family Thanksgiving feast...with certain off-world twists.

Fox and Zebra brought another salad, this time laden with fresh berries, and one of Zebra's delectable homemade cheesecakes; Romeo helped India whip up a couple of side dishes of a type he called her 'Korean soul food'—a platter of loaded cheese fries with sambal-laced sour cream and minced pickled garlic, and little kimchi Reubens sliced into finger-food appetizers. Entiyti ordered and brought several kitchen-sink pies from Trifle's Pizzeria—including a vegetarian pizza, to ensure it was kosher for Fox—as well as getting his hands on some sort of delectable chips or crisps popular on Emdali. And somehow little Doron managed to acquire ingredients and a kitchen to make what proved to be a delicious Edeptan specialty called grrk, though he had to use Earth potatoes instead of the traditional root vegetables used on Edeptis IV. "Still," the diminutive physician told them, "it turned out very similar. I am pleased."

Echo made a monster-sized cottage pie—minus the grated cheese over the potatoes, again for Fox—and a corn pudding. Omega baked a huge batch of the family-recipe Scottish shortbread, Southern-fried chicken, and a pot of fresh green beans with red-skinned potatoes—though the veggies came from the grocery, she wanted to show Entiyti what the dish was like. She and Echo also fetched a tray of cold cuts from the deli down the street, and four six-packs of chocolate stout from the market.

"And I'm making a pot of chicory coffee, too," Omega added, as the human males trundled Echo's dining table into Omega's dining area, then worked on reconfiguring both tables into one large table. Meanwhile, Zebra

287

and India loaded Lord Entiyti down with plates and flatware from Omega's cabinet, preparatory to setting the table.

"I'd say we have a damn fine meal, honey," Zebra said with a smile, coming to Omega and hugging her gently. "And congratulations for being back on the active list."

"Thanks, hon, for everything," Omega murmured, hugging the physician in return. "That goes for Romeo and India, too, AND all of Medical. Y'all kept me going until Echo could get back with Doron; I know that, and don't think I'm not appreciative."

"That makes two of us," Echo noted, looking up from the table reconstruction, a serious expression on his face.

"No maudlin discussions," Entiyti decreed, setting a stack of plates down on the kitchen counter. "This is a celebration!"

"Yeah!" Romeo enthused, snapping a lock into place. "There! It's done! Meg, get th' cloth on th' table, set out th' food, an' let's eat! I'm starved!"

"Oh, you're always starved," India said, poking him in the stomach as she moved past to help Omega spread the tablecloth, while Entiyti, Fox, Echo, and even little Doron doubled back to Echo's quarters to fetch the rest of the dining chairs.

Moments later, the big table was spread, set, and fairly groaning with food. Eight beings, from three different worlds, sat around it. Omega had intended to give Lord Entiyti and Fox the places of honor at the head and foot, but instead she found herself at the head of the table, Echo facing her from the other end.

"...Because that is as it should be, dear girl," Fox decreed. "This is your home, and you share it with Echo, after a fashion. And this meal is about..." he broke off. "I started to say Alpha One, but that isn't quite right. This is about the two of you, whether you're functioning as Alpha One or not."

A chorus of "Hear, hear! Yeah! What 'e said!" went around the table.

"All right," Omega acquiesced. "I get it. But...since this is the closest thing I have to a family any more...as the father figure, Fox, would you say grace?"

Fox blinked in some surprise, and stared at Omega for a moment...until Zebra, wearing a gentle smile, nudged him in the ribs with her elbow. "Go ahead, honey," she murmured.

"I...right," Fox began. "Forgive me, Omega; I'm afraid you caught me a bit off guard." He held out his hands, to right and left. Moments later, the table was ringed in a circle. "Barukh ata Adonai Eloheinu melekh ha'olam borei minei mezonot," he intoned. Then he paused for a moment, thinking, before adding, "U-modeh lekha Adonai al mishpakha zu."

"Amein," Zebra murmured.

"Amen," the whispered chorus followed.

There was a respectful pause, as they all looked at each other.

"Let's eat!" Romeo declared eagerly, and the solemn mood was instantly broken with laughter, as Omega reached for the first serving dish, to set it in motion around the table in the Southern tradition.

* * *

"That...was very good," Doron said, as they rose and retired to Omega's den, some with second bottles of stout, others with mugs of fragrant coffee.

"It was indeed," Entiyti agreed, patting his belly. "I told you, years ago, Doron, that humans really know how to cook."

"I remember, and you were right," Doron agreed. "Omega, how do you feel?"

Omega settled into one end of the couch, Echo easing down beside her, as the others all found seats. She didn't answer immediately, and the others' attention focused on her.

"You ARE feeling okay, aren't you, dear?" Zebra asked, brows knitting.

"Yeah, I can run get my medikit in my quarters if I need to—it's just around the corner," India offered. Omega raised a forestalling hand, smiling slightly.

"It's okay, guys, I'm fine," she told them. "I was just trying to come up with the right words to answer Doron. But," she shrugged, "I know several Earth languages, and I still can't come up with the right words to say how good, how...CONTENT, how happy...I feel right now. Echo might know some, or Pulgey, but..." She shook her head, then grinned and pointed at her mouth. "Will this do?" she asked. Everyone laughed.

289

"It will do, Omega," Doron averred, smiling back.

"It certainly will," Fox agreed. "And tomorrow, you are back on full, active duty. I won't have anything for Alpha One immediately, so you can just help me keep an eye on things. But I think I have an assignment coming up in a few days, that you should be able to sink your teeth into."

"That sounds good, Fox," Omega decided, missing the knowing glances that Fox, Entiyti, and Echo exchanged. "You know, it was rough. Damn rough. But we did it," she declared. "We made the contact, determined they really were sons of bitches—no offense to puppy dogs—kept 'em from getting Echo, and everybody survived to tell the tale."

"Except the aforementioned sons of bitches," Echo added.

"Yes," Entiyti affirmed. "And yes, it was rough. But it was also well and bravely done."

"Everything Pul said, and then some," Fox said.

"And now we put it behind us and look forward," Echo decreed.

"And now we put it behind us and look forward," Omega agreed.

* * *

"So, do you feel better about everything, after the marathon session the other day with Zz'r'p?" Echo asked Omega, as they headed out in the Corvette on a routine patrol the next day.

"That's funny. I was about to ask you the same thing," Omega responded with a grin.

"I must've read your mind," Echo grinned back. "Ladies first."

"Yes, I do feel better," she said, in all seriousness. "Now I don't have to worry about..."

"Violating others the way you once were?" a perceptive Echo finished for her.

"Yes—even accidentally. I guess you're relieved."

"I suppose so," Echo shrugged, hiding the disappointment he actually felt, "but we'd have been a helluva team with a mental link."

"I thought we already were 'a helluva team,'" she said.

Echo gave her a sidelong glance and saw her grin.

"We do pretty damn well, at that," he acknowledged.

"Echo? I got a question..." Omega's voice was suddenly very subdued,

290

with an odd, half-hurt, half-puzzled quality in the tone, and Echo glanced at her quizzically. Her face had grown serious.

"What's on your mind, Meg?" he asked, suspecting what was coming.

"You...didn't tell me...goodbye..."

Echo let out a long exhalation. *Bingo,* he thought. *I knew this was gonna hit, sooner or later.*

"...No." He shook his head. "No, I didn't."

"But...you promised me. You PROMISED me, Echo."

"I don't recall making that statement."

Omega just gazed silently at her partner. The pained expression in the blue eyes said more to Echo at that instant than words ever could.

"Besides," Echo continued, meeting those eyes for a moment as he drove, "if I remember right, what you actually asked me to do was to tell you when it was time to stop fighting. It wasn't time."

"But it would have been so much easier—on both of us—to just...let me go..."

"Meg, let's get something straight: When it comes to the life of my partner, I have never—and WILL never—take the easy way out. And I NEVER...STOP...FIGHTING. I don't expect YOU to, either. After all, you didn't, when it was MY life on the line."

"But, Echo—"

"No buts, Meg. Not this time. Not on this. Not ever on this."

They were silent for a long while, as the New York streets went by, and an expectant Echo watched his partner's thoughtful face out of the corner of his eye as he drove.

"I'm waiting," he told her quietly.

"For what?" she asked, startled.

"For the rest of your question. For you to ask me why I left. Why I didn't let someone else go after Doron. Why your partner wasn't there for you...like he 'promised.'"

"No," Omega replied simply. "I don't need to ask. I already know why."

Echo cocked his head, inviting her to elaborate.

"I don't know of anyone else that could've pulled it off," Omega told him, frank. "That was a real..." she laughed, *"tour de force.* As for your not being there for me...to coin a phrase, 'you must learn not to think in three-dimensional terms,' Echo. My partner may have been on the far side of the galaxy, but he was still backing me up, 'talking' to me, even giving me a 'transfusion.' No, Echo, you WERE there for me—in every way that mattered."

She laid her arm along the back of the car seat, allowing her hand to rest on his shoulder for a minute, rubbing, then patting it lightly. "Thanks, Echo. For everything."

"'It's what partners do.'" His voice was a soft murmur.

"Yes, it is," she agreed.

* * *

"By the way," he told her after a moment, "before I forget, be at Hangar 16 at the Chicago Station spaceport day after tomorrow at 09:00 D1. It's time for Doron to go home. His people need him."

"Oh...okay. Hangar...16, huh...? Does it...does it HAVE to be there?"

"Get back up on the horse, Meg."

"What?"

"When a horse throws you, you pick yourself up and get back in the saddle. Otherwise, you can let it get to you, and you won't be able to ride again. Fox and I deliberately decided on the hangar location."

"I really wish you'd checked with me first." She ran a distracted hand over her hair.

"Just be there, Meg. It'll be okay. I promise."

"What about you? Aren't we both going to the hangar?" she asked anxiously.

"Of course. I'm the pilot."

"Oh."

Echo watched Omega out of the corner of his eye as her face fell.

"Besides," he continued softly, "I've got a horse of my own to re-mount."

* * *

Omega shot a swift, somewhat startled look at Echo, and saw the shadow in his eyes as he returned her gaze. She nodded, musings turning inward.

Only Echo will ever fully understand what Chicago Hangar 16 represents to me. No one else could. No one else could even BEGIN to understand. And only I can understand what it is to him. Echo is right. We have to face it.

"No hunches this time, I hope?" he asked then, meaningfully, watching her thoughtful face. "I want you to tell me, if you do. Hunches, visions, dreams—from here on out, TELL me. I swear I'll listen from now on." He nodded at her. "So...go ahead an' check, I guess, if you can. If...you wouldn't mind."

Omega raised her eyebrows in understanding, offered him a smile of appreciation, then closed her eyes and tried to relax in the passenger seat, opening up mentally and waiting to see if anything came to her. Nothing did; she opened her eyes and looked at Echo, shaking her head.

"No. Not this time," she told him.

"Good."

They drove on through the streets of New York.

* * *

Late that evening, after Omega had popped up to the rooftop observatory to do a quick observing session—Pulgey Entiyti having expressed a conveniently-timed wish to see her at work there—Echo slipped into her bedroom, thence into the bathroom. He rummaged through her things, confiscating a few bits from the vanity's surface, then moved back to the bedroom.

There, he rifled her dresser drawers, grabbing several handfuls of neatly-folded lingerie and stuffing them into a small black duffel he produced from a warp pocket; small bulges in its side indicated the items already contained within.

Then he sat down on the edge of the bed and glanced over the articles on her nightstand. Reaching for her father's Bible, he stopped for a moment, blinking in some surprise. Then he picked up the object next to it.

It's the rose, he realized in shock, looking at the blossom held, frozen, within the transparent pink cube of resin. *The one I brought to the medlab on Valentine's Day. She found it! And it's preserved...and sitting beside her*

293

bed!

Suddenly he galvanized into action, scrabbling across the surface of the nightstand, searching. Not finding what he wanted, he jerked open the top drawer and foraged through it. Lifting the small framed family portrait, he froze.

Then he reached in and lifted out a small, brightly-colored Valentine card.

She kept it, he thought with a smile, something inside his chest trying to tap-dance. *She kept all of it. And this...this is tucked away with her birth family's portrait, like it's something special, too.*

Echo paused, and swallowed hard. Then he slipped everything very carefully back into its designated place with such accuracy—borne of long years' practice—that it would have required detailed, highly sophisticated equipment to even know it had been disturbed. The top of the bedside table, too, was set in order...though he held the rose cube in his hand for long moments, staring into it, thoughtful.

I dunno, he considered. *It means something important to her, obviously. After all, I'm part of the new family she's constructed around her, here in the Agency. I'd like to think it means she loves me...but I can't assume that. Not yet. Not that way, at least, not IN love with me—though I think it probably DOES mean that she loves me as family. Maybe, though, sometime soon, I can 'fess up about it, let her know that I care, that it was the closest I could get to a proper date with her on that day.*

He drew a deep breath. *Or maybe not. Best friends and all; maybe she viewed it as her best bud letting her know he was thinking about her. It was that, too, of course. But it was a lot more than that, at least to me.*

Echo gazed at the cube, considering, then raised it to his lips and pressed a light kiss to it.

There, he decided. *There's her good night kiss, every night, until something more, something better, comes along...if it ever does. And even if it doesn't, I'm here, right here beside her, for as long as she'll let me stay. And if that's for the rest of our lives, I'll be content.*

He eased the resin block back onto the nightstand's top, nudging it until he was satisfied with its positioning. Then he rose, smoothed the bedspread, and looked around.

"The rest will have to wait 'til later," he decided. "She'll notice, otherwise."

And Echo slipped out of Omega's bedroom, through the back door, and into his own bedroom.

When he emerged into his den, the small black duffel was gone.

* * *

When Omega returned from the observatory on the roof, she never noticed that anything had been disturbed.

Epilogue

Two days later, Omega found herself back in the exact same spacecraft hangar that had seen her literal trial by fire. But instead of a Cortian craft, a sleek silver saucer sat in its place. Fox stood beside her, Pulgey Entiyti next to him—and the entire Alpha Line department, who had turned out en masse to properly send off the medic that had saved their chief's partner. The seven other teams, plus eight brand-new ones, now formed a kind of honor guard gauntlet—one end next to Fox, Entiyti, and Omega; the other, at the hatch of the waiting spaceship.

Omega wasn't as uncomfortable in the setting as she had expected to be. All signs of the Cortian incident had been erased by the efficient Agency Facilities department, and in the end, one spacecraft hangar looked much like any other. A subdued Echo entered with Doron, and they walked up to Fox as Alpha Line stood at attention. She watched as Entiyti, who was there merely as a courtesy during his informal visit, eased back, allowing the Agency Director to take the lead; Entiyti and Doron had finished catching up in private the evening before, at another relaxed little dinner held in Fox's quarters, vowing to stay in touch better, now that Doron's home system was officially a member of PGLEIA.

"Well, Doron," Fox told the alien with a friendly smile, "it was VERY good to see you once more, but it looks like it's time to get you back home. We deeply appreciate what you did for Omega. And thank you for teaching our medics the regeneration technique. I hope we'll never have to use it again—at least not like that—but it's good to know, just in case."

"Indeed, Director," the alien healer agreed. "I am also glad to have seen you again, and to find you now in such a position of importance; you always seemed to me to be a being of much potential. I am happy to see I was correct. And I was pleased to be of use, and to save Agent Omega and help restore her to health. But I am glad to be returning to my own people. They need me as well."

Romeo and India moved forward from the head of the gauntlet then, and each touched one of Doron's arms.

"Thanks, man," Romeo said quietly.

"What he said," India murmured, waving her hand between herself and Omega. "Um, just because we're not genetically related, Meg and me...I mean, we're still family, you know...?"

"Hush," Doron shushed them. "I understand. It was ever my honor." A beatifically-smiling Doron nodded to them both, then turned to Omega as she stepped forward.

"Doron, I..." she began, voice cracking slightly.

Doron raised a quelling hand, and she paused.

"Your eyes speak for you," he said with another slight smile. "On my world, there is a saying: *Jpk.* 'It is enough.' Walk in health." He turned to Echo. "Agent Echo, I...believe I understand a little better now."

"Understand what?" Omega wondered, puzzled by the comment.

"Never you mind, Omega," Doron said, serene. "A little conversation, that is all. And I, too, have learned something from all this: Not all things require explaining."

"Let's go, Doron," Echo said quietly, and he and Doron turned and headed for the Division One saucer's hatch. They walked silently between the parallel rows of Alpha Line Agents, who respectfully saluted the two men, the human and the alien.

Fox, Entiyti, Omega, Romeo, and India watched them go from the head of the ranks. Omega sighed inaudibly.

Left high and dry again, she thought, discouraged.

* * *

At the hatch, Echo turned, seeing his forlorn partner standing beside Fox.

"Meg?" he called. He struggled to hide a grin.

"Yes, Echo?"

"Well??"

"'Well' what?" she asked, confused. Fox smiled slightly, but kept watching Echo.

"Are you coming, or aren't you?" Echo asked her.

297

Omega's eyes widened in surprise, and she shot a glance at Fox, who grinned. Behind him, Pulgey Entiyti displayed a toothy smile, pupil slits dilated in amusement. Romeo and India were grinning from ear to ear, as Fox nodded and waved her after Echo.

"Alpha One—comprised of the Alpha Line department chief and assistant chief—was officially assigned as Doron's escort detail, per the request of Alpha Line's chief," Fox told her, and Entiyti nodded.

"Across the galaxy...? My first offworld assignment, and I'm going... ACROSS THE GALAXY?" Omega said, stunned. Then she did a double-take. "Waitaminit. WHAT did you say?! ASSISTANT chief??"

"Indeed he did," Entiyti murmured. "That was not a hard promotion to pass through the Ennead."

* * *

"Get it in gear, Meg. We don't have all day. The launch window closes in an hour," Echo told her, no longer even attempting to suppress the grin, as he watched her face light up.

Without a moment's hesitation, Omega began sprinting across the hangar deck, between the rows of smiling, applauding Agents. Echo met her at the foot of the ramp, still grinning, as he put an arm across her shoulders to lead her into the spacecraft.

"Come on, partner," he told her. "Let me give you a guided tour of what's 'out there.'"

Author Notes

There are, as always, the usual suspects to thank: my husband, Darrell Osborn, and my parents, Steve and Colene Gannaway. There are also my beta readers, Dr. James K. Woosley, Evelyn Hively, and Larry Bauer. In addition to reading the finished manuscript and helping me polish, they all helped me brainstorm several things at various points in the story development. Larry is also by way of being something of a manager for me, so more thanks to him for putting up with all my crap, which crap sometimes includes panic attacks and bouts of, "What do I think I'm doing? I can't write!"

Once more, Nitay Arbel came to the rescue for matters of Hebrew blessings and appropriate ways to handle Jewish matters in a multi-planetary setting. Thanks, Nitay!

I'd also like to especially thank Tom Knighton and the members of Sarah's Diner and Lady Osborn's Pub, groups on Facebook, for the in-the-blind brainstorming they did with me on a few things here! Occasionally I get stuck on something and need an outside perspective, but it can be hard to describe what the problem is without giving out spoilers! These folks were game for throwing out ideas to help me solve my problem, and ultimately Tom's was the one I ended up using. So many thanks.

About the Author

Stephanie Osborn is a former payload flight controller, a veteran of over twenty years of working in the civilian space program, as well as various military space defense programs. She has worked on numerous Space Shuttle flights and the International Space Station, and counts the training of astronauts on her resumé. Of those astronauts she trained, one was Kalpana Chawla, a member of the crew lost in the *Columbia* disaster.

She holds graduate and undergraduate degrees in four sciences: Astronomy, Physics, Chemistry, and Mathematics, and she is "fluent" in several more, including Geology and Anatomy. She obtained her various degrees from Austin Peay State University in Clarksville, TN and Vanderbilt University in Nashville, TN.

Stephanie is currently retired from space work. She now happily "passes it forward," teaching math and science via numerous media including radio, podcasting, and public speaking, as well as working with SIGMA, the science fiction think tank, while writing science fiction mysteries based on her knowledge, experience, and travels.

For more, go to http://www.stephanie-osborn.com/.

A sneak peek at *Trojan Horse*, Book 5 of the Division One series, by Stephanie Osborn!

"...It's worth a try, Echo," Omega told him, as they brainstormed quickly. "Just let me do it."

"...Okay, Meg," Echo said, grudging. "Go ahead and give it a shot."

Omega keyed the broadcast switch.

"PGLEIA *Trojan Horse* to unidentified vessel. We are on a peaceful training mission. Why have you fired upon us?"

"*Trojan Horse*, this is the Cortian vessel *Pindar*. Your subterfuge is useless. We are aware that the Alpha One team of the so-called Pan-Galactic Division One crews this vessel, and that you caused the destruction of our flagship *Trindak* approximately thirty Earth days ago. We are here as a police action. Surrender or prepare to be destroyed."

Echo leaned over and pushed Omega's hand off the comm switch. "This is agent Echo. My partner had no part in the battle which destroyed the *Trindak*. Let her go, and I'll surrender."

"NO, Echo!" Omega cried.

"That is unacceptable," came the reply. "Communiques from *Trindak* before its destruction indicate your partner was heavily involved in the altercation which led to *Trindak*'s final battle. In any event, you are both prime acquisitions and should make excellent stock."

The two agents looked at each other in something akin to horror.

"They think of us as animals," Omega whispered, then her blue eyes blazed. "Echo—I've been a lab rat once before. Not again. Not ever again." She buckled in and booted the targeting computer. "Strap in, Echo. Fly this bird like you've never flown before. These damn sons of bitches are about to become part of the nebula."

Echo stared at his partner in shock for a moment. He heard the harsh epithet from the normally-smiling lips, saw the cold, hard, merciless expression in the sapphire gaze, and wondered. *Meg, what the hell happened to you? What exactly did my old enemy do to you...? TELL me, baby, don't keep it bottled up like this.*

"Echo! Break right, Ace! They've got a target lock! NOW!!"

Echo dropped into the pilot's seat and grabbed the controls, slamming their craft into a hard starboard translation maneuver, just as the green Cortian ray weapons sliced through their previous location.

In response, Omega's skilled fingers flitted over the weapons console, and purple beams lanced from the *Trojan Horse*. They struck the *Pindar*, and little puffs of atmosphere exited, before the alien ship's self-repair systems kicked in.

"Good shot," Echo remarked, as he put their ship into a hard loop, dogfight-style. "Here's another one for you, right up their...engines."

"Got it," Omega replied shortly, setting up and triggering another firing sequence. This time, when the purple beams touched the Cortian ship, a series of small explosions raced outward from the contact point. "Looks like we're in good shape so far, Ace."

"So far," Echo answered in a noncommittal tone, watching the enemy slave ship intently as they passed it by. "They just kicked it into high gear. Hang on."

The *Pindar* turned to follow the PGLEIA saucer as it shot by on its follow-through. Echo executed a series of evasive maneuvers, plunging into the heart of the nebula—the very densest of the gas and dust clouds that comprised the star-forming region—for cover as green beams peppered space around them. The artificial gravity of the *Trojan Horse* strove to compensate.

"Umph," Omega grunted as she bounced hard in her seat, five- point harness digging painfully into her shoulders, which were only protected by a layer of thin cotton and another layer of silk. "Nice job, Ace," she said, voice and expression ferocious. "They won't lay a finger on us, with you at the helm."

Echo ignored the comment for the moment, busy avoiding the deadly beams.

"Coming around for another pass, Meg. Be ready."

"I'll make it a strafing run..." She released the shoulder straps, rubbing her bruised right shoulder as she reached for the weapons controls. The trans-warp boson cannons fired, and this time Alpha One saw hull panels cartwheel away from the slaver ship.

"Echo," Omega said then, "sensors are showing they've sustained serious damage. Do you want to give 'em a chance to back down?"

Good. I've got my Meg back again, Echo thought, showing no reaction, but reaching for the comm. *The bloodthirsty version is gone. Can't say as I blame her, though. I felt that way myself about the* Trindak *when they toasted her.* He keyed the mike. "*Trojan Horse* to *Pindar*. Our sensors show you have sustained heavy damage. Do you wish to break off the engagement?"

The only answer was a barrage of green rays which Echo swiftly dodged.

"Okay, Meg," he growled, "take 'em out."

"With pleasure."

Echo brought the *Trojan Horse* in for a close pass as Omega targeted the areas already damaged on the alien spacecraft.

"Firing...now." The boson beams lanced outward at Omega's command, digging deep into the wounds of the *Pindar*, and abruptly a blinding white flare erupted from the damaged vessel. "Whoa—looks like I hit a sore spot..."

"Shit—she's going!" Echo exclaimed, watching the Cortian vessel seem to detonate. He kicked the *Trojan Horse* into a hard right-angle maneuver at maximum thrust, headed away from the *Pindar*, calling, "Hold on tight, Meg! Shields at max?"

"Affirm!" she responded. "Shields at one-oh-two and undamaged."

"Sensors aft," Echo barked.

"Sensors aft. Virtual heads-up?"

"Do it."

A 3-D tactical display of the sensor readings materialized in front of Echo. It showed a dense wave of shrapnel and debris rapidly advancing on their saucer. Echo wedged his legs between the seat and the console, bracing himself in lieu of the straps he'd never had a chance to don.

"Too close!" he exclaimed. "Meg, we're gonna get—"

A severe impact rocked the vessel, and Echo fought to stay seated as intense pain shot through one shin. Wrestling with the stick, he called to his partner.

"DAMN! We took a hit to the entire prop system! Meg, bring me up a navigation display! I need to see what's out there in this glowing pea soup!" He continued to fight the unresponsive controls, as a massive shadow gradually formed in the cloud ahead of them. "Meg, I need that—" Echo glanced at his partner. "Oh, shit," he whispered.

Omega was slumped across the copilot's panel, unconscious, a sticky red liquid trickling down the console's surface from the gash in her scalp.

Echo got off a mayday on the interstellar comm just before atmospheric entry. Then he tried desperately to re-establish enough maneuvering capability to soften their landing.

Unfortunately, it wasn't enough.

Don't miss any of these highly entertaining SF/F books by Stephanie Osborn!

Division One series:

Alpha and Omega

A Small Medium At Large

A Very UnCONventional Christmas

Tour de Force

Alpha and Omega by Stephanie Osborn

(ISBN: 978-0-9982888-0-2 ebook/978-0-9982888-1-9 print)

Dr. Megan McAllister was already a pretty unusual human—NASA astronaut, professional astronomer, polymath—when she encountered the man in the black Suit that night in west Texas. What Division One Agent Echo didn't know, when he recruited her to the Agency, was that she was even more special.

But he'd find out, soon enough.

Stephanie Osborn, aka the Interstellar Woman of Mystery, former rocket scientist and author of acclaimed science fiction mysteries, goes back to the urban legend of the unique group of men and women who show up at UFO sightings, alien abductions, etc. and make things...disappear...to craft her vision of the universe we don't know about. Her new series, Division One, chronicles this universe through the eyes of recruit Megan McAllister, aka Omega, and her experienced partner, Echo, as they handle everything from lost alien children to extraterrestrial assassination attempts and more. [First book in the Division One series.]

A Small Medium At Large by Stephanie Osborn

(ISBN: 978-0-9982888-2-6 ebook/978-0-9982888-3-3 print)

What if Sir Arthur Conan Doyle was right all along, and Harry Houdini really DID do his illusions, not through sleight of hand, but via noncorporeal means? More, what if he could do this because...he wasn't human?

Ari Ho'd'ni, Glu'g'ik son of the Special Steward of the Royal House of Va'du'sha'ā, better known to modern humans as an alien Gray from the ninth planet of Zeta Reticuli A, fled his homeworld with the rest of his family during a time of impending global civil war. With them, they brought a unique device which, in its absence, ultimately caused the failure of the uprisings and the collapse of the imperial regime. Consequently Va'du'sha'ā has been at peace for more than a century. What is the F'al, and why has a rebel faction sent a special agent to Earth to retrieve it?

It falls to the premier team in the Pan-Galactic Law Enforcement and Immigration Administration, Division One — the Alpha One team, known to their friends as Agents Echo and Omega—to find out...or die trying. [Second book in the Division One series.]

A Very UnCONventional Christmas (ISBN: 978-0-9982888-4-0 ebook/ 978-0-9982888-5-7 print) by Stephanie Osborn

It's Christmas in NYC, but for Alpha Line it's anything but a Silent Night: The Agency has a mole, leaking classified information to toy manufacturers and film producers alike, and the Agents are in danger of losing their anonymity. To complicate matters, the Prime Minister of Lambda Andromedae III, complete with entourage, has arrived to negotiate a new trade agreement with Earth. Worse, the more paranoid Division One field agents look at Omega's recent history with the Agency and suspect they have identified the mole!

Simultaneously, the discovery of a grim countdown in the most incongruous place possible — the Christmas tree at Rockefeller Center — augers the threat of horrific events on Christmas Eve itself.

Meanwhile, Omega is struggling to adjust to her very first Christmas in the Agency, made more difficult by the exposure of parts of her past long hidden from her conscious mind.

Will Omega be able to refute the accusations, or be punished for crimes she did not commit? Will the internal conspiracy expose the Agency? Or will efforts to thwart it see Echo — and Fox — caught up in the accusations as well? What is the meaning of the countdown to Christmas Eve, and will any of Alpha Line survive it? [Third book in the Division One series.]

* * *

Burnout: The mystery of Space Shuttle STS-281 by Stephanie Osborn (ISBN: 1-60619-200-0)

How do you react when you discover the next shuttle disaster has happened...right on schedule?

Burnout is a SF mystery about a Space Shuttle disaster that turns out to be no accident. As the true scope of the disaster is uncovered by the principle investigators, "Crash" Murphy and Dr. Mike Anders, they find themselves running for their lives as friends, lovers and coworkers involved in the investigation perish around them.

* * *

Sherlock Holmes: Gentleman Aegis series by Stephanie Osborn:
Sherlock Holmes and the Mummy's Curse

Sherlock Holmes and the Mummy's Curse by Stephanie Osborn (ISBN: 1-51888-312-5)

Holmes and Watson. Two names linked by mystery and danger from the beginning.

Within the first year of their friendship and while both are young men, Holmes and Watson are still finding their way in the world, with all the troubles that such young men usually have: Financial straits, troubles of the female persuasion, hazings, misunderstandings between friends, and more. Watson's Afghan wounds are still tender, his health not yet fully recovered, and there can be no consideration of his beginning a new practice as yet. Holmes, in his turn, is still struggling to found the new profession of consulting detective. Not yet truly established in London, let alone with the reputations they will one day possess, they are between cases and at loose ends when Holmes' old professor of archaeology contacts him.

Professor Willingham Whitesell makes an appeal to Holmes' unusual skill set and a request. Holmes is to bring Watson to serve as the dig team's physician and come to Egypt at once to translate hieroglyphics for his prestigious archaeological dig. There in the wilds of the Egyptian desert, plagued by heat, dust, drought and cobras, the team hopes to find the very first Pharaoh. Instead, they find something very different... (First book in the Gentleman Aegis series)

Sherlock Holmes and the Mummy's Curse is a Silver Falchion Award winner.

* * *

Displaced Detective series by Stephanie Osborn:
The Case of the Displaced Detective: The Arrival
The Case of the Displaced Detective: At Speed
The Case of the Cosmological Killer: The Rendlesham Incident
The Case of the Cosmological Killer: Endings and Beginnings
A Case of Spontaneous Combustion
Fear in the French Quarter

The Case of the Displaced Detective: The Arrival by Stephanie Osborn (ISBN: 1-60619-189-7) is a SF mystery in which brilliant hyperspatial physicist, Dr. Skye Chadwick, discovers there are alternate realities, often populated by those we consider only literary characters. Can Chadwick help Holmes come up to speed in modern investigative techniques in time to stop the spies? Will Holmes be able to thrive in our modern world? Is Chadwick now Holmes' new "Watson"—or more?

And what happens next? [First book in the Displaced Detective series]

The Case of the Displaced Detective: At Speed by Stephanie Osborn (ISBN: 1-60619-191-0)

Having foiled sabotage of Project: Tesseract by an unknown spy ring, Sherlock Holmes and Dr. Skye Chadwick face the next challenge. How do they find the members of this diabolical spy ring when they do not even know what the ring is trying to accomplish? And how can they do it when Skye is recovering from no less than two nigh-fatal wounds?

Can they work out the intricacies of their relationship? Can they determine the reason the spy ring is after the tesseract? And—most importantly—can they stop it? [Second book in the Displaced Detective series]

The Case of the Cosmological Killer: The Rendlesham Incident by Stephanie Osborn

(ISBN: 1-60619-193-4)

In 1980, RAF Bentwaters and Woodbridge were plagued by UFO sightings that were never solved. Now, McFarlane, a resident of Suffolk has died of fright during a new UFO encounter. On holiday in London, Sherlock Holmes and Skye Chadwick-Holmes are called upon by Her Majesty's Secret Service to investigate the death.

What is the UFO? Why does Skye find it familiar? Who—or what—killed McFarlane?

And how can the pair do what even Her Majesty's Secret Service could not? [Third book in the Displaced Detective series]

The Case of the Cosmological Killer: Endings and Beginnings by Stephanie Osborn

(ISBN: 1-60619-195-0)

After the revelations in *The Rendlesham Incident*, Holmes and Skye find they have not one, but two, very serious problems facing them. Not only did their "UFO victim" most emphatically NOT die from a close encounter, he was dying twice over—from completely unrelated causes. Holmes must now find the murderers before they find the secret of the McFarlane farm. And to add to their problems, another continuum—containing another Skye and Holmes—has approached Skye for help to stop the collapse of their own spacetime, a collapse that could take Skye with it, should she happen to be in their tesseract core when it occurs. [Fourth book in the Displaced Detective series]

A Case of Spontaneous Combustion by Stephanie Osborn
(ISBN: 1-60619-197-7)

When an entire village west of London is wiped out in an apparent case of mass spontaneous combustion, Her Majesty's Secret Service contacts The Holmes Agency to investigate. Once in London, Holmes looks into the horror that is now Stonegrange. His investigations take him into a dangerous undercover assignment in search of a possible terror ring, though he cannot determine how a human agency could have caused the disaster. Meanwhile, alone in Colorado, Skye is forced to battle raging wildfires and tame a wild mustang stallion, all while believing that her husband has abandoned her. Who—or what—caused the horror in Stonegrange? Will Holmes find his way safely through the metaphorical minefield that is modern Middle Eastern politics? Will this predicament seriously damage—even destroy—the couple's relationship? And can Holmes stop the terrorists before they unleash their outré weapon again? [Fifth book in the Displaced Detective series]

Fear in the French Quarter by Stephanie Osborn (ISBN: 1-60619-202-7) revolves around a jaunt by no less than Sherlock Holmes himself—brought to the modern day from an alternate universe's Victorian era by his continuum parallel, who is now his wife, Dr. Skye Chadwick-Holmes—to famed New Orleans for both business and pleasure. There, the detective couple investigates ghostly apparitions, strange disappearances, mystic phenomena, and challenge threats to the very universe they call home.

It was supposed to be a working holiday for Skye and Sherlock, along with their friend, the modern day version of Doctor Watson—some federal training that also gave them the chance to explore New Orleans, as the ghosts of the French Quarter become exponentially more active. When the couple uncovers an imminently catastrophic cause, whose epicenter lies squarely in the middle of Le Vieux Carré, they must race against time to stop it before the whole thing breaks wide open—and more than one universe is destroyed. [Sixth book in the Displaced Detective series]